Praise for *The Informers*

'Juan Gabriel Vásquez is one of the most original new voices of Latin American literature. His first novel, *The Informers*, a very powerful story about the shadowy years immediately following World War II, is testimony to the richness of his imagination as well as the subtlety and elegance of his prose' Mario Vargas Llosa

'It is deftly plotted and the author peels back layer after layer like the proverbial onion . . . We are drawn back ceaselessly into the past, from which a compelling revenge drama emerges. This is an impressive novel of betrayal, revenge, and redemption' *Literary Review*

'Anne McLean, who translated Javier Cercas's *Soldiers of Salamis*, has done a stupendous job of rendering Vásquez's intricate style into beautifully fluid English. *The Informers* deserves to be read not because its author has been named as part of a cabal of promising writers but because he has written one of this year's outstanding books' *Financial Times*

'For anyone who has read the entire works of Gabriel García Márquez and is in search of a new Colombian novelist, then Juan Gabriel Vásquez's *The Informers* is a thrilling new discovery' Colm Tóibín

'This is a subtle book about the ways in which the past can inform and shape the present . . . Anne McLean's well-turned translation brings these passages powerfully to life' *Daily Telegraph*

'A fine and frightening study of how the past preys upon the present, and an absorbing revelation of a little-known wing of the theatre of the Nazi war' John Banville

'Enthralling and frightening . . . With the authority of a historical document and the pacing of a thriller, Vásquez brilliantly and hauntingly portrays the impact of friendships and families, fear and suspicion, betrayal and redemption . . . An engrossing, intricately wrought novel that will continue to raise questions and fears in the reader long after the final page' *Sunday Business Post*

'What Vásquez offers us, with great narrative skill, is that grey area of human actions and awareness where our capacity to make mistakes, betray, and conceal creates a chain reaction which condemns us to a world without satisfaction. Friends and enemies, wives and lovers, parents and children mix and mingle angrily, silently, blindly, while the novelist uses irony and elipsis to unmask his characters' "self-protective strategies" and goes with them – not discovering them, simply accompanying them – as they come to understand that an unsatisfactory life can also be the life they inherit' Carlos Fuentes

'Vásquez handles this electric material efficiently and with some panache. Colombian writers must inevitably work in the shadow of the master, Gabriel García Márquez. But with this thrilling effort, Vásquez goes some way towards taking up the torch' *Spectator*

'In this dense, intricate book . . . . Vásquez shows a mastery of technique and language. The examination of the consequences that a single act can have not only for the person committing it but also, through the ripple effect, for many others brings us into the territory of Ian McEwan's *Atonement* . . . an extraordinary tale' *Guardian*

'An intricate tale of deceit, loyalty and tarnished relationships, told in beautifully restrained prose . . . *The Informers* provides a fascinating and detailed portrayal of wartime and post-war Columbia' *TLS*

'Juan Gabriel Vásquez, one of the most gifted writers to emerge from Latin America in recent years, fashions a misty and enigmatic mood of doubt, shadow and secrecy. His sombre city feels almost as if mature John Le Carré had wandered into the narrative labyrinths of Borges . . . A deft but never tricksy story-telling architecture of tales within tales' *Independent*

'From the opening paragraph of *The Informers*, I felt myself under the spell of a masterful writer. Juan Gabriel Vásquez has many gifts – intelligence, wit, energy, a deep vein of feeling – but he uses them so naturally that soon enough one forgets one's amazement at his talents, and then the strange, beautiful sorcery of his tale takes hold' Nicole Krauss, author of *The History of Love*

THE INFORMERS

Juan Gabriel Vásquez

Translated from the Spanish
by Anne McLean

B L O O M S B U R Y

LONDON · BERLIN · NEW YORK · SYDNEY

First published in Great Britain 2008
This paperback edition published 2009

Copyright © 2004 by Juan Gabriel Vásquez

English translation copyright © 2008 Anne McLean

This work has been published with the help of a grant from the Office of the Director
General of Books, Archives and Libraries of the Ministry of Culture of Spain

Bloomsbury Publishing Plc
50 Bedford Square
London WC1B 3DP

www.bloomsbury.com

Bloomsbury Publishing, London, New York, Berlin and Sydney

A CIP catalogue record for this book is available from the British Library

ISBN 978 0 7475 9651 6

10 9 8 7 6 5 4

Typeset by Hewer Text UK Ltd, Edinburgh
Printed in Great Britain by Clays Limited, St Ives plc

The paper this book is printed on is certified independently in accordance with the rules of
the FSC. It is ancient-forest friendly. The printer holds chain of custody

For Francis Laurenty
(1924–2003)

You will never wash out that stain;
you cannot talk long enough for that.

Demosthenes, 'On the Crown'

Who wishes to speak?
Who wishes to rake up old grievances?
Who wishes to be answerable to the future?

Demosthenes, 'On the Crown'

CONTENTS

I   The Inadequate Life   1

II   The Second Life   41

III   The Life According to Sara Guterman   105

IV   The Inherited Life   173

V   Postscript, 1995   253

      Historical Afterword   331

      Notes   337

I

The Inadequate Life

O N THE MORNING OF 7 April 1991, when my father
telephoned to invite me to his apartment in Chapinero
for the first time, there was such a downpour in Bogotá that
the streams of the Eastern Hills burst their banks, the water
came pouring down, dragging branches and mud, blocking
the sewers, flooding the narrowest streets, lifting small cars
with the force of the current, and even killing an unwary taxi
driver who somehow ended up trapped under the chassis of
his own vehicle. The phone call itself was at the very least
surprising, but on that day seemed nothing less than omi-
nous, not only because my father had stopped receiving
visitors a long time before, but also because the image of the
water-besieged city, the motionless tailbacks and dead traffic
lights and marooned ambulances and unattended emergencies would have sufficed under normal circumstances to
convince anyone that going out to visit someone was im-
prudent, and asking someone to come to visit almost rash.
The scenes of Bogotá in chaos attested to the urgency of his
call and made me suspect that the invitation was not a matter
of courtesy, suggesting a provisional conclusion: we were
going to talk about books. Not just any old book, of course:
we'd talk about the only one I'd then published, a piece of
reportage with a TV-documentary title – *A Life in Exile*, it
was called – that told or tried to tell the life story of Sara
Guterman, daughter of a Jewish family and lifelong friend of
ours, from her arrival in Colombia in the 1930s. When it
appeared, in 1988, the book had enjoyed a certain notoriety,

not because of its subject or its debatable quality, but because my father, a professor of rhetoric who never deigned to sully his hand with any form of journalism, a reader of classics who disapproved of the very act of commenting on literature in print, had published a savage review in the Sunday magazine of *El Espectador*. It's perhaps understandable that later, when my father sold the family home at a loss and took a lease on a refuge for the inveterate bachelor he pretended to be, I wasn't surprised to hear the news from someone else, even if it was from Sara Guterman, my least distant someone else.

So the most natural thing in the world, the afternoon I went to see him, was to think it was the book he wanted to discuss with me: that he was going to make amends, three years late, for that betrayal, small and domestic though it may have been, but no less painful for that. What happened was very different. From his domineering, ochre-coloured armchair, while he changed channels with the solitary digit of his mutilated hand, this aged and frightened man, smelling of dirty sheets, whose breathing whistled like a paper kite, told me, in the same tone he'd used all through his life to recount an anecdote about Demosthenes or Gaitán, that he'd spent the last three weeks making regular visits to a doctor at the San Pedro Claver Clinic, and that an examination of his sixty-seven-year-old body had revealed, in chronological order, a mild case of diabetes, a blocked coronary artery – the anterior descending – and the need for immediate surgery. Now he knew how close he'd been to no longer existing, and he wanted me to know too. 'I'm all you've got,' he said. 'I'm all you've got left. Your mother's been buried for fifteen years. I could have not called you, but I did. You know why? Because after me you're on your own. Because if you were a trapeze artist, I'd be your only safety net.' Well then, now that sufficient time has passed since my father's death and I've finally decided to organize my head and desk, my documents and notes, to get this all down in writing, it seems obvious that I should begin this way: remembering the day he called me, in the middle of the most intense winter of my adult life, not to mend the rift between us, but in order to feel less alone when they opened his chest with an electric saw and sewed a vein extracted from his right leg into his ailing heart.

It had begun with a routine check-up. The doctor, a man with a soprano's voice and a jockey's body, had told my father that a mild form of diabetes was not entirely unusual or even terribly worrying at his age: it was merely a predictable imbalance, and wasn't going to require insulin injections or drugs of any kind, but he would need to exercise regularly and observe a strict diet. Then, after a few days of sensibly going out jogging, the pain began, a delicate pressure on his stomach, rather resembling a threat of indigestion or something strange my father might have swallowed. The doctor ordered new tests, still general ones but more exhaustive, and among them was a test of strength; my father, wearing underpants long and baggy as chaps, first walked then jogged on the treadmill, and then returned to the tiny changing room (in which, he told me, he'd felt like stretching his arms, and, realizing the place was so small he could touch the facing walls with his elbows, suffered a brief attack of claustrophobia), and when he'd just put on his flannel trousers and begun to button up the cuffs of his shirt, already thinking about leaving and waiting for a secretary to call him to pick up the results of his electrocardiogram, the doctor knocked on the door. He was very sorry, he said, but he hadn't liked what he'd seen in the initial results: they were going to have to do a cardiac catheterization immediately, to confirm the risks. And they did, of course, and the risks (of course) were confirmed: there was an obstructed artery.

'Ninety-nine per cent,' said my father. 'I would have had a heart attack the day after tomorrow.'

'Why didn't they admit you there and then?'

'Because the fellow thought I looked really nervous, I suppose. He thought it'd be better if I went home. He did give me a very specific set of instructions, though. Told me not to move all weekend. Avoid any kind of excitement. No sex at all, especially. That's what he said to me, believe it or not.'

'And what did you say to him?'

'That he didn't need to worry about that. I wasn't about to tell him my life story.'

As he left the office and hailed a taxi amid the confusion of Twenty-sixth Street, my father had barely begun to confront the idea that he was ill. He was going to be admitted to hospital without a single symptom that would betray the urgency of his condition, with no discomfort beyond the frivolous pain in the pit of his stomach, and all because of an incriminating catheter. The doctor's arrogant spiel kept running through his head: 'If you'd waited three more days before coming to see me, we'd probably be burying you in a week.' It was a Friday; the operation was scheduled for the following Thursday at six in the morning. 'I spent the night thinking I was going to die,' he told me, 'and then I phoned you. That surprised me, of course, but now I'm even more surprised that you've come.' It's possible he was exaggerating: my father knew that no one was apt to consider his death as seriously as his own son, and to that, to thinking about his death, we devoted that Sunday afternoon. I made a couple of salads, made sure there was juice and water in the fridge, and began to look over his latest income-tax return with him. He had more money than he needed, which isn't to say he had a lot, just that he didn't need much. His only income came from his pension from the Supreme Court, and his capital, that is, the money he'd received when he'd sold off the house where I'd grown up and my mother had died, had been invested in savings bonds and the interest from them was enough to cover his rent and living expenses for the most ascetic lifestyle I'd ever seen: a lifestyle in which, as far as I could tell, no restaurants, concerts, or any other means, more or less onerous, of entertainment entered into the picture. I'm not saying that if my father had spent the occasional night with a hired lover I would have found out about it; but when one of his colleagues tried to get him out of the house, to take him out for a meal with some woman, my father refused once and then left the phone off the hook for the rest of the day. 'I've already met the people I had to meet in this life,' he told me. 'I don't need anyone new.' One of those times, the person who invited him was a trademark and patents lawyer young enough to be his daughter, one of those large-breasted girls who don't read and seem to go through an inevitable phase of curiosity about sex with older men. 'And you turned her down?' I asked. 'Of course I turned her down. I told her I had a political meeting. "What party?" she asked. "The Onanist Party," I told her. And off she went quietly home, and never bothered me again. I don't know if she found a dictionary in time, but she seems to have decided to leave me alone, because she hasn't invited me to anything since. Or who knows, maybe there's a lawsuit against me, no? I can almost see the headlines: Perverted Professor assaults young woman with biblical polysyllables.'

I stayed with him until six or seven and then went home, thinking during the whole trip about what had just happened, about the strange twist of a son seeing his father's home for the first time. Was it just the two rooms – the living room and bedroom – or was there a study somewhere? I couldn't see more than a cheap white bookcase leaning carelessly against the wall that ran parallel to Forty-ninth Street, beside a barred window that hardly let any light in. Where were his books? Where were the plaques and silver trays with which others had insisted on distinguishing his career over the years? Where did he work, where did he read, where did he listen to that record – *The Mastersingers of Nuremberg*, a title I wasn't familiar with – the sleeve of which was lying on the kitchen table? The apartment seemed stuck in the 1970s: the orange-and-brown carpet; the white fibre-glass chair I sank into as my father recalled and described for me the map of his catheterisation (its narrow highways, its back roads); the closed, windowless bathroom, lit only by a couple of transparent plastic rectangles on the ceiling (one of which was broken, and through the hole I could see two neon tubes in their death throes). There was soapy foam in the green washbasin, the shower was dark and didn't smell too good, and from its aluminium frame hung two pairs of recently washed underpants. Had he washed them himself? Didn't anyone come to help him? I opened drawers and doors held shut with magnets, and found some aspirins, a box of Alka-Seltzer and a rusty shaving brush that no one had used for a long time. There were drops of urine on the toilet bowl and on the floor: yellow, smelly drops, telltale signs of a worn-out prostate. And there, on top of the tank, under a box of Kleenex, was a copy of my book. I wondered, of course, if this might not be his way of suggesting that his opinion had not changed over the years. 'Journalism aids intestinal transit,' I imagined him telling me. 'Didn't they teach you that at university?'

When I got home I made a few calls, although it was too late to cancel the operation or to pay any attention to second opinions, especially those formulated over the phone and without the benefit of documents, test results, X-rays, etc. In any case, talking to Jorge Mor, a cardiologist at the Shaio Clinic who'd been a friend of mine since school, didn't do much to calm me down. When I called him, Jorge confirmed what the doctor at San Pedro Claver had said: he confirmed the diagnosis, as well as the necessity of operating urgently, and also the luck of having discovered the matter by chance, before my father's asphyxiated heart did what it was thinking of doing and suddenly stopped, without warning. 'Rest easy, brother,' Jorge told me. 'It's the simplest version of a difficult operation. Worrying from now till Thursday won't do anyone any good.' 'But what could go wrong?' I insisted. 'Everything can go wrong, Gabriel, everything can go wrong in any operation in the world. But this is one that's got to be done, and it is relatively simple. Do you want me to come over and explain it to you?' 'Of course not,' I said. 'Don't be ridiculous.' But maybe if I'd accepted his offer I would have kept talking to Jorge until it was time to go to bed. We would have talked about the operation; I would have gone to sleep late, after one or two soporific drinks. Instead, I ended up going to bed at ten, and just before three in the morning I realized I was still awake and more frightened than I'd thought.

I got out of bed, felt in the pockets of my jeans for the shape of my wallet, and dumped its contents under the lampshade. A few months before I turned eighteen, my

9

father had presented me with a rectangular card, dark blue on one side and white on the other, which gave him the right to be buried with my mother in the Jardines de Paz – and there was the cemetery's logo, letters like lilies – and asked me to keep it in a safe place. At that moment, like any other teenager, I couldn't think of anywhere better to put it than in my wallet; and there it had stayed all that time, between my ID card and my military card, with its funereal aspect and the name typed on an adhesive strip now wearing away. 'One never knows,' my father had said when he gave it to me. 'We could get blown up any day and I want you to know what to do with me.' The time of bombs and attacks, a whole decade of living every day with the knowledge that arriving home each night was a matter of luck, was still in the distance; if we had in fact been blown up, the possession of that card wouldn't have made things any clearer to me as to how to deal with the dead. Now it struck me that the card, yellowed and worn, looked like the mock-ups that come in new wallets, and no stranger would have seen it for what it actually was: a laminated tomb. And so, considering the possibility that the moment to use it had arrived, not due to any bombs or attacks, but through the predictable misdeeds of an old heart, I fell asleep.

They admitted him at five o'clock the next afternoon. Throughout those first hours, already in his green dressing gown, my father answered the anaesthetist's questions and signed the white Social Security forms and the tricolour life insurance ones (a faded national flag), and throughout Tuesday and Wednesday he spoke and kept speaking, demanding certainties, asking for information and in his turn informing, sitting on the high, regal mattress of the aluminium bed and nevertheless reduced to the vulnerable position of one who knows less than the person with whom he's speaking. I stayed with him those three nights. I assured him, time and time again, that everything was going to be fine. I saw the bruise on his thigh in the shape of the province of La Guajira, and assured him that everything was going to be fine. And on Thursday morning, after they shaved his chest and both legs, three men and a woman took him to the operating room on the second floor, lying down and silent for the first time and ostentatiously naked beneath the disposable gown. I accompanied him until a nurse, the same one who'd looked blatantly and more than once at the patient's comatose genitals, asked me to get out of the way and gave me a little ammonia-smelling pat, saying the same thing I'd said to him: 'Don't worry, sir. Everything's going to be fine.' Except she added, 'God willing.'

Almost anyone would recognize my father's name and not only because it's the same as the one on the front of this book (yes, my father was a perfect example of that so predictable species: those who are so confident of their life's achievements that they have no fear of baptizing their children with their own names), but also because Gabriel Santoro was the man who taught, for more than twenty years, the famous Seminar on Judicial Oratory at the Supreme Court, and also the man who, in 1988, delivered the commemoration address on the four hundred and fiftieth anniversary of the founding of Bogotá, that legendary text that came to be compared with the finest examples of Colombian rhetoric, from Bolívar to Gaitán. *Gabriel Santoro, heir to the Liberal Caudillo*, was the headline in an official publication that few know and no one reads, but which gave my father one of the great satisfactions of his life in recent years. Quite right too, because he'd learned everything from Gaitán: he'd attended all his speeches; he'd plagiarized his methods. Before he was twenty, for example, he'd started wearing my grandmother's corsets, to create the same effect as the girdle that Gaitán wore when he had to speak outdoors. 'The girdle put pressure on his diaphragm,' my father explained in his classes, 'and his voice would come out louder, deeper and stronger. You could be two hundred metres from the podium when Gaitán was speaking with no microphones whatsoever, pure lung power, and you could hear him perfectly.' The explanation came accompanied by the dramatic performance, because my father was an excellent mimic (but where Gaitán raised the index finger of his right hand, pointing to the sky, my father raised his shiny stump). 'People of Colombia: For the moral restoration of the Republic! People of Colombia: For your victory! People of Colombia: For the defeat of the oligarchy!' Pause; ostensibly kind question from my father: 'Who can tell me why this series of phrases moves us, what makes it effective?' An incautious student: 'We're moved by the ideas of . . .' My father: 'Nothing to do with ideas. Ideas don't matter, any brute can have ideas, and these, in particular, are not ideas but slogans. No, the series moves and convinces us through the repetition of the same phrase at the beginning of the clauses, something that you will all, from now on, do me the favour of calling *anaphora*. And the next one to mention ideas will be shot.'

I used to go to these classes just for the pleasure of seeing him embody Gaitán or whoever (other more or less regular characters were Rojas Pinilla and Lleras Restrepo), and I got used to watching him, seeing him squaring up like a retired boxer, his prominent jaw and cheekbones, the imposing geometry of his back that filled out his suits, his eyebrows so long they got in his eyes and sometimes seemed to sweep across his lids like theatre curtains, and his hands, always and especially his hands. The left was so wide and the fingers so long that he could pick up a football with his fingertips; the right was no more than a wrinkled stump on which remained only the mast of his erect thumb. My father was about twelve, and alone in his grandparents' house in Tunja, when three men with machetes and rolled-up trousers came in through a kitchen window, smelling of cheap liquor and damp ponchos and shouting 'Death to the Liberal Party', and didn't find my grandfather, who was standing for election to the provincial government of Boyacá and would be ambushed a few months later in Sogamoso, but only his son, a child who was still in his pyjamas even though it was after nine in the morning. One of them chased him, saw him trip over a clump of earth and get tangled up in the overgrown pasture of a neighbouring field; after one blow of his machete, he left him for dead. My father had raised a hand to protect himself, and the rusty blade sliced off his four fingers. María Rosa, the cook, began to worry when he didn't show up for lunch, and finally found him a couple of hours after the machete attack, in time to stop him bleeding to death. But this last part my father didn't remember, they told him later, just as they told him about his fevers and the incoherent things he said – seeming to confuse the machete-wielding men with the pirates of Salgari books – amid the feverish hallucinations. He had to learn how to write all over again, this time with his left hand, but he never achieved the necessary dexterity, and I sometimes thought, without ever saying so, that his disjointed and deformed penmanship, those small child's capital letters that began brief squadrons of scribbles, was the only reason a man who'd spent a lifetime among other people's books had never written a book of his own. His subject was the word, spoken and read, but never written by his hand. He felt clumsy using a pen and was unable to operate a keyboard: writing was a reminder of his handicap, his defect, his shame. And seeing him humiliate his most gifted students, seeing him flog them with his vehement sarcasm, I used to think: You're taking revenge. This is your revenge.

But none of that seemed to have any consequences in the real world, where my father's success was as unstoppable as slander. The seminar became popular among experts in criminal law and postgraduate students, lawyers employed by multinationals and retired judges with time on their hands, and there came a time when this old professor with his useless knowledge and superfluous techniques had to hang on the wall, between his desk and bookshelves, a kind of kitsch, colonial shelf upon which piled up, behind the little rail with its pudgy columns, the silver trays and diplomas on cardboard, on watermarked paper, on imitation parchment, and also chipboard plaques with eye-catching coats of arms in coloured aluminium. *FOR GABRIEL SANTORO, IN RECOGNITION OF TWENTY YEARS OF PEDAGOGICAL LABOUR . . . CERTIFIES THAT DOCTOR GABRIEL SANTORO, BY VIRTUE OF HIS CIVIL MERITS . . . THE MAYORALTY OF GREATER BOGOTÁ, IN HOMAGE TO DOCTOR GABRIEL SANTORO* . . . There, in that sort of sanctuary for sacred cows, the sacred cow who was my father spent his days. Yes, that was his reputation: my father knew it when they called him from city hall to offer him the speech at the Capitolio Nacional, that is, to ask him to deliver a few commonplaces in front of bored politicians. This peaceable professor – they would have thought – ticked all the right boxes for the event. My father didn't give them anything they expected.

He did not speak about 1538. He did not speak about our illustrious founder, Don Gonzalo Jiménez de Quesada, whose pigeon-shit-covered statue he passed every time he went to have a coffee-and-brandy in the Café Pasaje. He did not speak about the twelve little huts or the Chorro de Quevedo, Quevedo's stream, the spot where the city had been founded, which my father used to say he could never mention without his mind being invaded by the image of a pissing poet. Contravening the commemorative tradition in Colombia (this country that has always liked to commemorate everything), my father did not make his speech a politicised version of our childhood history primers. He did not abide by the terms of the agreement; he betrayed the expectations of a couple of hundred politicians, peaceful men who desired only to be swept along for a while by the inertia of optimism and then to be freed promptly to go and spend the 7 August holiday with their families. I was there, of course. I heard the words spat out into mediocre microphones; I saw the faces of those listening to him, and noticed the moment when some of them stopped looking at the orator to look at each other: the imperturbable eyebrows, the stiff necks, the hands with their wedding rings straightening their ties. Afterwards, they all commented on the courage it took to pronounce those words, the act of profound contrition, of intrepid honesty there was in each one of those sentences – all of which, I'm sure, held no importance for my father, who wanted only to dust off his rifles and take his best shots in the presence of a select audience – none of them, however, could recognize the value of that exemplary model of rhetoric: a valiant introduction, because he relinquished the chance to appeal to his audience's sympathies ('I'm not here to celebrate anything'), a narrative based on confrontation ('This city has been betrayed. Betrayed by all of you for almost half a millennium'), an elegant conclusion that began with the most elegant figure of classical oratory ('There once was a time when it was possible to speak of this city'). And then that final paragraph, which would later serve as a mine of epigraphs for various official publications and was repeated in all the newspapers the way they repeat Simón Bolívar's *I shall go quietly down to my grave* or *Colonel, you must save our nation.*

Somewhere in Plato we read: 'Landscapes and trees have nothing to teach me, but the people of a city most certainly do.' Citizens, I propose we learn from ours, I propose we undertake the political and moral reconstruction of Bogotá. We shall achieve resurrection through our industry, our perseverance, our will. On her four hundred and fiftieth birthday, Bogotá is a young city yet to be made. To forget this, citizens, is to endanger our own survival. Do not forget, citizens, nor let us forget.

My father spoke about reconstruction and morals and perseverance, and he did so without blushing, because he focused less on what he said than on the device he used to say it. Later he would comment: 'The last sentence is nonsense, but the alexandrine is pretty. It fits nicely there, don't you think?'

The whole speech lasted sixteen minutes and twenty seconds – according to my stopwatch and not including the fervent applause – a tiny slice of that 6 August 1988 when Bogotá turned four hundred and fifty, Colombia celebrated one hundred and sixty-nine years less a day of independence, my mother had been dead for twelve years, six months and twenty-one days, and I, who was twenty-seven years, six months and four days old, suddenly felt overwhelmingly convinced of my own invulnerability, and everything seemed to indicate that there where my father and I were, each in charge of his own successful life, nothing could ever happen to us, because the conspiracy of things (what we call luck) was on our side, and from then on we could expect little more than an inventory of achievements, ranks and ranks of those grandiloquent capitals: the Pride of our Friends, the Envy of our Enemies, Mission Accomplished. I don't have to say it, but I'm going to say it: those predictions were completely mistaken. I published a book, an innocent book, and then nothing was ever the same again.

I don't know when it became apparent that Sara Guterman's experiences would be the material for my first book, nor when this epiphany suggested that the prestigious occupation of a chronicler of reality was designed to fit me like a glove. (It wasn't true. I was just one more member of an occupation that is never prestigious; I was an unfulfilled promise, that delicate euphemism.) At first, when I began to investigate her life, I realized that I knew very little about her; at the same time, however, that my knowledge exceeded the predictable or the normal, for Sara had been a regular visitor at my house for as long as I could remember, and many anecdotes from her always generous conversation had stayed in my head. Until the moment when my project came about, I'd never heard of Emmerich, the little German town where Sara was born. The date of her birth (1924) barely seemed less superfluous than that of her arrival in Colombia (1938); the fact that her husband was Colombian and her sons were Colombian and her grandchildren were Colombian, and the fact that she had lived in Colombia for the last fifty years of her life served to fill out a biographical record and give an inevitable sense of substance to the particulars – you can say many things about a person, but only when we expose dates and places does that person begin to exist – but their utility went no further. Dates, places and other information took up several interviews, characterized by the ease with which Sara talked to me, without allegories or beating about the bush, as if she'd been waiting her whole life to tell these things. I asked; she, rather than answering, confessed; the exchanges ended up resembling a forensic interrogation.

Her name was Sara Guterman, born in 1924, arrived in Colombia in 1938?

Yes, that's all correct.

What did she remember about her final days in Emmerich?

A certain well-being, first of all. Her family made their living from a sandpaper factory, and not a bad living either, but rather what would have been considered quite a comfortable one. It took Sara some thirty years to realize just what a good living the factory gave them. She also remembered a light-hearted childhood. And later, maybe after the first boycott affected the factory (Sara was not yet ten, but waking up for school and finding her father still at home made a deep impression), the appearance of fear, and a sort of fascination at the novelty of the emotion.

How did they get out of Germany?

One night in October 1937, the town's operator called the family and warned that their arrest had been scheduled for the next day. It seems she had overheard the order while transferring a call, just the way she'd found out about Frau Maier's adultery (Sara didn't remember the first name of the adulterous woman). The family fled that very night, slipped over the border into Holland to a refuge in the countryside. They stayed hidden there for several weeks. Only Sara left the refuge: she backtracked as far as Hagen, where her grandparents lived, to tell them what was happening (the family thought a thirteen-year-old girl had a better chance of travelling unimpeded). She remembered one particular detail about the train – it was the fast train of its day – she was given consommé to drink, which was quite a novelty at the time, and the process of the little cube dissolving in the hot water fascinated her. They settled her into a compartment where everyone was smoking, and a black man sat down beside her and told her that he didn't smoke but he always sat where he saw smoke, because smokers were better conversationalists and people who don't smoke often don't talk during the entire journey.

Wasn't it dangerous to go back into Germany?

Oh yes, very. Just before arriving she noticed that a young man of about twenty had gone into the next compartment and that he'd followed her each time she'd escaped to the dining car to drink consommé. She feared, of course, that it was someone from the Gestapo, because that's what people feared at that time, and when she got to Hagen Station she left the train and walked past her uncle who was waiting for her and instead of greeting him, asked him where the ladies' was, and he, luckily, understood what was going on, went along with the act, accompanied her to the back of the station and despite the protests of two women went in with her. There, Sara told her uncle that the family was safe and nevertheless her father had now decided to leave Germany. It was the first time the idea of leaving was mentioned. While he listened to the news, her uncle scratched at a poster that someone, probably a traveller with too much luggage, had stuck there: *Münchener Fasching. 300 Künstlerfeste*. Sara asked her uncle if she needed to change trains to go from Hagen to Munich, or if there was a direct train. Her uncle didn't say anything.

Why Colombia?

Because of an advertisement. Months earlier, Sara's father had seen the sale of a cheese factory in Duitama (an unknown city), Colombia (a primitive country) advertised in a newspaper. Taking advantage of the fact that he still could, that the laws did not yet prevent him from doing so, he decided to travel to see the factory in person and returned to Germany saying that it was an almost unimaginable business, that the factory was rudimentary and employed only three girls, and nevertheless it was going to be necessary to consider the voyage. And when the emergency happened, the voyage was considered. In January 1938, Sara and her grandmother arrived by ship in Barranquilla and waited for the rest of the family, and there they received news of the persecutions, arrests of friends and acquaintances, all the things they'd been spared and – which seemed even more surprising – would continue to be spared in exile. A couple of weeks later they flew from Barranquilla to Bogotá's Techo Airport (in a twin-engine Boeing plane of the SCADTA fleet, as she was later informed, when, at sixteen or seventeen years old, she began to ask questions and reconstruct their first days in the country), and then, from Sabana Station, they took the train that left them in what for the moment was nothing more than the village of cheeses.

What did she remember about the rail journey across Colombia?

Her Aunt Rotem, an old, almost bald woman whose authority, in Sara's eyes, was diminished by her lack of hair, complained during the whole trip. The poor old woman never understood why first class, in this train, was at the back; she never understood why the girl, travelling by land across the new country, kept her nose in an album of contemporary art, a book with translucent pages that had been her cousin's and had got into her luggage by mistake, instead of commenting on the mountains and plantations and the colour of the rivers. The girl looked at the reproductions and didn't know that in some cases – that of Chagall, for example – the originals no longer existed, because they'd been incinerated.

What were her first impressions upon arrival in Duitama?

She liked several things: the mud that built up at the door to the house, the name of the cheese factory (Córcega, that word with its French flavour, and which also summoned up the charms of a sea so close to her birthplace, the Mediterranean that she'd seen on postcards), the paint they had to rub on to the Gouda cheese to distinguish it from the others, the very slight mockery her classmates subjected her to during the initial months, and the fact that the nuns of La Presentación College, who didn't seem able to comprehend the stubborn ignorance of the little girl, went wild with joy talking about the Death and the Resurrection, Good Friday and the Coming of Our Lord, and on the other hand they choked on scandalized gasps when they found Sara explaining circumcision to the daughters of Barreto, a barrister and old friend of former President Olaya Herrera.

And that was how, at the end of 1987, I wrote a couple of pages, and was surprised to find, while looking through old papers, the index card on which I'd written, years earlier, a sort of quick writing course provided by my father upon discovering that I had started to write up my degree thesis. 'First: everything that sounds good to the ear is good for the text. Second: in case of doubt, see first point.' Just as when I was writing up my thesis, that card, pinned to the wall above my desk, served as an amulet, an incantation against fear. Those pages contained barely a fragment of that recounted life; there, for example, was the way the soldiers imprisoned Sara's father, Peter Guterman; there were the soldiers, who smashed a plaster bust against the wall and sliced open the leather armchairs with their knives, but to no avail, because the identity cards they were searching for were nowhere in that house, but rather creased inside her mother's corset, and eight days later, when Peter Guterman was released but his passport was not, allowed them to cross the border and embark, with their car and everything, at Ijumiden, a port on the canal a few minutes from Amsterdam. But the most important thing about those two pages was something else: within them was the confirmation that all that could be told, the suggestion that I could be the one to tell it, and the promise of that strange satisfaction: giving shape to other people's lives, stealing what's happened to them, which is always disordered and confused, and putting it in order on paper; justifying, in some more or less honourable way, the curiosity I've always felt for all the emanations of other bodies (from ideas to menses) and which has driven me, by a sort of internal compulsion, to violate secrets, reveal confidences, show interest in others the way a friend should when deep down I'm just interviewing them like a vulgar reporter. But then I've never known where friendship stops and reporting starts.

With Sara, of course, things were no different. Over the course of several days I kept interrogating her, and did so with such devotion, or such morbid insistence, that I began to divide in two, to live the substitute and vicarious life of my interviewee and my original daily life as if they were distinct, and not a tale set in a reality. I witnessed the fascinating spectacle of memory kept in storage: Sara kept file folders full of documents, a sort of testimony of her passage through the world as legitimate and material as a shed constructed with wood from her own land. There were open plastic folders, plastic folders with flaps, cardboard folders, both with and without elastic closures, pastel-coloured folders and others that were white but dirty and others that were black, folders that slept there with no specific plans but prepared and very willing to exercise their role as second-rate Pandora's boxes. In the evenings, almost always towards the end of the conversation, Sara would put the folders away, take the cassette on which I'd recorded her voice over the last few hours out of the machine, put on a record of German songs from the thirties (*Veronika, der Lenz ist da* or perhaps *Mein kleiner grüner Kaktus*) and offer me a drink, which we'd sip in silence listening to the old music. I liked to think that from outside, from an apartment whose curious tenant was spying on us, this would be the image: a fluorescent rectangle and two figures, a woman well settled into the imminence of old age and a younger man, a student or perhaps a son, in any case someone who was listening and was used to doing so. That was me: I kept my mouth shut and listened, but I wasn't her son; I took notes, because that was my job. And I thought later, at the right moment, when the raw material of her tale had finished, when the notes had been taken and the documents seen and opinions heard, I would sit before the dossier of the case, of my case, and impose order: was that not the chronicler's single privilege?

One of those days, Sara asked me why I wanted to write about her life, and I thought it would have been easy to evade the question or throw out any old witticism, but to answer with something approaching the truth was as essential to me as it seemed to be, at that moment, to her. I could have said that there were things I needed to come to understand. That certain areas of my experience (in my country, with my people, at this time that I happened to be living) had escaped me, generally because my attention was taken up with other more banal ones, and I wanted to keep that from continuing to happen. To become aware: that was my intention, at once simple and pretentious; and to think about the past, oblige someone to remember it, was one way of doing it, arm wrestling against entropy, an attempt to make the disorder of the world, whose only destiny was a more intense disorder, stop, be put in shackles, for once defeated. I could have said that or part of it; in my favour I point out that I avoided these grandiloquent lies and chose more humble lies, or rather, incomplete lies. 'I want his approval, Sara,' I told her. 'I want him to look at me with respect. It matters more than anything ever has.' I was going to complete the incomplete truth, to speak to Sara of the phrase with which my father once described her – 'She is my sister in the shadows,' he told me. 'Without her I wouldn't have survived a week in this world of madness' – but I didn't manage to. Sara interrupted me. 'I understand,' she said. 'I understand perfectly.' And I didn't insist, because it seemed only normal that the shadow sister should understand everything without detailed explanations; but I noted on an index card: *Chapter title: Sister in the Shadows*. I never managed to use it, however, because my father was not mentioned in the interviews or in the book itself, despite having formed an important part – at least as far as could be seen – of Sara Guterman's exile.

I published *A Life in Exile* in November 1988, three months after my father's famous speech. The following is the first chapter of the book. It was titled, in bold italics, with four words that have been filling up across the years and that today, as I write, threaten to overflow: *The Nueva Europa Hotel.*

The first thing Peter Guterman did when he arrived in Duitama was to paint the house and build a second floor. There, separated by a narrow landing, were his office and his bedroom, arranged just as they had been in the house in Emmerich. He had always liked to keep his work and his family within a few metres of each other; furthermore, the idea of starting a new life in an old place seemed like taking his luck for granted. And so, he set about refurbishing. Meanwhile, other Germans, those in Tunja or those in Sogamoso, advised him time and again not to do so much work on a house that didn't belong to him.

'As soon as you have it looking nice,' they told him, 'the owner will ask for it back. You have to be careful here; these Colombians are cunning.'

And that's how it went: the owner demanded the house back; he alleged a fictitious buyer and barely even apologized for the inconvenience. The Guterman family, who hadn't been in Colombia for six months yet, had to move again already. But then came the first stroke of luck. In those days something was going on in Tunja. The city was full of important people. A Swiss businessman from Berne, who was negotiating setting up pharmaceutical laboratories in Colombia, had become a friend of the family. One day, at around ten in the morning, he arrived at the house unexpectedly.

'I need an interpreter,' he said to Peter Guterman. 'It's more than an important negotiation. It's a matter of life or death.'

Peter Guterman could think of no better solution than to offer his daughter, the only one in the family who could speak Spanish as well as understand it. Sara had to obey the Swiss man. She knew perfectly well that the will of an adult, and an adult who was a friend of her father's, was law to an adolescent like herself. On the other hand, she always felt insecure in that sort of situation: she had never managed to feel at ease with the unspoken rules of the host society. This man was European, like her. How had crossing the Atlantic changed his ways? Should she greet him as she would have greeted him in Emmerich? But this man, in Emmerich, would not have looked her in the face. Sara had not forgotten the occasional snubs she'd received over the last few years, or what happened to Gentiles' faces when they spoke of her father.

She went to the lunch, and it turned out the man for whom she was to convert the Swiss man's words into Spanish was President Eduardo Santos, recognized friend of the German colony; and there was Santos, who had so much respect for Sara's father, squeezing the hand of the adolescent interpreter, asking her how she was, congratulating her on the quality of her Spanish. 'From that moment I felt committed to the Liberal Party forever,' Sara would say many years later, with a sharply ironic tone. 'I've always been like that. Three set phrases and I'm overcome.' She interpreted during a two-hour lunch (and in another two she'd completely forgotten the content of the words she'd interpreted), and afterwards she mentioned the move to Santos.

'We're getting tired of moving from one house to another,' she said. 'It's like living in shifts.'

'Well, set up a hotel,' said Santos. 'Then you can be the ones to evict people.'

But the matter couldn't be so simple. At that time foreigners were not allowed to practise, without previous authorization, occupations other than those they'd declared upon entering the country. Sara pointed this out to the President.

'Oh, don't worry about that,' was the answer. 'I'll take care of the permission.'

And a year later, the cheese factory sold at a generous profit, they opened the Hotel Pensión Nueva Europa in Duitama. When the President of the Republic attended the opening of a hotel (everyone thought), that hotel was destined to be successful.

Sara's father had intended to baptize the hotel with his name, Hotel Pensión Guterman, but his associates let him know that a surname like his at a time like that was the worst start you could give to a business. Just a few months earlier, a Bogotá taxi company had contracted seven Jewish refugees as drivers; the taxi drivers of Bogotá organized an elaborate campaign against them, and all over the place, in the shop windows downtown, in the windows of cabs and even some trams, could be seen posters with the slogan: *We support the taxi drivers in their campaign against the Poles*. That was the first sign that the new life wasn't going to be much easier than the old. When the Gutermans heard about the taxi drivers, Sara's father's despair was so intense that the family reached the point of fearing something serious. (After all, one of his friends had already hanged himself in his house in Bonn, shortly after the pogrom of 1938.) Peter Guterman spoke warily of the spurious national identity the popular voice had assigned him: it had cost him several years to get used to the loss of his German citizenship, as if it were some object that had gone missing by mistake, a key fallen out of a pocket. He didn't complain, but he acquired the habit of cutting out the statistics that regularly appeared on the inside pages of the Bogotá newspapers: 'Port: Buenaventura. Ship: *Bodegraven*. Jews: 47. Distribution: Germans (33), Austrians (10), Yugoslavs (3), Czechoslovakians (1).' In his scrapbook there were Finnish vessels, like the *Vindlon*, and Spanish ones, like the *Santa María*. Peter Guterman paid attention to this news as if part of his family was arriving on the steamers. But Sara knew that these clippings were not familial announcements but emergency telegrams, actual reports on the discomfort the new arrivals caused among the locals. What's important is that the matter ended up justifying the name of the hotel. Peter Guterman's associates were Colombians; the word *Europa* sounded to them like a panacea in three syllables, as if the mere mention of the so-called civilized world would bring with it the definitive solution to their Third World problems. In a letter that later passed into the family's private history, into that collection of anecdotes with which aunts and grandmothers the world over fill domestic lunches as if trying to transmit clean blood to their descendants, his father told them, 'I can't understand why you people are so fascinated by the name of a cow.' And they read the letter and laughed; and they kept reading it, and kept doubling over with laughter, for a long time.

The Hotel Nueva Europa was in one of those colonial houses that had been convents since Independence and were then inherited by seminaries or religious communities with no great interest in maintaining them. All the constructions were the same: they all had an interior patio, and in the centre of the patio, the statue of the founder of the order or some saint. In the future hotel, Bartolomé de las Casas was the presiding statue, but the friar ceded his place to a stone fountain as soon as was possible. The fountain of the Nueva Europa was a circular pool large enough for a person to lie down in – over the years, more than one drunk would do – where the water picked up the taste of the stone and the moss that accumulated along its walls. At first the water was filled with little fish, golden and dancing; then with coins that gradually rusted. Before the fish, however, there hadn't been anything: nothing except the water and a pool that filled up with birds in the mornings, so many that it was necessary to shoo them away with the broom, because not all the guests liked them. And the guests had to be humoured: the place was not cheap. Peter Guterman charged 2 pesos 50 for bed and board with five daily meals, while the Regis, the other hotel of the moment in the region, charged a peso less. But the Nueva Europa was always full; full, especially, of politicians and foreigners. Jorge Eliécer Gaitán (who, incidentally, hated birds with the same passion he put into his speeches) and Miguel López Pumarejo were among the most regular clients. Lucas Caballero was neither a politician nor foreign, but he went to the hotel whenever he could. Before arriving he'd send a telegram that was always the same, word for word: 'ARRIVING NEXT THURSDAY STOP REQUEST ROOM WITHOUT BALLOONS STOP'.

The balloons he was referring to were eiderdowns, which Caballero didn't like. He preferred heavy wool blankets, the kind that collect dust and make allergy sufferers sneeze. Peter Guterman would have his room made up according to these specifications, issuing orders in German so urgently that the hotel employees, girls from Sogamosa and Duitama, managed to learn some basic words. Hairpeter, they said. Yes, Hairpeter. Right away, Hairpeter. Señor Guterman, professional obsessive, understood and accepted the obsessions of his most valued guests. (When he was expecting Gaitán, he'd have a scarecrow set up among the roof tiles of the mansion, even though he thought it detracted from the roof's folkloric charm.) Sara had to intervene all the time, serve as translator and conciliator, because Spanish was a terrible effort for her father from the start, and he never did master it very well; and, since we're also talking about a man accustomed to impossible levels of efficiency, he very often lost his temper, and would occasionally roar like a caged animal, leaving his employees in tears all afternoon. Peter Guterman was not a nervous man; but it would make him nervous to see the President, candidates to the presidency and the capital's most important journalists fighting over the rooms in his hotel. Sara, who with time had begun to get a better sense of her new country, tried to explain to her father that *they* were the nervous ones; that this was a country where a man ruled the roost simply by virtue of coming from the north; that for the majority of his guests, pompous and ambitious as they were, staying in the hotel was somehow like being abroad. That's how it was: a room in the Guterman family's hotel was, for the majority of those pretentious Creoles, the only opportunity to see the world, the only important role they could have in their minuscule play.

Because the Nueva Europa was, first and foremost, a meeting place for foreigners. North Americans, Spaniards, Germans, Italians, people from all over. Colombia, which had never been a country of immigrants, at that moment and in that place seemed to be one. There were those who arrived at the beginning of the century in search of money, because they'd heard that in those South American countries everything was still to be done; there were those who arrived escaping from the Great War, most of them Germans who'd been scattered around the world trying to make a living, because in their country this had become impossible; there were the Jews. So this turned out to be, no more no less, a country of escapees. And that whole persecuted country had ended up in the Hotel Nueva Europa, as if it was the true House of Representatives for the displaced world, a Universal Museum of the *Auswanderer*; and sometimes it felt like that in reality, because the hotel guests gathered each evening in the reception room downstairs to listen to the news of the war on the radio. There were confrontations, words exchanged, as was to be expected, but always prudently, because Peter Guterman managed quite early to convince people to leave their politics at the reception. That was his phrase; everyone remembered it, because it was one of the few things the hotel owner learned to say fluently: '*Bitte*, leave your politics at reception,' he would say to people arriving, without even giving them time to set down their suitcases to sign the register, and people accepted this pact because the momentary truce was more comfortable for everyone than coming to blows with the people at the next table every time they came down for a meal. But maybe that wasn't the reason. Maybe it was true that there, in that hotel on the other side of the world, people would share a table with people who in their country of origin would have thrown stones through the reception windows. What brought them together? What neutralized the merciless hatreds that arrived at the Nueva Europa like news from another life?

And the fact is that during those first years the war was something heard on the radio, a sad spectacle from elsewhere. 'The blacklists came later, and the hotels turned into luxurious jails,' says Sara, referring to the concentration camps for citizens of the Axis nations. 'Yes, that happened later. It was later that the war on the other side of the ocean came home to those of us on this side. We were so innocent, we thought we were safe. Anyone can confirm it for you. Everyone remembers it perfectly well: it was very difficult to be German at that time.' In the Guterman family's hotel things happened that destroyed families, disrupted lives, ruined futures; but none of that was visible until much later, when time had gone by and the ruined futures and disrupted lives began to be noticed. Everywhere – in Bogotá, in Cúcuta, in Barranquilla, in miserable towns like Santander de Quilichao – it was the same; there were places, however, that seemed to work like black holes, invoking chaos, absorbing the worst of a person. The Gutermans' hotel, especially at a certain point in time, had been one of them. 'Just thinking of it makes me sad,' Sara Guterman says now, calling up those events forty-five years later. 'Such a beautiful place, so dear to people, where such horrible things could happen.' And what things were those? 'It was as it says in the Bible. Brother shall betray brother, and the father the son; and children shall rise up against their parents.'

Of course, writing words such as *Auswanderer* or *blacklists* demands or should demand some sort of guarantee on the part of the one writing them. These were unreliable words and the book was full of them. I know this now, but then I barely suspected it: in manuscript, these pages had appeared so pacific and neutral that I never considered them capable of making anyone uncomfortable, much less of provoking disputes; the printed and bound version, however, was a sort of Molotov cocktail ready to land in the middle of the Santoro household.

'Ah, Santoro,' said Dr Raskovsky when a nurse intercepted him to ask how the surgery had gone. 'Gabriel, isn't it? Yes, it went very well. Wait here. In a moment we can go in and see the patient.' But then, it had gone well? The patient was alive? 'Not just alive, much more than that,' said the doctor, already on his way and spouting automatic phrases. 'You should see the heart he's got, just like new.' And after the sort of dizziness that hit me when I heard the news, something strange happened: I didn't know if my name, pronounced by the doctor, referred to the patient or the patient's son. I looked for a bathroom to wash my face before going into Intensive Care. I did it thinking of my father, not wanting him to see me like this, because I couldn't remember the last time one of the two had seen the other looking so out of sorts. In front of the mirror I took off my jacket. I saw two butterflies of sweat under my arms, and surprised myself thinking of Dr Raskovsky's armpits, as if we were close friends; and later, as I waited for my father to wake up, that intimacy I'd been seeking seemed detestable, perhaps because my father himself had taught me never to feel in debt to anyone. Not even to the one responsible for him still being alive.

Despite the doctor having spoken in the plural, I went into Intensive Care, that torture chamber, by myself. The monitors blinked like owls on the surrounding walls and tables; there were six beds, arranged with odious symmetry and separated by opaque partition walls like the ones in public lavatories, with aluminium rails that reflected glints of neon light. The monitors each beeped in their own rhythm, the respirators breathed, and in one of those beds, the last one on the left, the only one that faced the board where the nurses wrote the day's instructions in red and black markers, was my father, breathing through a greyish corrugated tube that filled his mouth. I lifted his gown and saw for the second time in one day (after never having seen it in my whole life) my father's penis, resting on his groin, almost at the level of his mutilated hand, and circumcised, unlike mine. They'd fitted him with a catheter so he wouldn't have to be disturbed when he needed to urinate. That was how it was: my father was communicating with the world through plastic tubes. And through electrodes arranged like patches on an animal's coat across his chest, on his forehead. And through needles: the one that was injecting him with tranquillizers and anti-biotics disappeared into his neck, the one for the drip into the vein of his left arm. I sat on a round stool and said hello. 'Hi, Dad. It's all over now, everything's fine.' He couldn't hear me. 'I told you, remember? I told you everything would be fine, and now it is. It's all over. We got through this.' His respirator was working, his monitor kept beeping, but he had absented himself. The tube in his neck was taped to his face, and stretched the loose flesh of his cheeks (his sixty-seven-year-old cheeks). The effect underlined the tiredness of his skin, of his tissues, and I, closing my eyes a little, could see the speeded-up film of his decomposition. There was another

34

image I tried to summon up, to see what I could learn from it: that of a plastic heart the size of a fist, that had sat for a whole month on my biology teacher's desk.

At four in the afternoon they asked me to leave, although I'd spent no more than ten minutes with the patient, but I went back the next day, first thing, and after confronting the aggressive bureaucracy of the San Pedro Clinic – the trip to the administrator's office, the request for a permanent-access pass that included my name and identity card and which I should keep well visible on my chest, the declaration that I was the patient's only relative and, therefore, only visitor – I stayed until after twelve, when I was kicked out by the same nurse who'd kicked me out the night before: a woman with thick make-up whose forehead was always sweaty. By my second visit, my father was beginning to wake up. That was one of the changes. The other was told to me by the nurse as if she were answering exam questions. 'There was an attempt to remove the respirator. He didn't respond well. Fluid collected in his lungs, he lost consciousness, but he's a bit better now.' There was one more tube wounding my father's body: it filled with bloody fluid and emptied into a bag with numbers on it to measure the quantity. Yes: it was a drain. Fluid had got into his lungs and they were draining it off. He moaned about different pains, but none as intense as that from the tube inserted between his ribs, which obliged him to lie almost on his side despite the fact that this was precisely the most painful position for the incision in his chest. He couldn't speak for the pain: sometimes his face would contract into dreadful grimaces; sometimes he rested, making no sounds about what he was feeling, not looking at me. He didn't speak; and the tube in his mouth gave his complaints a tone that in other circumstances would have been comical.

The nurse came, changed his oxygen, checked the drainage bag and left again. One time she stayed for three minutes exactly, while she took his temperature, and asked me what had happened to my father's hand.

'What does it matter to you?' I said. 'Just do your job and don't be nosy.'

She didn't ask me any more questions, not that first day or in the days that followed, during which the routine was repeated: I took up all the visiting hours, exploiting the fact that my father had insisted on keeping the operation secret, so no relatives or friends came to lend support. Nevertheless, something seemed to indicate that this wasn't ideal. 'Isn't there anyone outside?' was the first thing he asked me on the morning of the third day, as soon as they took the tube out of his mouth. 'No, Dad, no one.' And when the evening visiting hours began, he pointed to the door again and asked, through the haze of the drugs, if anyone had come. 'No,' I said. 'No one's come to bother you.' 'I've been left all alone,' he said. 'I've managed to end up all alone. That's what I've endeavoured to do, I've put all my efforts into it. And look, it's come out perfectly, not just anyone could manage it, look in the waiting room, *quod erat demonstrandum*.' He remained silent for a while, because it was an effort to speak. 'How I wish she were here,' he said then. It took me a second to realize he was referring to my mother, not to Sara. 'She would have kept me company, she was a good companion. She was so good, Gabriel. I don't know if you remember, why would you remember, I don't know if a child realizes these things. But she was wonderful. And a fellow like me with her, imagine. The way life goes. I never deserved her. She died and I never had time to deserve her. That's the first thing I think about when I think of her.' I, on the other hand, thought about a misdiagnosed pneumonia, I thought about the clandestine manoeuvres of the cancer; I thought, most of all, of the day my parents received the final diagnosis. I had been masturbating over a lingerie catalogue, and the impression made by the coincidence between the illness and one of my first ejaculations was so powerful that I was feverish that whole night; and the following Sunday, when I stepped inside a church for the first time in my life, I had the bad idea to confess, and the priest thought it obvious that my perversions were responsible for what was happening to my mother. Only much later, well into, even comfortable in, what they call the age of majority, could I accept my innocence and understand that the illness had not been a punishment from on high nor the chastisement that corresponded to my sin. But I'd never spoken of that to my father, and the variegated scene of Intensive Care, that seedy hotel of bad omens, didn't seem the ideal setting for such frankness. 'I dreamt about her,' my father was saying. 'You don't have to tell me,' I said. 'Rest, don't talk so much.' But it was too late: he'd started talking. 'I dreamt I went to the cinema,' he said. In the stalls, sitting three rows in front, was a woman who looked very much like my mother. The film was *Of Human Bondage*, which seemed incongruous given the cinema and also the audience; during the scene where Paul Henreid walks by himself in a poor area of London (it's a silent, nocturnal scene), my father could stand it no longer. From the darkness of the aisle, kneeling to keep out of people's way, he made out his wife's profile in the intermittent light from the film. 'Where were you?' he asked her. 'We thought you had died.' 'I'm not dead, Gabriel; what silly things you say.' 'But that's what we believed. We thought you had died of cancer.' 'You're both so silly,' said my mother. 'When I'm

37

going to die I'll let you know.' One of the darkest frames then appeared on the screen, maybe the black sky or a brick wall. The stalls went dark. When daylight reappeared in the film, my mother was walking between the rows towards the exit, without touching the knees of the people in the seats. Her sculptured face turned to look at my father before she left, and she waved goodbye.

'I wonder if it means something,' my father said. And I was going to answer that it didn't – you know full well, I was going to say to him, in a rather impatient tone, that dreams don't mean anything, don't let the surgery fill your head with superstitions, they're electric impulses and nothing more, the synapsis of a few disordered and confused neurons – when the patient took in a gulp of air, half opened his eyes and said, 'Maybe we could let Sara know.'

'Yes,' I said. 'If you want.'

'Not for me,' he said. 'It's more for her. If we don't tell her there'll be hell to pay later.'

I can't say I was surprised. The fact that we'd both thought of her in the space of a few days was less a coincidence than symptomatic of the discreet importance she had in our lives; once again I had the feeling about her that I'd had on several previous occasions, the notion that Sara Guterman was not the innocuous friend she seemed to be, that inoffensive, almost invisible foreigner, but that there was something more behind her image, and the confidence my father had always had in the image was moving. 'I'll call her tonight,' I said. 'She'll be very pleased, that's for sure.' I was about to say, *She'll be very pleased that you've survived*, but stopped myself in time, because confronting my father with the notion of survival could be even more harmful than a failed survival. That was him: a survivor. He'd survived the machete-wielding men and then his heart — that capricious muscle — and, if he could talk to me about this, he'd say he'd also survived this city where every landscape is a *memento mori*. Like a hostage who had been freed by his kidnappers, like a woman saved from a bomb blast by altering her itinerary at the last minute (by not doing her shopping at Los Tres Elefantes, by going for lunch with a friend instead of going to Centro 93), my father had survived. But suddenly I found myself wondering: what for? Why does a man want to keep living who at sixty-seven years of age could be said to be a superfluous element, someone who had completed his cycle, someone who had nothing pending in the world? His life didn't seem to hold much meaning any more; at least, I thought, not the meaning that he would have wanted it to provide. Seeing him looking so small, nobody, not even his own son, would have guessed at the private revolution that was beginning to take shape inside his head.

II

The Second Life

THAT'S HOW THE inevitable perversion began, the
moment one ends up becoming father to one's own
father and witnesses, fascinated, the disrupted authority
(power in the wrong hands) and out of place obedience
(the one who was strong is fragile and accepts orders and
impositions). Sara, of course, was with us by the time they
discharged my father, so I could lean on her to get through
those initial difficulties: the transfer of the patient to his own
bed, the atmosphere of the apartment seeming inhospitable
and even hostile compared to the elegance, the comforts,
the *intelligence* of a hospital room. By the time we returned
to his apartment, it was as if after the surgery his body was
even more shrunken: the trip from the car door to his bed
took us fifteen minutes, because my father couldn't take
two steps without having to stop to catch his breath,
without feeling his heart was going to explode, and he
said so, but saying so also made him short of breath, and the
paranoia began all over again. His leg hurt (where they'd
extracted the vein to make the graft), his chest hurt (as if the
stitches were going to burst from one moment to the next),
he asked if we were sure the veins had been well sewn up
(and the verb, with its connotations of manual trades, of
craftsmanship, of a slapdash hobby, terrified him). As soon as
we got him under the covers, he asked us to close the
curtains but not to leave him alone, and he turned on his
side, like a foetus or a frightened child, maybe out of habit
from the tube stuck between his ribs for so many days,

43

maybe due to the way bodies have of making themselves small when there is danger.

Sara took charge of the injections at first, and I, instead of just letting her get on with it, watched her closely: with her black skirts down to her ankles, her knee-high boots and long sweaters – dressed like a forty-year-old – moving through my father's apartment with her swimmer's hips, Sara belied the three children she'd had, and from the back no one would have thought her any older if it weren't for the luminous grey of her hair, the perfect bun like a ball of nylon: her silhouette, in all its details, made the crisis my father was undergoing seem even starker. At some moment I wondered if the inescapable contrast between this woman's buoyant energy and his own crude deterioration mightn't be too much for him, but a sort of complicity soon became evident between the two of them, a current of collusion that there, in the theatre of fondness and support and affection that any convalescence is, seemed to become more intense. There was more than one reason for it, as I found out later: Sara had also had her quota of impertinent physicians. Ten or so years before, she had been diagnosed with an aneurysm, and she, like the wilful and sceptical woman she was, had taken a decision contrary to the one her children seemed to prefer: she refused to undergo surgery. 'I'm too old to have my cranium opened,' she'd said, and the impertinent one, as well as his colleagues, had conceded that it was not in any way possible to guarantee the success of the operation, and confessed that among the possible outcomes was partial paralysis or being reduced to a state of permanent stupidity for the rest of her life. That, however, wasn't the problem, but rather that Sara had *also* refused the other option the doctor proposed: to go and live in a warm climate, as close to

44

sea-level as possible, because in Bogotá at two thousand six hundred metres the altitude multiplied the pressure with which her own blood threatened the weakened wall of one of her veins. 'Suppose I've got ten years left to live,' she apparently said. 'Am I going to spend them on the coast, an hour by plane away from my children, from my grandchildren? Or in one of those towns, La Mesa or Girardot, where there's nothing but half-naked people and flies the size of Volkswagens?' So she'd stayed in Bogotá, aware as she was that she was carrying a time bomb in her head and frequenting the same places as ever, the same bookshops as ever, the same friends as ever.

The fact is that there was something fascinating in the showy familiarity between them. On the third day of the convalescence, as soon as the doorman announced Sara over the intercom, my father took the unused serviette out from under his plate, handed it to me and dictated a welcome note, so when Sara came in she received the following caption, written at speed in one long blue word: *From the anterior artery to the antagonistic aneurysm: long live bloody-minded blood vessels.* Later there were other assonances, other alliterations, but this first serviette is still the one I remember best, a sort of declaration of civil conduct between the two oldies. If she was already there when I arrived to see my father, what I found was not a friend paying a visit to a sick man, with all its weight of worried questions and grateful answers, but a scene that seemed not to have moved for whole centuries: the woman sitting in a chair, her eyes fixed on the crossword puzzle she was working on, and the patient lying on his bed, as quiet and alone as the stone figure on a papal tomb. Sara didn't hug me, she didn't even stand up to say hello, she just took my face in her two dry hands and pulled it towards her and kissed me on the cheek – her smile didn't show her teeth: it was prudent, sceptical, reticent: she gave nothing away – and made me feel as if I were the visitor (not the son), as if she were the one who'd been taking care of my father all these days (and now she was grateful for my visit: how good to see you, thanks for coming, thanks for keeping us company). My father, for his part, was lost in his fog of medication and exhaustion. However, liberated from the corrugated tube that had breached his mouth, his face had now recovered some normality, and I could occasionally get the memory of his violated ribs and the draining of his lungs out of my head.

Until then, it had never seemed so evident that my father had entered his final years. He couldn't move without help, standing up on his own was out of the question, speaking left him breathless, and there Sara and I were to help him to the toilet, to interpret his few words. Sometimes he coughed; to keep him from screaming in pain and disturbing the neighbours, Sara held a towel rolled up and held tight with two pieces of masking tape, like a scale model of an old-fashioned sleeping bag, across his chest. In the mornings he sat in his underwear on the toilet and I helped him wash his armpits. Thus I eventually confronted the wound I had preferred to avoid out of fear of my stomach's reaction; the first time, my memory, which likes to do these things, superimposed the image of the shrunken, naked, vulnerable man with one of a certain photo from his youth in which my father appears standing like a guard, his hands crossed behind his back and his chest held high. In that image not only was his hair black, but that black hair was everywhere: it covered his chest and his flat belly, and also – this didn't show in the photo, but I knew it – a good part of his back. For the operation, the nurses had shaved his chest and smeared a yellow liquid over it; these few days later, the hair began to grow again, but some of the pores were blocked. What I saw then was the inflamed vertical incision (an incision made not just with a scalpel, but also with a saw, although the severed bones were not visible), the same red as the two or three infected hair follicles, and lifted in certain areas by the pressure of the wire with which the surgeons had closed the rupture in the sternum. At that moment I felt, without false empathy, that punctual pain, the puncture of the wire — a foreign body — beneath the damaged skin. And nevertheless I washed him; all those days, more successfully each time, I kept washing him. With one hand I held his arms up in the air, lifting them by the elbow, for they were incapable of lifting themselves; with the other I washed the straight, smelly hairs in his armpits. The most difficult part was rinsing the area. At first I tried to do it by cupping my hands, but all the water spilt out before it touched my father's skin, and I felt like an inexpert painter trying to paint a ceiling. Then I started using a sponge, slower but also gentler. My father, who remained silent during the whole process, out of reserve or due to the unpleasantness of the situation, one day finally asked me to put a bit of deodorant on him, please, cut out this degrading procedure, please, and get him back to bed, please, and let's pray I wouldn't have to wash even more private parts.

Every day, Sara asked him *if he'd moved his bowels*. (I don't know what shook me more the first time I heard her say it: the adolescent euphemism or the intimacy that the question, in spite of the euphemism, revealed.) Every day, I took charge of the simvastatin and the baby aspirin, ridiculous names like those of all medicines, and after a while began to administer the injections as well. Once a day I lifted his pyjama top and pinched the loose flesh of his waist with one

47

hand and stuck the hypodermic into it with the other. The needle disappearing into the skin, my father's shouts, my own trembling pulse – the thumb pressing the dense liquid out of the syringe (into the flesh) – all that became shockingly habitual, because the routine of inflicting pain cannot be comfortable for anyone. The injections had to be given for a week; during this time, I stayed with him. I used to do it in the mornings, after my father woke up, but before that I was careful to talk to him about something, anything, for half an hour, so his day wouldn't start with a needle. A physiotherapist came mid-morning and made him sit up in bed, facing her, and imitate her movements, at first as if they were playing a mirroring game and later as if the woman were, in fact, in charge of transmitting to the patient knowledge that is innate and instinctive to everybody else, not learned in morning classes: how to raise an arm, how to straighten one's torso, how to make a pair of legs take you to the bathroom. Gradually I came to know that her name was Angelina, that she was from Medellín but had come to live in Bogotá after completing her studies, and that she was over forty but under fifty ('Us, the ones on the fourth floor,' she said once). I would have liked to ask her why, at her age, she wasn't married, but I was afraid she'd be offended, because the day of the first session she'd entered the apartment the way a bull enters a ring, demonstrating at once that she was here to do her work and that she didn't have time to look or any desire to be looked at, even though she wore brightly coloured blouses with buttons that looked like mother-of-pearl and even though later it didn't seem to matter too much to her if her breasts – if those buttons straining over her breasts – brushed my father's back during the massage, or if drops fell on to the faded sheet, on to the pillow from her freshly washed, very black hair.

It was one of those days, after Angelina had said goodbye until the following morning (she only had a couple more days of work with my father and his problematic muscles), that we talked about what happened after his 6 August speech. My father was learning to move again at the same time as he learned to talk to me. Having me as an interlocutor, he discovered, implied another way of speaking, different, daring, radically risky, because his way of addressing me had always been dominated by irony or omission, those strategies of protection or concealment, and now he realized he was able to look me in the eye and speak direct, clear, *literal* sentences. I thought: If the heart-attack scare and the operation were the prerequisites for this dialogue, I should bless the anterior descending, raise an altar to its incriminating catheterization. That's how we started, without any warning, to talk about what had happened three years before. 'I want you to forget what I said,' said my father. 'I want you to forget what I wrote. I'm not good at asking things like this, but that's how it is. I want you to erase my comments from your head, because what's just happened to me is special, a second chance, Gabriel. They gave me a second chance, not everyone gets so lucky, and this time I want to carry on as if I hadn't published that review, as if I hadn't actually gone as far as doing that cowardly thing I did to us.' He turned over, heavy and clumsy and solemn like a warship changing direction. 'Of course, it may be that those things can't be corrected, that the thing about a second chance is a pure lie, one of those things they invent to deceive the unwary. That had occurred to me; I'm not that much of an idiot. But I don't want to admit it, Gabriel, and no one can force me to;

being mistaken is still one of our inalienable rights. That's how it has to be, at least if you're going to stand a chance of staying reasonably sane. Can you imagine? Can you imagine if you couldn't take back anything you said? No, it's unthinkable, I don't believe anyone could stand it. I'd take the hemlock or commit suicide in Calauria, or any of those elegant Panhellenic martyrdoms.' I saw him smile half-heartedly.

'Does it hurt?'

'Of course it does. But the pain is good. It keeps me aware, makes me notice things.'

'What do you have to notice?'

'That I'm alive again, Gabriel. That I still have things to do around here.'

'You have to recover,' I said. 'Then there'll be time to do whatever you want, but first you have to get out of that bed. That alone is going to take you a few months.'

'How many?'

'As many as it takes. You're not telling me that now you're in a hurry.'

'No, no hurry, not at all,' said my father. 'But it's really strange, don't you think? Now that you mention it, it seems strange. It's as if it's been given to me whole.'

'What has?'

'This second life.'

Six months later, when my father was dead and had been cremated in the furnace of the Jardines de Paz, I remembered the atmosphere of those days as if within them was encoded all that would come afterwards. When my father spoke to me about the things he had to do, I suddenly noticed he was weeping, and his tears – clinical and predictable – took me by surprise, as if they hadn't been forecast in sufficient detail by the doctors. 'For him it'll be as if he'd been dead,' Dr Raskovsky had said, rather condescendingly. 'He might get depressed, might not want to have the curtains open, like a child. All this is normal, the most normal thing in the world.' Well, it wasn't; a weeping father almost never is. At that moment I didn't know it, but that weeping would recur several times during the days of his convalescence; it stopped shortly afterwards, and in the next six months (six months that were like a premature and unsuccessful rebirth, six months that passed between the day of the operation and the day my father travelled to Medellín, six months that covered the recuperation, the beginning of the second life and its consequences) it never happened again. But the image of my father weeping has remained irremediably associated with his desire to correct old words, and, although I cannot prove that was the exact reason – I haven't been able to interrogate him for this book, and I've had to rely on other informers – I feel that it was at that moment my father thought for the first time what he thought in such detail and with such bad luck he thought again later: *This is my chance.* His chance to correct errors, to rectify faults, to ask for forgiveness, because he'd been granted a second life, and the second life, as everyone knows, always comes with the inconvenient obligation to correct the first one.

His errors and their corrections happened like this:

In 1988, as soon as I received my copies of *A Life in Exile*, I took one to my father, I left it with the doorman and sat down to wait for a call or an old-fashioned, solemn and perhaps moving letter. When neither the letter nor the phone call arrived, I began to wonder if the doorman had misplaced the package; but before I had time to pass by the building and find out, rumours of my father's comments began to reach me.

Were they really as unpredictable as they seemed to me? Or was it true, as I sometimes thought over the following years, that anybody would have seen them coming by simply taking off the blindfold of family relations? The prophet's kit – the tools of prediction – was within my reach. My decision to write about current things had always elicited from my father inoffensive sarcasm, which nevertheless made me feel uncomfortable; nothing caused him as much mistrust as someone concerned with things contemporary: spoken by him, the word sounded like an insult. He preferred to talk about Cicero and Herodotus; actuality seemed like a suspect practice, almost infantile, and if he didn't perpetrate his opinions in public it was out of a sort of secret shame, or rather to avoid a situation where he'd feel obliged to admit that he too had read, at the time, *All the President's Men*. But none of that allowed me to foresee his displeasure. The first of his comments, or the first, at least, that I heard of, my father made openly enough to hurt me: he didn't choose a meeting of colleagues, or even a corridor chat, but waited till he found himself in front of the whole group who attended his seminars; and he didn't even choose his own epigram (he did have some quite venomous ones), but preferred to plagiarize an eighteenth-century Englishman.

'This little book is both very original and very good,' he said. 'But the part that is good is not original and the part that is original is not good.'

As had to happen, and as he perhaps hoped would happen, one of the people at the seminar repeated the comment, and the chain of breaches of confidence, which in Colombia is so efficient when it comes to damaging someone, soon reached an acquaintance of mine. Then, with the false and petty compassion common to those who inform on others, that acquaintance, a court reporter on *El Siglo*, very aware of the little respect I deserved, reproduced the phrase for me, enunciating like a good actor and openly studying my face for reactions. The first thing I imagined was my father's roar of laughter, his head thrown back like a neighing horse, his baritone voice resounding through the auditorium and the offices, capable of penetrating closed wooden doors; that laugh, and the stump of his right hand looking for a pocket, were the signs of his victory, and could be seen every time he made a good joke along with his eyelids squeezed shut and most of all the disdain, the talented disdain. Like a vulture, my father could find his opponent's weak spot at a glance, the emptiness of his rhetoric and personal insecurities, and pounce on them; the unexpected thing was that he'd use that talent against me, although sometimes he wasn't wrong in his complaints. 'The photos. The photos are the most irritating. Actors from soap operas and folk singers belong in magazines,' he used to say to anyone who'd listen, 'but a serious journalist? What the hell is a serious journalist doing in a mass-market magazine? Why do readers need to know what he looks like, if he wears glasses or not, if he's twenty or ninety years old? A country's in trouble when youth is a safe conduct, let alone a literary virtue. Have you read the reviews? The young journalist this, the young journalist that. Shit, is there no one in this country capable of saying whether he writes well or not?'

But something told me it wasn't really the photos that bothered him, that his objections ran deeper. I had touched something sacred in his life, I thought at that moment, a sort of private totem: Sara. I had got involved with Sara, and that, due to rules I hadn't managed to figure out (that is, due to rules of a game that no one had explained to me: this became the most useful metaphor when thinking about my father's reactions to my book), was unacceptable. 'Is that it?' I asked Sara one day. 'Are you a taboo subject, an X-rated film? Why didn't you warn me?' 'Don't be silly, Gabriel,' she said, as if waving away a fly. 'You're acting like you don't know him. You're acting like you don't know how he gets when an apostrophe goes missing.' It wasn't impossible that she was right, of course, but I wasn't satisfied (there are lots of things missing in my book but the apostrophes are all present and accounted for). *Dear Sara,* I wrote on a piece of notebook paper that I put into an airmail envelope, because it was the only one I could find, and sent by local post, instead of going to give it to her myself. *If you're as surprised as I am by my dad's attitude, I'd like to discuss the matter with you. If you're less surprised, then I'd like it even more. In other words: after all our interviews, there is one question I forgot to ask. Why, in two hundred pages of information, does my father never appear? Answer it, please, in no more than thirty lines. Thanks.* Sara replied by return of post (that's to say, her envelope reached me in three days). When I opened the envelope I found one of her visiting cards. *Yes, he does. Page 101, lines 14 to 23. And since you allowed me 30, you owe me 21.* I found the book, looked up the page, and read:

It wasn't just learning a language. It was buying rice and cooking it, but also knowing what to do if someone fell ill; how to react if someone insulted you, to keep it from happening again, but also to know how far you could go in insulting them back. If Peter Guterman was called a 'Polack shit', it was necessary to know the implications of the phrase. Or, as a friend of the Guterman family said, 'where the geographical error ended and the scatological one began'.

Beyond the fact that it was true (yes, there was my father, present only with his Cheshire cat grin), it was obvious that Sara was not prepared to take me seriously. That was when I decided to go to the source, to take the offended party by surprise: I'd attend his seminar unannounced the following day, just as I had so many times when I was still a student, then invite him for a drink afterwards at the Hotel Tequendama to talk about the book face to face and, if necessary, with the gloves off. And there I was the next day, punctually seated in the back row, by the translucent windows, by the yellow light that reflected off the International Centre.

But the class ended without me daring to speak to him.

I went back the next day, and the next, and the next as well. I didn't speak to him. I couldn't speak to him.

Nine days went by, nine days of clandestine presence in my father's classroom, before something (not my will, obviously) broke the inertia of the situation. By then the rest of the students had become used to my being there; they put up with me, without recognizing me, the way initiates put up with the presence of a dilettante. That day, as far as I remember, there were fewer people than on other occasions. It seemed obvious, though, that fewer of them were current students and more were recent graduates, a collage of smooth faces with a smattering of ties, the odd briefcase, a few attentive or mature expressions. The light of the lecture hall had always been insufficient, but that day one of the fluorescent tubes flickered till it went out just after my father settled his overcoat on the back of his chair. So, in the gloomy half-light of pale neon, all the faces had bags under their eyes, including the professor's; some faces (not the professor's) yawned. One of the students, the nape of whose neck would serve as my landscape during the class, caught my attention, and it took a moment to understand why: on top of his desk was a book, and I'm sure I choked – though nobody noticed – when I realized it was mine. (The title, more than legible, was insolent; my own name seemed to be shouting at me from the too colourful rectangle of the cover.) The air was a mixture of chalk dust and accumulated sweat – the sweat of so many people listening to so many lectures all day long – my father was far away, with his good hand fingering the buttonholes of his jacket in one of his Napo-leonic gestures. He greeted the room in two words. He didn't need any more to generate a wave of terrified silence, to paralyse the chairs and open all eyes.

He began the class talking about one of his favourite speeches: 'On the Crown' was not only Demosthenes' best speech, it was also a revolutionary text, although that ad-jective is applied to other things these days, a text that had changed the vocation of public speaking as much as gun-powder had changed warfare. My father told how he'd learned it by heart when he was very young – a brief autobiographical interlude, not at all usual in this man who jealously guarded his privacy, but nothing too surpris-ing; or that's what I thought, at least, under the strange gloom of that afternoon – and he said the best way to memorize someone else's words was to get a job far away from where you lived, as he did when he was twenty, taking advantage of simultaneous transport and oil-workers' strikes, accepting a three-month job for 85 pesos a month, driving a fuel tanker between the Troco plants in Barrancabermeja and the buyers in Bogotá. It was an anecdote that I'd already heard on several occasions; when I was a teenager, the tale had conjured up legendary images of the open road, but there was something obscene or exhibitionist in its public retelling. 'On those trips I learned more than one important text by heart,' he said. 'I spent many hours on the road, and the assistant I'd been assigned was the closest thing to a mute I've ever met. But he wasn't an impoverished student like me, or even a miner, but the son of the truck's owner, perfectly useless, he did nothing but listen to me when he wasn't asleep. Anyway, driving a truck full of gasoline I learned a good part of "On the Crown", a very particular speech, because it's the speech of a man whose political career has failed, and who finds himself at the end of his life forced to defend himself. And without wanting to, which is worse. Only because one of his political allies decided to nominate him for a prize, while another, an enemy, a certain Aeschines, opposed it. That was the situation. Demosthenes, poor guy, hadn't even wanted to be decorated. And he was faced with this terrible task – impossible for anyone, of course, except the greatest. Any senator would have been daunted. Aeschines himself would have run away in fright. Convincing the public of the nobility of one's own errors, justifying disasters one is responsible for, apologizing for a life that one might know to be mistaken, is that not the most difficult thing in the world? Did Demosthenes not deserve the crown for the mere fact of examining his past and subjecting it to trial?' My father took a smooth, perfect, luminous square out of his breast pocket, a neon handkerchief, and dried his forehead, not wiping it, but with delicate little pats.

I was pleased to see he didn't seem bothered by the sustained murmuring of movement: the chairs against the floor, the rustle of clothing, papers torn or crumpled up. His voice, perhaps, prevailed over those trivial distractions, and also his figure. He was elegant without being solemn, firm without being authoritarian, and that was plain to see; much more so, in fact, than I was. My father had not noticed my presence. He hadn't pointed me out like he had on other occasions; he looked straight ahead, at a point somewhere above my head, on the wall or out of the window. 'I see we have a guest today.' 'I'm going to take the opportunity to introduce someone.' He said none of that; then, while I listened to him explain how Demosthenes invoked the gods to begin his speech – 'the intention is to create an almost religious atmosphere that will influence the state of those who are listening to him, because he should be judged by gods, not by men' – I had the unequivocal sensation of invisibility. I had stopped existing in that precise moment; I, Gabriel Santoro the younger, had just evaporated from that date in history (which I no longer remember) and from that precise place, the lecture hall of the Supreme Court of Justice, on the corner of Seventh Avenue and Twenty-eighth Street. I saw myself suddenly tangled in that misunderstanding: maybe he hadn't seen me (after all, it was dark and I was in the last row); maybe he'd chosen to ignore me, and it wasn't possible to make myself noticed without looking ridiculous and, which was worse, without interrupting the class. But I had to risk it, I thought; at that moment, knowing whether my father was ignoring me on purpose monopolized my attention, my decimated intelligence. And when I was about to ask him something, anything – why did Demosthenes insult Aeschines so brutally and call his father a slave, or why did he begin speaking, for no reason, of the ancient battles of Marathon and Salamis – when I was about to break with these questions the spell of invisibility or of non-existence, my father had again begun to talk of other times, the times of his youth, when speaking was important and what someone said could change someone else's life, and only I knew his words were for me, that they searched me out and chased me with the relentlessness of a guided missile. Professor Santoro was speaking to me through a filter: the students were listening to him unaware that my father was using them the way a ventriloquist uses a dummy. 'None of you have felt that terrible power, the power to finish some-one off. I've always wanted to know what it felt like. Back then we all had that power, but we didn't all know that we had it. Only some used it. There were thousands, of course: thousands of people who accused, who denounced, who informed. But those thousands of informers were just a part, a tiny fraction of the people who could have informed if they'd wanted to. How do I know? I know because the system of blacklists gave power to the weak, and the weak are the majority. That was life during those years: a dictatorship of weakness. The dictatorship of resentment, or, at least, of resentment according to Nietzsche: the hatred the naturally weak feel for the naturally strong.' Notebooks opened, students made a note of the reference; one, beside me, underlined *Federico Nietzsche* twice, with the first name in Spanish. 'I don't remember when I heard of the first case of justified denunciation. On the other hand, I clearly remem-ber an Italian who dressed in mourning for a funeral, and was then included on the blacklist for wearing the uniform of Fascism. But I have not come here to talk of these cases, but to keep quiet. I have not come to talk of my experience. I have not come to talk about the enormous error, about the misunderstanding, about how my family and I suffered for that error, that misunderstanding. The moment when my life was impounded: I have not come to talk about that. My grant suspended, my father's pension turned off like a water tap, those many months in which my mother had nothing to live on: I have not come to talk about that. I can tell you perhaps that my work as a truck driver enabled me to carry on my studies. I can tell you that Demosthenes, the great Demosthenes, enabled me to carry on my life. But I have not come to break the silence. I have not come to break the pact. I have not come to make cheap accusations, nor to set myself up as a victim of history, nor to list the many ways that life in Colombia can ruin people. A joke made at the wrong moment in front of the wrong people? I'm not going to talk about that. The inclusion of my name on that inquisitors' document? I'm not going to give details, I'm not going to delve into the subject, because that is not my intention. I have spent several years now teaching people to speak, and today I want to speak to you about what is not said, what is beyond the tale, the account, the reference. I cannot prevent other people from speaking if they believe it useful or necessary. So I shall not speak out against the parasites, those creatures who use the experience of those of us who have preferred not to speak for their own ends. I shall not speak of those second-rate writers, many of whom had not even been born when the war ended, who now go around talking about the war and about the people who suffered during the war. They do not know the courage of those who have preferred not to speak: they'll not learn of it from me. They do not know that it takes strength not to make use of one's own suffering: they'll not learn it from me. They especially do not know that making use of others is one of the lowest occupations in humanity. No, no, they'll not learn it from me. The things they do not know they'll have to learn on their own. Today I have come to keep quiet and protect the silence of those who have kept it. I shall not speak . . .' And, in fact, he didn't speak. He didn't speak of one title in particular, or of one author; but the system of ventriloquism he'd installed in his lecture hall had suddenly transformed into a searchlight, and the violence of that dazzling beam fell on me. The accusations of the ventriloquist-searchlight had taken me by surprise, so much so that my head overlooked the revelations about my father's past – a persecuted man, a victim of unjust accusations as the result of an unimportant joke, a frivolous comment, an innocent bit of sarcasm, the content of which had already begun to take various forms in my head – and concentrated on the possible defence of my right to ask questions, and, of course, Sara Guterman's right to answer them. But the auditorium was not the most conducive setting for that debate, so I started to consider the best way to escape (the way to do so without calling attention to myself, or the way to do so by calling attention but not revealing my identity to the rest of the audience, without demolishing what little dignity I had left), when my father grabbed his overcoat from the back of his chair with a slightly clumsy movement, and the lining of his sleeve got caught on the back of the chair, which crashed on to the wooden floor with an angry reverberation. Only then did I understand that the controlled tone and measured surface of my father's words concealed, or at least masked, an interior disorder, and for the first time in my life I associated the notion of recklessness with my father's behaviour. But he had already left. The class was over.

I had to take some time to recover, like someone who's just been in an accident – like a pedestrian stepping out of the shadow, the screech of brakes, the violent collision — because I felt queasy. I held my head in my hands and the noise of students getting up gradually subsided. I went out, looked for my father and didn't see anyone. I walked around in front of the building, under the insufficient light of the walkway, and I could have sworn I saw him cross Seventh between buses and minibuses, jog with his overcoat folded over his arm, despite the cold, towards the International Centre, but a second later the illusion had crumbled: it wasn't him. (That momentary confusion functioned as a symbol of bad literature. That's it, I thought. Now I've started to see my father when he's not there, to confuse him with my image of him, now I've started to unlearn his silhouette, for I'd realized I would have to unlearn his life: one revelation, just one fucking revelation, and already my father is a crude hologram, a phantom in the streets.) When I turned round and began to walk south, thinking of taking the first street that went down to Seventh and thus doubling my chances of finding a taxi at that hour, I ran into a student. A street light lit him from the back — a saint and his halo — and it took me a second to recognize him: it was the student who had my book; at the beginning of the class the fetishistic attention he was paying my father had already bothered me, and now he seemed anxious to confirm that attention.

'You're *el junior*, aren't you?' he said. 'Your old man's well hard, brother. You're a lucky guy. Too bad there aren't more sons of bitches like him.'

Half an hour later I arrived at the house of my father, *el senior*, the hard man, the stranger. But he must have taken a slower route, because he wasn't home yet, so I crossed the street and settled down to wait for him on the corner, sitting on one of those milestones you still find all over Bogotá, those rough, angular stones that used to mark the streets and for some reason they haven't taken away, although many of them now have incorrect information (*Boulevard* where it should say *Avenue*, *Nineteen* where it should say *Thirty*). And all that time, while I was freezing to death and watching a dirty yellow cloud swallowing the night sky, I was thinking: Why has he never told me about what happened? And *what had happened*? What was the unfortunate joke made at the wrong time, that someone had taken too seriously? Who was the humourless person who'd made the accusation; who was the informer? Had he ever told my mother? Was there anyone else who knew about this? That was the first thing I asked when he arrived with his collar undone (disorder struggling to the surface) and unenthusiastically tolerated my following him upstairs and sitting down when he sat down. I also asked him if he'd seen me; I asked him if, after seeing me, he'd recognized me. He chose to answer my questions out of order. 'Of course,' he said. 'I saw you were there at the back, sitting there from the start. I've always seen you. Sometimes I let you know, sometimes I don't. You've been there all week, Gabriel. How do you suppose I wouldn't notice?'

'I would've liked to know,' I insisted then. 'You never told me. You never talked to me about that.'

'And I'm never going to tell you,' he said. He didn't seem to be choking anything back; nothing seemed to be moving him deep down inside, but therein lay the maladjustment, and I knew it. 'Memory isn't public, Gabriel. That's what neither you nor Sara have understood. You two have made things public that many of us wanted forgotten. You two have recorded things that many of us took a long time to get out of sight. People are talking about the lists again, they're talking about the cowardice of certain informers, about the anguish of those unjustly informed on . . . And those of us who'd made our peace with that past, those who through prayer or pretence had arrived at a certain conciliation, are now back to square one. The blacklists, the Hotel Sabaneta, the informers. All words that many people rubbed out of their dictionaries, and you come along, white knight of history, to display your courage by awakening things most people prefer to let lie. Why hadn't I told you? No, that's the wrong question: better to ask why talk about things that don't deserve attention. Why did I say what I said today? Why refuse to speak in public as I did today? Was it to teach you a lesson, so you'd realize the nobility your father keeps hidden, that schmaltz? Was it to invite people to forget your book, to act like it had never been published? I don't know, both intentions strike me as childish, absurd as well as chimerical, a lost battle. But there's one thing I want you to know: I would have done the same if I hadn't seen you there. I am not going to speak of those denunciations, but I can tell you one thing: in a parallel reality I would have denounced you and your parasitical book, your exploitative book, your intrusive book. That's the only clear thing in all of this: the men who have remained silent did not deserve to have your reportage inflicted on them. Keeping silent is not agreeable, it demands character, but you don't understand that, you, with the same arrogance as all the rest of the journalists in the world, you thought the world could not manage without Sara's life. You think you know what this country is, that this country and its people no longer hold any mysteries for you, because you believe Sara is all there is, that you've known her and you've known us all. That's why I would have denounced you, as a con man, and as a liar. Yes, I would have done it even if I hadn't seen you. And anyway, what were you doing there? Why didn't you tell me you were coming? No, don't answer, I can imagine. You went so we could talk about the book, right? You went so I could give you my opinion. And that's what you're here for now; deep down you still want me to talk about you. You still think I'm going to congratulate you, I'm going to encourage you and say you were born to write about Sara's life, or rather that Sara was born and went through her whole life, through the Nazis and exile, through wartime in a strange country, through forty years of life in this city where people kill each other out of habit, so that you could come now and sit down comfortably with your tape recorder and ask her idiotic questions and write two hundred pages and our happiness would be so irrepressible we'd all start masturbating. Aren't you good? That's what you expect people to say. That's why you wrote it, so everyone would know how good and compassionate you are, how indignant you feel when these terrible things happen to humanity, no? Look at me, admire me, I'm on the side of the good guys, I condemn, I denounce. Read me, love me, give me prizes for compassion, for goodness. Do you want my opinion? My opinion is that you've got every right to investigate, to ask questions, even to write, but not to publish. My opinion is that you should have put that manuscript in a drawer and locked it, and then tried to lose the key. My opinion is that you should have forgotten the matter and that you are going to do so now, even though it's too late, because everyone is going to, everyone is going to forget your book in less than two months. It's that simple. I've nothing more to say. My opinion is that your book is shit.'

And then the unthinkable happened: my father made a mistake. The man who spoke in perfect paragraphs, who

65

communicated during the course of a normal day in quarto sheets ready for press, had mixed up his papers, confused his objectives, forgotten his speech and didn't have a prompter handy. The man who forecast the oblivion of my book lost control and ended up doing everything possible so that my book would be remembered. On its own merits, *A Life in Exile* would have gone unnoticed; my father – or rather his disproportionate, impetuous, unthinking reaction – took care of putting the book centre stage, and focusing all spotlights on it. 'He's going to publish a review,' Sara warned me. 'Please tell him not to, tell him that's no way to behave.' I replied, 'I'm not saying anything. Let him do what he likes.' 'But he's mad. He's gone mad, I swear. The review is terrible.' 'I don't care.' 'You have to convince him; he's going to hurt you. Tell him the book was an accident. Make him see reason. Tell him that publishing the review is against his own interests. If he publishes it, it's going to attract people's attention. Explain that to him. He doesn't realize. This can be avoided.' Then I asked her why she was so worried. 'Because this is going to hurt you both, Gabriel. I don't like to see you hurt each other. I love you both.' Her explanation struck me as odd; or rather, it struck me as superfluous, and therefore incomplete. 'You'd rather the book wasn't spoken about,' I said to Sara. 'That's not true. I'd rather *he* wouldn't speak of the book. I'd rather he wouldn't speak about the book *like that*. He's going against you, but that's not it. It's that all this is contrary to his own intentions, don't you see?' 'Of course I see. So what?' 'I've never seen him react so pathologically. Who knows what'll happen afterwards. This isn't Gabriel.' 'Tell me something, Sara. Did you know?' 'Did I know what?' 'Don't play the fool. Did you know? And if you knew, why isn't it in the book? Why didn't you tell me during the interviews?' It's an odd debating strategy that I've forgotten the name of: if your opponent demands something, respond with even more aggressive demands. 'Why did you hide it from me? Why did you give me incomplete information?'

The review appeared a few days later:

As the subject for his first book, the journalist Gabriel Santoro has chosen one of the most difficult and, at the same time, one of the least original. Jewish emigration in the 1930s has been, for several decades, the talk of as many journalists as there are places in the journalism schools. Santoro wanted, undoubtedly, to appear audacious; he would have heard that audacity is one of the journalistic virtues. But to write a book about the Holocaust, in this day and age, is as audacious as shooting a sitting duck.

The author of *A Life in Exile* imagined that the mere announcement of his theme – a woman who escaped from Hitler as a young girl and settled permanently in our country – was sufficient to generate terror and/or pity. He imagined, as well, that a clumsy and monotonous style could pass for a direct and economical one. In short: he counted on the reader's inattentiveness. Sometimes it's sentimental: the protagonist is a woman 'of fears and deliberate silences'. Sometimes it's wordy: in Colombia, her father feels 'distant and welcome, accepted and foreign'. Anyone will notice that the metaphor and the chiasmus aim to reinforce the ideas; anyone will notice that they manage only to weaken them. These are not the only occasions where this happens.

Of course it would all work better if the intention in general wasn't so obviously opportunistic. But the author tells us that emigrating is bad, that exile is cruel, that an expatriated man (or, in this case, woman) will never be the same. The pages of this book are rife with the clichés of sociology, while more thought-provoking truths, such as the capacity of men to reinvent themselves, to remake their destiny, remain submerged. They haven't interested the author; perhaps this is why the book doesn't interest us.

Finally, *A Life in Exile* is little more than an exercise: a commendable exercise, some will say (although I don't know with what justification), but an exercise after all. I won't point out that its tropes are cheap, its ethos questionable, and its emotions second-hand. I will say, however, that as a whole it is a failure. This verdict is clearer and more direct than the best inventory of the book's shortcomings, the listing of which would be as futile as it would be exhausting.

The text was signed with the initials *GS*. There was not a single reader unaware of the name they stood for.

By December 1991, that is, three years after those words, my father's recovery was complete, and after several conversations, and the recollection of those scenes, the retraction of his mistaken words seemed definitive. On Sundays, Sara invited us over for *ajiaco* with chicken, not prepared by her, but ordered in and delivered in separate bags like the ones they use to carry live fish, containing the cream, the capers and the corn on the cob, all packed into a little polystyrene box. Having a regular routine arranged and having his son present, as a participant and not as a witness or prosecutor, was for my father a confirmation and almost a prize (pats on the back from a pleased teacher): 'If it was necessary for me to be opened up like a frog so we could spend Sundays together, well fine, I'll happily pay that price. In fact, I'd pay double, indeed I would. I would have paid four angioplasties, in order to eat this *ajiaco* in this company.' Sara lived in an apartment that was too big for the needs of its sole occupant: it was a sort of large eagle's nest built into the fifteenth floor of a building on Twenty-eighth Street, across from, or rather above, the bullring, and it had windows on two sides, so on clear days, leaning out of the window, you could see the blot of blue tempera of the church of Monserrate, and from the other window, if you looked down, the rough, dun-coloured circle of sand. The dining room had fallen into disuse, as often happens in the houses of people living on their own, and now Sara used the table to assemble three-thousand-piece jigsaw puzzles of Alpine scenes, so we'd help ourselves to *ajiaco* in deep bowls and take it on trays to eat in the living room, and we'd switch on the radio and listen to whatever concert HJCK was broadcasting that afternoon while we ate our lunch. As the weeks went by, it gradually became more possible and less surprising that we could finish eating without having spoken during the whole meal, enjoying each other's company in ways it wasn't necessary to verbalize, nor even to make known by the usual codes, friendly smiles or polite glances. At times like those, I used to think: These two are all I have. This is my family.

The Sunday that my father told Sara and me about Angelina, the physiotherapist, and what was going on with her, wasn't just any Sunday, because the final phase of the Advent season was just about to start, and so, while in the rest of Bogotá Catholics got ready to sit down beside a nativity scene and read prayers from a pink book that was once given away free with any purchase in Los Tres Elefantes, Sara

69

insisted we get her grandchildren's Christmas tree out of the cupboard and help her set it up in a corner of the living room. 'This is what I get for being a liberal,' she'd said to me once. 'I just wanted to raise my children without religion of any kind, and look, they end up doing the same Christian nonsense as everyone else. When it comes down to it, I might as well have carried on with my Jewish nonsense, no? Mama didn't want me to marry the way I married: you'll end up converting, you'll lose your identity. I never believed her, and now look at me: I have to put the wretched tree up. If I don't do it now, there'll be no putting up with my sons later. These things are important, Mum. Traditions, symbols. Just excuses. What they want is to save themselves the lumberjack's job of setting up one of these nuisances.' And my father and I, who after my mother's death had gradually left aside these practices of trees and donkeys and oxen and mirrors that simulate lakes and moss that simulates fields and plastic babies lying on fake hay, we who had developed together an affectionate indifference towards all the paraphernalia of Christmas in Bogotá, suddenly found ourselves kneeling on the carpet, putting the branches of a tree into order by size and spreading out the instruction page across our knees. It wasn't an easy job and the amount of irony it brought with it wasn't inconsiderable either, and maybe that's why we did it with less reticence than might have been expected, along the lines of, *Who would have imagined* or, *If so-and-so could see us now*. Sara had started talking about her grandchildren. That was an area my book hadn't touched on, because it was inaccessible; no matter how hard Sara tried, she could never explain the distance between her own German childhood and that of her grandchildren. If her sons were strangers, her grandchildren were doubly so, people as far removed from

Emmerich, and from the Emmerich synagogue, as it was possible to be. 'How old is the youngest?' I asked.

'Fourteen. Thirteen. Around there.'

'Fourteen,' I repeated. 'Same age as you when you arrived.'

Sara thought for a moment; she seemed not to have noticed that before. 'Exactly,' she said, but then she fell silent, organizing with her aged hands the green and yellow and red spheres of fragile glass, frosted or shiny, opaque or clear, which she was going to hang on the tree when my father and I had finished it. 'Other people look at their children and see themselves in them,' she said. 'Your dad sees himself in you, he'll see himself in your children. That'll never happen to me: we're different. I don't know if it matters.'

'Well, there's genetics as well,' said my father.

'How so?'

'They look like you, and, unfortunately for them, that's definitive.'

That afternoon, my father seemed invulnerable to the traces of his past. He remembered the words they'd be praying all over the place that week, those verses that had always made him burst out laughing: *O King of the Gentiles and their desired One / O Emmanuel, our Protector / O Holy One of Israel / Shepherd of Thy flock.* He recited them (for he knew them by heart, all the verses of all the days of the novena, and some of the prayers as well), and attached a branch to the tree trunk, and then he recited another one, and picked up another branch and spun it round to see where it fitted. And all the time he seemed happy, as if these holidays, to which he'd always been immune, suddenly affected him. And then he confirmed the feeling I'd had earlier: one of the consequences of the second life was a brutal nostalgia, the notion, so very democratic, so universally accessible and at the same time so surprising, of time lost, even though we might have suffered more in that time than in the present. I knew it thanks to my recordings, which at that moment and in that instant seemed to justify every second I'd invested in that curious fetish: conserving other people's voices.

Another of those Sundays I'd tactlessly brought to Sara's house one of those cassettes that I guarded like a state secret. After we'd poured our coffee, I asked them to sit round the sound system and keep quiet, and in the open space that served as a living room, the three of us listened to Sara talking about their hotel. 'The war was in the hotel, we carried it in our pockets,' we heard her say. 'I can't tell you all the things I saw, because there are people who are still alive, and I'm no informer; I don't want to destroy reputations or dig up anything that someone wants to keep buried. But if I could, if we were alone in the world, you and I, in this house, if a bomb had fallen and Colombia no longer existed and only we existed, and you asked me what went on, I could tell you everything . . . Later you'd be sorry you knew. One gets contaminated by this kind of knowledge, Gabriel; I don't know how better to tell you, but that's how it is. If they'd asked me, I would have said, I prefer to close my eyes, not to see those things. But of course, no one asked me. Who would have had the decency? In spite of my father being the owner of the hotel, no? Because if there was any logic in the world, an angel of the Annunciation should have appeared in the Nueva Europa and warned my father that this would happen, that that would happen. No, not logic: justice. A warning would have been fair at the very least but of course, one can't count on such things, that clause is not in the contract. The contracts are written up there and you sign them without complaint, and later things happen and who do you talk to if you're not satisfied . . . Anyway, I can't tell you everything, but I can tell you about the hotel, about the hotel and the war and the effects on my life, because one is also the spaces where one has grown up.

'You ask me if I regret anything. Everybody regrets something, don't they? But you ask and right there I get the image of the face of old lady Lehder in my head. She was one of the Germans from Mompós. That's what we called the German Nazis in Mompós. Some of them had been regular clients of the hotel before 1940; several of them knew Eduardo Santos. Much better than I did, as well. That's why it was so strange, Gabriel. That's why it was so surprising that woman should come looking for me. It was the beginning of 1945. She came to find me to ask me to intercede on behalf of her husband. That's how she said it, it's not my fault, she'd said *intercede on his behalf*. Herr Lehder had just been confined to the Hotel Sabaneta. No, I refuse to speak of a 'concentration camp'; language can't play those tricks on us. One thing is one thing and another thing is something else. The thing is that Frau Lehder was living alone in her house in Mompós, her servants had left, she'd had her electricity cut off. And her husband was in the Sabaneta. That's why she came to see me, to ask for help. I told her to go away, maybe more politely, but that's what I said to her. And she told me about her son in the Wehrmacht, a young man of your age, she said to me, he's just a boy, he fought at Leningrad until he was wounded. I just want to be allowed to listen to the radio, to know if anyone has news of my son, whether he froze to death in Leningrad, Fräulein Guterman. It seems the soldiers have to urinate in their trousers to feel a little bit of warmth. I

73

said no. I didn't even let her sit down to listen to the radio. Later I heard that the Lehders had found a lawyer friend in the Ministry of Foreign Affairs, and so they were able to return to Berlin. In any case, I remember that: having refused to let old lady Lehder sit down by the radio and see if anyone mentioned her little soldier. I didn't give a damn about the little soldier or about old lady Lehder. But that wasn't the worst. The worst thing is that even today I wouldn't help her. You ask me if I regret anything and I think about that, but the way to fix it, today, would be for it not to have happened. There's no other way. Because if it happened again, I'd do the same. Yes, I wouldn't think twice. It's terrible, but that's how it is.'

The power of those recordings. That afternoon, listening to them, my father aged twenty years: maybe he would have thought, as I was thinking, that Sara Guterman's every sentence evoked the treachery of which he'd been the victim, every sentence contained it, but also managed to empty it of meaning, for neither Sara nor I could grasp his experience, feel what he'd felt as a young man. He never asked us to turn the machine off, or to change the cassette, nor did he stand up with some excuse to escape to the bathroom or the kitchen. He silently endured that recording, which must have been at the very least uncomfortable and sometimes even painful, because it brought back to life for him the circumstances that he'd kept secret for such a long time and to which, under the spur of my book, he had alluded in public, to the unease (and sometimes admiration) of his students; he endured it as he'd endured the catheter, with his eyes wide open and fixed on the hanging lamp, the scrawny wire, the metallic shade. When the first side finished and I asked if they wanted me to turn it over, he said no, no thanks, why didn't we put on a little music and chat for a while, Gabriel; wasn't it better to take advantage of these moments to talk? His voice, thin and raspy as a paper kite, was barely audible; in a single sentence, my father managed to complain, draw attention to himself like a badly brought-up teenager, and cast the authority of his tantrums over the atmosphere: if there were things he preferred to forget, it was incomprehensible and even obscene that others might want to remember them. And for the rest of the afternoon, the company of that bitter and pale old man, which would have annoyed me in a stranger, struck me as pitiful and pathetic. That's what I discovered that afternoon: my father was incapable of wrestling with the facts of his own life; the notion of his past bothered him like a raspberry seed stuck in the teeth. Those conversations recorded five years earlier (about things that had happened half a century ago) damaged him from within and sucked at his blood, left him as exhausted as if he'd just come out of the operating room.

But on the afternoon I'm talking about, my father was back to being the force he used to be. His mind was again functioning as it had done at the height of his powers, and the hypothesis of the second chance seemed as much in evidence as if there were a horse in the room. I remembered the recorded words, raised my head to look at the people with whom I was sharing a meal – my family – and thought what always seems incredible: *This happened to you two.* This, which happened half a century ago, happened to you, and you're still alive, acting as tangible testimony to events and circumstances that will perhaps die when you die, as if you were the last human beings able to dance an Andean folk dance that no one else knows, or as if you knew by heart the words to a song that had never been written down and will be lost to the world when you two forget it. And in what physical state did these memory receptacles live? How deteriorated were they, how much time did the world have to try to extract their knowledge? Every movement, every word from my father was like a little banner saying: *Don't worry, everybody calm down, nothing's happened here*. And Sara, it seemed, thought the same.

'The truth is you've come out as good as new,' Sara said to my father. 'I wonder if I should have one of those things too.'

'No such thing as reincarnation?' my father said. 'No karma? No one's going to convince me of that any more, my dear; from here on in I declare myself a Hindu.'

'I can't stand this,' said Sara. 'Now I look older next to you.'

It was a slight exaggeration, of course, because Sara, with her loose linen slacks and a white shirt that came down to her knees, still looked solid, as though she'd been let off half her years for good behaviour. She seemed to have settled into a comfortable solitude, seemed resigned to the days passing her by and content to look up, with something that might be called submission but also habit, to watch them go. Her face underlined the years she'd lived with no more responsibility than her own sustenance. Her earlobes were pierced, but she wore no earrings; she used bifocals for reading, the frames gold and discreet, the lenses a coppery colour. Her body, it seemed to me, had lived at a different rhythm: it didn't show the marks of time, the tiredness of the skin; it didn't show the tensions, of course, or the way pain marks people's faces, scratches their eyes and forces them to wear glasses, contorts the corners of mouths and scores their necks like a plough. Or was it perhaps more precise to speak of memory: Sara's body accumulated time, but had no memory. Sara kept her memory apart: in boxes and files and photographs, and in the cassettes of which I was the custodian, that seemed to absorb Sara's history and at the same time withdraw it from her body. The cassettes of Dorian Guterman. The files of Sara Gray.

As for him, it was true that over these last six months his transformation had been remarkable. I knew that one of the immediate consequences of the operation was a sudden invasion of oxygen into an unaccustomed heart, and therefore levels of energy the patient had forgotten existed, but seeing him through the eyes of our hostess, watching him as his contemporary watched him, I thought that yes, the cliché was true, my father had come out *as good as new*. Over the last few months I would have forgotten if not for the image of the scar blazoned across his chest, that corporeal memorandum, and the restrictions imposed after the operation, still in effect – although only my father remained aware of those private disciplines – which surfaced at lunch and dinner, just as they came up that afternoon, while we ate *ajiaco* in that Christmassy apartment with a view of Monserrate.

'And what are you going to do now?' said Sara. 'What are you going to do with your new life?'

'For the moment, not count my chickens. Or rather count them, but very quietly. I have to take good care of myself just to stay as I am. The diet is very strict but I have to stick to it. It's pretty good, though, being twenty again.'

'What an insufferable fellow you are! Something will happen to you, for being so arrogant.'

The new Gabriel Santoro. Gabriel Santoro, corrected and improved version. The reincarnated orator stood up all of a sudden and made a beeline across the living room, arrived at the wooden bookcase and with his left hand picked up a cardboard sleeve the size of a wedding invitation and with the thumb of his stump he took the disc out of the sleeve and put it on the record player and set the speed at 78 rpm and lowered the needle, and then one of the German songs Sara had made me listen to years before began to play.

Veronika, der Lenz ist da,
die Mädchen singen Tralala,
die ganze Welt ist wie verhext,
Veronika, der Spargel wächst.

I had closed my eyes and leant back on the sofa, and begun to let myself drift into post-lunch drowsiness, after the heaviness of the *ajiaco* on a Sunday afternoon, when I thought I heard my father singing, and discounted the idea as impossible and unbelievable, and immediately I seemed to hear his voice again underneath the old music and static from the speakers and the 1930s instruments. I opened my eyes and saw him, with his arms around Sara (who had started washing up the plates), singing in German. The fact that I hadn't heard him sing more than three times in my entire life was less odd than seeing him sing in a language he didn't know, and I immediately remembered a scene from when I was small. For a few months, my father had put on a wig and changed his glasses and worn a bow tie instead of a normal tie: the fact of belonging to the Supreme Court, even though he wasn't a judge, had made him *interesting*, and he'd received his first threats, a couple of those calls so common in Bogotá and to which we've become accustomed and don't pay much attention. Well anyway, the first time he arrived home in disguise, he called hello from the stairs as he always did, and I went out and found myself with this unfamiliar figure, and was afraid: a brief and soon dispelled fear, but fear it was. Something along the same lines happened as I watched him move his mouth and emit strange sounds. It was, in truth, another person, a second Gabriel Santoro.

> *Veronika, die Welt ist grün,*
> *drum lass uns in die Wälder ziehn.*
> *Sogar der liebe, gute, alte Grosspapa,*
> *sagt zu der lieben, guten, alten Grossmama.*

When the old folks came to sit back down in the living room, one or the other noticed my shocked face, and they both started to explain that, among other things, my father had spent the last few months learning German. 'Do you think it absurd?' he said. 'Because I do, I confess. Learning a new language at sixty-something: what for? What for, when the one I already have isn't much use to me? I'm retired, I'm retired from my language. And this is what we retired people do, look for another job. If we get given a second life, then the urge is even stronger.' That was when, in the middle of the treatise on that way of reinventing oneself, in the middle of the spectacle of his remodelled words, in the middle of these sung phrases whose meaning I would find out later, my father spoke to Sara and me about Angelina, about how he'd got to know her better in these months – it was logical, after seeing her every day for so long and benefiting from her massages – how he'd gone on seeing her after the therapy was finished and his health restored. That's what he told us. My father the survivor. My father, with the capacity to reinvent himself.

'I'm sleeping with her. We've been seeing each other for two months.'

'How old is she?' asked Sara.

'Forty-four. Forty-five. I don't remember. She told me, but I don't remember.'

'And she hasn't got anyone, right?'

'How do you know she hasn't got anyone?'

'Because if she did, someone would be throwing it in her face. That sleeping with old men is against the rules. The age difference. Whatever. She must have a good story.'

'Oh, here we go,' said my father. 'There's no story.'

'Of course there is – don't give me that. First of all, she's got no one to protest. Second, you get evasive when I ask you. This woman has a hell of a story. Has she suffered a lot?'

'Well, yes. You've got the makings of a great inquisitor, Sara Guterman. Yes, she's had a shitty life, poor thing. She lost her parents in the bombing of Los Tres Elefantes.'

'That recently?'

'That recently.'

'Did they live here?'

'No. They'd come from Medellín to visit her. They got to say hello, and then they went out to buy some nylon stockings. Her mum needed some nylon stockings. Los Tres Elefantes was the closest place. We passed by there in a taxi not long ago. I can't remember where we were going, but when we got there Angelina's hands were numb and her mouth dry. And that evening she was a bit feverish. It still hits her that hard. Her brother lives on the coast. They don't speak to each other.'

'And when did she tell you all this?' I asked.

'I'm old, Gabriel. Old-fashioned. I like to talk after sex.'

'All right, all right, a little decorum, if you don't mind,' said Sara. 'I haven't gone anywhere, I'm still right here, or have I become invisible?'

I patted my father on the knee, and his tone changed: he put aside the irony, he became docile. 'I didn't know what you'd think,' he said. 'Do you realize?'

'What?'

'It's the first time I've ever spoken to you about anything like this,' he said, 'and it's to tell you what I'm telling you.'

'And without giving the rest of us time to cover our ears,' said Sara. And then she asked, 'Has she stayed over at your house?'

'Never. And don't think I haven't suggested it. She's very independent, doesn't like sleeping in other people's beds. That's fine with me, not that I need to tell you. But now she's taken it into her head to invite me to Medellín.'

'When?'

'Now. Well, to spend the holidays. We're going next weekend and coming back the 2nd or 3rd of January. That's if she gets the time off, of course. They exploit her like a beast, I swear. It's the last week of the year, and she has to fight tooth and nail.'

He thought for a second.

'I'm going to Medellín with her,' he said then. 'To spend Christmas and New Year with her. I'm going with her. Damn, it does sound very odd.'

'Odd, no, it sounds ridiculous,' said Sara. 'But what can you do? All adolescents are ridiculous.'

'There is one little thing,' my father said to me. 'We need your car. Or rather, we don't need it, but I said to Angelina that it's silly to take a bus when you can lend us your car. If you can, that is. If you're not going to need it, if it's not a problem.'

I told him I wasn't going to need it, although it was a lie; I told him it was no problem, partly because his whole being,

81

his voice and his manner, was speaking to me with an unprecedented affection, as if he was asking a special favour of a special friend.

'Take the car and don't worry,' I said. 'Go to Medellín, have a good time, say hi to Angelina for me.'

'Are you sure?'

'I'll stay with Sara. She'll invite me over for Christmas and New Year.'

'That's right,' she said. 'Go along and don't worry. We won't miss you. We're going to stay here and have our own party. Drinking what you can't drink, eating saturated fats and talking about you behind your back.'

'Well, that sounds perfect,' said my father. 'My back doesn't usually mind that.'

'Are you going to drive?' said Sara.

'Not all the time. My hand tends to be a bit of a risk factor on roads like that one. She'll probably do most of the driving, I guess. I can't guarantee she's good at it, but her licence is in order, and anyway, who said you have to drive well to drive in Colombia? How dangerous can it be? I'm in no position to make demands; if a Virgil falls into your life, you don't start cross-examining.'

'What do you mean?' I asked. 'Was it your idea?'

'Don't bring Virgil into this,' said Sara. 'Delusions of youth, that's what it's called.'

'Ah ha, the green-eyed monster is among us. Are you jealous, Sarita?'

'Not jealous, no, don't be silly. But I am old, and so are you. Stop pretending you're not. Eight-hour car trips. Making love with schoolgirls. You're going to have a heart attack, Gabriel.'

'Well, it'll be worth it.'

'Seriously,' I said. 'What does she think?'

'That any co-driver is a good co-driver.'

'No, about your age. What does she think about your age?'

'She thinks it's fine. Well, I imagine she thinks it's fine, I haven't asked her. Fundamental rule of forensic interrogation: don't ask questions you don't want to hear the answer to, watch out for boomerang questions, as the ancients used to say. No, I don't want answers that are going to hit me in the back of the neck. I haven't asked her what she thinks about my hand either, if it bothers her, if she has to make an effort to forget it. What do you want me to say? I'm a good guy, I'm not going to hurt her, and that alone must seem like a fortune to her. It's stupid, but I feel like taking care of her. She's forty-four but I want to take care of her. She's convinced the world is shit, that everyone was born with the sole objective of giving her a hard time. It's not the first time I've heard the argument, but it's the first time it's come so close to me. And I spend all day and half the night trying to convince her of the opposite, Plato, *homo homini Deus*, all that stuff, and she never picks up a book even by accident. I've lived a long while, I've seen what there is to see. But this is by far, far the most unpredictable thing that's ever happened to me in my life.'

He forgot that life likes to outdo itself. Life (the second life) waited a week before reminding him, and did so with a wealth of detail.

Now I like to think about that week over and over again, because it's the closest thing I've got to innocence, to a state of grace, because at the end of that week a whole idea of how the world should be ended. At that moment this book did

83

not exist. It could not exist yet, of course, because this book is an inheritance created by the death of my father, the man who looked down on my work (writing about other people's lives) while he was alive and who after he died left me as a legacy the subject of his own life. I am my father's heir and I am also his executor.

While I write I see that, over the course of several months, instead of the things and papers that I need to reconstruct the story it has been the things and papers that *prove the existence* of the story and that can correct my memory, if necessary, that have been accumulating on my desk. I am not sceptical by nature, but nor am I naive, and I know very well the cheap tricks memory can avail itself of when it suits, and also, at the same time, I know that the past is not stationary nor is it fixed, in spite of the illusion of documents: so many photographs and letters and films that allow us to think of the immutability of what we've seen, what we've heard, what we've read. No: none of that is definitive. It can take just a tiny detail, something that in the grand scheme of things we consider insignificant, to make a letter relating trivialities become something that determines our lives, to make the innocent man in the photo turn out to have always been our worst enemy.

My desk was once my mother's. The wood has softened from being smeared with so much furniture polish, but no other strategy has occurred to me to protect this block (that looks recently carved from a wet tree trunk) from wood-worm attacks. There are rings from glasses and cups that nothing short of sandpaper could now shift. The corners are chipped or split, and I've got more than one splinter from carelessly brushing my hand across it. And, most of all, there are things, things whose principal function is evidential.

Every once in a while I pick up one of those cassettes and make sure they're still there, that they still contain Sara Guterman's voice. I pick up a magazine from 1985 and read a paragraph: 'When the Japanese attacked the US naval station at Pearl Harbor, in December 1941, Colombia finally decided to break relations with the Axis Powers . . .' I pick up the December 1941 speech, with which Santos broke relations with the Axis: 'We are with our friends, and we are firmly with them. We will fulfil the role corresponding to this policy of continental solidarity with hatred towards none . . .' I pick up a letter from my father to Sara, a letter from Sara to my father, a speech by Demosthenes: this is my evidence. I am heir, I am executor and I am also prosecutor, but before this I have been archivist, I have been organizer. Looking back – and back means a couple of years ago as well as half a century – events take shape, a certain design: they mean something, something that doesn't necessarily come as given. To write about my father I've been obliged to read certain things that despite his tutelage I had never read. Demosthenes and Cicero are the most obvious, almost a cliché. *Julius Caesar* was no less predictable. Those books are also compelling pieces of evidence, and each one of them figures in my dossier, with all the annotations my father had made in them. The problem is that interpreting them is not within my powers. When my father notes, beside Brutus's speech, 'From verb to noun? Here you lost.' I don't know what he might have meant. I feel more comfortable with facts; and death, of course, is the densest of facts, more meaningful, less susceptible to being perverted or misappropriated by different interpretations, relative versions, *readings*. The rule says that death is as definitive as anything can be on earth. That's why it's so disconcerting when a man changes after death, and that's why biographies and memoirs get written, those cheap and democratic forms of mummification.

The process of my father's mummification was only possible from 23 December 1991, when the accident happened. At that moment I was at home, comfortable and calm and in bed with a friend, T, a woman I've known since I was fifteen and she was twelve, with whom I get together every two or three months to make love and watch a movie, for, although she is married and relatively content, we've always had the idea that in another life we could have been together, and we would have liked that. I still see T as a little girl, and perhaps there's a perversion there that we allow ourselves for a few hours. We touch, go to bed, watch a movie and sometimes go back to bed after the movie, but not always, and then T has a shower, dries her hair with a hairdryer I bought just for her, and goes home. That's how it was that night: according to my calculations, we were watching the movie, and maybe Marlon Brando was dying of a heart attack in the garden in front of his grandson, but it's possible that the film had ended and I was seeking T's mouth, which is wide and always cold. Sometimes I've gone as far as considering the possibility of this coincidence: that T was sitting on top of me and sliding up and down my erection the way she often does just at the moment when my car (driven by my father) and an Expreso Bolivariano bus (driven by a certain Luis Javier Velilla) went over the cliff together a few kilometres outside Medellín, on the way to Las Palmas. The car was on its way out of Medellín; the bus was arriving. Five passengers survived the accident. I'll never understand how my father, the great survivor, was not among them.

★   ★   ★

Boomerang questions began to accumulate almost immediately in my head, and I, with a negligence the rhetoric professor would have reproached me for, allowed that to happen. What was my father doing on the road to Las Palmas, that is, coming back from Medellín? Why was he driving at night, when he knew that road's terrible reputation? Why hadn't he let Angelina drive? These questions (the most physical, the most circumstantial) and the others, those concerning the blame for the accident (the most likely, I thought then, to come back and hit me in the back of the neck), came flooding in without warning when I received Sara's phone call and as I heard her tell me the news, or rather read it word for word from the newspaper, while I listened to her somewhat distractedly with the fleeting altruistic regret one tends to feel when listening to news of someone else's death in Colombia. Then she told me my father's name was in the newspaper's list. 'That can't be right,' I said, still standing beside the bedside table. 'He's in Medellín. He's not coming back until January.'

'The licence plate of the car's there, Gabriel, and the name,' she said. She wasn't crying but her voice sounded nasal and uneven like the voice of someone who'd only just stopped. 'I wanted it to be a mistake too. I'm very sorry, Gabriel.'

'What about her? Was she with him?'

'Who knows?'

'If she wasn't with him, maybe it wasn't him. Maybe it was someone else, Sara.'

'It's not someone else. I'm so sorry.'

In my left hand I had a white T-shirt with a doctored photo of the Caribbean and the slogan: *Colombia nuestra*, and in my right a travel iron, a fist-sized contraption that I'd got on special offer in an electrical shop in Sanandresito. I'd just ironed the shirt and unplugged the iron, but after I hung up, as I sat down distractedly on the unmade bed, I rested it on my leg, and the burn was brutal. By the time I got dressed, half incredulous and half dizzy, and called a taxi, an oblong blister the colour of watery milk had formed above my knee. The operator who took my call gave me two numbers, a code and the identification number for my mobile, those security strategies that we ingenuous Bogotanos trust to evade criminals; but my father had just died – the pain of my burnt skin did nothing but remind me, like a testimony to those two bodies, his and his lover's, perhaps burnt as well, the skin converted into a single bag of white water – and as I got into the taxi I realized I'd forgotten the numbers I had to say for the taxi driver to accept me. 'Code?' the driver asked and then repeated, and the glistening down on his upper lip, his narrow eyes said the same thing. I suddenly feared something was wrong with me, I began to have trouble breathing and barely had time to think, in the midst of an intense physical pain, of the loss that had just invaded my life and the darkness of what was left of my reasoning, that I was about to suffer an anxiety attack.

I got back out of the taxi. I told the driver to wait for a second, please, but he must not have heard me: as soon as he saw me lie down on the ground, he put the car in gear and pulled away. On a nearby wall were some geraniums; they reminded me, as was to be expected, of the walls of the houses you see on the way down into Medellín from Las Palmas, and as soon as that image came into my head so did the first wave of nausea. I knelt beside the wall and threw up a thin, rust-coloured, almost odourless phlegm (I hadn't eaten anything that morning), and stood up as soon as I felt that my legs, which go weak when I vomit, would be able to support me, because it seemed the minimal dignity of enduring these experiences standing up – the vision of the buildings with their windows falling on top of me, the pressure of clothing on my chest – would somehow help me to get through this week in which Sara, merciful and braver than me, would take charge of the formalities with the ease of a professional gravedigger, but with the kindness a gravedigger would have forever lost. One of her sons called me during those days. 'Why don't you take care of these things yourself?' he said over the phone. 'My mum isn't up to looking after other families' deaths, that should be obvious.' I thought it was a strange form of jealousy, because Sara was duplicating the measures she'd taken when her husband died; her son didn't seem to like it very much. But Sara paid him no attention. Sara went on doing what needed to be done. She drafted an announcement for the two Bogotá news-papers, the ones we open to see what deaths we have to attend that day, and decided, for reasons she didn't seem too clear about, to leave her own name out of the text, despite my request that she include it along with mine. So Gabriel Santoro invited mourners to the funeral of Gabriel Santoro; and in the drum roll of the duplicated name and surname there was something solitary and sad, because many of those who attended the mass, people who didn't know me, had the impression of a printer's error. Sara apologized many times for not having included our second surnames, as we normally do in this country, which has always seemed strange to her. Of course, that would have prevented any confusion, but I didn't blame her, I couldn't have blamed her. She had taken on even the most trivial tasks, which are, for that very reason (because they take us away from the gravity, the solemnity, the rite) the most painful, and, after an off-the-cuff comment in which I'd mentioned I'd rather have the body cremated out of fear of the renewed pain of the anniversaries and cemetery visits and flowers bought at the roadside, Sara had negotiated with the administrators of the Jardines de Paz and managed to get them to change the plot – the plot whose title I'd carried around in my wallet for so many years the way others carry the wrinkled telephone number of their first girlfriend – for the right to cremation.

The service was held on the following Thursday. The mass, in the gloomy Cristo Rey Church, was a marvel of religious vacuity, an inventory of the absurdities in which some people seem to find solace. 'Our brother,' said the priest, and looked back at his notes to refresh his memory, 'Gabriel Santoro, has died to live in us. We, through the love of Christ, through his infinite and eternal charity, live in him.' Later I found out that before the mass he'd been asking for me, looking for me to ask some questions, and Sara had dealt with him in my place. The priest had approached her with a little book bound in black leather in his hand, open and ready like a journalist's. 'What was the deceased like?' he asked Sara. She, accustomed to these procedures, answered with the supposed attributes of his star sign: he was a kind, affectionate, generous family man. The priest took notes, shook Sara's hand, and she watched him return to the sacristy. 'Those of us who knew Gabriel,' he said later, from the microphone, 'appreciated his kind and warm personality, his infinite affection for his loved ones, his boundless generosity to friends and strangers alike. May the Lord receive him in His Holy Kingdom.' And the sea of heads nodded: they were all in agreement, the dead man had been a good person. 'Gathering here to remember our brother is also to ask ourselves how we can perpetuate what he has left in us; it is to measure the intensity of the loss, and the consolation of the Resurrection . . .' The priest asked in public the question I'd been asking myself privately for so long, not just since the instant I knew my father was no more, but long before, and his words felt intrusive. I thought of my father's possible legacy; I felt at first I'd received nothing, nothing but the name, nothing but the timbre of our voices; but I ended up considering that in many ways my life was no different from his: it was a mere prolongation, a strange pseudopodium.

Three of my father's colleagues helped me to lift the coffin – without a window of any kind, as advised by Sara – and carry it to the door of the church; then, a squadron of men dressed in mourning cut off our path; there was a rustling of papers, the coffin rested on a gilded stand, and a stranger began to read. He held the paper with a ringed hand (rings on three fingers). The man was the spokesman for the Mayoralty of Greater Bogotá; at the end of each sentence his heels lifted two or three centimetres from the ground, as if he was trying to stand on tiptoe to get a better view.

Ladies and gentlemen, friends, compatriots all:
 Gabriel Santoro, notable citizen, thinker, professor and friend, was in his advanced years the standard-bearer, or let us say, the very paragon of the impartial and honest man, because every moment of his life was distinguished by his pure and noble patriotism, his moral integrity, robust personality and temperament, his devotion and fondness, the strict and upright fulfilment of his duties and, furthermore, by the cordial, affectionate nature of his human relations.
 Born in Santa Fe de Bogotá, bountiful land of his illustrious ancestry, Sogamoso was the cradle of his

forebears and source of the clear water of his understanding. Shaped by politics, science and culture in a home of Christian virtues, he cultivated and assessed them with conscientious unction, as is customary in societies which practise healthy ideas with profound conviction. Religion, the principles of the philosophical ideal were the centre, nerve and motor of his intellect, projecting it with emanations of grandeur towards the immediate future. And, of course, faith grew in his spirit and brought him the intimate proximity of God; his wisdom and peace of the soul reflected the living miracle of a select, worthy and civilized person.

And with all of this, breathing scents of eternity with the eminent breezes and incense of holy patriotic inspiration, with the joy of youth, athletic, elegant and upstanding, transcending the classrooms of his Alma Mater, which received him like a beacon showing the way in these days of dark designs and ambiguous omens. Solicitous, disciplined and diligent, with the uprightness of an honest man, Gabriel Santoro worshipped everlasting philosophy; the tranquil attitude of a great orator illuminated the born leader, fixed his eye on the horizons of the beloved country. In this setting we, the people of Bogotá, single out Gabriel Santoro to place him, in honour of his illustrious trajectory, in the pantheon of the nation's notables.

For his life, from the illustrious moment when he received his honours degree in jurisprudence, was forever assuming the role of pilot in the storm, educating generations of men to honest labours and diaphanous ideas, and transmitting the most illustrious treasure of our species, the language we revere with its use each day of our lives. And for all that he shall be recognized in the annals of our nation, since in these very moments of exemplary pain the nation is preparing the official recognition and its decrees shall honour Doctor Gabriel Santoro with the Medal of Civic Merit. So it is declared and shall be carried out by due process of the law.

Peace be upon the tomb of the famous teacher and worthy citizen, Doctor Gabriel Santoro. The festive and joyful tricolours wave in heaven, welcoming the orator and man. May the perpetual light shine on him.

Santa Fe de Bogotá, the 26th day of the month of December, 1991.

At that moment, when the speech ended and the box slid across the fuchsia-coloured carpet of the hearse and the driver closed the door, taking the greatest possible care to avoid my gaze, people began to walk towards me, to murmur condolences and offer open hands that emerged from black sleeves, and the leaden rhetoric of the duty-roster orator (those anacolutha, those subversive gerunds, those dangling participles) was the least of my worries. In any case, this I remember well: I didn't want to shake anyone's hand, because my own right hand was still feeling the weight of my father and his coffin, and I had got it into my head to make the pressure of the copper handle on my palm last for a few minutes. Later, by one of those curious associations a mind under pressure is capable of, I thought of the handles and the carpet of the hearse when the coffin began to enter the cemetery's crematorium. The door of the furnace was copper and the handles of the coffin were copper. The heat in the room, around the flowers and their putrid smell, the white ribbons, the gold letters on the white ribbons, was no different from the heat I'd felt in the car park of the funeral home, with the sun hitting the thick cloth of my jacket and my sweaty neck. And now, at the same time as I let myself be overwhelmed by these small annoyances, I thought about my dead father. At some point I thought I'd never, as long as I lived, be able to think about anything else. I was alone; there was no one left between me and my own death. Filling out the cremation forms, I had written, for the first time in a long while, my father's full name, and the automatism of my hand made me shudder, that it had memorized those movements over years of writing Gabriel Santoro, but always referring to myself, not to a dead man. The contents of my own name, that which seems immutable to us (although only through force of habit), were being transformed. Of all the changes we go through during our lifetimes – I thought, or I believe I thought – of all the changes imposed on us, what could be more violent?

In that box, behind the hatch, was his body. I could not know in what state, I could not know what damage the accident had done to him, nor had I wanted to find out the causes of death. Maybe he'd broken his neck, maybe he'd suffocated, or maybe, like one of the passengers of whom news had emerged, he'd been crushed by the chassis, or maybe the impact of the car (against the mountain, or the bus, or some tree trunk) had thrown him forward with such force that his seat belt or the steering wheel or the dashboard had broken his ribs. The doctors had said that the bones of his chest would take a year to regenerate after the operation; now the cut made by the saw irritated my imagination much less than the images summoned up by the accident. And in a few minutes, after the clothing and skin, after the soft tissues – the eyes, the tongue, the testicles – after the renewed heart, those bones would be melted by the heat of the furnace. What was the temperature in there? How long did the whole process take, the transformation of a professor of rhetoric into ashes to fill an urn? Would the wire the surgeons had used to reconnect the bones of his chest melt too? And while I thought about this the few people who had come to the cremation spectacle kept approaching me, and the numbness of my hands and my tired words seized me again, as if to prove one more time what I've always known and never needed to prove: that I am not equipped to grieve for the dead, for no one ever taught me the words of sorrow or the conduct of mourning. Then a woman came to greet me – to convey her personal inventory of consoling phrases, of meaningful embraces, of *prêt-à-porter* sympathy – and only when she was a metre away did I recognize Angelina, who had accompanied us in silence throughout the day, timid and half hidden, reluctant to participate in any of the ceremonies, as if embarrassed to be what she would always be: the deceased man's last lover.

She was wearing a shawl that served her well as camouflage, black and loose like a Bedouin's djellaba, and her unmade-up face, under the material, was again that of a woman any mature man might take a fancy to. She had decided to come as soon as she managed to find out that my father was, in fact, among the dead; the accident had spoilt her Christmas, she said with a certain coolness (I thought she was protecting herself from her own sadness), but she wasn't going to allow it to spoil her New Year, that was for sure, and as soon as she could she was going on holiday somewhere, as far away from all this as possible. She was the one who pointed out, on the way out of the cemetery, that I didn't have keys to my father's apartment, and she did. There would surely be a few things I'd like to get, she suggested, and it was unlikely, or rather impossible, that we'd see each other again. She didn't mind going there with me and giving me the keys, she went on saying in the tone of a professional conciliator, as long as I would allow her to stay in the apartment for a while, while she packed up cardigans, rings, women's magazines and even packets of sweetener that had piled up there over the course of six months of dates with my father, and that it would now be pointless to waste.

'Look, the truth is I'm not really up to it right now,' I said. 'But why don't we meet tomorrow and then we'll have all the time we want.'

And that's what we did. The next day, in the middle of the afternoon, Angelina and I went into my father's apartment together and sat down to talk with the look and feel of long-lost twins. We found the door double-locked: the door of someone who'd gone away on a trip. Inside, the impression was the same: the curtains closed, the clean plates stacked on a wooden draining rack and one dirty glass in the sink (the orange juice one drinks before an early start, planning to have breakfast along the way). I had sat down in the ochre armchair, and she, after smoothing her skirt with her hands (a movement touching her bottom, her thighs), on one of the dining-room chairs. The pale light from the street marked her face, free now of the shadow of the djellaba, with the shadows of the window bars. When a car went past on Forty-ninth the reflection of its windshield projected across the ceiling of the apartment, mobile, luminous, a searchlight looking for escaped prisoners. 'I asked him not to go,' Angelina told me. 'And it went in one ear and out the other. At that hour, you know? How could he go so late? At least three buses have gone over the cliff on that road. Of course I told him. I told him and he ignored me.' She was talking with her face hardened and a voice that seemed to accuse my father or suggest it was all his fault. 'No, not three buses, many more, tons. The last not long ago. Everyone was killed.'

'But not this time,' I said. 'Didn't you know? There were people who survived.'

'I haven't read the papers, I didn't want to see them, it hurts too much. But they tell me things, people tell me things even though I don't want them to. There's no way to get them to respect you.'

'What things?'

'Well, stupid things, that's all.'

'What stupid things?'

'For example, that the bus was driving with its lights off, that it only had those little yellow lights up above turned on, you know the ones? That's the kind of shit that comes out in the newspapers. I don't know who the driver was, but I hate that son of a bitch. Maybe it was his fault.'

'Don't say that. Whose fault it was . . . I don't know if it really matters.'

'Well, it might not matter to you. But a person wants to know, don't you think? What if it was Gabriel's fault?'

'He's driven on highways all his life. He used to drive trucks as big as a house. I don't think it was his fault.'

'What trucks?'

'Troco trucks.'

'And what does that mean?'

I was talking to her now as if we were brother and sister. As if she should know as well as I did my father's whole life.

'Nothing,' I said. 'It's the name of a company. Like any other name. It doesn't mean anything.'

Angelina thought for a second.

'Liar,' she said then. 'Gabriel means God's warrior.'

'Oh yeah? And what does Angelina mean?'

'I don't know. Angelina is Angelina.'

She closed her eyes. Squeezed them as if they stung.

'The thing is, he'd just gone out,' she said. 'Why did he have to go out so late? Men are so stubborn. They never listen.'

'And you?'

'What about me?'

'Why weren't you with him?'

'Oh,' she said. A pause. Then, 'Because I wasn't.'

'Why not?'

'He wouldn't let me go with him. It was his business.'

'What was?'

'His business.'

'What business?'

'Oh, I don't know,' said Angelina, angry and a bit anxious. 'Don't ask me any more questions, don't be a drag. Look, I didn't stick my nose into his business. We barely knew each other.'

'But you were a couple.'

It wasn't the right word, of course. Angelina didn't mock me, but she could have done.

'A couple, doesn't that sound nice? Like on the soaps. Is that what people say about us, that we were a couple? It's nice, I think I'd like that, though what's it matter now? He was more worried than I was about what to call us. He was always asking me what we were.'

'And what were you?'

'Incredible, you're exactly the same, chip off the old block, isn't that what they say? I don't know, we slept together once

98

in a while, we kept each other company, I think we loved each other a little; in six months you get to love someone a little. I loved him, I know that for sure, but that's life, isn't it? You're a grown-up, Gabriel, you know a person doesn't go to bed with someone and immediately become part of their life. If he wanted to go, what was I supposed to do? Nothing, right? Let him go.'

'But it was so late,' I said.

'So what? Oh yeah, I would have liked to go with him and get myself killed with him, how romantic. But he didn't invite me, what do you want me to do?'

'And in Medellín. What the hell was he going to do there? He didn't even like that city, he had an aversion to it.'

'He'd never been there.'

'He disliked it anyway.'

'Oh, that's a good one,' said Angelina. 'Take a dislike to places you've never been.' And then, 'He'd never been there.'

She began to cry, discreetly, silently. I wouldn't have noticed but for the movement of her index finger that swept the line of her lashes and then wiped the mascara on her black skirt. 'Silly fool,' said Angelina. It was normal that she should cry as one does cry in the days following a death, when the whole world is little more than an empty shell, and the intensity of the loss seems unmanageable, but I couldn't help but think that her quiet weeping, devoid of show and all despair, had different qualities, and then it occurred to me for the first time that Angelina was hiding something from me, and immediately I saw it, I saw it as if it were written in neon lights on a dark wall: my father had hurt her. She was crying out of resentment, not sadness. My father had hurt her. It seemed incredible.

'And did you have plans?' I asked.

Angelina looked at me (or rather her piercing eyes looked at me, as if separated from her body) with something that was uncertainty but also hostility, as if she was a little girl and I was trying to cheat her in a shop.

'What plans?' she said.

'To move in together, I don't know, for him to stay in Medellín. He didn't really tell me very much, you know? One day he came out with the thing about the trip. Just like that, out of the blue. That he was going away with you to spend the holiday, that's all he told me. That was it.'

'Well then, that was it. Christmas and New Year, those were the plans.'

'And then?'

'Listen to this guy. Then nothing. Why are you asking me so many questions, I'd like to know.'

'I'm sorry, Angelina. It's just that he . . .'

'How should I know what went through his head? What do you think I am, a fortune-teller?'

'No, of course not. I'm not asking —'

'Do you know what I'm thinking right now? Let's see, let's see if you're so great. What am I thinking?'

She's thinking of her pain, I said to myself. *She's thinking everyone wants to hurt her. And the man who seemed to be different hurt her too.* But I didn't say it, among other reasons because I couldn't prove it, because it was impossible for me to imagine the circumstances of that injury.

'What am I thinking?'

'I don't know.'

'You don't, do you? See, so why do you think that I can know what your dad was thinking? Sure, it would make things easier if it was like that, wouldn't it? Knowing what other people are thinking, fantastic. Well, you know what? If you could see what other people were thinking, you'd be too terrified to leave your house.'

Angelina was defending herself, although it wasn't too clear what from. I, for my part, left it there; I accepted that an argument, or a grudge, or a disagreement between my father and his lover (the resolution of which was interrupted by death, that great meddler), was no concern of mine; I accepted that the least important aspect of my father's death was the fact that he'd died in a traffic accident, and the least important aspect of the accident was its location or the distribution of responsibility. So we spent the rest of the evening doing what we'd planned. She collected her things, every sign of her passage through the life of a dead man, and said goodbye with a distant and formal handshake, perhaps thinking of what she'd said to me at the cemetery: we'd never see each other again, because there was no reason in the world why we should. I watched her walk slowly down the stairs, carrying under her left arm a cardboard box that we'd emptied of newspapers to fill up with the sweetener and the sweaters and the magazines, a baseball cap that my father had forbidden her to wear the first time he'd seen her in it, and a plastic bag full of hair conditioner, seaweed skin creams and packets of sanitary towels. I closed the door when I heard her say goodbye to the doorman; then, for an hour or two more, I walked around the apartment, opening drawers, cupboards, doors, lifting up shirts and peering behind books, with all the movements of someone looking for a hidden treasure but with no intention of finding it: just wanting to make sure my father hadn't kept savings or valuable documents in some secret place and that later, when what was necessary was done with this place, the documents or savings wouldn't be lost among the rubbish or stolen. That's how I found an old ticket to a Leonardo Favio concert, beside a half-empty box of condoms, and, in spite of the faded letters on the paper, I could see the concert had been the year my mother died, which undoubtedly explained why my father had submitted himself to the unbearable torture of popular ballads; and that's how I realized, as I went through his meagre and amateur collection of similar records – some still with their tissue-paper sleeves intact – that there were no cassettes in this house, because there was no machine to play them on, and I was struck by a notion I hadn't considered until that moment: my father left behind two or three texts, but his voice was not recorded anywhere. I would never hear his voice again.

Days later, in Sara Guterman's house, where I had gone to spend New Year's Eve, I again thought of this small tragedy, and told her. Sara gave me all the sympathy she could, but obviously couldn't contradict me or disprove the fact that my father's memory would gradually disappear little by little, and his disappearance would be pinned on circumstances as impalpable as the non-existence of a recording, at the same time as her voice had been generously consigned to remain for ever on a dozen cassettes. Her television was on, because we'd agreed that we'd pay little attention to the toasts and Colombian traditions of eating grapes and wearing yellow for luck, and we'd go from one year to the next watching the celebrations in other cities, and there were the images, the black skies suddenly filling with dense and luminous fire-works like candyfloss, the noise and the kisses, the clocks playing their starring roles in Delhi, in Moscow, in Paris, in Madrid, in New York, in Bogotá, and the people of those cities chanting a countdown that in those moments was the most important thing in the universe. No German city featured in the televised inventory, and I thought of asking Sara if there was anyone in Germany – or Belgium, or Austria – with whom she would have liked to celebrate, relatives or friends she'd be with right now if she didn't live here but there, if she'd never emigrated. I was about to embark on that dangerous pastime, the speculation about an alternative life, and to thank her for her company on this night that I wouldn't have been able to get through on my own, when she cut me off in mid-sentence and put her hand on my arm, and the longest New Year's Eve of my life was formally inaugurated at that moment: Sara began to tell me about rumours circulating in the Bogotá media that week, according to which Angelina had accepted a large amount of money from an important magazine, the name of which she did not yet know, in exchange for revealing in an interview that Gabriel Santoro, the man who was honoured during his funeral and would in the near future be formally decorated, the lawyer who had distinguished himself as an orator for thirty years, not only by his talent but also by the high moral standards of his conduct, was not in fact what everyone had thought: he was an impostor, a liar and a faithless lover. 'This changes everything,' Sara said to me. 'Because there are things I'd rather you heard from me than had to read out there.'

III

The Life According to Sara Guterman

'CHRISTMAS 1946. Well, not the 24th, but just a couple of days before. Almost exactly forty-five years ago, imagine, and I'm not one to dwell on anniversaries. Nothing odd in remembering a date like that, do you think? Everybody remembers things that happen at Christmas, and so do I, even though in my house we didn't celebrate the same things or on the same days. But Mama always paid a lot of attention to Christmas, partly, I think, because she wanted to blend in with her new country, the whole recent-arrival complex. When in Rome, et cetera. It would be odd if I did forget the date, even for a second, or if I couldn't remember exactly what happened that day, what I was wearing, what was in the newspapers. The problem is that I remember what happened the day before and the day after, a month before and a month after, because it was a very unusual period, and even as I was living through it I realized my life was changing. To witness the moment when your life changes forever is a very strange thing, I swear. And I have it here in my head, it's like a film that I can't turn off, that I've seen a thousand times. Sometimes I'd like to turn off the film, lose it forever. But then I think: I can't do that to Gabriel. When it was obvious that he was going to forget it all, that his intention was to erase his part in the film come hell or high water, I thought I would become his memory, the idiotic idea of being someone else's memory occurred to me, and stayed stuck in my head. Now you can go down to the corner and buy memory, right? At least my grandchildren have done. They get a taxi and go to the computer shop and buy memory – I'm sure you've done it too – I don't even know what a computer is, I haven't wanted to learn, and asking my grandchildren how these things work is to subject myself to their impatience. So anyway, I was Gabriel's memory, although I couldn't talk about that to anybody. I was and maybe still am such a terrible thing: a memory forbidden from admitting that it remembers. My sons don't let me remember either. I'm not allowed to speak to my grandchildren about what happened in those years. I thought about that just a little while ago, I'd never realized: I've gone through life heeding people who forbid me to remember; is that not the strangest thing in the world? So the film in my head ended up existing only in my head. Like those Chaplin films that were lost for so long and that they now say they've found, I don't know if you saw the news anywhere. Anyway, that's what I was, a reel, a spool, a roll, I don't know what you call it, a can of film that gets lost, and no one cares that it remains lost because no one intends to show it, and if someone did show it I swear no one would go to see it. What we did go to see was *Of Human Bondage*, which was showing then, before Christmas. I loved Paul Henreid, we were all a little annoyed with him because he'd taken Ingrid Bergman in *Casablanca*, and hadn't left her to Rick who was so charming. And we went to see it. Gabriel didn't like it. Of course, he'd read the novel. Who wrote the novel?'

'Somerset Maugham.'

'Yes, that one. And he hadn't liked the novel either. Anyway, that was at the beginning of December. A week later, when I had managed to convince him to see it again, to see if he liked it this time, we received the news. Konrad Deresser had killed himself. Konrad, Enrique's father. I'm not even sure you know who I'm talking about.'

'Enrique Deresser, yes. Dad's friend, no? I think he met him at your hotel. Yeah, he talked to me about Enrique Deresser a couple of times, especially when I was about twelve or thirteen, and one time he told me about the death of Konrad Deresser. But then he didn't any more. He stopped mentioning the subject. Just like that, all of a sudden. As if Deresser was the Christ child or Santa Claus, you know? As if my father had said to me, Children talk about these things, but for an adult they are ridiculous characters. That happened with him.'

'Tell me what you know.'

'I know that Enrique's father went broke. I know he killed himself, took I don't know how many sleeping pills and washed them down with a cocktail of liquor and gunpowder. I also know that it all happened in a dive of a hotel, no, in a boarding house on Twelfth Street, on Twelfth around Fifth or Sixth, because one time we were walking past there and Dad told me. Look, this is where Deresser's father killed himself, he told me. I remember it very clearly, we were walking down Fifth Avenue towards Luis Ángel Arango. We were going to look for a couple of books that he thought were *absolutely crucial* for my thesis. Longinus's *On the Sublime*, and *The Art of Persuasion in Greece* by Kennedy. He thought my thesis was for a different degree, I guess.'

'That's incredible, you remember the titles? How can you? What an amazing memory.'

'One always remember titles, Sara. When my mum died I was reading *The Man with the Golden Gun* by Ian Fleming. When I graduated I was reading *Clandestine in Chile*. García Márquez. When they killed Lara Bonilla I was reading *Hiroshima*. John Hersey. One always remembers, or at least that's how I am. Not you? Don't you remember what you were reading on important dates? Let's see, what were you reading when your husband died?'

'I don't know. I remember there was a bullfight on. It was Pepe Cáceres. The bull caught him but he wasn't hurt. I saw it all from up here. And I don't even like bullfighting.'

'But no books.'

'No. I guess I'm not like that.'

'Well, anyway, Longinus and Kennedy. Those were my authors when Dad told me about Konrad Deresser.'

'I didn't know he'd told you. It's strange. Anyway, let me tell you the rest: Gabriel was in the hotel that weekend. I had kept on working in the hotel after the war, with more and more responsibilities, because suddenly the ability to speak Colombian Spanish had made me indispensable. What a word: indispensable. Your dad and I were twenty-two years old, and Enrique a little older, twenty-four or twenty-five, already grown-up. Twenty-two, can you imagine? Who's indispensable at the age of twenty-two? My grandson's that age, or at least somewhere around there, and I see him and think: We were that age? Weren't we children? Of course, back then we were already people at twenty-two, we were adults, and these days a thirty-year-old is still a child. But it doesn't matter, we were young. How was it that the things that happened to us happened? Aren't there things that a person only does when they're older; is there not a minimum age for doing certain things, especially the ones that mark your life? I've spent so many years asking myself these questions that the answers now matter very little to me. Now what I want is for no one to answer them, because an unexpected or strange reply would make me revise my life. And there comes a time when we're no longer up for revisions. I'm no longer up for revisions. Gabriel tried to revise, for example, and I don't know what his girlfriend thought about that, but things aren't that simple. You can't start revising your life and rest easy. It's forbidden to revise and rest easy. That should be inscribed on our birth certificates, so we know what to expect, so we don't go through life doing silly things.

'Your father was at law school, but even so he managed to come out to Boyacá every weekend. When he couldn't catch a bus, I'd look through the reservations for someone we knew, and he would always get a lift, as if guests' cars were for hire. I'd just give him the phone number, and he'd take care of the rest: he'd call, put his case in his Don Juan voice, and the guests would end up offering him a place in their car. Gabriel had this ability: he managed to get people to do things for him. It wasn't just that he knew how to talk, no. People believed him, people trusted him. Even Papa would let him stay in the hotel without paying the full rate, which would have been out of Gabriel's reach, something he might've been able to afford three times a year. And so he'd arrive with his contracts and administrative procedural textbooks, and he'd study for a while, almost always in the mornings, and then we'd go out for a walk, when my work in the hotel allowed. This wasn't in term time, and in the holidays Gabriel would normally get some job, driving trucks all over the country as if Colombia were the size of a ranch. Of course, they hired him because he had the stamina of an ox and he could sit behind a steering wheel for twenty straight hours, without sleeping, hardly even stopping to eat. That year he drove fuel tankers during the transport workers' strike . . . but you know about that, don't you?'

'Yes, he told me about that several times as well. "On the Crown". The trucks.'

'Well, that Christmas there weren't any trucks to drive, there wasn't any work, because the strike was over. Gabriel couldn't bear staying at home. He never talked to you about that, I'm sure. He couldn't stand your grandmother. And I have to say I could see why. Doña Justina was already puritanical before they killed her husband, and from that moment on she went to unbearable extremes, especially for her only child. So it was the most normal thing in the world for Gabriel to ask me for asylum, I'm not exaggerating, that's the word he used, holiday asylum, because his mother, to celebrate Christmas, got together with three old maiden aunts, and for each novena they said the rosary with such fervour that after her death the doctors found one of her kneecaps was dislocated and said it was from spending so much time kneeling during the second half of her life. Gabriel made fun of her in public. It was a little painful to watch.'

'I never knew her.'

'No, of course not. When she died you would have been two or three years old, and Gabriel never wanted to take you to her house for her to see you. The old lady sent everybody to tell him that she wanted to meet her grandson, that she didn't want to die without seeing her grandson, and Gabriel didn't react at all. With time I came to realize that he was throwing it back in her face . . . it's just a saying, of course, because in that family they never faced up to things, they didn't talk about illness or misunderstandings or anything. Do you know what he reproached her for? – well, what I think he reproached her for behind her back – That she should have let herself die after the death of her husband. That she buried herself alive at the age of thirty-five – because I don't think she could have been any older when they killed your grandfather. Let's see, Gabriel was ten or twelve, probably twelve, so she was just barely into her thirties, yes, she was already dead and in mourning at that age, and Gabriel said that sometimes her mourning was for her own death. He talked to me about that several times. He'd come back from his Catholic school and come home to rooms darker than those of the priests, the furniture all covered with sheets so the upholstery wouldn't get worn, an enormous crucified Christ in every room, all identical, the ones with lots of blood and open eyes, you know? The ones that usually have crosses made of corrugated wood, if you can say it like that. Have you seen those?'

'I think so, I've seen them somewhere. The ones that aren't smooth. The sort of irregular ones, like chocolate braids.'

'Before they killed your grandfather, Doña Justina taught Gabriel how to make the crosses, because at the house in Tunja the child had a lot of free time and there was more than enough wood. And afterwards, for a time, she still forced him to go on making them. Making wooden crosses until he was twelve or thirteen. How he hated her for that. He remembered those crosses all his life. After that he hated all manual labour, I think partly because of that. Or did you ever see him painting the house, or trying to learn how to play an instrument, or fixing the plumbing or a cupboard door, or cooking?'

'But I always thought that was because of his hand.'

'Ah, his hand.'

'That had to affect his life, no? It dictated what he could and could not do, defined his interests. He didn't even write, Sara. And he was always telling me about his childhood complexes, about the effects of the deformity on a child . . .'

'No, wait. One thing at a time. There wasn't any effect, nothing like that.'

'How so?'

'What happened to his hand was later. And it didn't happen the way you think it did. He grew up with both his hands intact. That Christmas, his hand still existed, and it existed for a few days more. Or rather, what happened was just a little after what I'm telling you about. But I don't understand, you told me you knew about the trucks. How was he going to drive one of those monstrosities with a mutilated hand? No, no, that day, when Gabriel came down to breakfast and found out that Konrad was dead, all his fingers were intact, he was an intact man. People were gathered around the radio, I remember, but not because they'd just broadcast the news, simply because we'd got used to the idea that that was the meeting place for certain things. How I wish I knew what ever happened to that radio. It was one of those Philips that look like a doctor's bag, the most up-to-date model, with its little wicker screen and everything. Papa told me the news and asked me to tell Gabriel. He knew how close Gabriel and Enrique were, everyone knew. It was obvious that Gabriel would have wanted to be informed. In half an hour he'd had something to eat so as not to travel on an empty stomach, packed, put on his new shoes, a pair of moccasins with leather soles as smooth as baby's skin, and he was ready to ask the first person leaving for Bogotá for a lift. "But he's already been buried," Papa told him. "It was almost a week ago." Gabriel didn't pay him any attention, but it was obvious he was hurt. His friend's father had died, and no one had told him, no one had invited him to pay his last respects. He asked me to come with him, of course, and he did it there, in front of Papa: that was a measure of the confidence he had, of the trust Gabriel inspired even when he was so young. I asked what we were going for, and he said, "What else? To pay our last respects to Señor Konrad." "But they've already buried him, Gabriel," Papa said again. And Gabriel, "Well, it doesn't matter. We'll pay our respects in the cemetery."

'But we didn't go to the cemetery. We got to Bogotá that very afternoon, around four, caught the tram at Seventy-second, but when we got to Twenty-sixth Gabriel sat still in his seat, without making the slightest move. I asked him what was going on, weren't we going to the cemetery? "Later," he said. "First I have to talk to someone." And that was how I found out that Konrad Deresser had been living with a woman at the time of his death, but what was more shocking was that Gabriel knew and I didn't. Not that he knew her, but he knew of her existence. Her name was Josefina Santamaría and she was from Riohacha. And we showed up unannounced, we showed up to visit her in the boarding house at Eighth and Twelfth where Deresser had lived. Josefina was a black woman, taller than Gabriel. The only thing I knew about her life was that she'd arrived in Bogotá six months previously and that she went to bed for good money with members of the Jockey Club. I didn't know anything more because that afternoon we didn't talk about her, but about Deresser. She was the one who told us, second by second, how he'd killed himself. "Of course I knew, love, how could I not know," Josefina told us. "You could see in his face that he was half dead." "And why didn't you do something?" asked Gabriel. "And how do you know I didn't? When I saw him go out that morning, I went out after him and followed him. I followed him all morning, what more was I supposed to do? What happened was that he took me by surprise. He was a lively one, my little monkey."

'That morning, like every morning back then, Deresser had left late, around ten, to have coffee and brandy for breakfast across the square from the Molino. "He always sat there," said Josefina, "to watch the students' girlfriends, I think." But Josefina wasn't jealous, just the opposite: when she saw him off in the mornings, she said give my regards to the girls, let's hope the wind picks up and lifts one or two of their skirts. That morning he stayed longer than ever, as if someone had stood him up and he didn't know what to do. He walked back and forth across the plaza, he walked towards the *Espectador* building and waited to see the news on the blackboard. "Ever since they started bringing out that board, he'd stopped buying the newspaper," Josefina said. They stopped doing that blackboard thing later, but for many it was the perfect solution while it lasted: a guy came out of the window at certain times with the most important news items written there, by hand, as they happened, it was great. Deresser didn't have any money to buy the newspaper, and had become a regular client of the news board. That morning the street in front of the newspaper office was full, but full of ladies, who wanted to know how and where they were going to pay tributes to the Archbishop, who was celebrating the fiftieth anniversary of his ordination. Deresser approached them, tried to speak to one or two, and was unwelcome, of course. No one wanted to be approached by a bearded man who looked like he hadn't slept and almost always smelt of sweat and sometimes of urine, even if he did carry a leather briefcase that looked like it had seen better days, even if he did still have those green eyes that had made him famous among the women who worked at the Nueva Europa. And

Deresser repeated the routine, walking back to the Garcés shop and returning to the front of the newspaper offices, not once, not twice, but several times.

'If he had arranged to meet someone there, that person didn't show up. If he was waiting for someone, that person didn't come. Deresser went into the Molino twice, walked through looking at the tables, and both times he stopped under Sancho Panza and from there looked around at all the tables again, but nothing. Nothing he wanted. So he kept walking, he crossed the plaza and went south on Sixth. "He was walking right up against the wall," said Josefina, "as if the rest of the people were lepers, or he was." Josefina saw him go into a pawnshop, the kind that used to be more common then than they are now, and come out again without his briefcase. At first she thought the obvious, that he'd just pawned that ugly briefcase for which he couldn't have got much, but later she found out that he'd also taken the last luxury he had left, and that was, in any case, a useless luxury: a record of classical music. It was useless because days before he'd pawned the turntable he used to listen to it. For Deresser that moment, the moment he pawned his last record, had to mean something terrible. People who are going to kill themselves cling to silly little things, construct symbols out of everyday items to mark a date. Pawning that record marked a date for Deresser, not just because with this gesture he marked the closure of his life, but also because it was probably that money he later used to buy the sleeping pills from the Granada Pharmacy.

'Deresser was a failed musician but one who had taken that failure well. He'd set up a glassworks to keep his family fed when he realized that in Colombia it was going to be impossible to make a living from teaching the piano. That

117

was back in 1920, when he'd recently arrived in Bogotá. But a few years later, after meeting people in the terrible process an immigrant goes through, he gradually began to get into the National Radio Service, and eventually to work there. He decided what they played and when, he told the presenters about Chaliapine or Schoenberg and they would repeat on air what he'd told them two hours earlier. For those who knew the Deressers, that was the family's best time, a few years when no one would have imagined a personal disgrace awaited them, a time that ended or began to end in '41, when Santos broke with the Axis. Among the first things they went after were the broadcasters. There could not be any German or Italian or Japanese people near the airwaves. And Deresser arrived one morning to find he didn't have a job and furthermore some people looked down on him. The family was left as it had been before: depending on the glass they sold. And they didn't do badly, the glass made good money, and besides, Deresser stayed in contact with the two programmers at the station who didn't reject him, and they saw each other once in a while and he made recommendations. But music, at least for Deresser, was no longer a source of work. After that, between '41 and '46, Deresser listened to music, though less and less, and he finally accepted that things in his life weren't going to go as he had wanted them to, accepted that someone had taken his life out of his hands. In October he found out that the first Nazis were going to be hanged in Nuremberg in the middle of that month, and the first thing he did was to get a record by Wagner, who he'd detested all his life, and call his friends at the station. They saw him at the boarding house, as far as Josefina recalled, his friends came without making any comment about the place or the company he was in, but you could see the sorrow on their faces. Deresser showed them the record and talked about it with such enthusiasm, or feigning enthusiasm with such talent, that his friends left the boarding house promising they'd play it one of these days, thanking him for introducing them to a little-known work by a rarely broadcast composer, asking him to keep in touch, to keep making suggestions, contributions . . . Deresser asked them one more thing. He asked them as a special favour to please broadcast it on the 15th of October, and he said that day was Enrique's birthday, and that the Wagner piece was one of his favourites and it would be a good birthday present, and they believed the whole lie, they left feeling moved and making new promises. They fulfilled them. They played the record on the 15th of October, the day of the hangings in Germany. The Wagner piece was called *The Mastersingers of Nuremberg*. Half the Germans in the city called up indignantly. The other half called up to ask who'd been responsible because they wanted to congratulate him. Josefina said it was the last time she saw Deresser more or less happy, although it was for mocking half the world without the other half knowing.

'After pawning *The Mastersingers*, Deresser must have known what he would spend the money on. He went down Seventh then headed north, walking slowly like a tourist. "He stood for about half an hour in front of the Granada," said Josefina. Not right in front of it on the same side of the street, but on the opposite sidewalk, as if he was about to shoot an elephant and was keeping an eye on it from a distance. But when he did go into the pharmacy, when he finally made up his mind, he went in and came out again in two seconds. "I think it was when he came out that he noticed. I was really hidden. I was there in Parque Santander, behind a tree, don't know how my little monkey did it, but I think that's where he saw me." And then again the same thing, but in reverse: again south on Seventh, passing in front of Gabriel's office, though no one can ever know if Deresser thought of Gaitán at that moment, even if purely through the power of suggestion. He kept going down to the Plaza de Bolívar, as if this time he did have an appointment. A few blocks before arriving, he could already hear the noise of the people gathered in the Plaza de Bolívar, even if those people weren't shouting or singing or protesting. The ladies were really quiet, very decent they were, all of them standing facing the cathedral and some already with rosaries in their hands, the older ones, especially. For Josefina, these were strange spaces, strange and even hostile, and she didn't usually go anywhere near them. The last time she'd passed through this plaza, though it was only a few blocks from her house, she'd been like a zombie following the people who came to hear the *Te Deum* and to wave flags and shout things the day the war ended.

'It was a quarter past three in the afternoon. The homage to the Archbishop had started not long before, certainly, because when the ladies at the front began to move towards the Palacio, there were a few at the back who were still feeding the pigeons little bits of bread, crouched down, holding their parasols in one hand, stretching out the other gloved hand, full of crumbs. Josefina looked at them, dying of envy, because she liked pigeons but was allergic to them. And for a second, a single second, she watched one of those ladies, one who was wearing a wide-brimmed black hat with pink flowers, and who wasn't giving the pigeons bread-crumbs, but grains of hard yellow corn, and she stood watching the corn that bounced around when a fat, reddish pigeon pecked at it on the ground. She was jealous of the lady with the black sun hat for the ease with which she could approach the pigeons. When Josefina, recently arrived in Bogotá, had tried to do the same, her eyes had begun to water and her nose to itch so badly that she'd had to sit on the steps of the Capitolio because she couldn't see where she was going for the tears. Later, in the afternoon, she'd come out in a terrible rash on her neck, and she didn't know and no one wanted to tell her where she could buy calamine lotion to put on to stop her scratching so much. Three days. Three days it took her to discover the Granada, which was so close to her boarding house. There she could get calamine when she no longer needed it, when she wasn't itchy any more and already knew that she could never go near another pigeon in her life. And thinking about this, about the lotion and the Granada Pharmacy, she looked up again, after this briefest of seconds, and noticed that Deresser wasn't there any more.

'She looked all around, swept the plaza with her gaze. She circled round the little group of women who were now moving. She went among them and endured their insults. They called her everything, insulted her the way those on the inside usually insult someone on the outside. But she didn't see him, she couldn't find him, she'd lost him. All she could see were black hats and dresses as if she were suddenly in the middle of a funeral, everyone wearing gloves, as if touching each other disgusted them, but among these easily disgusted people she didn't manage to find Deresser, only two or three faces that looked at her in horror, two or three mouths that said, A negress, a negress. She went all around the square, twice passed the window out of which Bolívar had leapt to keep from being cut to pieces in his own bed and didn't think of Bolívar, or of anyone other than Konrad Deresser, a man who was fleeing from her, who was hiding from her, but at no point did it occur to her to recover her dignity, be guided by pride and stop looking for someone who at that moment did not want to be with her. It didn't occur to her that Deresser might have gone off with another woman, because that had never mattered to them, so he had no reason to hide such a thing from her. It didn't occur to her that Deresser might be mixed up in some shady business, because, in spite of having reasons to go mad with fury against this crazy country, which had broken his life and his family into pieces, in spite of all that, Deresser had never been one of those who take matters into their own hands. Quite the contrary, he was gentle, gentle as a lamb, too gentle for the world he got stuck with after '41. No, none of that occurred to her. Looking for him through La Candelaria and then down Seventh, Josefina was thinking about him the way you think about a sick child: more worried about him than about herself, less worried about losing him than about the fright the child will get when he realizes he's lost.

'She arrived back at the boarding house just after five in the afternoon. On her way she'd passed a group of men going to pay homage to the Archbishop just as their wives had done a couple of hours earlier, and she thought how odd the people of Bogotá were, that they did everything like that, the men on one side, the women on the other, it was a miracle they hadn't gone extinct. Among the men she'd seen Don Federico Alzate, with whom she had an appointment later, and she acted as she always did when she ran into one of her clients in the street, looking down at her sandals, and her white toenails, counting her toes, because she thought that this way, thinking about something else and not about pretending, the other's shame and her own pretence would no longer be visible in her face. And now in her room she lay down to wait. She couldn't wait by the window, because her room didn't have any windows. "I realized that people without windows wait differently," she told us later. At ten to seven, when Federico Alzate arrived, she was still waiting. Josefina normally insisted her clients take her somewhere else, out of a tacit agreement with Deresser and because it also seemed wrong to her to sleep in the same bed she used to earn the money to pay for it. But this time she chose to stay. She had time to get the job done. It was hours later, when her client had left and Josefina was washing, that she heard shouts on the stairs. It was the owner of the hardware store on the ground floor. He came repeating like a parrot what he'd just been told: Deresser had been seen laid out on Jiménez Avenue, three blocks from there, swimming in his own vomit.

'He wasn't dead, but when Josefina found him there was nothing to be done. The smell was that of a dead man, in any case, or at least that's the memory she was left with. Josefina discovered then that she'd grabbed the money she'd just earned on her way out the door, and she wanted to give the ironmonger a peso to help her get Deresser to a hospital, but the ironmonger was already walking away and pretending not to hear. Josefina stopped two taxis, and neither of them wanted to take her even though she offered them the whole three pesos she had in her hand. Then she felt something on her leg, and lifting up her skirt discovered she hadn't put on any underwear, and a mixture of water and semen was running down her thigh making her kneel down and retch, and at the same time, as if the world had come to an agreement, a fellow with an open umbrella though it wasn't raining came over and said to her, "Don't trouble yourself,

baby. You can see from here he's already on the other side."
Later, when it was dark, when first the police had come and
then the detectives to take the body away, a journalist was
listening to the statements of a witness. "I saw him running
over there," he said and pointed towards Third, "as if he was
drunk, and covered in sick, and shouting, he was shouting
that his stomach hurt." It seems, as was later discovered, that
Deresser had gone to sit in the Chorro de Quevedo, pre-
sumably after giving Josefina the slip, and in all likelihood it
was there that he took the pills, although no one knows or
ever will who got the gunpowder-laced alcohol for him. It's
incredible that he actually managed to walk from the Chorro
to the place where they found him, near the Parque de los
Periodistas. That's what had the most affect on Gabriel, the
image of Konrad Deresser running half asleep and feeling the
mixture burning his guts instead of anaesthetizing him and
killing him silently as he'd expected. "He must have been
very frightened, and sleeping pills take longer to work in a
frightened person," years later a doctor told Gabriel, after
he'd explained the case without naming any names, as a
hypothetical case, just out of interest. "And would it be very
painful?" asked Gabriel. "Oh, yes," replied the doctor. "It
would hurt worse than death."

'That day we ended up leaving the boarding house very
late. We realized we hadn't eaten anything since breakfast,
and of course Josefina had nothing to offer us. Although it
was obvious, I said to Gabriel that it was too late to go to the
cemetery, and asked him if he wanted to go the next day. But
his mind was elsewhere. He didn't look at me, didn't hear
me, and he was walking three steps ahead of me as if I were
his bodyguard. I thought he was going to suggest we go to
the Parque de los Periodistas, or to look for the physical space

where Deresser had died, but he didn't. And then I began to think what I later managed to put into words: Gabriel hadn't taken me to see Josefina to find out what she knew, or at least that wasn't his only reason. We'd gone to see her, and had listened to her talk and talk and talk for a whole afternoon, to confirm what she didn't know. Because it was perfectly obvious that this woman had lived all those months with Konrad Deresser without it mattering a damn to her where he came from or where he was going or why he was in the mess he was in or how he thought he'd get out of it. If she hadn't asked, we were both thinking, why was he going to explain. "If he didn't explain it to her," Gabriel said to me then, "that means he hadn't explained it to anyone." That's what he said. And I agreed, of course. It was the most logical explanation. And in spite of being so logical, and in spite of me agreeing, I didn't ask Gabriel why all that seemed so important to him. Most of all, why confirming that had seemed more urgent than going straight out to find his friend. Although the following day he did. He went to look for Enrique and didn't find him, he didn't find anybody. Much later we found out that Enrique had left home. Later, that he'd left Colombia. That was what your dad found out. But he didn't find out where he'd gone.

'I didn't want to go with him that time. I was too overwhelmed by all that had happened. I'd seen more than one case like that, of course. I'd seen my fair share of failures, of people who'd gone under, but this was different. I'd never seen anything like that up close and never anyone who'd killed himself. Yes, I'd heard of people who'd killed themselves; in those years it wasn't such an exotic thing. News from Germany, but also from immigrants. But what do you want me to say? When something like that happens to someone you know, who you've spoken to and seen and touched, it's like finding out for the first time. As if up to that moment you didn't know that was possible, to kill yourself because of problems. Konrad's case stood out, not because it was odd, but because it was close. Thousands of Germans went through the same thing with the blacklists, then their assets were frozen and put into trusts. Thousands were left absolutely ruined, watched for five years as their money went up in a puff of smoke. Thousands. After the blacklists, getting sent to the Fusagasugá internment camp was child's play; for old Konrad it was almost a rest, because by the time they sent him there his inclusion on the blacklist had left him almost bankrupt. Those interned in the camps were fed, and they didn't have to worry about utility bills, and all those things. In theory, the government took their expenses out of their accounts, but if the internee had no money, what were they going to do, starve him to death? No, they went on giving him what they gave the others, and that's what must've happened with the old man. In any case, these ones were almost lucky; that's what you can see over time. One hundred and fifty, two hundred Germans, almost all upper class, were guests of the state under the pretext of having links with the Nazis, or that they were spreading propaganda, or whatever, and of course, sometimes it was true. In that place there were people of the worst sort just as there were harmless little men who wouldn't hurt a fly. Some had already been on the lists, but not always. The old man had, and that's what matters. The punishment of the lists was suffered by thousands, like I said, but we only saw one fall from start to finish like that, like a plane, like a duck that had been shot, and that was Enrique's dad. Old Konrad, who wasn't old. We called him that because his hair was grey, but he was only about fifty-five when he killed himself. I've known people just starting out at that age.

'I remember the piece of paper, as if I had it right here; worse, it's strange that I don't have it. I suppose I got the collecting bug later, no? No one grasps the importance of what's happening when it's actually happening. If a genie appeared and offered me three wishes, that's what I'd ask for, to know how to recognize things that are going to be important later. Not for other people, that's easy. We all knew that with Gaitán that was it. When they killed him, we all knew this country would never recover. No, with public things it's different; I'd like to recognize them when they happen to me, that phrase your best friend says, that thing you see by accident – one doesn't know that it's important. I'd like to know it. Well, later the lists appeared in books, facsimiles, as they call them, and we could see them, the ones who wanted to could see what those little pieces of paper that buggered us up so much, pardon my French, looked like. The circulars the gringos sent, and all, you know? The heading, the name of the country between two lines, the month in English and the translation. The thirty or forty pages of names. The names, Gabriel, the thousands and thousands of names all over Latin America. Hundreds of names in Colombia. That was the important part.

'Nice and organized, in alphabetical order, not in order of warrant, or degree of danger. The owner of a bookshop in Barranquilla where Nazis held meetings and where they gave away free copies of *Mein Kampf* to everyone who came in – that man's name would be alongside a poor Japanese green-grocer who'd sold a few potatoes and carrots to the Spanish Embassy, and for that alone, just for exchanging a few of his vegetables for a bit of cash from the Franco regime, they put him on the blacklist. What power a list can have, no? That column down the left with all the letters exactly the same, all capitals, one after another, it's always fascinated me. I've always found lists enthralling, why should I deny it? There's nothing wrong in that either, I suppose, nothing reproachable. A telephone directory was the best thing I could have when I was little; I'd put my finger at the top and slide it down a page where they were all *l*s or *m*s, where they were all *u*s. The feeling of tranquillity that gives you. The feeling that there is an order to the world. Or at least that it can be put into order. Take the chaos of a hotel, for example, and you put it down on a list. I don't care if it's a list of things to do, of guests, the payroll. *Everything that needs to be is there and what's not there isn't because it shouldn't be there.* And you breathe easy, sure of having done things as they need to be done. Control. That's what you have when you make a list: absolute control. The list is in charge. A list is a universe. What isn't in a list doesn't exist for anyone. A list is proof of the non-existence of God. I said that to Papa once and he slapped me across the face. I said it to sound interesting, a bit to see what would happen, and that's what happened, a slap. But deep down it's true. Well anyway, in December 1943, on page 6, Enrique's father's name appeared on the list. Above him was "DeLaura, Luciano, PO Box 199, Cali". Below him was "Droguerías Munich, Tenth Avenue no. 19–22, Bogotá". And in between those two, in that space so neat and orderly, was Enrique's father. "Deresser, Konrad. Cristales Deresser, Thirteenth Street no. 7–17, Bogotá." That simple, all on one line, name, business and address, and they didn't even have to use two lines, didn't even have to break into the margin the way they do when a single item occupies two lines in a list. That always bothers me, taking up two lines when one is sufficient, because it looks ugly. Old Konrad would have agreed with me. Old Konrad was always very orderly.

'A few days later, even before I knew about the matter, Margarita Deresser phoned the hotel. That was Enrique's mother's name. She was from Cali, with very pale skin and very long surnames, you know what I mean. I answered. She wanted to talk to my father, she explained to me. They needed witnesses. Deresser had requested an appointment with the Consultation Committee and they'd just got back from the interview; it had been at the United States Embassy. That was a new thing. Before it was only the Embassy that could decide if a person should be included on the list or not. Now there was a committee. "It didn't do any good," Margarita said. "It won't do any good, you'll see. What they want is our money, Sarita. And they'll take it with or without a committee, with Doctor Santos or with López or whoever. This very thing has happened a thousand times already. Not to people we know, but you hear about these things." They'd been offered *tinticos* and *tecitos*, a little coffee, a little tea, those diminutives people in Bogotá like to use to seem friendly, and they'd been asked why the gentleman thought his name should be removed from the list of nationals with their assets frozen. They'd been listened to for fifteen minutes while they tried to explain that it was all a misunderstanding, that Señor Deresser didn't have any kind of economic or personal relations that could possibly go against the interests of Colombia or the United States, that he was no supporter of the Führer, far from it, he felt loyal to President Roosevelt, and all so that finally an assistant or ambassadorial secretary could tell them that Señor Deresser's relations with enemy elements were more than proven, as was his sympathy for propaganda activities. That's how it was, they were very sorry, they weren't going to be able to reconsider the matter, it wasn't up to them, but to the State Department. "I don't know what we're going to do," said Margarita. "Konrad of all people, that's what bothers me. If this happened to your father I know he'd work it out. But Konrad is weak, he lets life get him down. Someone has to explain it to them, Sarita. Tell them he hasn't got anything to do with the Axis or anyone, that he doesn't know anything about politics, he's only interested in music and being able to make his panes of glass in peace. Your father has to write to them. He has to tell them what Konrad's like, what we're all like. Important people have stayed in the hotel: you're not going to tell me they can't pull some strings, are you? We have to get him off that list, Sarita. We'll do whatever it takes, but we have to get him off that list. If not, this family's going to the devil." I asked, "And what does Enrique say?" And she told me, "Enrique doesn't want anything to do with it. He says that's what we get for mixing with Nazis."'

Of course (said Sara Guterman) then I knew where it all came from. Actually, the fact that Enrique had turned his back on Konrad seemed normal to me, because they'd never got along very well. But for him to wash his hands of something so serious was not so normal, because being on the list was going to affect him as well, no doubt about it. The truth is, I couldn't understand it. 'Nobody knows Enrique,' your dad said to me around that time. 'Not you, not me, not his mother. Nobody has any reason to expect anything from him. You find that surprising? Well, you'll just have to swallow it, and learn not to expect things from people. Nobody's what they seem to be. Nobody is ever what they seem to be. Even the simplest person has another face.' Yes, as a philosophy that's fine, but there was nothing in the way Enrique was, nothing in his persona or his talk that could lead anyone to expect this. For me it was a betrayal, to put it frankly. The word is very strong. Betraying your father is something that only happens in the Bible, and that's how I saw it. But suddenly what your dad said was true, and we simply hadn't looked as closely at Enrique as we should have. And we'd known him for quite a while. He'd spent Holy Week in the hotel every year since 1940, more or less, maybe earlier. Old Konrad had been granted a sort of private tender, which was how my father did things in the hotel. Out of nationalistic preferences, or immigrant solidarity, or whatever you want to call it, the fact was that from the very beginning, it was Konrad who took charge of the four hundred and fifty-nine panes of glass for the renovation of the Nueva Europa. Imagine. Every mirror and every window, every rectangle of every glass door, bevelled or otherwise, smoked for the boudoirs, frosted for the bathrooms and silvered glass for the chandelier in the dining room. In reality, Enrique didn't care a fig for the hotel and his father's glass. Other things mattered to him. For example, the hotel was full of women, and Enrique was convinced that women existed on the face of the earth only so he could pick and choose between them as if they were avocados. Of course, sometimes it seemed he wasn't wrong. He'd arrive at the hotel in his elegant Everfit suits, with his Parker 51s, carrying flowers and moving with the self-confidence of a bolero singer and looking like an archduke, and the women would melt, it was embarrassing. But he was a fascinating guy — even I could never deny that. And not only because he had foreign airs, something which has always gone down well here or because he moved as though he'd been offered the world and declined it out of modesty, or because he was able, simply by walking into the dining room with his hair slicked back and the manners of a nobleman's son, to evoke obscene comments from the female employees and secret favours from the guests' wives, but also because his voice seemed lie-proof. Enrique's words didn't matter – his authority mattered. I swear, Enrique made his interlocutors feel they were outside their lives for an instant, as if he'd rescued them and put them on an operatic stage. (But no, Enrique didn't like opera. Just the opposite, he looked down on it, he looked down on that music to which his father devoted his free time and some of his work time too.) And when you talked to him, he looked in your eyes and at your mouth, your eyes and mouth, with such intensity that at first people wiped their moustaches, thinking they had crumbs there, or took off their spectacles to see whether there was something on the frames. Then you'd figure out that no, it was just the attention he gave. That was what it was like to talk to him. A war could break out in the garden, and he wouldn't take his eyes off you.

Enrique never spoke German in public. He'd learned it at home, it was the language he spoke with his father, but outside, working in the glassworks or when he was at the hotel, he would answer in Bogotá Spanish even though old Konrad had asked in Swabian German. For your dad all this was a sacred mystery. The first time he went to the Deresser's house for dinner, that big, comfortable house in the neighbourhood of La Soledad, he thought it was so strange. When he arrived it was like his friend, when he changed languages, was no longer the same person. Enrique was talking and he didn't understand. He was talking in his presence and he had no way of knowing what he was saying. At first he was taken aback, and then he became suspicious. But later Gabriel went off thinking it was the most fascinating spectacle he'd ever seen, and the next time he asked me to go with him. A sort of guide to German customs, or occasional interpreter. Now I think he wanted witnesses. After dinner, Enrique asked old Konrad, 'Would you go back for good?' He answered evasively and immediately started to speak about the language he'd been born into and then about Spanish, which seemed so difficult to him. He'd read some poet saying that slang was like a wart on the common language. That's what stayed with me, a wart. 'No matter how hard we try,' he said, 'that's what we immigrants are, producers of warts.' Then he closed the conversation, and it was almost better that way, because Enrique was apt to say very harsh things that he'd never allow himself to say about other things, about romantic composers or Bohemian glass. Enrique said he was never going to teach his children German, and he repeated it to your dad and to me on several occasions. I understood him, of course, because my father received letters from acquaintances or colleagues or distant relatives. In them people explained to us how terrible it was talking familiarly, using the language affectionately or to say pretty things, when for all practical purposes, it was the language of National Socialism.

Of course, Enrique began to realize that his father's language was dying in his head, not only because he didn't use it outside the home, but because he didn't speak it with people his own age, and his idioms, sayings and set phrases were all thirty years out of date. And that's how he saw the contradictory and even unbearable situation of being enclosed in a language that didn't think like he did, but like his father: that's where those desires to rebel against his own home came from. It was very strange. It was like a will to be a character without a landscape, you know? Someone with no relation whatsoever between his body and the carpet, between his body and the dining-room walls. In the house there was a piano rented by the day and a portrait of a Prussian military officer, some illustrious ancestor, I think. Enrique didn't want to have anything to do with that. He wanted to be a character with no backdrop. A flat, two-dimensional creature, with no past. And when he went out, it was like he wanted to be new. Language was just one of the things that allowed it. With his looks, speaking Colombian Spanish was like putting on a wetsuit and diving into the water, that feeling of comfort, of being in a strange medium but one in which you could move more easily than in your own. He was always going to make the most of it, no? Even if he was a fool. Enrique, for the first time, found out what your dad always knew: you are what you say, you are how you say it. For old Konrad things were exactly the opposite.

Margarita would sit me down in one of the velvet arm-chairs in the living room and offer me tea and biscuits or one of the cakes from Frau Gallenmüller's shop, the one at Nineteenth and Third, and talk to me about that; she'd start getting nostalgic right there, talking about her husband, and always end up telling me how different he was when he first arrived in Colombia, how he'd changed since then. She said time had betrayed him. It had betrayed both of them, everyone. Instead of returning to her husband the security that everyone feels in their own land, and that an exile gradually gains little by little, time had taken it away from Konrad. He had been forbidden spontaneity, Margarita said, the capacity to react unthinkingly, to make a joke or ironic remark, all the things that people who live in their own language can do. Partly due to this, old Konrad never had a normal relationship with a Colombian. What he said was too meditated or stilted to forge a friendship with anybody. Or complicity, at least. Complicity is very gratifying, but it's impossible if you don't speak properly. Enrique was lucky enough to figure that out and understand it, in spite of being very young. Konrad Deresser was always a very insecure person, and Enrique, from a very early age, became obsessed with creating the opposite sort of mask, inventing himself as someone able to trust in himself, develop the security that would allow him to talk to others as he did later talk to them. Without blinking. Without stuttering. Without thinking twice about a word. I've never known who learned it from whom, whether he learned it from your dad or your dad from him. At the beginning of 1942, a family of Germans came to live in Bogotá from Barranquilla. You have to imagine what it meant to someone like the old man to talk to people from his country. I know, I can imagine, because my father felt the same way for a long time. Exactly the same. He'd run into a German and be in heaven. It was the best thing that could happen to him. Speaking continuously, fluently, without noticing his own grammatical mistakes on the other person's face, his clumsy conjugations, without thinking his pronunciation was going to make his neighbour burst out laughing from one moment to the next, without fearing rs and js more than thieves, without that feeling of vertigo every time he put the stress on the wrong syllable.

The family that arrived was called Bethke, husband and very young wife. He was about thirty, maybe a bit older, about the age you are now, and she would have been twenty, like us. Hans and Julia Bethke. It was at the time of the first restrictions. Citizens of the Axis nations out of the radio stations. Axis citizens off the newspapers. Axis citizens away from the coasts. Yes, that's how it was. All the Germans who lived in Buenaventura or Barranquilla or Cartagena had to go and live in the interior. Some went to Cali, others to Medellín, others came to Bogotá. Bogotá filled up with new Germans at that time. It was wonderful for the hotel, Papa was happy. Well anyway, the Bethkes were among these, from Barranquilla. For *Buss und Bettag* in 1943, the Deressers organized a small dinner, very low-key. Your dad was very surprised that they invited us. We were both about to turn twenty, but we were still babes, that's obvious; at that age one feels like the saviour of the world, and it's a miracle we survive our own mistakes. There are those who don't survive, of course, there are those who at sixteen or seventeen or eighteen commit the only mistake they'll ever make and they're wound up for the rest of their lives. At that age you realize that everything they've told you up to then is pure rubbish, that the world is another entirely different thing. But does anyone give you up-to-date instructions, or at least a guarantee? Not at all. Figure it out as best you can. That's the cruelty of the world. It's not being born that's cruel – that's psychoanalysis for beginners. Nor losing your family in an accident. Accidents don't mean anything. What's cruel is that they let you reach the conclusion that you know how things work. Because that's the age of majority. A woman gets her period, and four or five years later feels sure there'll be no more surprises. And that's when the world arrives and tells you, None of that, Miss, you don't know a thing.

When they invited us, I explained the obvious to Gabriel: that Konrad Deresser owed heaven and earth to my family. If it hadn't been for my father, who gave him the contract for all the glass in the hotel, old man Deresser wouldn't even have enough money to eat, let alone to invite people to dinner. When they dismissed him from the radio station, my father paid the cook's son to find the twenty or thirty smallest windows in the hotel and break them without being seen. And then he ordered new ones from Deresser and paid the full price for them, and he also had to pay for two stitches to the boy's thumb, which he cut while trying to break a window in a bathroom on the second floor. So of course I was invited, since I was the daughter of Herr Guterman. Herr Guterman, by the way, was also invited. How could he not be. But he said no, no thank you. He sent me to be polite, and Gabriel came with me, but Papa made excuses because he was perfectly aware the Bethkes were Nazis. There are photos of meetings in Barranquilla, a swastika the size of a cinema screen and these people on their white-painted wooden chairs, all with their hair very neat. And on the platform or stage, whatever you call it, people in their well-pressed brown shirts, hands behind their backs, standing to attention. Or in meetings, all sitting round a table with its embroidered tablecloth, drinking beer. The Bethkes right there, he in white suit and tie, with his armband, and she with a brooch on her chest. In the photo you can barely see it but I remember perfectly: the eagle was gold and the swastika was onyx, a very well-made piece of jewellery. And I went to dine with these people one evening. It wasn't such an odd thing, believe it or not. I dined with swastika brooches, with armbands on several occasions. It wasn't exactly a regular occurrence at the hotel, of course, but before 1941 no one hid, none of them concealed anything, so it wasn't the most unusual thing in the world either.

So, why did he send me? If Papa preferred not to go himself, for the very understandable reason of disagreeable company, why didn't he mind me going? I wondered at the time, and later the answer was obvious. My father was an idealist. Only an idealist goes so confidently to a country like Colombia. People say the idealists are all dead, because they were the ones who stayed, hoping things would sort themselves out. I've never agreed. Those were the unfortunate ones, that's all. Or the ones who didn't have money. Or the ones who didn't get the papers to enable them to leave Germany or visas for the United States or wherever. On the other hand, the idealists packed their bags one night and said life's better somewhere we've never been. My father was a rich man in Germany. And one night he said, I'm sure we'll be better off selling cheese in the jungle. Because that's what Colombia was to a fellow like Papa, the jungle. Some of my schoolfriends wrote me letters asking if there were lifts to take us up to the treetops, I swear. That is idealism, and that's why it seemed necessary to him that I represent the family and sit beside a fellow they said had a portrait of Hitler hanging in his living room. Here in Colombia it's another life, here we're all Germans, he'd say, here there are no Jews or Aryans, he'd say in the hotel, and in the hotel it worked for him. Yes, you'd have to be very naive, very short-sighted, I know. What about his friends hanged in the public squares in Germany? And those who'd spent years by then with a yellow star sewn on their clothes? Oh, yes, my father wasn't often wrong but he was wrong about that. He believed, like so many other Jews, that Nazism abroad was a game, that exiles couldn't seriously be Nazis, no matter how many meetings they held, how much propaganda they spouted, how much evidence there was. We helped to build this country, didn't we? People were fond of us, no? Spirits were tempered here, people became more civilized and rational. Who could prove to him that the opposite was the case? Anyway, he wasn't the only one. The Jewish community was expert in denying the hatred of others, or whatever you want to call it. Of course, there would always be some guest to confirm those stupid ideas, because hotel guests aren't going to tell the owner what they think of his nose, are they? Guests aren't going to paint a swastika on the walls of their room, are they? No, at that time my father was a lamb. Old man Seeler, a horrible fellow, one of the patriarchs of anti-Semitism in Bogotá, stayed in the hotel one time, and my father accommodated him with the excuse that he saw him arrive with Isaac's novel *María* in his hand. And I could give you thousands of examples like that. What can I say? From the beginning he thought he couldn't raise me to be resentful, he told me that often, that with me they'd have to cut their losses and start afresh, and besides (he didn't tell me this, but I can well imagine), he couldn't send out the idea that there were people with whom you do not sit, and much less Germans like us. Like us, you see. In Colombia the enemy was less of an enemy. That's what the lamb my father sometimes was would have thought. Besides, remember in Colombia nothing was ever said about the camps in Europe, about the trains or the ovens. All that just was not in the Colombian press. We found out about it later, and those who knew about it while it was happening were on their own; the newspapers paid no attention to them. The fact is I served as ambassador for Herr Guterman the idealist, and that's how I ended up sitting between your dad and Herr Bethke, and facing Enrique Deresser, who was seated between the two women, Julia Bethke and Doña Margarita. At the head of the table, presiding but without any authority, was old Konrad, who looked smaller than he was when he was sitting down, but maybe it was the company that made him shrink.

Hans Bethke's perfectly shaven face, his little spectacles, everything about him said: I'll smile at you, but turn round and I'll stab you in the back. He had curly, blond, slicked-down hair, and it formed little spirals at his temples. His whole head was a whirl, like sharing a table with one of Van Gogh's trees. And the tree talked. It talked a mile a minute. He used the little he'd done in his life to put down anyone else. Before we'd finished our drinks in the living room, we already knew that Bethke had travelled to Germany when he was twenty, for a short stay, sent by his family to get to know the land of his ancestors, and he'd returned to Colombia more German than the Kaiser. You would have said he wore his passport on his sleeve if his passport wasn't still Colombian. He had very small hands, so small that the salad fork looked like the one for the main course when he held it. Small hands, I don't know why, always make me sort of suspicious. Not just me, your father feels the same way. It was as if they were made to slip into the pockets of the people sitting next to him. But he didn't slip them anywhere. Bethke handled his cutlery as if he were playing the harp. But when he spoke it was something else. Bethke had a column in *La Nueva Colombia*, although I only found that out later. And hearing him talk was like hearing that, a column in a Fascist newspaper. Yes, that's what the man on my right was, a talking newspaper. Don't tell me it's not the height of irony.

With the aperitif still in his hand, Bethke started to tell Konrad about the things he'd brought back from his trip. Records, books, even two charcoal drawings by names that meant nothing to me. I said I liked Chagall very much. Just to participate in the conversation, that's all. And Bethke looked at me as if it was time for my bottle. As if I should brush my teeth and go straight to bed. He said something about decadent art, something I didn't really catch, to tell the truth, and then he spoke to Konrad as prudently as he could, but if he was trying to hide his indignation he did it very badly. He was either a bad actor or a very good one; I never figured it out. 'I'll tell you something, Herr Deresser,' he said. 'I wouldn't be here, having a drink with you, if I knew that sort of decadence could take hold in Germany. But I'm not concerned, and I won't deny the reason. I'm calm because the Führer is looking after us; he looks after you and he looks after me, he reminds us what we are. There's something in the air, Herr Deresser. It's there for whoever wants to notice it, and I want to be part of it, here in Colombia or wherever, it doesn't matter; a man takes his blood everywhere he goes. No, no one renounces his own blood. Why should a German have to forget himself when he arrives here? Have you forgotten who you are, have my parents forgotten? Quite the contrary. What happens to their children is another matter. Do you know what I think of all these Germans who don't speak German, with their Hispanic names and their reactionary customs, the ones who show up late because people here are always late, who do sloppy work because here they're slapdash, who lie and swindle because that's normal here? They are sick. They're sick and they don't realize. They're like lepers. They're falling apart. They wanted to assimilate and they've done so downwards. The ironic thing about this business is that people like me had to come along, people who first stepped on German soil at the age of twenty, to explain all this, to correct the path.'

I don't think Gabriel would have really understood what he was talking about. But I didn't have to explain it to him, first because I didn't even understand it very well, I heard these things and it was like they were talking to me underwater, and second because Gabriel, during the lecture, had been upstairs in Enrique's room, listening to the first few chapters of *La vorágine*. They were broadcasting a reading, or rather a performance, of the novel on the radio, with sound effects and everything. There was thunder and rain, Gabriel said, and people walking through grass and the sound of monkeys and of people working, it was fascinating. When they came down to the dining room they were still talking about it, and Konrad had to suggest to Enrique the possibility that the rest of us hadn't heard the programme, that continuing to talk about the programme in front of us might not be very polite. Among other reasons, because talking about *La vorágine* was interrupting Herr Bethke. And that was a no-no. It might be the end of the world, but Herr Bethke would take his message to the other side of the table. That's what old Konrad seemed to be saying. He seemed to be saying, We're not aware of how lucky we are. He seemed to be saying, This table doesn't know how lucky it is. And all for the fact that sitting there with us was a man who knew Emil Pruefert, the famous Emil Pruefert, leader of the Colombian Nazi Party. Pruefert had been one of the first Germans to leave the country. We didn't know if they were friends, but Bethke talked about Pruefert as if they'd shared the same wet-nurse as babies, as if they'd drunk milk from the same breast. And old Konrad was pale, pale with admiration maybe, or maybe with respect, in spite of knowing that Pruefert had left before Colombia and Germany had broken off relations, and even too long before, which some thought strange and others just cowardly.

We'd never seen him like that, neither Gabriel nor I, and the impression was very shocking. It was as if he'd been emptied of himself. He couldn't hold his head up, that had to be it, it couldn't be agreement. That wasn't politeness, or diplomacy. It wasn't the good manners of a host towards his guest. And I don't know if Enrique was pretending, making out he'd never seen his dad as that spectacle of disgusting obsequiousness, but he also looked shocked. 'This is German,' Bethke was saying. 'To be able to sit down to a meal and talk of our land without complexes. Why should this country forbid us to use our language? What's already happened is terrible, but for us to let it happen is unthinkable. Why should we allow it, Herr Deresser? The government is closing German schools wherever they are. The German Secondary School of Bogotá? Closed. The Barranquilla Kindergarten? Closed. What, seven-year-old children are a threat to the empire of the United States? You'll have read the comments by Struve, the Communist priest. The honourable Minister didn't close a school, but an institute of political propaganda. And then there are these cheap harangues. No more Nazi teachers. Declare Spanish the official language of instruction. Let's make a bonfire on the patio and burn all the Nazi propaganda. And what is this material? History textbooks. That's what Arciniegas, the Minister, is looking for, that's what President Santos wants, to burn German history books, to persecute and extinguish the German language in this country. And what are the Germans doing about it? They're letting it happen, it seems clear to me.' Margarita interrupted him, or tried to interrupt him, talking about some association that was doing good things. Bethke heard her but didn't look at her. 'Katz, a mechanic,' he said. 'Priller, a baker. Is that the great society? Are those the "Free Germans"? There is poison in the blood of these Germans, Herr Deresser. The source of that poison must be cauterized, it must be done in the name of our destiny, that's what I say.' At that moment your dad leaned over to me and said very quietly, 'Liar, he didn't say it. It's from a very famous speech. Everyone in Germany knows it.' To tell you the truth, it didn't surprise me that he should know things like that. But I couldn't follow it up, or ask him any questions, whose speech it was, what else it said, because Bethke never stopped talking. 'Only a few dare to raise their voices, to protest, and I am one of them. Are you not proud of your German blood, Herr Deresser? And that that blood flows through your son's veins?' And that was when Enrique spoke for the first time. 'Don't bring me into it,' he said. He didn't say anything more, and it didn't seem like he would say anything else, but those five words were enough to make Konrad sit up straighter: 'Enrique, please. That's no way to talk to a . . .' But Bethke cut him off. 'No, let him, Herr Deresser, let him speak, I want to know the opinions of our young people. Young people are the reason for our struggle.' 'Well, don't tire yourself on my account,' said Enrique. 'I can take care of myself.' Old Konrad interrupted. He obviously knew too well how far his son could go. 'Enrique is a romantic,' he said. 'It's his Latin blood, Herr Bethke. How can you expect . . . of course, you understand, those born in Colombia . . .' 'I was also born in Colombia,' said Bethke, cutting him short, 'but that was an accident, and in any case I don't forget where I come from and what my roots are. At this rate Germany is going to be finished, Germany is going to lose the war, not against the Americans, not against the Communists, but against every *Auslandsdeutsche*. No, one cannot stand around with one's arms folded watching the extinction of one's people. Everyone knows how human beings work. The mother always takes charge of raising the children, to a large extent by custom, and it's the mother's language the child adopts most naturally. Your wife knows it. Your son is the living proof. They rob us of our own blood, sir, they steal our identity. Every German married to a Colombian woman is a line lost for the German people. Yes, sir. Lost to *Germanness*.'

He said that last bit looking down at his own plate to scoop up a spoonful of broth. No, it wasn't broth, it was cream of tomato soup, as thick as custard, that Margarita had had served with a little spiral of cream adorning the surface. In the centre of the spiral, where there was a sprig of parsley, landed a whole bread roll, one of those the size of a fist, with a hard crust, you know the ones? Enrique had thrown it hard, as if he'd wanted to kill a fly perched on the parsley. The bread stayed there, held up by the density of the tomato soup, and the tomato soup landed on Herr Bethke's shirt and tie and slicked-back hair. And I got splashed a little too, of course, inevitably. I don't have to tell you I didn't mind in the slightest.

Old man Konrad stood up as if his chair had a spring, shouting things in German and waving his arms around like a swimmer. In extreme situations, he would call Enrique by his German name. And this situation was extreme. Old Konrad shouting in German at his son Heinrich and wiping off Herr Bethke's shoulders. 'Don't bother, don't trouble yourself,' Bethke said with his jaw clenched so tightly that it was a miracle we could make out the words. 'We were just going in any case.' And his wife, the invisible Julia, stood up then, and she did so as she'd done everything all evening: without making a single sound. Her cutlery didn't make any noise, her spoon never touched the bottom of the dish, her serviette never made a sound when Julia wiped her little lips. She stood up, went to her husband's side. Two seconds later we heard the door. We heard Konrad saying goodbye. 'I'm so sorry, Herr Bethke. Something like this, a person like yourself will know how to forgive . . .' But we didn't hear anything from the guests, as if they'd turned their backs on the apologising old man. There was the sound of those little bells that shake when the door is opened, when it's shut. We did hear that. The jingling. And then we saw old man Konrad return to the dining room, red with rage but without letting a single growl, a single insult escape. He kissed Margarita on the forehead and began to climb the stairs without looking at Enrique and without looking at us; we had stopped existing or we existed as a disgrace, like a finger pointing at him. It seemed incredible to me that he wasn't going to say anything, and then he said four words, four little words, 'That won't happen again,' and he said them in the same tone someone else might have used to say, 'Tomorrow's market day.' 'It will happen again,' Enrique said, 'every time you invite a son of a bitch into the house.' Margarita was crying. I noticed your father had turned away from her, probably so as not to make her feel worse. I thought it nice that it had occurred to him. Meanwhile old Konrad stood still on the first step, as if he didn't really know how to get to his room, or as if he was waiting on purpose for Enrique to say what he said, 'I wonder when you'll ever be able to stand up to anybody.' 'Enrique, love,' said Margarita. 'Or doesn't it matter to you?' said Enrique. 'Doesn't it matter if someone insults your wife in front of you?' 'No more,' said Margarita. Old Konrad began to go upstairs. 'You're a coward,' Enrique shouted. 'A coward and a toady.'

Have you ever seen the staircases in those houses in La Soledad? They were very special, because some of them, the most modern ones, didn't have banisters. If you are on the first floor watching someone climb the stairs, the person's body gets cut off a bit with each step, I don't know if you've ever noticed. On the first step you see the whole body. By the fourth the head's no longer there, because the ceiling cuts it off. Further up the torso's gone, and further still all you can see are two climbing legs, until the person climbing the stairs disappears. Well anyway, the stairs of that house were like that. I'm telling you all this because Enrique shouted what he shouted when old Konrad was nothing but a pair of legs. 'A coward, a toady.' The climbing legs stopped, I think with one knee up, or at least that's how I remember it. And then they began to come back. One step down. Then another. Then another. The body of old Konrad was reappearing to us. His torso, his head. Until he was back on the first step. No, he didn't come all the way down the stairs. It was as if he wanted to assure us that in spite of his having returned to say something, the dinner was over, the evening had been cancelled. And there, standing on one of the first steps, in profile for those of us who were sitting in the dining room, he looked at his son, at the son who had called him a coward and a toady, and he just burst, the dam gave way. He spoke in Spanish, as if he wanted to say to Enrique, Now I'll play by your rules. I don't need advantages, I don't need condescension, what I want is for you to get it once and for all. And Enrique got it, of course. We all got it. 'Yes, I am a coward,' old Konrad said, 'but that's because I'm not what I want to be. I am a coward for staying here, here I am, that's the cowardly thing. Every day Germany is humiliated, read *El Diario Popular* and you'll see. Look what Roosevelt's lackeys are saying every day. Do they think nobody notices? They call us fifth columnists, they stone our legation, break the windows of our shops, forbid our language, Enrique, they close the schools and deport the principals. Why is Arciniegas closing our schools? Is it for political or religious reasons? It's not because there are Nazis, it's because there are laymen, and the ones who aren't secularists are Protestant. We don't know who's closing the German schools, whether it's the government or the Holy See, and meanwhile Arendt and his traitors call themselves Free Germans, and I'm just supposed to rest easy. Bethke does what I am incapable of imagining; he is a true patriot and not ashamed to say so out loud, to speak aloud, the German language was made to be spoken aloud. Even if a person is mistaken. Yes, he is surely mistaken, but he is mistaken on behalf of Germany. I've been ashamed of being German, but that is not going to last forever; all cowardice has its limits, even mine. I tell you, I am not going to remain quiet and calm. Germany has friends everywhere. You don't love Germany, of course, you have no roots. Do you know what it means to be German, Fräulein Guterman, or are you a rootless one as well? Your language forbidden, literature stolen from the German schools and burnt in public by the priest? But there are people working so that these things will stop happening. I don't care if a government of backward people considers them dangerous, I don't care, a patriot is never dangerous. In Colombia there are people who pray for Germany to win. I am not one of them, but that doesn't matter, because German destiny is greater than its leaders, yes indeed, German destiny is greater than the Germans. And that is why we are going to resist in spite of ourselves. Sometimes a person has to do unpleasant things, and who is going to judge you, that's all that matters, who is the judge of your life is the only important thing. Hitler will pass, like all tyrants, but Germany remains, and then what?

We have to defend ourselves, don't we? And we will resist, I have no doubt about that. However and by whatever means necessary.'

So later, when they put old Konrad on the blacklist, I had to remember that in order to understand why Enrique had vanished as if it was nothing to do with him. And it still shocked me, because such disdain is always shocking, no? At first I thought: When their business is left without customers is he not going to suffer the consequences too? Does he think this is a game, that people will keep buying from them in secret, that they'll risk being blacklisted as well? When they were forbidden from buying even a light bulb, when they were no longer able to pay the salaries of their two or three employees, what was Enrique going to do? That's what happened, of course: and it happened more efficiently than we had imagined. Fear works very well with things like this, nothing like fear to get things moving. In a week, an office-equipment shop in Tunja had already cancelled their orders for five-metre-by-four display windows so special that they'd had to bring in new casts through Panama. And also the display windows the Klings had ordered for their jewellery shop, smaller but also thicker, remained in storage in the warehouse, and later the suppliers of carbonates and lime-stone stopped sending their products, but they didn't bother returning the money they'd already been paid. Margarita told me all this. It was as if she felt obliged to keep me up to date. As if I were a shareholder of Cristales Deresser, or something like that. 'We have to have the kilns checked. I call the fellow who usually does it, and you know what he tells me? That he doesn't want to get into trouble. He asks me to please understand, not to hold a grudge, that when all this is over we'll most certainly do business again, of course. But it was just that an acquaintance of his was working for Bayer, got fired and now he can't find work anywhere. What do I care about his acquaintances? Not that I'm insensitive to other people's problems, but we're in no position, you understand, Sarita. This fellow has a signed contract with us. The most terrified one is Konrad. He just can't believe it. The agreements, he says to me, they've given their word. Does this no longer matter to anyone?'

It was around then that Margarita wrote a letter to the senators. She was looking for help, and someone had suggested these names to her. And my father was useful for that, because Leonardo Lozano had stayed at the hotel several times. He wasn't what you'd call a regular client, but he knew my father and he liked to go and talk to him, blunder along in German and convince himself my father understood his blunderings. So, after the holidays, as soon as the official offices reopened, Papa delivered that letter in person. Although I didn't see that one in particular, I saw dozens of similar letters during those years, letters of pure controlled desperation, letters wearing straitjackets. It was always the same procedure, so I can tell you more or less with certainty. Margarita's letter, if it resembled the ones the rest of the people wrote, would have been addressed to one or more senators of the opposition. The most privileged wrote to ex-President Santos, but that didn't always work. Sometimes it was better to appeal to less high-ranking people, because the gringos were afraid of debates in the Congress. Fear of the hostility of an important politician. Fear of disrepute, because that led, I suppose, to loss of diplomatic power. There were senators famous for their opposition to the lists and for having got several Germans removed from them. Margarita must have written to one of these. The letter would have started off saying that she was a Colombian citizen, that her father was so-and-so and her father's profession was such-and-such, the more Colombian the better. Then she explained that her husband was German, but that he'd arrived in Colombia long before the war, his roots in the country were undeniable, they even had a Colombian son. And then, the proof: we go to Catholic mass every Sunday. Spanish is spoken in the home. Her husband had adapted to the customs of our country instead of imposing those of his own. And most of all: he had never, never ever had sympathies for the Reich, not for the Führer nor for his ideas. He is convinced that the war had to be won by the Allies, he admires and respects the efforts of President Roosevelt to protect world democracy. So the inclusion of her husband (or her son) on the list is completely unjust, an aberration as a result of his nationality and surname but not of his actions or his ideas, because furthermore neither her husband nor her son had ever participated in politics, those affairs had never mattered to him, and the only thing he wanted was for the war to be over so he could carry on living in peace in this country he loved as if it were his own, et cetera, et cetera, a long et cetera. The letter would have said all that, always the same; if someone had been quick enough they could have made a fortune selling printed prototypes. A plea of Colombianisms, or of Colombiaphilia, however you want to put it. It was pathetic to read these letters, doubly so if they hadn't been written by an intermediary but by the interested party himself. And at the same time, by pulling strings or by whatever means, there were propagandists of the Reich who managed to get off the list with public apologies and bouquets of flowers from the government.

A week later, Margarita received a stamped and franked reply on official headed notepaper. Lozano's personal secretary regretted that the senators could not be of any help, something like that. It seemed they'd done several similar favours and now everyone was appealing to them, everyone looked to those who had opposed the lists in the Senate, and there came a time when Santos tired of sending messages, of giving references, of speaking well of Germans so they would be taken off the lists. Margarita arrived when the strings that could be pulled had worn away. Because influence wears out too, everyone knows that. The Deressers were out of luck. They simply got there too late, that's all. If all this had happened in 1941, when the lists were new and not so radical and people did things to revoke unfair inclusions, things would have been different. But it didn't happen in 1941. It happened in 1943. Two little years. And that made all the difference. Margarita sent a couple more letters, but didn't even receive replies. Well, that's not quite true: the first didn't receive a reply, but the second did. The reply was that old Konrad was going to be confined to the Hotel Sabaneta, in Fusagasugá, in the department of Cundinamarca, until the end of the war, due to his links with propagandists affiliated with the government of the Third Reich, and given that reports led to the consideration that his civic and professional activities could be prejudicial to the security of the hemisphere. With all this pomp, with all this ceremoniousness they informed him, and two days later a bus from the General Santander School came to pick him up.

'And Margarita? What happened to her?'
  'Well, she made a choice. She had two options, to go or to stay, and she made a choice. I don't remember exactly when she left home, or when we found out, rather. For some reason, that fact has disappeared from my head, me, who

never forgets anything. At the end of '44, or was it already the next year? How long had the old man been in the Hotel Sabaneta, six months or a year? Of course, what happened was that the failure of the company and of the family was kept secret, as was normal back then. Everyone saw the decline, everyone knew when they sold the machinery and the least necessary bits of furniture, but the details weren't visible from the outside. And then Margarita left home. The first weekend after she'd gone, Papa took us to Fusagasugá, to visit old Konrad. "And if they put me on the list for this," he said to me, "let them. Having friends doesn't infringe on anybody's democratic security, as far as I know. If one is forbidden from having friends, it would be better to know it once and for all." "But they say he's got Nazi sympathies," my mother said. And he said, "We don't know that. It's not been proven. If it's shown to be true, Konrad will not hear from us again. But it has still not been proven, we can still go and visit him and keep him company. His wife has left him, that's no small thing. We're not going to look the other way." I thought he was right, of course. And also, there was a pro-Nazi demonstration during those days in Fusagasugá, a large number of students went to shout slogans against the imprisonment of the Germans, and no one did anything. There weren't even any arrests.

'Enrique didn't go, of course, even though we offered him a lift. No, he stayed home, and we didn't even try to insist. By then he'd distanced himself from everyone. He wasn't speaking to his father, didn't go to visit him even when someone offered to take him to Fusagasugá. He'd even distanced himself from us. He didn't return messages, didn't call, didn't accept any invitations. When Margarita went away, he lost the only bond he had left. "The saddest thing," my father said, "is that all this will be over one day. Things are going to go back to normal again. This has to end sooner or later. And who will fix this family? Who will tell Margarita to come back, that everything will be fine from now on?" And it was true. But I don't blame her, Gabriel. I didn't blame her then, but now I blame her less. I've passed the age that she was then. Now I'm older, much older than Margarita was when she left her husband and son, and I confess that I'd have done exactly the same. I'm sure of it. One doesn't have to wait until things work themselves out, because that could take a year but it could also take twenty. My father asked, "Who will tell Margarita to come back?" And I thought, without saying so: And if she comes back, and if she stays with them and waits, and if it turns out that the internment camps are still there fifteen years hence, and the Germans are still stuck in the Hotel Sabaneta, who's going to pay her back those lost years? Who's going to give her body back the years that it lost waiting for abstract things, a new law, the end of a war?

'That day at the Hotel Sabaneta was one of the strangest experiences of my life. It was a luxurious place. In normal times it must have been more expensive than ours, and that was saying something. Well, I don't know, I can't be sure, but it was a first-class place. Of course, it's hot over there, and that changes everything. Where we had a fireplace and heavy ponchos for the guests, they had enormous gardens with people sunning themselves in bathing suits. There was a huge swimming pool, something I'd hardly ever seen, and even fewer times had I seen so many blond heads atop semi-naked bodies; it was a holiday resort like the French Riviera. Since the men spent most of their time alone, they saw no reason not to lie in the sun almost completely naked, and on visiting days the wives would find themselves with these people red as beets, some of them almost had sunstroke. That day the place was full. Imagine, a hundred and fifty families in a hotel where there was normally room for no more than fifty. It was like being in a bazaar, Gabriel. No one would have called those fellows prisoners of war. But that's what they were, no? Prisoners of war taking the sun. Prisoners of war sitting on a blanket eating roast chicken, an enviable picnic. Prisoners of war strolling with their daughters and wives along the most picturesque little gravel paths. Prisoners of war doing callisthenics in the gymnasium. Among them were some older men, who walked around all day long properly dressed, in white suits and ties, felt hats. Old Konrad was one of those, wearing a collar and tie in spite of the heat. The only ones more overdressed than him were the police on guard duty, with their police caps and sabres at their waists, the most pathetic little figures. Konrad was sitting on a balcony on the second floor. There was another person sitting about two metres away from him. Papa recognized him: "Shit, I didn't know Thieck was here." That's what he said, he said it in German, complete with vulgarity. He was very startled to see that Thieck. He was one of the important men of the Barranquilla colony. He worked at Bayer. He must've stayed at the hotel once or twice, I don't remember any more, but the important thing is that he was sitting two metres away from Konrad and not a word passed between them, and a place like the Sabaneta really fostered sociability. Anyway, Konrad was there, with his back turned to the other man. We waved to him as soon as we got out of the car, as enthusiastically as possible, and he didn't even lift his hand, as though the newspaper was weighing him down.

'That visit was terrible. The old man was disturbing us all with his unbearable repetition of the same old story: "I have not done anything, I swear, I am a friend to Colombia and to democracy, I am an enemy of all the dictatorships of the world, I am an enemy of the tyrant, I love this country that has been my host," et cetera, et cetera. And he showed us a shadow he had under his eye. It seems he had come to blows with someone who dared to speak of Himmler with respect. There was no way to make him shut up for a second, or for him to see a stranger and not immediately leap on him to tell him his woes and convince him of his innocence. It was a lamentable spectacle. And all the time he was carrying that briefcase he carried till his death, he took it everywhere, all around the hotel, and if you weren't careful he'd sit down beside you and take out all the documents concerning his case and show them to you. He'd take out the letters he'd written explaining the misunderstandings, the letters his wife had written, the replies they'd received, the newspaper from the day his name appeared on the list. He carried all that everywhere he went, "In case I run into a good lawyer by chance," he said. And that time it was our turn; for the old man we were the closest thing to confidants. We were sitting on that balcony, above a climbing bougainvillaea, watching the people swimming in the pool and spreading towels on the grass to sun themselves. Our rented paradise, no? Then at some point my father got up to go over to talk to another of the internees, a Jewish man from Cali he knew by name. The old man was speaking in German, as he always did when he spoke of emotions, of feelings, since he felt less vulnerable in his native tongue. "In these papers there's one thing missing, Sarita. Do you know what that is? I'll let you guess. Go on, guess. I've got everything here, see, things about myself that even I didn't know. Let's see if you knew, Sarita, did you know that I'm connected to platinum traffickers? I bet you didn't, did you? But that's how it is, Cristales Deresser is suspected of collaborating in the trafficking of platinum to Hamburg, ah, yes, see what a well-organized business we've set up. The platinum comes from Cali, arrives in Bogotá and, by way of Cristales Deresser, gets sent to Barranquilla and then shipped to Europe. It seems I'm linked to my associates in Barranquilla by mutual friendship with Herr Bethke. What it is to have friends in common, eh? It's good to be with your own people abroad; the language is our homeland and all that. Let's see what else I have here . . . I can always find more interesting documents, this briefcase is infinite. Look, I can tell you that my company is mentioned in letters from the Legation, yes, the Bogotá Legation writes to the Lima Legation and mentions me, I must be important. Of course, I also have documents that don't mention me, but rather my good friends, you know who I'm referring to. *El Siglo*. November of the year of Our Lord 1943. Yes, we do get the newspapers here, don't think they keep us uninformed. Let's see, under *b* for Bethke, let's see what the list says, yes, *b* for Barranquilla. Did you know he was a member of the German Club? Did you know he lives in El Prado? Yes, here in my briefcase I've got all this, but something's missing, can't you guess what it is? I'm going to tell you and don't be startled. It's a letter of farewell." Then he went from irony to tears. You should have seen him, he seemed like a lost child. "I don't care if it's written in pencil on a paper napkin, there is no note here that says I'm going. You don't know what that means, arriving home one day and that happens . . . Living with someone is many things, one day you'll find out, but one of them is waiting for homecoming time, because everyone has a time they get home, everyone who has a house has a time for coming home to it. It's not a routine, it's something that gradually takes over. I suppose it must be an animal instinct, no? A person wants to get to the place where he's safe, where it's least likely something bad will happen to him." Enrique had written to him a few days earlier to tell him that Margarita had left. "One day she didn't come home, Sarita, just like that. How could she do that to her family? I close my eyes and imagine Enrique awake and waiting for her, Sarita, hearing noises, and then the telephone rings, and it's her, Sarita, there she is telling her son she's not coming home any more, that she'll write to me later to say goodbye. Like that, nothing more, she left me a message, she left me a message and she went away, and of course she never did say goodbye, not even a letter of farewell. I don't know where she is, or who with, I don't know what her life's like any more, I'm never going to know ever again. I pray to heaven nothing like this ever happens to you, Sarita. I wouldn't wish this on anybody."

'He told me all that. But he didn't stop there. He told me about the first days. They'd been horrifying, he explained. Horrifying the first time the hotel administrator looked at him pityingly after having found out, and then, when everyone at the table must've known, horrifying the first time a letter arrived he didn't immediately recognize. He took it, sure it would be from Margarita, and it turned out to be from the Spanish Embassy, in charge of German assets during those years. They were notifying him of the state of his reserves. When he looked up he noticed that everyone else was watching him, not trying to hide it at all. They'd all stopped playing bridge or reading the paper and were watching him; they wanted to know if Margarita had come back too. Or rather they knew the letter wasn't from Margarita and they wanted to see poor Konrad's face. "They were making fun of me. They were laughing behind my back." Most of the Germans that were held there were people with money, and many could allow themselves the luxury of buying a house in the village so their families could live near by. For them things were easier. With a permit, which wasn't so difficult to obtain, they could go and sleep in their houses. They had family. They had wives, they had children. Konrad didn't have any of that any more. "They all looked at me with pity, but inside they were laughing, they were killing themselves laughing, and I'm sure the laughter exploded as soon as I went to my room. The people in this place are the most despicable I've ever had the misfortune to know. Even the Italians, Sarita, even the Italians laugh at me. My disgrace is better than a book for them, I'm their melodrama, I keep them entertained. I'm alone here, Sarita, I don't have anybody." Everything he would have liked to say to the Committee, to the US Ambassador, he said to me in the Sabaneta. And not many could endure that. There was Konrad spewing out his personal tragedy, and there's nothing less bearable than hearing disgraces one hasn't requested. Until I stood up and said, "I'm sorry, Herr Konrad, I can't stay any longer. I'm going to find my father. We have to go back to Bogotá and then on to Duitama. Think of the trip we have ahead of us. I've got work to do, you see, you know what a hotel's like," and I left, I cut him off in mid-sentence and I left. It wasn't true that we were going to go back at that time, of course. We were planning to stay the night in a guest house in Fusagasugá that a local opportunist had opened for precisely that purpose, because there were lots of families who came from Bogotá to see their fathers. We had reserved a room, we were going to return to the Sabaneta the next morning to say goodbye to the old man, but I begged that we should go straight back to Bogotá. "What an ill-mannered girl," my father said, but I thought something worse: What a cynical girl. I had already started turning that way. Well, cynical and all, I insisted so much that in the end that's what we did. We didn't see Konrad again. After that day, I never visited him again. My father went a couple more times, but I refused. I'm quite sure I couldn't have stood it.

'The worst thing, as you can imagine, is that the old man wasn't exaggerating. Seeing him was pathetic because of his lack of courage, but all that was happening to him was real, it wasn't invented. By the time the war ended and the inmates came out of the Hotel Sabaneta, old Konrad was alone. Without Margarita, of course, and to all intents and purposes without Enrique, who wasted no time in setting up his own place, as if he'd waited his whole life to get rid of his parents. Konrad found that life had left him behind. When he got out, he couldn't sell the family home, because it was still held in trust, and the house was eventually auctioned in mid-1946. The money never got to Konrad's pocket, obviously, but rather covered the expenses of his enforced vacation, and also war damages, which the government claimed out of the Germans' accounts. I don't know how or when he met Josefina, but she obviously saved his life, or at least helped him postpone his death. Many of the interned left the country. Some returned to Germany, others went to Venezuela or Ecuador to do the same thing they'd been doing in Colombia but starting from scratch, and that made all the difference. Starting over again, no? That's what breaks people, the obligation to start all over again one more time. Konrad, for example, could not. He devoted himself to slowly dying over the course of a year and a half . . . I can imagine it perfectly, lying with Josefina as if that woman were a shipwreck's raft, dividing the day between his opera records and coffee-and-brandy in any old café. Yes, the more I think about it the more convinced I am that Margarita did the right thing in leaving him. She died in Cali, in 1980, I think. She remarried, this time a Colombian, after Konrad's death. I think she had two children, a boy and a girl. A boy and a girl who are older than you and probably have their own children by now. Margarita, a grandmother, incredible. Maybe it's cruel to say, but look: what could she have done with that weakling of a husband? Could anyone have believed that Konrad might come out on top eventually? The lists stayed in effect for a year after the end of the war, and during that time Konrad fell to pieces. By the time they were abolished it was too late: the old man was already almost a beggar, but he was by no means the only one. There were those who survived the lists. I knew several. Some were in the Sabaneta, and of those a few really were Nazis. Others weren't even confined to the hotel, but went broke the way the old man did. And many of them remade themselves. They never again had the life they'd had before the lists. They never got their money back, and even today they think about those losses. The old man was one of the ones who couldn't. He couldn't manage it. That's the way the world is, divided between those who can and those who can't. So don't talk to me about Margarita's responsibility or anything like that. Sure, she left her family behind, and sure, in some way the old man's suicide has something to do with her. But she managed to live, no? Or does a person get married in order to be a guardian of the weaker one? Margarita had a second life, as your father would say, and that one came out right. With children, with grandchildren. I suppose anybody would like that.

'Of course Margarita didn't come to Konrad's funeral. Understandable, no? After all that had happened, to have to deal with a suicide and a concubine . . . Concubine is a pretty word; it's a shame people don't use it any more. Now they say lover and leave it at that. Concubine, cohabitation, it's pretty, don't you think? They're pretty sounds. Maybe that's why: people don't like that such a pretty word means such a thing. Suicide, on the other hand, isn't pretty. *Selbstmord*, in German, and I don't like that either. Sure, I say these things as if they're my ideas, when in reality it was your dad who made me appreciate it. We'd only just said goodbye to Josefina when he was already saying to me, "Concubine sounds better than lover, don't you think? I wonder why that is." But he said it sadly. Not cold or distant, not at all; not indifferent to everything we'd found out that afternoon, old Konrad's terrible death, the idea of the pain he must have felt, all that . . . It made a very deep impression on me. He didn't deserve such a death, I'm quite sure of that, but who says what kind of death we deserve? How is that measured? Does it depend on the good you've done, on your merits, or on what you did wrong, your mistakes? Or is it a balance? You atheists have a really hard time on this one; that's why it's good to be a believer. The arguments I used to have with your dad about this. He always won, I don't need to tell you. For a long time he used to use Konrad as an example. "The old man turned Catholic, and what good did it do him? You know thousands of Germans who converted in order to get along better in Colombia, to be more accepted by their wives and their mothers-in-law and their friends. And did it help them at all?" And I would say nothing, because it occurred to me, although I could never have proved it, that if old Konrad had remained a Protestant he would have committed suicide all the same. Not just that, he would have committed suicide *sooner*. I mean, it was his Protestant side that said, Take those pills, get yourself out of this mess. But who can prove that? And anyway, what good would it do, what damn difference would it make?

'That night, after talking to Josefina, we stayed at your dad's house, because it was too late by then even to think about getting back to Duitama. Your grandmother, wrapped in a black shawl as always, made up the bed in the guest room for me. She said hello and looked after me with that sad face that ghosts have in films, while Gabriel went upstairs and locked himself in his room, almost without a word. The house was in Chapinero, above Caracas Avenue. It was one of those two-storey houses, with staircases covered in worn red carpeting tamped down with copper rods. I'm not going to say, Shame you never knew it, or anything like that, because that house gave me the creeps. The silliest things made me uncomfortable, like those copper rods and rings that held the carpet in place, or the parrot on the back patio, who shouted "Roberto, Roberto", and no one knew who Roberto was or where the parrot had got hold of that name. In any case, that night I had a hard time getting to sleep, because I wasn't used to the noise of traffic either. What do you expect, I was a small-town girl; a city like Bogotá was a terrible change for me. And in your grandmother's house it was as if everything was working against me, as if everything was hostile. All the furniture in my room was covered in sheets and you could still smell the dust. It was as if the whole house was in mourning, and we had just been talking to Josefina, and all that mixed together . . . I don't know, I eventually got to sleep but it was very late. And when I woke up, your father had gone out and come back with the news that Enrique was not at home. "What do you mean he's not there? Is he lost?" "No. I mean he's gone. He left everything and went away. And no one knows where." I asked him who told him and he got impatient. "The policeman on his block, who heard from the girls who work for the Cancinos. What does it matter who told me? His father has just killed himself, his mother left a while ago, it seems logical that Enrique's gone too. He wasn't going to stay in that house by himself." "But without saying goodbye." "Saying goodbye, saying goodbye. This isn't a cocktail party, Sara. Don't be so silly."

'Then his bad mood passed and we were able to have breakfast in peace, without speaking but in peace, and before noon we caught the train at Sabana Station. It was a foul day, it rained the whole way home. It was raining in Bogotá, raining on the way out of the station, raining when we arrived back in Duitama. And all the time I was thinking of reasons someone might have to go away like that, leave everything behind without even saying goodbye to their friends. I didn't say anything because your dad would've been at my throat; he was very upset, you could see that. In the train he pretended to sleep, but I looked at his closed eyes, and his eyelids were moving very quickly, trembling the way a person's eyelids tremble when they're very worried. Seeing him like that made me feel bad. I loved him like a brother then. Gabriel was like a brother to me, and we'd only known each other for about five years, but you see, I stayed at his house, he stayed at the hotel . . . Always keeping up appearances, of course. I was a young lady with a reputation to take care of, et cetera. But rules were bent as far as they possibly could be, it seems to me. And that's because we were like brother and sister. In the train, when I saw he was pretending to sleep, I fell asleep myself. I leant my head on his shoulder, closed my eyes, and the next thing I knew Gabriel was waking me up because we'd arrived in Duitama. He woke me up with a kiss on my hair, "We're here, Sarita," and I felt like crying, I suppose from so much stress, or from the contrast, no? Stress on one side, affection on the other. Or on one side worry for your father, who might have lost a friend for ever, and on the other the way he had of taking care of me as if the one who'd suffered a loss was me. Yes, I almost burst into tears. But I held them back. I've always been good at holding back tears, always, since I was a little girl. Papa made fun of me until he died of old age. He made fun of my pride, which wouldn't even allow me to look sad or angry in public, let alone cry. A woman crying in public has always seemed to me absolutely pathetic. Yes, sir, that's me: champion at suffering in silence.

'When we arrived at the hotel it was still raining, and the sky was so dark that all the lights were on though it was mid-afternoon. It was that typical grey sky of Boyacá, you feel like you could touch it if you stood on tiptoes, and the water kept falling as if something had given way up above. Your dad refused to share my umbrella. He let me walk ahead while he got soaked walking behind. I'm sure it had been raining all day there in Duitama too, because the fountain was full to the brim; at any moment the water was going to spill over the edges. But it was pretty to see the rain hitting the water in the fountain. And even prettier if we were watching it from the dining room, nice and dry and drinking hot chocolate. Papa was there with a guest. He introduced us to him saying he was José María Villarreal and was just leaving. I immediately knew who he was, because Papa had spoken of him several times. "He's a *godo* to watch out for," he told me once, with more respect than usual in him. They'd been seeing a lot of each other, because they shared a sort of passion for Simón Bolívar, and Villarreal didn't seem to mind coming from Tunja once in a while to talk about the subject, believe it or not. We exchanged greetings with the *godo* to watch out for and sat down, Gabriel and I, to warm up our hands with a cup of hot chocolate by the glass door to the dining room. There was a fire in the grate, outside it was still pouring with rain, and in the dining room it felt wonderful. Even my father seemed content seeing his friend to the door and probably talking about the Pantano de Vargas or one of those things. He was like a child with a new toy. Incredible, no? Incredible that we were such a short time away from disaster, Gabriel. I think about it and wonder why the world didn't stop at that moment. Who did we have to bribe to get the world to stay still just there, when we were all fine, when each of us seemed to have survived the things that life had thrown at them? Who should we have asked to pull those strings? Or were those strings worn out too?

'According to what Gabriel told me the next day, in the afternoon, when we were able to be alone for the first time since he woke up from the anaesthesia, it happened more or less like this:

'After the hot chocolate he'd gone up to his room with the idea of resting from the train journey and reading a little. In a week or so he had to take his first preparatory exam: all the subjects from civil law in one exam, a sort of continuous firing squad, like being shot and then shot again another ten times. So he opened his books on the desk and began to study the ways to acquire dominion over property, which were at least well-written articles, full of rhetorical devices, which on a good day made him laugh out loud. Gabriel's classmates thought he was odd. Those poor guys couldn't understand the humour he found in the stipulations on the gradual and imperceptible subsidence of the waters, defined in pure poetry, or the dove that flew from one dovecote to another without any reprehensible guile on the part of the new owner. "But I couldn't concentrate," he told me later. "I tried to read about the dove and I'd see old Konrad lying on the street vomiting, I'd move on to the gem set in the ring and I'd see Josefina in her sandals, with fresh semen trickling down her leg, and I'd start retching too. So I stood up, closed my codes and notes, and went out for a walk." I didn't hear him leave, because I was in my parents' room listening to a strange piece of news. Before the beginning of the war, a Hungarian architect had disappeared along with his wife, and someone had just found them in the mountains. There were some tourists walking up in the mountains and a guy came out from somewhere and asked them how the war was going. It seemed he'd fixed up a cave and had spent all that time hidden there. He fished for food and got water from the river. When they told him the war had ended a year and a half ago, he went down to Budapest, went to see his family and returned to his house, but as soon as he arrived he realized he wasn't going to be able to do it. His wife agreed. So they packed up some clothes and utensils and went back to their cave. Papa liked the story. "I'll bet you anything you like they're Jews," he said. And while we listened to the rest of the programme, Gabriel went downstairs and out for a walk. But before leaving he went to the kitchen and asked for a big *pandeyuca* to take with him. He told María Rosa, the cook, that he'd be back in an hour.

'It was dark by then. Gabriel walked under the balconies and the eaves, dashing from beneath one balcony to the next, from the eaves of one house to the next, trying to stay as dry as possible. But it wasn't raining so hard any more, and it was pleasant to breathe in the fresh, clean air, it was pleasant to walk through empty streets. "I turned up my collar," he said. "I thought about eating my *pandeyuca* in two bites, so I could put my hands in my pockets, but then I thought it could keep my hands warm since it was fresh from the oven. I was determined to have a good long walk, even if I gave myself pneumonia. It was just so quiet, Sara, I wasn't going to miss it." It was simply a matter of walking cautiously, taking care not to slip on the paving stones, which were terrible when it rained, and he was focussing all his attention on that. And so, looking down at the ground and walking steadily forward like a horse with blinkers on, with a warm *pandeyuca* in the pocket of his jacket, he ended up at the plaza, among other reasons because all the streets in a small town like ours lead to the plaza, to such an extent one wonders why they bother giving it a name. Plaza de los Libertadores, the Duitama one's called, but no one in the history of the town has ever had to say the full name. The plaza is the plaza. That day it was all decorated for the recent holidays, images of the baby Jesus hanging on doors and balconies and leaning in the windows of the cafés. And Gabriel walked around the plaza looking in the shop windows, the café windows, and inside the cafés a few people were sheltering, most of them farm labourers freezing to death and smelling of wet ponchos. From one of those cafés, where there weren't any peasants but people in ties who worked in the town hall, someone called him, firmly but without raising his voice. It was Villarreal, Papa's friend.

'He asked him what he was doing out there in the rain, if he needed anything. He had his car around the corner, he said, he could give him a lift somewhere. "He spoke to me so courteously that I immediately forgot the most incredible thing: that he'd called me by name, by my full name, having only heard it once, and only in passing." But Villarreal was like that with everybody. When Gabriel explained that he was just out for a walk, that he liked strolling at night because there were never any people in the streets in Duitama, Villarreal seemed to understand completely, and he even began to recommend routes to him, not just in Duitama, but also in Tunja and in Soatá and in the centre of Bogotá. He was an extremely cultured man, who knew, or seemed to know, the history of every corner. They talked about the church that was still under construction, right there, on the other side of the plaza. "A few days ago, on a Sunday, I went into the building site to see it from inside," said Villarreal. "If it works out as planned, it's going to be *bellísima*." Gabriel liked the way he pronounced his double *l*s, that liquid sound that has been lost; no one pronounces their double *l*s like that any more. And maybe it was because of those double *l*s, or maybe it was Villarreal's manners, but afterwards, after they'd said goodbye, Gabriel carried on walking around the edge of the plaza under the eaves and the balconies and the colonial street lamps, which were lit though they didn't cast any light, and he crossed the road and looked around to make sure no one could see him. It was absurd, because going into a building site shouldn't be illegal. "But when I thought that, it was already too late, I was already inside. And I don't regret it, Sara, I'm not sorry. The nave of a cathedral under construction is a staggering thing to see."

'He was sheltered by immense walls, but it was colder than outside. It was the dampness of the cement, of course, it was cold cement in his nostrils when he took a deep breath. Near the altar, or near the place where the altar would be, there were two piles of sand as high as a man and a smaller one of bricks, and beside them was the mixer. By the door side were stones, beams, more stones and more beams. The rest was scaffolding, scaffolding everywhere, a seamless monster that went right round the nave and rose up to the windows without their stained glass. There inside, it was as if he'd become colour-blind. All was grey and black. And then there was the silence, such perfect silence that Gabriel held back an urge to shout to see if a nave under construction had an echo. "I felt good," he told me later. "I felt calm for the first time for days. Almost blind and almost deaf, that's how I felt, and it was a kind of serenity, as if someone had forgiven me." He wanted to sit down, but the ground was wet, there were buckets and trowels all over the place, there was unmixed cement and sand, and from one corner came the smell of urine. So he stood. At that moment he remembered the *pandeyuca*, took it out, pulled off a couple of threads that had stuck to it from his pocket, and began to chew.

'It was cold by then, of course, but it tasted good. Gabriel ate slowly, taking small unhurried bites, trying with all his might not to think about old Konrad's death but about anything else at all, about the taste of cassava and cheese, for example, about the smell of the cathedral cement, about the arrangement of the pews when they put them in, about the pulpit and the priest, about how long it would take to build, and he thought about all that and then he thought about the hotel, he thought about me, thought he loved me, thought about my father, thought about Villarreal, thought about Bolívar, thought about the battle of the Pantano de Vargas, thought about the name of the plaza, Liberators, and that's where he'd got to when the men appeared. The place was so dark that Gabriel didn't manage to see their faces beneath their hats, and didn't know which one asked him if he was Santoro, the one from Bogotá. Maybe the one who asked was the same one who took out his machete first; it seems quite logical. Question, answer, machete. They'd come in through the cathedral door, or rather through the space for the door, so Gabriel had to start running towards the altar, confident he'd be able to escape out of the back of the building site. He slipped on the gravel but didn't fall, he kept running over the loose boards of the scaffolding, but he had to get through between a column and a pile of sand, and when he stepped on the sand his foot sank in and his shoe slipped and Gabriel fell to the ground. He lifted up his right hand to protect himself from the machete blow, but closed his eyes when he saw the blade coming down, and then he didn't open them again.

'When dinner was served in the hotel dining room, María Rosa went to look for Mama and asked her what we should do with Don Gabriel's place. Should we wait for him, wasn't he going to be coming? Mama came up to my room and asked me the very same question. I didn't even know Gabriel had gone out, I thought he was still in his room. "He went out two hours ago. He told María Rosa that he wouldn't be long. Why don't you put on a coat and ask her to go with you?" She had already put on a poncho when I came down, and told me my father had already left. "I wonder if he got hit by a car, Señorita Sara," she said. That was just what I was afraid of and I was not at all pleased to hear that the same idea had occurred to her. María Rosa started walking towards the plaza and I went the other way, like when you go to the lake by car. I walked around, asked the few people I saw, but I didn't even know what to look for, where to look, I'd never been in such a situation before. Besides, I was scared. All of

Duitama knew who I was, and if so inclined I could go out alone at four in the morning, but that night I was scared. So after a little while I was back at the hotel. Mama was sitting on one of the benches on the patio, in spite of the cold, and told me as soon as I came in that María Rosa had found him near the church. "He was attacked," she said. "He's hurt. Your father took him to Tunja; he's there with him now, so don't worry."

'But she didn't tell me they cut four of his fingers off with a machete. She didn't tell me he'd almost bled to death. Gabriel told me all that the next day, when Papa brought him back to the hotel. He also explained the symptoms of septicaemia to me. "We have to be vigilant," he said. All that when he was getting better, after the hours he'd spent unconscious. The Duitama doctor came, examined his injury, insisted how lucky we'd been, and I liked that he addressed us in the plural, that he saw us all together. That's how I felt, at least at that moment: I had been maimed as well. Gabriel's hand was bandaged, but just from the shape of the dressing, or rather from the shape of what was under the dressing, I could see how serious the matter was. "But who did this to you?" I asked him. It was just a manner of speaking, one of those questions you ask just because you do, you know, not expecting a reply. But I was immediately sorry, I felt panic-stricken, because I realized that Gabriel knew who had done that to him and furthermore he knew why. "No, don't tell me," I said, but he'd already started talking. "Enrique sent them," he said. "My friend sent them. But don't worry, I deserved it. This and much more. I killed the old man, Sara. I fucked up their lives. It's all my fault." '

IV

The Inherited Life

THE LIFE I RECEIVED as my inheritance – this life in which I'm no longer the son of an admirable orator and decorated professor, or even of a man who suffers in silence and then reveals his suffering in public, but of the most despicable of all creatures: someone capable of betraying a friend and selling out his family – began one Monday, a couple of weeks after New Year, when, at about ten at night, I microwaved myself a meal, sat down cross-legged on my unmade bed, and, just before starting a quick glance through the newspaper of the day that was ending, got a phone call from Sara Guterman. Without even saying hello, Sara said, 'They're showing it.' That meant, *It's happening.* What we had expected was happening. These things don't usually need to be coaxed: turn on the television and feel how your life changes, and if you have a little camera, take it out and film yourself, record for posterity the transformation of your face.

I had spent the day, and the whole week, busy with the second transformation of my father's memory. The first time, a mendacious, manipulated confession had begun to move the past around; now, the potential of real events (those false dead, those cataleptic bodies) was modifying the precarious truth and also the version my father had formulated (no, imposed) through a few words improvised in a classroom. But had he really improvised them? Now I had begun to think he had probably planned them with the subtlety with which he planned his speeches, because that's what it had been, an elaborate speech, which my father had used to change his memory of events, and thus change or pretend that his own past was changed, a past in which, he had believed, Gabriel Santoro would no longer be guilty of a friend's disgrace, and he would from then on be converted into a victim, one victim among many in that time when speaking mattered and a couple of words could ruin someone. I was occasionally moved by the confidence my father had in his own phrases, the blind faith that it was enough to tell a tampered-with story – change the positions of the characters, like a magician does, transform the betrayer into the betrayed – so the exchange imposes itself over the past, more or less like that Borges character, that coward who by force of believing in his own courage manages to believe that his courage existed. 'The *Summa Theologica* denies that God can unmake the past,' says the narrator of this story; but he also says that to modify the past is not to modify a single fact, but to annul the consequences of the fact, that is, to create two universal histories. I can never re-read the story without thinking of my father and of what I felt that Monday night: maybe my task, in the future, would be to reconstruct the two histories, uselessly to confront them. It occurred to me at some point that, much to my regret, I would end up devoting myself to revising memories, trying to find the inconsistencies, the contradictions, the barefaced lies with which my father protected one tiny act – or rather, pretended it did not exist – one action among thousands in a life more filled with ideas than actions.

On the sofa in my living room, lined up like infantry, were the tapes of my interviews with Sara. After our conversation on New Year's Eve – which lasted until six-thirty in the morning, since after the revelations already recorded came my questions, my protests and then more questions – I listened to them again, pursuing in Sara's voice as well the covering up, or the complicity, or the references to other denunciations, other absurd inclusions on the blacklist, other family catastrophes that would have been caused in some remote way by that amateur inquisition. And the day of the programme, before Sara's call, I'd been listening to one of the last. In the recording, I asked her if she would have ever returned to live in Germany if the opportunity had arisen, and she answered, 'Never.' And when I asked her how she could be so sure, she said, 'Because I did go back once, so I know what it feels like.' In 1968, she told me, she'd received an invitation from the municipality of Emmerich, her home-town, and she had travelled there with her father and her eldest son – by plane to Frankfurt and train to Emmerich – to attend one of those ceremonies of public atonement certain sectors of German politics used at the time to try in vain to do what we all try to do all the time: correct mistakes, alleviate the damage done. 'It was strange to be there,' the recorded voice was saying, 'but we'd arrived by night, and I thought the next morning everything would seem even stranger to me when I saw in the light of day things I hadn't seen for thirty years. Although we didn't know if they'd still be there, because during the war Emmerich was one of the most bombed cities.' Herr Strecker, the man who had helped them escape in '38, was there to welcome them. He had also left Germany, but a year later, said Sara, then lived in Montevideo for a few years. 'He and Papa embraced and almost wouldn't let go of each other,' said Sara, 'but on the plane my father had told us we were forbidden from crying in Germany, so I made an effort, it wasn't so difficult. Ceremonies are more or less what we know they're like.

We visitors were assigned a local youngster, one for each exiled couple; since I'd gone without my husband, Papa and I were a twosome. The strangest thing was how their mouths filled up with the word "exile" and all its synonyms, in which the German language is generous; we have no lack of words to call those who leave. We were supposed to talk in a school or a university about our experience, and my father said, "I don't know if there are enough schools in Emmerich for all its exiles to speak." And just think, the same thing was happening in other cities, all over the country. I don't know, sometimes I think I don't really know what all that was in aid of. What was the aim of calling all those from abroad and reminding them of where they were from? As if they were claiming them, no? Like an absurd demand, to put it like that.

'A friend of Papa's had died three years earlier, and no one had informed us, and when we arrived they gave us the news. The widow asked us if it was worth it to go and live in Colombia. She kept repeating that she had every intention of going somewhere else, and she smiled at me and consulted Papa about the options. She asked us what Colombia was like. Sometimes she thought about Canada. What did we think of Canada? I felt sorry for her, because it was obvious she didn't want to leave. I still don't know why she tried to convince people she did. For my part, I met a schoolfriend. It was the strangest thing in the world. I asked her what had happened to so-and-so and somebody-or-other, and most of all I asked about Barbara Wolff, who had been my best friend at Daughters of the Sacred Cross, yes, what a name, and what a school, as well: it was run by a community of aristocratic nuns; up to that moment I'd never imagined such a thing could exist. A blue-blooded nun, imagine that. Well anyway, this friend looked at me with such surprise, until she couldn't stand to hear any more praise from me for my friendship with Barbara Wolff. "But she made you suffer so," she said. It seems that everyone remembered how Barbara tormented me, took advantage of me, talked about me behind my back and made up stories, all those things little girls do. And I had no choice but to believe her, but it startled me, because I remembered absolutely nothing of what she told me. I had such a lovely memory of Barbara, and at that moment I didn't know what to think. I was a bit sad about that. You wouldn't expect to make such a trip to receive bad news; imagine if someone showed up now and told you your dad abused you and you don't remember. Tell me your world wouldn't start to change. Mine wasn't so serious, but almost, because in any case it was as if the world from before emigration was no longer trustworthy. I watched Papa closely, saw how necessary the journey had been for him. One of the reasons, the most obvious, was to confirm that he had made the right decision. Imagine if thirty years later you realized it would have been much better to stay. No, we needed confirmation of how bad things had been before we left, confirmation of how much the Jews who stayed had suffered. I couldn't do so with Barbara, because she was living in England at the time; it seems she was or is a biologist. What would I have said if I could have called her? Let's see, Barbara, do you remember treating me badly when we were little? No, ridiculous. But still, if I did feel like crying, I'd get in the car and drive to Holland, cross the border, because I had Papa's rule very clear in my head: no crying in Germany. And I went along with the rule at all times, even when he didn't demand it. I didn't even cry when we visited the grave of my older sister Miriam, who died of meningitis when she was seven. I barely remembered her. However it was, at those moments I began to think I understood why God had sent us to Duitama. I thought he had made us work so hard so we wouldn't dwell on bad memories. Not now, now I think that was hugely stupid, not only because Papa is dead now too, and his presence was what allowed me that religiosity when I was young, but rather because of something more difficult to explain. One gets old and symbols lose their value, things become only what they are. One tires of representations: that this represents such-and-such and that represents something else. The ability to interpret symbols has gone for me, and God goes with that. It's as if it were extinguished. One gets tired of looking behind things. Behind a priest's glasses. Behind a communion wafer. Maybe for you young people it's hard to understand, but that's what God is for old people: a fellow we've been playing hide-and-seek with for too long. You'll have to decide if you want to leave all this nonsense in the book. Maybe you shouldn't: who's going to be interested in this blather? Yes, it would be better if I stuck to my own story. If not, you'll get tired of my silliness and turn off the tape recorder. I don't want that to happen, I like talking about all this.

'The mayor gave the welcoming address. A real experience, because through that speech I discovered how much it cost to get out of Germany when we did. I discovered how rich my parents had been, because only the wealthy could afford to pay the *Reichsfluchtsteuer*. That's what they actually called it, desertion of the Reich tax. I discovered the fortune they'd left behind to go to Colombia. We went to the synagogue, a solid block of concrete with round copper domes like a Russian church. There, at some point, I accepted that Germany was no longer my country, not in the sense, at least, that a country belongs to normal people. Papa took that trip very hard. It did nothing but remind him of the laws of 1941. I told him that almost thirty years had gone by and a person has to forget about those things, but he couldn't.'

'The laws of 1941?' This is my recorded voice. I don't recognize myself in it.

'We were in Colombia, an ocean away from Germany, and one fine day we woke up and weren't Germans any more. You don't know what that means until your passport expires. Because then, what are you? You're not from here, but you're not from there either. If something bad happens to you, if someone does something to you, no one's going to help you. There is no state to defend you. Wait, I'm going to show you something.' There is a pause in the recording, while Sara looks among her papers for a letter my father wrote to her from Bogotá dated with the inscription: *1 Av 5728.* 'The Jewish date was another gesture typical of that pedant of a father of yours,' Sara said. 'There was no way to explain to him that religion had also gradually disappeared from my life, and never came to exist in those of my children. I don't even remember what month that was, or what year.'

'Can I keep it?' says my voice.

'That depends.'

'Depends on what?'

'Are you going to put it in the book?'

'I don't know, Sara. Maybe, maybe not.'

'You can keep it,' she said, 'if you don't put it in.'

'Why?'

'Because I know Gabriel. He would not be amused to see himself in a book without anyone asking his permission.'

'But if I need . . .'

'No, no, none of that. You can take it if you promise. If not, the letter stays with me.'

I decided to keep it. I have it here.

If I were you I wouldn't worry too much [my father wrote to Sara]. A person is from wherever they feel best, and roots are for plants. Everyone knows that, don't they? *Ubi bene ibi patria*, all those ready-made sayings. (Still, ready-made by the Romans, so they can at least qualify as antiques.) Speaking for myself, I've never even left this country, and sometimes I think I never will. And I wouldn't mind, you know. Lots of things are happening here; more than that, here is *where things happen*; and although I'm sometimes disappointed by the provincialism of the South American Athens-in-its-dreams, I tend to think that here human experience has a special weight. It's like a chemical density. Things people say seem to matter here as much as what they do, I suppose partly due to a reason that is quite stupid when looked at closely: everything is yet to be constructed. Here words matter. Here you can still shape your surroundings. It's a terrible power, isn't it?

I've read it several times, I'm reading it now, while I write, and I read it that night, just before Sara called me to warn me that my father's fall from grace was just starting. My father, the man who had never left this country and who never would, the man who seemed to give as much importance to words as to deeds. What would he have thought if he had seen what I was seeing on television? Would he have regretted what he wrote on 1 Av 5728? Would he have forgotten it on purpose? For me, innocent reader of that letter, it was obvious that my father, when he wrote it, must have thought of Deresser, and that would undoubtedly be

182

one of the many inventories that I should draw up starting with the contributions of Sara's testimony: every phrase spoken by my father, every offhand and seemingly trivial comment, every reaction to someone else's comment, would soon be on a list, the list of moments when my father was thinking of Deresser and, especially, of what he'd done to him. *It's a terrible power, isn't it?* Yes, Dad, it's terrible, you would know, you were remembering what you'd done, what your words had caused. (But what words, and how spoken? To whom in exchange for what? In what circumstances? How had my father played his part as informer? And I'll never know, because there were no witnesses.) And now, publicly, you are paying for your words.

So it was on television. It wasn't by means of a written interview, as Sara had believed at first and had made me believe, that Angelina was going to begin the task of bringing down, with the collaboration of the people of Bogotá's hunger for sensationalism, my father's reputation; it was not a magazine that required her services, but one of those programmes of rigorously local interest, of intense, late-night journalism centred on Bogotá, that are now so common but in the year 1992 were still a novelty for the citizens of the illustrious capital. Some of my colleagues, I should admit, succumbed to these first programmes, real journalists who managed to acquit themselves decently with a keyboard, good investigative reporters and acceptable writers, and who instead ended up perpetrating little theatrical pieces for two actors (a presenter and a guest), plays filmed with two cameras, to keep costs down, and in front of a black background, to accentuate the dramatics. They were a mixture of forensic interrogation and show-business interview; the guests could be – in fact, had been – a congressman accused of embezzlement, a beauty queen accused of being a single mother, a racing driver accused of using drugs, a city councillor accused of links to drug traffickers: all from Bogotá, originally or by adoption, all susceptible to being recognized as symbols of the city. That was the programme: a space to debate unproved accusations, to debunk more or less sacred figures, which, as everyone knows, is one of the Bogotá viewing audience's favourite pastimes. If my father were alive, I thought, he would occupy the place of the guest: a moralist accused of betrayal. In his place was Angelina Franco, ex-lover and witness for the prosecution, the woman who had attended the fall. The dramatic plot – from glory to disgrace, all that and romance too – was quite clear; the journalistic potential would have been obvious even to a novice, and you could almost feel the waves of the electromagnetic spectrum vibrating with Bogotá's thrill at the prospect of the haughty being dishonoured, the arrogant brought down a peg or two.

Angelina was sitting in a swivel chair, facing the presenter and separated from him by a modern office table, an inelegant slab that might have been Triplex or simply covered plastic; the presenter was Rafael Jaramillo Arteaga, a journalist known for his aggression (he would say his frankness) and for his lack of scruples when it came to making damaging revelations (he would say exposing hidden truths). The set was designed to intimidate: the illusion of mysterious, hidden, illegitimate things. There was Angelina, confident and complicit, dressed in one of her bright, straining blouses – this time it was fuchsia – and a skirt that seemed to be troubling her, because all the time she had to keep adjusting it, lifting up her hips and tugging at the hem. The camera was focused on the interviewer. 'Not everyone remembers one of the most unclassifiable, most paradoxical episodes of our recent history,' he said. 'I'm referring to the Proclaimed List of Certain Blocked Nationals, regrettably famous among historians, regrettably forgotten by the wider public. During the Second World War, the US State Department issued blacklists with the aim of blocking Axis funds in Latin America. But everywhere, not just in Colombia, the system lent itself to abuses, and in more than one case the just paid for sinners. Today we present the story of one of those abuses. This, esteemed viewers, is the story of a betrayal.' Cut to commercials. When they return, a photo of my father appears, the same one that had appeared in *El Tiempo* with his obituary. A voice off-camera says, 'Gabriel Santoro was a lawyer and prestigious professor here in our capital. For more than two decades he devoted his time to teaching techniques of public speaking to other lawyers as part of a programme at the Supreme Court of Justice. Last year he died in a tragic traffic accident on the Bogotá–Medellín highway. He had travelled to the city of eternal spring to spend the holidays in the company of his lady friend, Angelina Franco, native of that city.' Then Angelina's face appeared on the screen with her name in white letters. 'But as soon as they arrived, Angelina Franco realized that her companion had not told her the whole truth. She has now found out the truth, and is here to tell it.' And that she did: she told. She told without stopping, she told as if her life depended on it, she told as if there was someone under the table pointing a gun at her. Among the things that came out of the speakers – that dialogue between the sniper and his own rifle – there was a lot of rubbish, I supposed, a lot of barefaced invention, but there was nothing that would not help me devise a portrait of my father's lover, because even lies, even a person's rudest inventions with respect to herself, tell us valuable things about her, and perhaps more valuable than the most honest truths. Transparency is the worst deception in the world, my father used to say: one is the lies one pronounces. Any journalist learns that after conducting two interviews, any lawyer after two cross-examinations, and especially, any orator after two speeches. I thought all these things; nevertheless, during the elongated hour the programme lasted, the sixty minutes, including the advertisements, of the beating and careful defenestration of the memory of my father, my perplexity did not cease for one second. Why was she doing it? While Angelina told what she was telling, while she looked occasionally towards the back of the set, fascinated by the blue neon lights that formed the programme's name, I could only concentrate on that question: *Why was she doing this to my father?*

I would have liked to have known then what I later found out. Nothing new, nothing original: it happens to us all, and it happens all the time. To understand that little piece of theatre, the fall from grace of a semi-public figure, the disenchanted physiotherapist's impromptu, I would first have to understand other things, and those things, as often happens, would only arrive later, when they were less useful or less compelling, because life is not as orderly as it seems in a book. Now that I know what I know, my question seems almost naive. The reasons Angelina had for doing what she was doing were no different, no more elegant or subtle or bookish or sophisticated than anyone else's, by which I mean to say that her motivations responded to the same concerns we all have, no matter how elegant and subtle and sophisticated we consider ourselves. My formulation had been, *Why was she doing this to my father?*, but I could have asked, simply, *Why was she doing this?* She was doing it because a man (an anonymous man, whichever: if it hadn't been my father, it would have been whoever took his place) came to embody for her everything in her life that was dreadful and odious, and she wanted revenge. She was doing it out of revenge, a posthumous revenge, the benefit of which only Angelina could perceive. She was doing it because my father condensed, involuntarily, every little tragedy Angelina had suffered in her life. How do I know? I know because she told me herself. She gave me the information, and I, out of some sort of already inevitable addiction, agreed to receive it.

But first I had to put up with more blows: these came from the screen, from the interviewer and the interviewee. I have reconstructed them as follows.

Was she aware of Gabriel Santoro's reputation?

No. Well, when Angelina met him, Gabriel was tucked up in bed like a baby, and that doesn't enhance anybody's appearance, even the President would look diminished and common reduced to pyjamas and bedclothes. Angelina knew, however (or rather in time she gradually came to know), that her patient was a very cultured person, but cultured in a good way, able to explain anything with great patience. With her, in any case, he had a lot of patience: he would explain things to her two or three times if necessary, and in this Angelina saw the mark of a good teacher. Of course, he had already retired when they met, but one never stops being a teacher, or at least that's what he said. But prestige, local fame, she'd only found out about all that after he died. Gabriel didn't talk about those things; when they spent a whole evening together in his apartment, for example, Angelina would snatch up those prizes they'd given him one by one and ask him for explanations. And what's this one for? And this one? That's how she found out about the Capitolio speech, that's how she heard about all those strange things Gabriel said about Bogotá. That's how she found out who Plato was and that Bogotá was four hundred and fifty years old. That's how she found out many people had thought that speech was very good and that Gabriel could have been a very important judge if he'd accepted the offers. Anyway, that didn't mean he was an important person.

But she did know that Santoro was going to be decorated?

Yes, but that didn't mean much to her. She didn't know what sorts of people got decorated, or why. For her, the medal was something that happened at his funeral, one more ritual, something false that everybody agreed to take as true. Just like the things the priest said.

How did they get romantically involved?

The same way anybody did. They were both very lonely people, and lonely people are interested in other lonely people and try to see if, with other lonely people, they can be less lonely. It's very simple. Gabriel was a very simple person, when all was said and done. He was interested in the same things everybody was interested in: being recognized for what he'd done well, being forgiven for what he'd done wrong, and being loved. Yes, that most of all, being loved.

How did she find out about what he'd done in his youth?

He told her all about it himself. But that was in Medellín already, when everything seemed to be going well, when it didn't seem likely that telling her old stories could affect the relationship they had. And it did affect her, of course, although right now Angelina couldn't explain things step by step, who can do that, see the chain of decisions that end up tipping a relationship into the shit? It had been like this:

Angelina had invited him to her city, she wanted to show it to him, take him around, partly out of the impulse lovers get to entrust their old life to the other, and partly because Gabriel very rarely got out of Bogotá, and in the last twenty years hadn't been further than four hours away by car. In a cultured person, that seemed almost an aberration to Angelina. And one day, after they'd been going out together for several weeks – they said *going out* although the scene of their encounters was never outside, but divided between his apartment and hers, two shoeboxes – Angelina came up with the idea and presented him with a gift-wrapped Manila envelope adorned with a red, fake-taffeta bow. In the envelope was a suggested itinerary: the thick stroke of a black felt-tip pen that roughly imitated the road, marked with perfect round points set out as a Tour of Colombia. Stage 1: Siberia Roundabout. Fill up the car and have a kiss. Stage 21: Medellín. I show you my parent's house and we have a kiss. Gabriel accepted immediately, asked his son if they could borrow his car, and one Friday in December, very early, they set off. At a prudent speed and making all the stops that Gabriel's health required, it took them less than ten hours to get there.

What happened in Medellín?

At first everything was going fine, with no problems. Gabriel insisted they stay in a hotel, as long as it wasn't too expensive – after all, what good was his pension if he couldn't treat them to a bit of luxury every once in a while – and the first night they crossed the street and ate dinner in a tourist restaurant decked out like a mule drivers' canteen: consciously down-to-earth and chaotic. The next day they crossed the city to look for the house Angelina had left at the age of eighteen, and found, on the first floor, where the living room used to be, a shop selling woollen stockings, and on the second, where the room she'd shared with her brother had been, a second-hand clothing storeroom. There were three little alleyways formed by long aluminium tubes that also served as racks, and, hanging from the tubes, were sweaters, coats, jackets, sequinned dresses, overalls, frock coats for hire, and even fancy-dress cloaks, smelling of dust and mothballs in spite of their plastic covers. And so, talking about empty clothes, blouses stiff with so much starch, coats hanging like carcasses in a butcher's shop, they returned to the hotel, tried to make love but Gabriel couldn't, and Angelina thought of the normal reasons, the combination of age and fatigue, but it never occurred to her that Gabriel might be nervous for reasons that had nothing to do with his physical state or hers, or that by that point his anxiety (anxiety about what he had planned) was so intense as to spoil a few minutes of good sex. That was when he talked to her of Enrique Deresser. He didn't call him that, because she, of course, couldn't care less about the name of this long-ago friend of the sixty-something man lying in bed with her, naked and now revealing secrets she hadn't asked to know. Gabriel told her the whole thing, told her what had happened forty years before, of his obsession to be forgiven; and so, with a politician's ease, talking the way most people breathe (but he was breathing with difficulty and pain), like someone shooing a fly away with a hand (even if it was an incomplete hand), he told her that his friend Enrique lived in Medellín, had been there for more than twenty years, and he, out of cowardice, had never decided to do what he was doing now: contemplating the possibility of leaping across forty years to talk to a man whose life he'd ruined.

What did she feel at that moment?

On the one hand, curiosity, a frivolous curiosity, quite similar to what anyone would have felt in her place. What was in his friend's head? Why hadn't he got in touch with Gabriel in all these years? Was there that much hatred, that much resentment? The reasons the reverse hadn't occurred were more obvious: according to what Gabriel had told her, at the beginning of the 1970s, when he found out his friend was in Medellín, he felt an urge to look him up, but he was scared. His wife was still alive then, and his only son was about ten; whether it was reasonable or not, Gabriel felt that approaching Enrique was the most dangerous thing he could do, something like staking the lives of his whole family on a game of blackjack. Of course he wasn't betting on anyone's life, but rather something as personal as his own image. But she couldn't judge him for that. A person gets used to the way other people look at him – and everything contained in that look: admiration or respect, commiseration or pity – and doing something to change that look was impossible for ninety per cent of humanity. And Gabriel was human, after all. Well anyway, at that moment and after those explanations the naked man said to her, 'I've never dared to do it, and now I'm finally going to do it. And it's thanks to you. I owe it to you. You're the one who gives me this strength, I'm sure of that. I wouldn't do it if I weren't with you. This is what I've been waiting for all this time, Angelina. I've been waiting for your support and your company, everything no one else could give me.' Yes, Gabriel said all that, he foisted those responsibilities on her.

Apart from curiosity, what else did she feel?

She felt proud but also a little betrayed. Proud to be the reason for this momentary courage: yes, she had believed him, had believed that without her Gabriel Santoro would never have come to Medellín. And betrayed for stranger reasons, less explainable, that had a lot to do with jealousy. Suddenly Enrique Deresser turned into something like a lover from the past, a girlfriend Gabriel Santoro had had in his youth. Angelina listened to Gabriel and what she heard was nostalgia for an old love affair; the desire to re-live those memories. Of course that's not how it was, but there, in Medellín, Angelina found herself suddenly having to compete with someone else for Gabriel's attention. Betrayal is an exaggeration, of course. She could have said jealousy, jealousy for a past that up till then had been comfortably non-existent. The most serious betrayals happen like that, with the tiniest things that for someone else would mean nothing. The most painful betrayals happen when they find your weak spot, something that doesn't matter much to other people but does to you. Well, that's what Gabriel did: found her weak spot. So – thought Angelina – this is why he'd come here with her. Until that moment, Gabriel had been for her a sort of act of faith in her own life, the proof that at almost fifty years of age a woman could still find happiness in company, and the proof, as well, that luck existed, because their meeting (the meeting of lovers) had been a matter of luck: a convalescing man and a physiotherapist are quite likely to end up together, of course, but it's less probable that a physiotherapist would be in such need of affection as she was and that the convalescent would be so disposed to give it as he was. Gabriel, she had thought more than once, was her life raft. And there, in the hotel in Medellín, Angelina suddenly thought her life raft had been using her. And she felt a sort of secret panic that she was very careful not to reveal.

What did this secret panic consist of?

It was the difference between what she thought and what she said. Inside she thought, very much in spite of what everything seemed to prove, that it was a lie that Gabriel loved her, the affection he'd shown her was false. Inside she thought Gabriel had used her to alleviate his weakness and also his cowardice. Inside she thought for the whole week he'd been making her believe that he was enthusiastic about the idea of going to Medellín, when his intentions were quite different. False. All false. Inside she thought what Gabriel Santoro really wanted from her was not a lover, but a heart doctor, a sort of nurse mixed with a psychologist, someone who would help him to make long overdue apologies, for he had always been too cowardly to make them himself. That is, someone to wait in the hotel while he went and did his long-postponed errand, found his friend and got forgiven and had a drink to toast old times and the disappearance of all the grudges. Inside she thought she was a mere extra in this film, a substitute in the game, a consolation prize. And if that wasn't bad enough, Angelina was watching Gabriel transform before her very eyes; the wise and mature, cultured and elegant man she'd known had turned into a traitor – betrayed a friend, betrayed a lover – yes, a manipulative, disloyal liar. But she endured it, she pretended, understood that perhaps she was blinded by emotion, like in the soaps. The disillusion and humiliation were very intense, and the mockery (yes, because that's what it all boiled down to, what was happening in that Medellín hotel room: it was life mocking her, life choosing Gabriel Santoro to show her there was no possible way out, that happiness did not exist and much less with a man, and looking for it was naive, and believing you'd found it frankly stupid). And nevertheless, Angelina endured it, as she had endured all her life, because she loved Gabriel and she wanted Gabriel to go on loving her. And she knew that jealousy blinds a person and that you could also be jealous of the past, even though Gabriel was going to leave her for a few hours to go and see a friend, not a lover, from his youth. Yes, that's how she split in half: inside she thought life had sent her Gabriel Santoro to demonstrate this to her, that Gabriel Santoro was the messenger of her humiliation. And outside she'd decided to withstand it, put on a nothing-to-do-with-me face and do the only thing she could do: congratulate Gabriel, praise his valour and his will to seek forgiveness. What a hypocrite.

The praise was not genuine?

No, no, no, no, no. What Gabriel had done to his friend was unforgivable; that seemed perfectly clear to her and everyone will agree. Yes, a long time had passed since the events of the war, since the business of the blacklists and the groups of informers or spontaneous informers; but time does not heal all, that is an absolute lie. There are things that stay with us: a brother's desertion, a lover's disdain, the death of parents, the betrayal of a friend or of his family. No one can ever get free of something like that, and it's good that things should be that way. Traitors deserve punishment, and if they somehow manage to betray with impunity, they at least deserve to be punished by their own guilt until they die. If it were up to Angelina, if she had had the tiniest bit of power over other people's actions (which she had never had), and especially if she hadn't been so in love, Gabriel would never have left the hotel, would never have gone to see his friend.

So he did finally go to see him?

Of course he went to see him. Or at least he left the hotel saying he was going to go and see him. Like a cowboy, no? As if he was saying, I'll just go out and kill him and come right back. That was the Sunday, Angelina remembered, because she'd stayed in the hotel watching cartoons all morning.

And what happened between the two men?

That Angelina didn't know, obviously, because she hadn't gone with him, as she said. It happened like this: after the confession, Angelina got up and went to the bathroom and looked in the mirror, because she'd seen that people look in the mirror when they want to solve their most serious problems, and in front of the mirror she said to herself, You have to look on the bright side. Depending on how you look at it, what he's doing is very nice. He's asked you for help. You're important to him. And then she managed to repress what she was feeling (what she'd been thinking deep down), and when she went back out, calmer then, the first thing she did was to embrace Gabriel and tell him, 'Congratulations, I think what you're doing is very brave. You'll see, your friend will take it well. No grudge lasts a hundred years.' And as soon as she said those words, she noticed how the atmosphere in the room changed. Affection once again, the tensions disappeared, yes, all that was needed was a little goodwill, control of negative emotions. And this time they could. They went back to bed: and they could. It wasn't the best sex they'd ever had, but it was good, there was the tenderness that comes when an explosive situation between a couple is diffused. Gabriel told her he loved her. She heard the words without responding, but feeling that she loved him too. And she fell asleep. She never saw him again.

He left without saying goodbye?

And why would he say goodbye, if his intention was to talk to his friend and come straight back?

*She had never suspected that Gabriel wasn't going to come back?
That possibility never crossed her mind?*

Yes, but only when it was already too late. The next day
Gabriel got up very early, and he must have left without
having a shower, because Angelina didn't hear him. She
didn't hear him get up, didn't hear him get dressed, didn't
hear him leave the room. When she woke up she found the
note. Gabriel had written it on the hotel stationery but not
on the writing paper, on an envelope, probably thinking of
propping it up against the lamp on the bedside table and
getting it to stay upright. *I might be a while. In any case, by this
afternoon I'll be free again. Thanks for everything. I love you.* She
re-read the *I love you* and felt happy, but there was something
that made her uncomfortable. *I'll be free again.* Free of her?
Would Angelina turn into a nuisance when her mission as
companion was completed? She thought what she had never
thought: *He's not going to come back.* No, that was impossible,
Gabriel wouldn't abandon her like that, not even if he'd used
her for a purpose, and that purpose had been accomplished.
No, it couldn't be. She endured it as best she could: turning
on the television and looking through the channels (a few US
channels, one Spanish, even a Mexican one) for a programme
that might distract her, and she found that cartoons, all those
hammer blows and point-blank gunshots, those explosions
and free falls, that is, those caricatured cruelties, precisely and
carefully performed the labour of obliterating the small
cruelties, the small uncertainties of real life. At midday she
went down to the pool and ordered a lunch fit for three
physiotherapists, all of them hungry, and asked them to
charge it to the room. And it was there, in front of the
wet children of a tourist from the coast, two ill-mannered
little boys who splashed her as they ran past with their

misted-up masks over their noses and their red water wings squeezing their biceps, that she realized as if they'd whispered it in her ear: He's not going to come back. He lied to me. He's going to do what he means to do and then he's going to go, he's going to leave me nice and comfortable in this hotel so I have a good time for a couple of days, but he's going to leave me. And that became more and more obvious as time went by, because the best proof that a person is not going to come back is that he doesn't come back, no? Angelina spent the afternoon stuck in the hotel, waiting for a call, waiting for a bellboy to come up to the room with a note, but that didn't happen, the wretched Gabriel hadn't even left her a note. And when she looked out of the window, as if she could see the road leading up to the hotel from the window, Angelina realized that she was in her city, in the place where she'd been born and lived for years and years, and that, nevertheless, she had nowhere to go. Once again, she thought. Once again men had conspired to convert a friendly city into a hostile city; to convert her, a stable woman with her feet firmly on the ground, into a stranger, an unsettled person, a foreigner.

Didn't she have any acquaintances left in Medellín?

Yes, there were people she knew, but it's not enough to know someone to ask them for a night's shelter, much less to explain the reasons why a person's been left where they were (she couldn't bring herself to say the word 'abandoned', it sounded pathetic to her, or at least too plaintive). She thought she could wander around the lighting displays that were everywhere in downtown Medellín at that time of year, stars and mangers and bells, all rustled up with coloured lights and wires covered in green plastic; she thought of going for a walk through the city and simply looking at display windows, considering that three days before Christmas all the shops would be open and full of people, noise, garlands, decorated trees, lights and Christmas carols; she thought of giving life an immediate chance to return to its course, to not go off the rails. She went down to the car park, saw that Gabriel had taken the car – and imagined him driving with his left hand and changing gears with the thumb of his mutilated hand – and found out that it had rained the night before by the rectangle of dry pavement you could still see where the car had been; and she went straight back up to the room, dumped everything of Gabriel's out of the suitcase onto the bed. That's how she spent the night, beside the clothes of the man who had left her. She didn't sleep well. At six in the morning she'd already called a taxi, and in less than fifteen minutes the taxi had picked her up and Angelina was on her way to the bus station.

So she also left without even leaving a note, without saying goodbye in any way?

Gabriel wasn't coming back, that was obvious. Why should she say goodbye? By leaving her dumped and rejected in a hotel, Gabriel had made it very clear that he didn't want to see her again: what kind of note could she have written? Of course, she didn't imagine she'd never see him again in her life; she thought back in Bogotá she'd track him down to demand an explanation, or at least she'd talk to him, and she never imagined Gabriel would die in the act of leaving her, wasn't that very ironic? Yes, there are accidents that seem like punishments, not that it made her happy, that would be a disproportionate punishment. Gabriel dead after leaving her, incredible. If he'd even suspected it, he would have left in a different way. Everyone has their ways of leaving and ways of leaving depend on a thousand things: where we're leaving, why we're leaving, who we're leaving.

How did she find out about his death?

From the newspapers. Of course, the most incredible thing was that she passed the very spot a few hours later, and didn't see anything. Her bus was an Expreso Bolivariano, just like the bus in the accident; it had left at seven in the morning, and Angelina was wide awake when they'd taken the road up to Las Palmas, but she hadn't noticed anything in particular, not the commotion of the morbid looking out of the window, or the traffic jams a more or less notorious accident can cause. And nothing in the world made her feel her world had changed, nothing warned her of this new absence, the disappearance, the hole in the order of things: that meant, of course, that her emotional links with Gabriel had broken completely and forever. Later, the rocking of the bus had made her sleepy, and then, half awake and half asleep, she'd thought again about the terrible story of the foreign family and their treacherous friend. At times it seemed impossible: Gabriel was too honest to act in such a cowardly way; too intelligent to do so out of ingenuousness or innocence. But maybe none of that was true, and the matter was just that simple: this man, who had used her to come to Medellín, who had slept with her, made plans for the future, told her he loved her, and all that just to leave her to her fate in a hotel room, this man was no different than his actions proved, and he'd kept the mask of a respectable person all his life at the expense of the credibility and affection of those around him. Everyone knows it: someone who betrays once will carry on betraying until he dies.

So she didn't believe in repentance?

She believed, all right, but she didn't think it possible that he had repented. Or maybe it was possible, but not un-questioningly commendable. In fact, if the repentance was genuine, and the desire to be forgiven genuine, Gabriel would not have had any reason not to carry on his relationship with her. The pretext of repentance was not a safe conduct for airing selfishness; nor did it exclude certain responsibilities, or, at least, certain human priorities. We'll never know now what reasons Gabriel had for ceasing to love her, for deciding that returning to the hotel did not figure in his plans. Was he justified in hurting her that way, lying to her and deceiving her (writing that he would come back when it was perfectly clear he had no intention of doing so), laying such a cruel trap for her, and all that without taking into account the revelation of his true nature to her, who would quite happily have lived with the deception in order to keep him?

What did she think happened between Gabriel Santoro and Enrique Deresser?

Supposing that they actually saw each other, no? Because we don't know that for sure either. The possibility that Gabriel, having got as far as Medellín, had lost his nerve, is quite real, it deserves to be taken into account. Angelina had thought of that during the funeral: What if Gabriel had repented of repenting? What if the fear of confronting his friend had been stronger than the possibility of forgiveness? What if Gabriel had sacrificed her, and then had died himself in the accident, and *it was all for nothing*? In the cemetery, Angelina had met Gabriel's son, the journalist, and had suggested they meet the next day in the dead man's apartment with the intention of telling him everything: tell him who his father had really been; release him from deception as well. In the end, she hadn't been able to. And that was why: the possibility that Gabriel had never actually seen his friend. Because at that moment, after the violence of the cremation, the sadness of the whole ceremony, the idea that Gabriel had died coming from Medellín (after leaving her, yes, but without having carried out the object of the trip) was, more than absurd, heartless. And Angelina was not a heartless person.

And if they did actually see each other, what might have happened between them?

Angelina didn't know. To tell the truth, she wasn't interested. She'd already left all that behind. She'd already begun to forget Gabriel. She wanted to get on with her life now, start a new life. A chat between two tired old men about subjects half a century old? Please, please. Nothing could matter less to her.

I, of course, felt just the opposite. During the single hour of the broadcast more things seemed to have happened than during all of my thirty years, or, to put it another way, from that moment on it seemed like nothing except that local television programme had happened in my life, and so many windows opened on to so many new rooms, so many traps, that instead of turning off the television and phoning Sara to talk about what Angelina had just revealed, which would have been the most logical thing to do, I allowed something resembling vertigo to take me outside, and I found myself driving down Seventh towards the bullring at eleven at night. Half my head was thinking of arriving unannounced at Sara's house, and the other half felt indignant, thought it almost treacherous (yes, the word had settled into my vocabulary, like a new font in a word processor) that Sara hadn't told me about Enrique Deresser. Enrique Deresser was alive; Enrique Deresser was in Medellín. Was it possible that she didn't know, either? Was it possible he'd also hidden it from her, as

Angelina had suggested? On television, his lover had elevated herself to the level of supreme confidante, the only person on earth my father trusted, or trusted sufficiently, at least, to share the secret with and ask for her help. And what had she done? After declaring that she understood him, telling him she admired his contrition and his bravery, the courage a man of his age with the life he'd led would need to undertake an eight-hour trip with the sole intention of asking for forgiveness, after all that, what had she done? She had thought about herself. She didn't know, any more than the rest of the world, the reasons my father had had for ending their relationship (in a rather inelegant way, it's true, but elegance belongs to those with self-respect, elegance is part of a lifestyle that my father, at that moment, had renounced). In a man's struggle with his errors, Angelina had only seen the man who'd walked out of her life without saying goodbye, and had decided to respond to the humiliation. That's what she'd done: she'd informed on him. After his death, when he could no longer defend himself, she'd informed on him.

Deresser in Medellín? Had he perhaps fooled them all, had he pretended to leave Bogotá and Colombia when actually he'd hidden and stayed hidden all these years? No, that was impossible. Perhaps he had really left, lived elsewhere – in Ecuador or Panamá, in Venezuela, Cuba, Mexico – before returning incognito and starting life like the creature without a past, with mixed blood and no fixed nationality he sometimes, in his youth, had wanted to be? While I drove, I found myself speculating about his life, what might have happened during those forty years, how many times had he been wrong the way my father had been wrong, how many errors had he committed, how many things had he repented of doing, how many would he like to be forgiven for? The idea of Deresser being alive also transformed his image, if you could call the squalid and incomplete portrait Sara had conjured up for me an image, and it began to get saddled with the effects of having carried on acting and doing; it took away that curious virginity that the disappeared have and that makes them invulnerable to error. It was obvious: one who disappears loses, first of all, the ability to continue making mistakes, the capacity to betray and to lie. His character remains steady, or rather fixed, like the light on the silver of a negative. To disappear is to leave a moral portrait of oneself. Deresser, who for several days had been an abstraction for me (an abstraction that lived in two spaces: in Sara's voice and in the 1940s), now became vulnerable again. He was no longer a saint; he was no longer, or he wasn't *only*, a victim. He had been someone able to do harm like he'd done to my father; he still was, that is, he had been for half a century more. That half-century, I thought, had been given to him to carry on doing harm. And probably – no: with total certainty – he'd taken advantage of it.

He would have got married in the first country he went to, Panamá or Venezuela, and in time he would have separated from his wife and also from his children due to those banal disagreements that turn into separations. Would he have changed his name when he married? In those days it wasn't too difficult, because the world was not as frightened as it is today of the identity of those who inhabit it, and Deresser could have, without much bureaucracy, called himself Javier, for example, or carried on being Enrique, but changed his surname. Enrique López would have struck him as common, and perhaps too common to sound convincing; Enrique Piedrahíta would have worked better, a personal but inconspicuous name, idiosyncratic but not visible. And so Enrique Piedrahíta would have left behind, once and for all, the detested Germanness that had caused him so many problems in Colombia, and with it he would have got rid of his father, of the memory of his father – that inherited memory that spoke of Germany as if the Kaiser were still alive, as if the Treaty of Versailles had never existed – and also the inherited faults, because Enrique Piedrahíta, finally free from that nostalgic family, could not be suspected of uncomfortable relations, and no one could inform any authority of those relations: no one could accuse his family of Nazi sympathies, or of putting the safety of the hemisphere in jeopardy, or of threatening, with his nationality and his language, the interests of democracy. And if someone, on the way out of a cemetery, saw him in a black shirt, they would think he was in mourning, not accuse him of Fascism; and if someone heard him speak German, or speak fondly of the place where his father was born, they wouldn't follow him home, or go through his papers, or close his glass-and-mirror factory; and if someone found among his papers a drunken note insulting Roosevelt, and if someone . . . and if someone . . . No, none of that would happen. No one would include him on blacklists, no one would send him to a concentration camp in Fusagasugá, no one would mix him up with those who did serve the Nazi Party from positions protected by the country's conservative newspapers, no one would identify him with Laureano Gómez and his support for Franco, no one would take him for one of those heart-and-soul Nazis who had talked to him at the German Legation or in meetings of the German community before whom he'd pretended to nostalgia, patriotism, Germanness that he did not feel. And he would be free, he would be Enrique Piedrahíta for the rest of his life and he would be free.

At some point, however, he would have made a mistake: out of an impulse for honesty under pressure, out of the need that, according to criminologists, pushes people into answering questions no one has asked them, he would have confessed to his wife that his surname was not Piedrahíta, but Deresser, and that he'd been born in Colombia, yes, just as his accent and habits and way of going through life indicated, but that half his blood was German. He would have confessed that his parents hadn't died in a plane crash – in the February 1947 accident in El Tablazo – but that his mother (whose name was Margarita) had abandoned them, and his father (whose name was Konrad, not Conrado), a coward, completely faint-hearted, had chosen to kill himself rather than try to recover from failure, rather than survive the desertion. None of what he confessed had been so grave, but his wife, a timid, quiet woman who had fallen in love with Enrique as naturally as everyone falls in love, would have become aware of this terrible threat; someone who could hide something like that for so long would keep on hiding things; and, in any case, the idea of trusting him seemed impossible, and in each disagreement, each conflict they had for the rest of their lives, she would be embittered by the notion that *maybe* Enrique was lying to her, *maybe* what he was telling her now wasn't true either. No, she couldn't stand it, and would end up leaving home just as her mother-in-law had done, whom she suddenly understood (it would be like a bolt of lightning, that solidarity between deceived women), whom she'd belatedly start to respect although she'd never met her.

Would Enrique have kept in touch with his mother? It wasn't very likely. No: it was downright impossible. But maybe he had written to her on a couple of occasions, first to reproach her for the desertion that had pushed his father into suicide and then sending out tentative probes to size up the possibility of a re-encounter; or maybe it would have been she who had looked for him, who had hunted him through the German consulates in all the capitals of Latin America until finding him and writing a letter that Enrique would not have deigned to read or answer (he would have recognized her handwriting; he would have torn up the letter without opening the envelope). And over time the voluntarily exiled memory of his mother would gradually fade like an old photo, and Enrique wouldn't even hear of Margarita's death, for no one had been able to find him to give him the news, and one day he would estimate the amount of time passed and the very high possibility that his mother, grown old who knew where and in what company, would be ill or would be dying or would have already died. And Enrique Piedrahíta, who by that time would have constructed a different life in Venezuela or in Ecuador, with friends and associates and enemies too, earned without great fault on his part – because, in spite of his having done all he could to go unnoticed, no one is exempt from slander and treachery, no one is immune from unwarranted hatred – would begin to consider what he had never considered: returning to Colombia.

He wouldn't have decided all of a sudden, of course, but after several days, several weeks of uncertainty, and perhaps he'd spent entire years before eventually deciding that the return was feasible. At some point he would have loathed this life full of decisions and possibilities and options: he would have been satisfied with a quiet, sedentary life in which he never had to ask himself where to go now or whether he should stay, what risks or what benefits awaited him if he moved. He would have doubted. And losing his friends? And losing the reputation acquired with the effort of the recent arrival, the foreigner, the immigrant, with that effort he had learned, through a sort of burlesque paradox, from his immigrant, foreigner father? All this he would have wondered about, and then he would have thought: Why not? None of his friends would compel him to stay, that was certain, he had never interested them that much; and the one who did would perhaps be the one who would later undermine him irreparably, would steal money from the firm, sleep with his new wife. Nothing tied him anywhere, and Enrique, out of fear of feeling exiled and stateless, would invent a pretext for leaving and perhaps he'd invent a destination: he was going to the United States; that's what he would have said. And he wouldn't have to justify it, because the reasons that everybody goes are always clear to those closest to them, and according to rumours (those same friends and relations would think sadly, because it's always sad when someone leaves, but also with the absurd envy of those who stay not out of choice but from lack of options), the United States is a country made to receive everyone, even exiles like him.

But he would discover when he arrived in Bogotá that this city was no longer his, that by going to Ecuador or Peru he had lost it for ever and a kind of gigantic ravine, a grand canyon of hostilities and bad memories and bloated resentments, separated him from it. Staying away for twenty years has its consequences, of course; and Enrique would have realized that the only way to ease his absence was by not returning to the place he'd left, just as the best way to correct a lie was by insisting on it, not by telling the truth. In Bogotá he would have found out that many of the Germans from Barranquilla had been able to return after the war, when the measures that forbade Axis citizens from living in coastal zones were lifted. But Barranquilla was not for him, not just because Barranquilla in his mind was the city of the Nazi Party, not just because the Bethkes had come from Barranquilla and might still be alive and remember that dinner when they talked about difficult subjects in front of Gabriel Santoro – who later informed those who wanted to be told about those subjects – but also because his blood was Bogotá blood and he was used to the constant cold and rain and the grey faces of the people of Bogotá, and would never feel comfortable where it was forty degrees in the shade. And then, just when the weight of uprootedness began to be too much, something had happened. Enrique Piedrahíta or Deresser, who at forty-something years of age was still as attractive as a Colombian Paul Henreid, would have fallen in love, or rather, a woman – maybe separated, or maybe a widow in spite of her youth – would have fallen in love with him, and he would have clearly understood that for exiles the best way to appropriate a city is to fall in love, that the feeling of belonging is one of the more abstruse consequences of sex. And then, in secret and almost incognito, he would have appropriated the city that fell into his lap this time, without a moment's hesitation.

Thirty years. Thirty years he would have lived in Medellín with his last wife and with a daughter, just one, because his wife knew that after a certain age more than one pregnancy is dangerous and even irresponsible. And many times, over those thirty years, he would think of Sara and Gabriel, and to avoid the urge to phone them he would have to remember the betrayal and the suicide and he would have to remember the faces of the men with their machetes when he paid them 40 pesos so they would do what they did (but Enrique wouldn't know the final result; for him, the aggression had an abstract character; in his imagination there were no amputated fingers or stump or solitary thumb). In those thirty years he would have written many letters; many times he would have written on an envelope: *Señorita Sara Guterman, Hotel Pensión Nueva Europa, Duitama, Boyacá*, and on a blank sheet of paper he would have repeated different openings, some of them resentful and others conciliatory, some of them pitiful and others insulting, sometimes talking only to Sara, sometimes including a separate letter for Gabriel Santoro, the treacherous friend, the informer. In it he would ask, not cleverly but sarcastically, if he still considered that Konrad Deresser was a threat to Colombian democracy merely for having welcomed a fanatic into his home, for listening to stupidities without raising objections, for adding his own nostalgia and cheap patriotism to these stupidities, for being German but also a coward; and whether those falsely altruistic conjectures were sufficient to ruin the lives of those who had cared for him; and whether he'd accepted money in exchange for the information he'd given the American Ambassador or whoever it had been, or if he'd turned it down when they offered it, convinced he was acting according to the principles of civic-minded valour, of political duty, of a citizen's responsibility. But he would never send that letter or any of the others (dozens, hundreds of drafts) he wrote as a hobby. And after thirty years the arrival of Gabriel Santoro had surprised him less, much less, than he would have imagined. Enrique would have agreed to see him, of course; he would have understood, with slight panic, that with time the resentment had disappeared, the disdainful phrases were no longer at the tip of his tongue, that the revenge had expired like the rights over unused premises; and above all, he would have accepted against his will that remembering Gabriel Santoro gave him an illegitimate and almost abnormal urge to see him and talk to him again.

That's how things would have gone, I thought, and meanwhile, without noticing, I had passed Sara's building. When I got to the bullring on Fifth Avenue, instead of turning left I ended up, out of distraction and a few seconds of indecision, heading down that narrow, dark corridor that leads to Twenty-sixth Street, and I thought of taking Seventh northbound and coming back a few blocks to go up to Sara's again. But that didn't seem to make much sense any more, or maybe I just couldn't see any in it, because if I kept going on Twenty-sixth I could get on to Caracas, and that was the route I'd taken from the centre each time I went to visit my father during the first few days of his convalescence, the route Sara would have taken for the same purpose, and the route that at this hour of the night would take me most quickly to his apartment. It was, to put it one way, a conspiracy of coincidences; and in a few minutes of speed and total disrespect for traffic lights – at a red light in Bogotá we take our foot off the accelerator, put the car into second and make sure no one's coming, but fear keeps us from actually stopping – I found myself in front of his building. Since my father's death I'd never driven that way, and I was impressed by how easy it was at that hour of night to get through those streets, which during the day are impossible. I thought the daytime traffic would remain associated with my father's recuperation, and the ease of the night, on the other hand, with this visit to the apartment of a dead man, more or less the way my father's death would always be associated with my old car while this one, bought second-hand from a garage with the insurance money, would always remind me that my own life (my material and practical life, everyday life, the life where I eat and sleep and work) would go on even though it might sometimes weigh me down. There was just one window with lights on and a silhouette, or perhaps a shadow, crossed it once and then back again before the light went out. The doorman raised his head, recognized me and relaxed again. Who would have said I'd end up coming here, alone and in the middle of the night? And nevertheless, that's what had happened. A brief distraction – not turning left, but going straight on – a vague respect for the inertia of coincidences, and there I was, entering the last place inhabited by my last living relative, and doing so with a very clear idea in my head: to look for Angelina's phone number in the only place I might be able to find it. It wasn't like a flash of inspiration, but a sudden and dictatorial necessity; to doubt her, who'd given me so much information, was foolish and even ungrateful. Angelina. Look up her number, call her, confront her.

'My condolences, Don Gabriel,' the doorman said; he didn't remember, or he remembered without it mattering, that he'd already given me his condolences two or three times since the day after the funeral. He also handed me the post that had kept on arriving even though a month had passed since the death of the addressee and even though that death had received more publicity than most; and I realized I didn't know what to do with the bills and the subscriptions, with the College of Lawyers circulars and notification from the bank. Reply to them one by one? Draft a standard letter, photocopy it and send out a mass mailing? I regret to inform you that Dr Gabriel Santoro died . . . please be kind enough, therefore, to cancel his subscription . . . Dr Gabriel Santoro recently passed away. He, therefore, will be unable to attend . . . The phrases were ludicrously painful, and writing them was just short of unthinkable. Sara would know how to do it; Sara would know the procedures. At her age, the practical effects of death are routine and no longer intimidating. That's what I was thinking as I opened the door, and as I went in I realized that I would rather have felt something more intense or perhaps something more solemn, but what hit me first, as was to be expected given the circumstances, was my own nature. I've never been able to avoid it: I've always felt comfortable with solitude, but being alone in someone else's house is one of my fetishes, something like a perversion that I would never tell anyone about. I am the kind of person who opens doors in other people's bathrooms to see what perfumes, or what painkillers, or what kind of birth control they use; I open bedside-table drawers, I search, look, but I'm not after secrets: finding vibrators or letters from a lover interests me just as much as finding an old wallet or a blindfold. I like other people's lives; I like to make myself at home and examine them. I probably violate several principles of discretion, of trust, of good manners in doing so. It's quite probable.

A month and the place was already beginning to smell closed up. The orange-juice glass I'd found on the day of my appointment with Angelina was still in the sink, and that's the first thing I did when I went in: wet the sponge and scrubbed the bottom of the glass hard to remove a bit of dried pulp. I had to turn the water supply back on, though I didn't remember having shut it off: that day, I thought, Angelina must have dealt with it. The curtains were still closed too, and I had the feeling that if I opened them they'd release a cloud of dust, so I left them as they were. Everything was the same as the last time I'd been there, and what remained most painfully immutable was the absence of the owner; on the other hand, that owner had begun to turn into someone else since his death and would perhaps continue his transformation, because once secrets start coming out, the twenty-year-old infidelity, the white lies – yes, like a snowball – no one can stop them. Except for my own book, everything in this place seemed to suggest that my father hadn't had a childhood, and even my book only suggested it in a tacit, indirect, lateral way. But was it the same book? *The first thing Peter Guterman did when he arrived in Duitama was to paint the house and build a second floor.* First sentence. *At that time foreigners were not allowed to practise, without previous authorization, occupations other than those they'd declared upon entering the country.* Another sentence. *In the Guterman family's hotel things happened that destroyed families, disrupted lives, ruined futures . . .* The sentences were no longer the ones I'd written, and it wasn't due to the violent irony that had begun to fill them: their words had changed too, *foreigner* didn't mean the same as it had before, nor did *futures*. The book, my book about Sara Guterman, was the closest thing to those years and the only thing able to suggest the (ill-fated) presence of my father; but it was also the proof a tricky prosecutor would have used to allege my father's non-existence, the Cheshire cat.

I looked over the blue and brown spines of the oldest books, looked over the disorderly colours of the more recent ones, and didn't find a single title I didn't recognize, not a single jacket flap or flyleaf that could have contained, at this stage, the slightest surprise. My father's meticulousness, his idea that a messy environment is one of the causes of a messy thought process, had obliged him to arrange all his lecture notes, his twenty years of speaking on how to speak well, on the same shelf; I chose one of the folders at random and examined it imagining I might find an incriminating document; I found nothing. Was there not in this place a single piece of paper that contained the dead man's youth, not a newspaper clipping about the blacklists or a book that might contain annotations, no reference to Enrique Deresser or his family or Bogotá in the 1940s? A man's private history irremediably obliterated: how could that be possible? In a manipulable world, a world susceptible to being reprogrammed by us, its demiurges, would there not have been an immediate need to remedy that? Thinking of that I picked up my book and opened it to the Appendices, chose an example of a report from the ones I'd found during the course of my investigation – the different ones they used in the cases of real infiltrators or active propagandists, and that later came to light, always partially censored by officials – and copied it by hand, adapting it to my uncertainties, on the blank pages that seem designed for such purposes between the printer's imprint and the flyleaf. I wrote: *Military Intelligence Division, War Department General Staff, Military Attaché Report.* And then:

Interviewed in El Automático café, the witness Gabriel Santoro declared that Konrad Deresser, proprietor of Cristales Deresser, has extremely close relations with supporters of the Colombian Nazi Party (with its headquarters in Barranquilla and elements infiltrated all over the territory) and on several occasions has demonstrated anti-American attitudes in the presence of Colombian citizens. It has been determined that the witness's word is trustworthy.

I turned the page. I wrote: *In accordance with Special Order No. 7 of the Military Attaché, Bogotá, Colombia, investigated the references with the following results.* And then:

Interrogated in the offices of the Embassy of the United States of America, Bogotá, the informant Santoro (NI. See below, Hotel Nueva Europa dossier) declared that Mr Konrad Deresser has very close relations with known propagandists (principally Hans-Georg Bethke, KN. See below, List of Blocked Nationals, updated November 1943) and on several occasions has demonstrated anti-American attitudes in the presence of Colombian citizens, as well as his employees, whom he regularly greets in German. His declarations have been verified against those of other sources. The word of the informant has been deemed trustworthy.

I put the book back in its place and discovered the universe hadn't been transformed by my falsifying the contents of those pages. My father was still incognito in his own memory, dead but also clandestine. But perhaps what would be impossible, in my father's case, was the opposite: a hole, a gap in the art of erasing fingerprints, a defect in the rigour of the most rigorous man in the world, an inconsistency in his powerful desire to erase Deresser the way Trotsky (just one example) was erased from the photos and encyclopedias of Stalin's time. If it was about revising his history, my father – my revisionist father – had achieved it with success. But then, he'd committed the error that we all perhaps commit: telling secrets after sex. I imagined the lovers. I imagined them walking around this apartment naked, going to the kitchen to get a drink or to the bathroom to throw away used condoms, or sitting like teenagers in this chair. She is naked on my father's lap like a ventriloquist's doll, and her recently shaved legs (her shins covered in goose pimples) hang over the arm of the chair without touching the floor; he is wearing his bathrobe, because there are certain levels of decency one never loses. 'Tell me about yourself, tell me about your life,' says Angelina. 'My life is of no interest,' answers my father. 'It will be to others,' says Angelina. 'I'm interested.' And my father: 'I don't know, I don't know. Maybe some other time. Yes, one day I'll tell you all about it.' Maybe if we go to Medellín, thinks my father, maybe if you accompany me to do what I cannot do alone.

On my father's desk, not on his bedside table, I found his telephone book, but Angelina's surname didn't pop into my head immediately, as happens with our own acquaintances, so it took me a moment or two to find her number among the squadron of scribbles jotted down with his left hand. It was after midnight. I sat beside the pillow, on the edge of the bed, like a visitor, like the visitor I was. At the foot of the lamp there was a film of dust; or maybe it was on every surface in the apartment, but here, due to the direct and yellow light, it was more visible and indecent. I opened the drawer and rummaged through HB pencils and 200-peso coins, and then I found a cheap little book, the kind they sell in supermarkets or pharmacies (displayed beside the razors and the chewing gum), that I hadn't noticed the last time. It was a gift from Angelina. *Books for Lovers*, it said on the laminated, greenish cover, and underneath: *Kama Sutra*. I opened it at random and read: 'When she holds and massages her lover's lingam with her yoni, this is Vadavaka, the Mare.' Angelina the mare, massaged my father's lingam, here, in this bed, and suddenly the elaborate diatribe I'd prepared at the back of my mind began to blur, and Angelina, far from embodying my father's fall from grace, turned into a vulnerable but shameless woman, sentimental and affected but also direct, capable of giving a withdrawn professor of classics in his sixties a cheap version of an illustrated sex manual. I hesitated, thought of hanging up, but it was too late, because the phone had rung two or three times, and I was the more surprised by the question I was pronouncing. 'Could I speak to Angelina Franco, please?'

'Speaking,' said the voice at the other end of the line, sleepy and a little irritated. 'Who is this?'

'Do you have any idea what time it is? You're crazy, Gabriel, calling at this time of night. You scared the hell out of me.'

It was true. Her voice was thick and accelerated. She coughed, took a deep breath.

'Did I wake you?'

'Well, of course you woke me up, it's after midnight. What do you expect? Look, if it's to give me a hard time . . .'

'Partly, yeah. But don't worry, I'm not going to shout at you.'

'No? Well, thanks a lot. The one who should be shouting here is me. The nerve!'

'Look, Angelina, I don't know how things were with my dad. But people don't do things like what you did to him, that seems obvious. Was it for the money –?'

She cut me off. 'All right, all right. No insults.'

'How much did they pay you? I would have paid you as much to keep quiet.'

'Oh yeah? And I would have been just as happy? I don't think so, dear, I don't think so. Do you want me to tell you the truth? I would have done it for free, yes, sir. People need to be told things as they are.'

'People don't give a damn, Angelina. What you did . . .'

'Look, I have to go to sleep. It's late and I have to get up early. Don't call me again, Gabriel. I don't have to explain myself to you or to anybody, ciao.'

'No, wait.'

'What?'

'Don't hang up on me. You know where I am?'

'Why should I care? No, really, don't tell me you called me to talk crap? I'm going to hang up, bye.'

'I'm in my dad's apartment.'

'Great. What else?'

'I swear.'

'I don't believe you.'

'I swear,' I said. 'I came here to find your phone number. I was going to phone you to insult you.'

'My phone number?'

'In my dad's phone book, I don't have your number.'

'Oh. Right, very interesting, but I need to go to sleep. We'll talk some other time, bye.'

'Did you watch the programme tonight? Did you see yourself on television?'

'*No*, I didn't watch the programme,' said Angelina, obviously annoyed. '*No*, I didn't see myself on television. They didn't call me, they said they'd call before showing it and they didn't call me, they lied to me too, OK? Can we hang up, please?'

'It's just that I need to know a couple of things.'

'What things, Gabriel? Come on, don't be a drag. I'm going to hang up. I don't want to hang up on you, hanging up on people is rude, but if you force me to I will.'

'What you did to my dad is serious. He . . .'

'No, no, wait a second. What he did to me, that was serious. Leaving without saying anything, dumping me there like an old rag. *That* is what you don't do to a person.'

'Let me speak. He trusted you, Angelina. Not even I knew those things, he hadn't even told me the things he told you. And that, obviously, affects me as well. All those things he told you. All the things you said on television. So I want to know if it's true, that's all. If you made some of it up or if it's all true. It's important, I don't have to explain why.'

'Oh, so now you're accusing me of lying.'

'I'm asking you.'

'With what right?'

'Without any. Hang up if you want.'

'I'm going to hang up.'

'Hang up, go on, hang up, don't worry,' I said. 'It's all lies, isn't it? You know what I think? I think my dad hurt you, I don't know how, but he hurt you, leaving you, getting tired of you, and you're getting even like this. Women can't stand anyone getting tired of them, and this is how they get even, like you're doing. Taking advantage of the fact that he's dead and can't defend himself. You've got a chip on your shoulder, that's all, that's what I think. You betrayed him in the most cowardly way, and all because the old man decided that this relationship wasn't worth carrying on, something anyone has the right to do in this bitch of a world. This is slander, Angelina, it's a crime and you can go to jail for it; of course you're the only one who knows if you're slandering him or not. What do you feel when you think about it, Angelina? Tell me, tell me what you feel. Do you feel strong, do you feel powerful? Sure, it's like sending an anonymous threat, like insulting someone under a pseudonym. All cowards are the same, it's incredible. The power of slander, eh? The power of impunity. Yes, slander is a crime, although no one's ever going to prove it in your case.

That's you, Angelina, you are the lowest of the low: a thief who got away with it.'

She was crying. 'Don't be mean,' she said. 'You know full well I didn't make any of it up.'

'No, the truth is I don't know. The only thing I know is that my dad's dead and you're dragging his name through the mud all over Bogotá. And I want to know why.'

'Because he left me in the worst way. Because he took advantage of me.'

'Please, don't be trite. My dad's incapable of taking advantage of anybody. He *was* incapable.'

'Well, that's what you think; it's not for me to tell you any different. But no one ever left you, you can see that for miles. I know what happened in Medellín, I know what he made me believe. He made me think he was coming back and he didn't come back, he told me to wait for him and left me there waiting, I know all that, and that was from the start, he planned all that, he needed my support and he thought: Well, she can come with me and once we get there and she's no use to me any more, I'll leave her there. He made me believe . . .'

'What did he make you believe?'

'That we were going away together. That we were a couple and we were spending Christmas together.'

'And didn't you go away together?'

'No, we went so he could take care of a little business. And once I'd completed my function I turned into a nuisance.'

'They're two separate things.'

'What are?'

'One: asking for help. Two: wanting to be helped.'

'Oh no, don't give me that crap. All men –'

'Where are your parents, Angelina?'

'What?'

'Where is your family?'

'No, just a moment. That's out of bounds, watch it.'

'How long has it been since you spoke to your brother? Years, right? And wouldn't you like to speak to him again, have someone who reminded you of your parents? Of course you would, but you don't because you've been estranged for a long time, and now it's hard to get close again. You'd like to, but it's difficult. Getting close to people is always difficult. People who are distant are frightening, it's completely normal. But you know what? It would be easier if someone helped you, like if I went with you to Cartagena.'

'Santa Marta.'

'If I went with you to Santa Marta and sat and had something to drink while you went and met your brother and talked out what you need to discuss. If things went well, there I'd be for you to tell me. If they went badly, if your brother told you to go to hell and said he didn't want anything to do with you, to go back where you came from, there I'd be. And we could go to the hotel, or wherever, and we'd lie down and watch television, if that helped you, or we'd get drunk, or screw all night, whatever. But there is another possibility: after going to see him, you decided for other reasons you didn't want to come back. That's something else, it wouldn't be a reason for me to go around slandering you afterwards. Get the message or shall I explain it more clearly?'

'I don't want to see my brother.'

'But don't be an idiot. It's an example, an analogy.'

'It might be what you say. But all the same, I don't want to see him.'

'That's not what we're talking about. Oh please, what an idiot. We're talking about my dad.'

'I have no interest in seeing my brother. Maybe he did, but I don't.'

Silence.

'OK,' I said. 'How do you know he's not interested?'

'No, I don't know, I imagine.'

'Why do you imagine that?'

'He didn't come to my parents' funeral. What else does that prove?'

'Don't cry, Angelina.'

'I'm not crying now, don't mess with my life, OK? And if I feel like crying, what's it to you? Leave me alone or I'm hanging up right now, let me –'

'Can I tell you something odd?'

'Or I'll slam the phone down?'

'I went to give blood. The day of that bomb, when they blew up Los Tres Elefantes.'

Silence.

'What blood type are you?' she said after a while.

'O positive.'

Another silence.

Then: 'Like my dad. Did you really donate blood that day?'

'Yes, I went with a friend who's a doctor,' I said. 'The person who would have operated on my dad if Social Security didn't exist. He forced me to go. I didn't want to.'

'Where did you go?'

'Most of the wounded were at the Santa Fe and the Shaio. The clinics closest to the store, and the best equipped, I imagine. I went to the Santa Fe.'

'Where do you give blood in the Santa Fe?'

'On the second floor. Or the third. Up some stairs, in any case.'

'And what's the place like?'

'Are you testing me?'

'Tell me what the clinic's like.'

'It's a big room with coffee-coloured sofas, I think, and there are little windows,' I said. 'You talk to a nurse, then they send you in.'

'To the back on the left?'

'No, Angelina, to the back on the right. There are cubicles, lots of people giving blood at the same time. They make you sit in very high chairs.'

'Those high chairs,' Angelina said. 'You gave blood. Gabriel never told me.'

'I'm sure he didn't know. He didn't follow my life that closely.'

'Amazing,' she said. 'I remember when Gabriel asked me about my parents and I told him, I got upset, he said so many nice things. He talked to me a lot that day, he even told me about his wife's illness, but he never told me this. How amazing, I'm amazed.'

'It's not such a big deal. Everyone in this city has given blood.'

'But it's the connection, you know what I mean? It's amazing, I swear. I don't know what my dad's cause of death was, I didn't want to know whether it was a blow, or . . . but if you –'

'Take it easy. Don't talk about that if you don't want to.'

'My mum was A positive. That's more difficult.'

'Did you get along well?'

'Average. Fine, I think. But not too close. They were there and I was here.'

'I guess people grow apart.'

223

'Yes, that's right. And the one time they come to visit me, they get hit by a drug lord's bomb. What rotten luck, man, I must be jinxed.'

'No, not really. Sooner or later it hits us all, and sorry for saying such stupid things. Are you happy here?'

'Oh, it doesn't matter, there're bombs in Medellín too, bombs wherever a person goes, Gabriel.' And then laughing: 'Like the moon.'

'But if they were alive, wouldn't you consider going back to Medellín?'

'I've been here for quite a few years now, I'm used to it. Moving is no fun, it's awful. I don't know about you, but people who are always moving don't seem trustworthy, like . . . like untrustworthy, that's the only word, I can't put it any better. To go away from where you were born isn't normal, is it? And going away twice from where a person's from, or leaving your own country, you know? Going to a country where they speak something else, I don't know, it's for strange people; rootless people can do bad things.'

'Yes. My father thought the same way. Can I ask you a question?'

'Another one?'

'How did you end up getting mixed up with my dad?'

Silence.

'Why? You don't think I'm good enough?'

'No, that's not what I meant, Angelina. It's just that . . .'

'He was such an intelligent, cultured person, no? And I'm a masseuse.'

'Masseuse?'

'When my boyfriend wanted to insult me he used to say that: "I don't know what I did to end up with a fucking masseuse." Sure, it's my own fault, because a true professional doesn't get involved with patients.'

'I asked you a question.'

'I don't know, your dad was just another patient, it's not like I get involved with all my patients. Things like that happen before you notice, you know? Suddenly, Gabriel crossed the line, and I told him no, that no one gets involved in my life, and he didn't listen to me. But he was the patient and I put up with the things he said to me.'

'Why? Why didn't you leave, if it bothered you so much, why didn't you get a replacement?'

'Because the therapy hadn't finished. It's not for me to say, I know, but I take my work seriously, you know? And I'm good at my job, because I like it. All I want is to help people move again, there's nothing simpler. Well, that's what he was, any old patient, one of so many, a block of time in my schedule – I have a schedule with all my visits – he was one more. I had no intention of letting him into my life, I swear, I'd been hurt too much by men, not that I'm so experienced either, don't get me wrong. You want to know why I opened the door to him and not to another.'

'You don't have to talk about doors.'

'I talk the way I like. If you don't like it, I'll shut up. I don't speak as well as you guys.'

'Sorry. Go on.'

'I had more than ten during those months. All men in their fifties, their sixties, two or three in their seventies. After heart surgery they need to learn how to move again, like newborn babies. So I get beside them and give them exercises to do, you feel sorry for people, I play with them a little and remind them they're not dead even if they sometimes feel like it, because they're so depressed sometimes, you feel sorry for them . . . Anyway, it's like a gift from God, I swear, dealing with these people who've come back to life. Their bodies have them disorientated. The body thinks it's dead and you have to convince it that it's not, because . . .'

'Yeah, they explained all that to me.'

'OK. I'm there for that too, to show them they haven't died, that they're still there. If you could see me, you should see the work it takes with some of them, especially the younger ones. Sometimes I get one like that, men who have a bypass at forty-something, like as young as me, and they don't accept it. And I explain and explain again.'

'What?'

'That it's at their age when they're at the highest risk. Didn't you know? Because at forty, forty-five, you still feel young, and you knock back the drinks, and smoke like a chimney and eat all that fried food. And exercise, I don't fucking need it, I'm still young. Well, your heart thinks otherwise. It's had a long time of drinks and cigarettes and doesn't want any more. And that's how accidents happen. It's good for me because it's a bit of variety, I like that they're not always so old, that I can touch bodies my own age once in a while, I'm still young. Oh, sorry, that's a bit familiar. I shouldn't be saying these things. Remind me that you're not your dad.'

'Why? You could tell him these things?'

'Well, of course. He loved to hear me talk about my work.'

'Yeah, well, you enjoy your work and you like to talk about how much you enjoy your work. I don't see what's strange about that.'

'It's that there are jobs you shouldn't enjoy too much, Gabrielito, don't play dumb with me. Especially if you don't do them in a normal way. If you were a gynaecologist you couldn't go around shouting, I love my job, I love my job. People wouldn't take it well; now you're going to tell me that's never occurred to you.'

'But you don't do what a gynaecologist does. Nothing even close.'

'I like to touch. I like to feel people. You can't go around saying that out loud. Other physiotherapists sit their patients down twenty metres away and from there tell them what they have to do. I get close, I touch them, I give them massages. And saying that I touch them and that I like it is not approved of. The clients would feel uncomfortable and the doctors would kick me out. You're not going to tell anybody, are you?'

'Don't be ridiculous.'

'I like contact, what can I do? After a weekend alone at home, I feel the lack. A person is very alone at home; you live alone, too, don't you? Well, I miss going out to meet someone. Oh, if the San Pedro cardiologist could hear me he'd kick me out on the street, I swear he would.'

'Well, I'm no cardiologist.'

'No, but I wouldn't say these things to your face either. Just as well we're talking on the phone.'

'Just as well.'

'I like getting into a packed lift. I don't feel alone, I feel calm. In places like that men brush up against a person. My friends hate that, but I like it. I've never told anyone that, ever. My boyfriend was claustrophobic, he didn't like things like that. And a massage isn't being touched but touching, caressing. I know people like it. Perhaps they're ashamed that they like it, but they like it, men especially. I know I'm still attractive.'

'When did you know?'

'That I'm still attractive?'

'That this was the job for you.'

'Oh, I don't know. You're imagining nonsense now, aren't you? Well, I didn't give my dolls massages, much less my girlfriends, for your information. Don't laugh, it's true.'

'I believe you.'

'If I'd had brothers close to my age, maybe I wouldn't have felt so alone, I was a lonely child. But my brother was six years older than me, well, he still is. He was never with me. He began to notice I existed when I was about eleven, around there. One time my chest was hurting, you know, when you first start to grow, and my parents were both at work, so I told my brother. He took me into the bathroom and sat me on the washstand. He was very strong and he lifted me up from the floor like that, in one go. And he started to touch me. "Does it hurt here? And here? Does it hurt here?" He touched my ribs – does me telling you this bother you? He touched my nipples. It hurt a lot, but I answered yes, no, a little. And then he went off to do his military service and those things didn't happen any more. I was eleven. Then, the first time he came home during his military service, something very strange happened to me, like a feeling of disgust, like a small disgust. It might have been his shaved head, I don't know. I didn't like the way he was talking either, that flashy ways soldiers talk, you know? And all the bloody crap, sorry, all the silly things he told us about his new military friends, people who'd come back from Korea three or four or five years ago, who told him such interesting things, interesting to my brother at least, and he showed up repeating them like a parrot. I was bored and my brother seemed like a jerk. When I went to take a shower, I locked the door and pushed the dirty-laundry basket up against the door. It was just a latch and if someone pushed hard enough it would open, not that my brother was going to break down the door to see me naked, but still. And then my brother arrived with the news that he was leaving home. He'd got his girlfriend pregnant and he was moving out. No one even knew he had a girlfriend. She lived in Santa Marta, worked in a travel agency, or a tourism office, and she was going to get him a job. As soon as he was settled into his job and had saved a bit of money he was going to invite us all to the coast. He promised all that, but then nothing. I remember my mum saying, "We've lost him." She'd done some calculations, and she was sure her grandchild must have been born by then, and my brother didn't say anything. "He's gone and we've lost him." That's what my mum said. For me, on the other hand, it was a relief. It's sad, but that's how it is.'

'It's not so sad. The guy was a heel, Angelina.'

'Yeah, but he was my brother. Imagine later when I told them I was leaving too. Of course, that was a long time later. I was doing my practical training, but all the same it hit them hard. I was the baby of the family. They busted their arses to send me to university, Gabriel, and what for, so I'd grab my diploma and head off to Bogotá. Ungrateful brat, no? But I was really good. It's not my fault I had magic hands.'

'Teacher's pet.'

'No, as a student I kept my head down, tried not to stand out. It was later, during my internship. It was in the Leon XIII. I would have stayed there my whole life if I hadn't come to Bogotá. It was the Leon XIII physiatrist who noticed I worked miracles with my hands. He assigned me an eighty-year-old patient who'd had three bypasses and in ten days I had him doing aerobics. When they transferred him to Bogotá, he practically dragged me with him. That's when we started seeing each other.'

'Name?'

'Lombana. He was the kind of guy who liked travelling and being in other places. He'd studied in the United States and he got along great, everyone liked him, he made thousands of friends. But I didn't. In this whole fucking city I only knew him, so I did what anyone would have done in my place: I fell in love. It took me three years to find out the guy was married. He was already married in Medellín. The transfer to Bogotá wasn't a promotion, he'd requested it, because in Medellín he'd married a girl from here. And do you think I told him to go to hell? No, I stayed right there working away, like an idiot, meeting him almost always in my apartment, and in the motels in La Calera for special occasions. He'd take me there to weaken me: sometimes I'd get hysterical, or threaten to finish with all that shit, and that was my consolation prize. I deserve it all, for my stupidity. I like the motels in La Calera. When there aren't any clouds, when the air is clean and the pollution's not too bad, you can see the Nevado del Ruiz volcano. I used to love to see the snow-capped peak. He used to say he was going to take me there one day even though it was dangerous. Of course I didn't believe him, I'm not that naive either.'

'No.'

'And that went on for ten years. Ten years, Gabriel. It sounds like a long time but for me it went by like a shot, that's the truth. Because there wasn't the wearing down that real couples have. I've never been married, and maybe I shouldn't talk about something I don't know, but I swear Lombana fought more with his wife than with me, I haven't got the slightest doubt. Because with the wife there's a

230

history. That's what a person had to avoid, that you build up a history with people, with friends, with lovers. You get close to a person and right there the resentments start to build up, things you say or do without meaning to, and that gets you into a history. You go to see your cardiologist and he takes out your medical history and without even meaning to he checks out everything: that you stopped smoking, yes, but not till you were forty. Your father had a heart murmur. Your great-uncle had arteriosclerosis. That's what Lombana told me, that with his wife it was like that, they went to bed and each and every grudge over their whole marriage went to bed with them. In the end he only made love to her from behind, because he didn't want to look at her face. He told me all that. With every possible detail. I didn't want that to happen to me, and I suppose that's why I put up with it for ten years without doing anything, anything serious, I mean. I didn't want to do things that would later fill me up with bitterness and grudges, you know how it is. I like sex face to face, like normal. I'm a decent girl.'

'How did they kill him?'

Silence.

'Right then, is there any part of my life Gabriel didn't tell you about? He was a newsreel, your dad. Well, I'm sorry, but I don't like talking about that.'

'Oh please, Angelina. You already told me your brother used to touch you up. You just told me how you like sex.'

'That's different.'

'It was downtown,' I said to her. 'It was in a nightclub.'

'And what does it matter to you?'

'It doesn't matter to me. I'm just curious.'

'Morbid.'

'Exactly, morbid curiosity, that's what it is. Was he into any dirty business, drugs?'

'Of course not. There was a fight and guns came out and he got shot, nothing more. The most normal thing in the world.'

'Were you with him?'

'No, Gabriel, I was not with him. I was tucked up safe in my apartment. I wasn't with him, and I wasn't with my parents later, OK? Yeah, I wish I'd been killed too by that fucking bomb, I wish I'd been killed in the shootout. I wasn't with him and nobody came to tell me because very few people knew I existed and all the ones who did know preferred to respect the wife and not tell her they killed your husband and besides he's had another woman for the last ten years, no, thirteen whole years, how about that. No, I found out on my own. He wouldn't let me phone his house and I had to go and stand there in front of it like a prostitute to ask him if he wanted to finish with me, or why had he disappeared like that, and when he didn't appear all day then I checked into things and eventually found out, but no one informed me because you all hide under the same blanket, fucking hypocrites. So, I wasn't with him, so what? Can we talk about something else?'

'Don't be like that. It's good to talk about these things. It's therapeutic.'

'That shit again. Your dad used to say the same thing. Why are you so arrogant? Does it run in the family? Look, if you guys go through life talking about everything and that works for you, fine, but tell me one little thing, why the fuck should it be the same for me?'

'No reason. Calm down.'

'Why would what works for you lot work for me as well?'

'Calm down. No one's saying that.'
Silence.
'You need to respect other people more, Gabriel.'
'Respect other people.'
'We're not all the same.'
'We're very different.'
Silence.
'Besides, I'm the therapist.'
'Yes.'
'Don't give me that shit.'
'No.'
Silence.
'Well, at least we're in agreement. Wait a second. Wait, wait, wait, wait . . . OK. Right, what were you saying?'
'What happened?'
'I was rolling a joint.'
'At this hour?'
'Yeah, right now. After what happened to my parents, this was the only way I could get to sleep.'
'And you rolled it there, in bed, without dropping the phone? What a pair of hands you've got, it's true.'
'I hold the phone with my shoulder, that's all. It's not that hard. Do you sleep well?'
'I suppose. I wake up early, though. Five in the morning and that's it, my brain wakes up in one second and keeps running all day. Or I get up to go to the bathroom. But everyone else can go back to sleep, I can't. While I'm pissing I think of my dad and then there's nothing for it. It'll last for a while, I guess, and then things'll go back to normal. Because things normalize, don't they?'
'Yes. Don't worry about that, Gabriel, things go back to normal. Here, have a puff of marijuana down the phone.'

'I can smell it from here, I'm so jealous.'

Silence.

'So, you're in your dad's apartment, eh? Sitting on your dad's bed. It's a little strange, to tell you the truth, you've got your strange side, you have.'

'What are you wearing, Angelina?'

'Oh no, but not so strange after all.'

'Are you under the covers?'

'No, I'm stark naked on top of the bedspread and I've got a red lamp shining on me. Of course I'm under the covers, it's fucking freezing in this fucking city. As usual. And you?'

'I'm taking my jeans off and getting under the covers too. It is cold. I think I'm going to stay here, I've never slept in this bed.'

'Aren't you scared?'

'Of what?'

'What do you think? That you'll get your feet pulled.'

'Angelina, what a thing to say. And you, a woman of science believing in such superstitions.'

'Science, my arse, I've had mine pulled. A friend from university died three years ago, of kidney failure, you know, one of those things they discover one day and three days later there's nothing to be done. And it was as if the poor thing hadn't had time to say goodbye to her friends. I was here, totally relaxed, and sound asleep, and I swear she pulled them. Dead people like to say goodbye to me.'

'Well, no one's ever said goodbye to me. And no one's ever come to pull my feet.'

'But in a dead man's bed. It's impossible that it doesn't make a bit of an impression on you. I couldn't do it. You're very brave. What sheets are on the bed?'

'They're white with checks.'

'I gave those sheets to your dad. He hadn't bought himself new sheets for ten years.'

'I'm not surprised.'

'Those are the last sheets Gabriel slept in.'

'OK, don't get mystical on me. I'm going to stay here and my dad's not going to come to scare me, I swear he's got better things to do.'

'Can I tell you something?'

'Tell me something.'

'You're very good, Gabriel, a lot better than I was. You're going to get over this quickly.'

'Don't be fooled. I act like I'm fine, but it's a defence mechanism. I'm an expert at that, everybody knows it. A poker face is a defence mechanism. Cynicism is a defence mechanism.'

'And isn't it hard to keep pretending?'

'I play poker in my spare time.'

'Sure, you make jokes about it, but I'm jealous. What I wouldn't give for a bit of a poker face. Can you learn that? Where do they teach it? No, I swear, it hit me really hard being alone, after the bomb, being on my own at night. Then your dad showed up and it was like he rescued me, I held on really tight to him. Maybe that was my mistake. And then to see that he left me too. That he was also capable of hurting me. The truth is that hit me pretty hard. Who told me to build up my hopes? Who told me to be so naive? But it was really hard.'

'I know. Enough to make you stab him in the back. And on television.'

'You think what you like, my conscience is clear. I only know one thing, that Gabriel was someone else. In the end he wasn't the person we thought he was.'

235

'Not him nor anyone else, Angelina.'

'Well, on television, I wasn't talking about him, I was talking about the other one.'

'Sophist.'

'What's that?'

'It's what you are. A shameless sophist.'

'Is that an insult? Are you insulting me again?'

'More or less. But I don't feel like fighting.'

Silence.

'Me neither. I've turned out the light now, I've got a nice buzz, I'm tucked up here as if everything was fine, as if the world was all peaceful, as if I didn't have problems, and I know I'm cold, but I don't feel it, or I feel it but it doesn't matter . . . No, I don't want to fight either . . . it's the first time I've felt good all day. Though I am cold.'

'Well, put on something else. What are your pyjamas like?'

'It's a long nightgown, long, down to my knees. Light-blue cotton with dark-blue edging on the sleeves, really pretty.'

'That explains it. Don't you even have any socks on?'

'Yeah, socks as well.'

'Have you finished smoking now?'

'A while ago.'

'Good. Are you sleepy?'

'Not too sleepy, no, I'm a little tired. You?'

'I'm wide awake. I have to stay and wait for my dad.'

'Don't even joke about that, Gabriel, don't say those things. Look, I've got goosebumps all over now.' Silence. 'On my arms and on my neck.' Silence. 'I really loved him.'

'I did too, Angelina.'

'Everybody loved him. People loved him.'

'Yeah.'

'I'm sure his German friend loved him.'

'Sure.'

'So why did he do that to him? Why didn't he ever tell anyone, not even you? Why did he tell me he was coming back if he was tired of me and didn't want to see me any more? Why did he tell us so many lies?'

'Everyone tells lies, Angelina,' I said. 'The worst thing is that we don't notice. That's what should never happen. Liars should be infallible.'

'I don't know about infallible, but I would rather not know. Carry on, like before. Wouldn't you?'

'I'm not sure,' I heard myself say. 'I have wondered about that, I have.'

A few days later I paid Sara a surprise visit, I dragged her out for a walk down Fifth Avenue to Fourteenth Street, and we walked down as far as the place where they killed Gaitán. That had happened one afternoon – 1948, 9 April, one o'clock in the afternoon: the coordinates formed part of my life, and my life actually began more than a decade later – and twelve hours earlier my father had been listening to the dead man's last speech, the summing up in defence of Lieutenant Cortés: a man who had murdered out of jealousy, a uniformed Colombian Othello. Gaitán had been carried out of the courtroom on men's shoulders; my father, who had been waiting for this moment to approach him and try to congratulate him without his voice trembling, was repelled by the mob surrounding him. It was a whole year before my father dared to set foot again in the place where we now were; he would later return with some frequency, and each time would stop for a few seconds in silence before he went on his way. The pavement of Seventh Avenue is broken at that spot by the tram tracks (that don't go anywhere, that get lost under the pavement, because the trams, those trams with blue-tinted windows that my father told me about, haven't existed for years), and as I, standing in front of the Agustín Nieto building, read the black marble plaque that describes the assassination in more sentences than strictly necessary, Sara, thinking I wasn't looking, crouched down at the kerb — I thought she was going to pick up a dropped coin — and with two fingers touched the rail as if she were taking the pulse of a dying dog. I kept pretending I hadn't seen her, so as not to interrupt her private ceremony, and after several minutes of being a hindrance in that river of people and putting up with insults and shoves, I asked her to show me exactly where the Granada Pharmacy had been in those years when a suicidal man could buy more than ninety sleeping pills there. A year and a half after Konrad Deresser's suicide, Gaitán's murderer had been taken by force inside the pharmacy to prevent the furious mob from lynching him, and from the pharmacy he'd been dragged by the furious mob, which had punched and kicked him to death and dragged his naked body to the presidential palace (there is a photograph that shows the body leaving a trail of shreds of clothing behind like a snake shedding its skin: the photo isn't very good, and in it Juan Roa Sierra is barely a pale corpse, almost an ectoplasm, crossed by the black stain of his sex). And there we were, standing where Josefina must have stood, facing the road along which, on that 9 April 1948, the ectoplasm of the assassin and the people who had taken it upon themselves to lynch him had gone. 'No, I didn't know Enrique was alive,' Sara was saying. 'And, see how things stand: if your dad wasn't dead, I wouldn't be able to believe it. I'd think it was one of that little woman's lies, a halfway intelligent fabrication to justify the grotesque action of selling herself for that interview. Actually, I'd prefer to be able to do what so many people do: convince myself. Convince myself that it's not true. Convince myself that it's all Angelina's invention. But I can't, and I can't for a reason: your dad is dead, and in some way he was killed for going to see him, for visiting Enrique. I bet you've thought of this: if Enrique weren't alive, Gabriel's death wouldn't mean anything.' Of course it had already occurred to me; she didn't need to say it, because Sara already knew. (Since our conversations for the book I got used to not saying things that to Sara would be superfluous. Sara *knew*: that was her mark of identity.) She went on: 'Of course you can get all philosophical, ask, for example, why should his death mean anything, does any death ever mean anything. We could be very nihilistic and very elegant. But none of that matters, because Enrique isn't alive for us. If he was, he would have called me by now, or he might even have come to the funeral, no? But, none of that. Alive or dead, in Medellín or in Seventh Heaven, it's all the same, because Enrique wants to be dead to me, he's spent fifty years willing it so. And I'm not going to be the one to spoil that now. I'm not going to be the one who meddles in his life without being invited, and much less now that your father's dead.'

From the pharmacy, or from its former location, we walked towards the Plaza de Bolívar, trying to follow the elder Deresser's route, not for fetishism or even for nostalgia, but because we were in unspoken agreement that nothing, not even the most skilful tale, could replace the world's potential for truth, the world of tangible things and people that rub against you and bump into you, and the smells of piss by the walls and people's sweaty clothes, and piss in beggar's sweaty clothes. We passed in front of the Civil Court

Building, where the lawyers' offices were where my father worked until, through a mixture of luck and talent, he was able to devote himself to the occupation that suited him best, and in the gallery that passes through the building, and that is usually full of pedlars selling sweets and plastic dolls and even second-hand hats, Sara wanted to look for some little present for her youngest grandson, and ended up buying a dented old toy truck the size of a cigarette lighter, a green truck with doors that opened and good shock absorbers on the back (the old man insisted on showing us how well they worked against the floor tiles of the gallery). And later, sitting on the steps of the cathedral, Sara took the little truck out of her handbag and tested its shock absorbers as she told me that once, when she was young, she had believed that in Bogotá the world was about to end, because the pigeons in the Plaza de Bolívar started dying all at once, and if you were walking across the plaza during the day a pigeon could easily have a heart attack in full flight and fall on your head. Later she found out that a whole ton of corn, the corn that the women in the plaza sold in cones of newspaper so children and old folks could pass the time feeding the pigeons, had been poisoned without anyone knowing why and without those responsible ever being found, or even pursued. Bogotá, Sara told me, had never stopped being a demented place, but those years were undoubtedly among the most demented of all. In those years, this was a city where poisoned pigeons announced the end of the world, where aficionados, bored by a bull's docility and perhaps that of the bullfighter, would invade the ring to tear the animal apart with their bare hands, where people killed each other in protest at another's death. Three days after that 9 April, Peter Guterman had brought his family to Bogotá, because he thought it necessary that his daughter should see the damage, touch the broken windows, enter the burnt ruins, go up to the terrace roofs, if they were allowed, where the sharpshooters had been stationed to fire on the crowds, and see the bloodstains on the same rooftops from a wounded marksman, and at least manage to glimpse all that which they'd manage to escape (they now knew) at the last moment. This sort of pedagogical expedition was normal for him, and it took Sara many years to realize that behind it there was nothing more than an impulse to justify himself: her father wanted to confirm that he'd done the right thing in leaving Germany; he hoped that the brutality of this country which was now his would condone or legitimate the right to escape from the old country, from the earlier brutality. That was why Sara hid from Peter Guterman the twenty metres of black alpaca that my father had bought for a quarter of the price after the looting and from which he had had a suit made, with a pleated skirt and short jacket, with buttons on the front, to give her as a birthday present. Of course, Peter would not have liked his daughter going around dressed in material stolen from a display window, much less stolen during riots: that had too many echoes, lent itself to too many associations. But wasn't it stupid or exaggerated – Sara had thought at the time – to see in the shop windows of Bogotá a reference, reduced yet tangible, to the shop windows of Berlin? Then she'd seen photographs of the looted shops in Bogotá, and had changed her mind. Kling's Jeweller's. Wassermann's Jeweller's. Glauser & Co., Swiss watches. The names weren't always legible on the broken glass; they were always, however, recognizable. Sara never wore the suit in her father's presence.

Later we looked for the boarding house where Konrad Deresser spent his final days, and were surprised to find it easily: in this city, which in six months can render itself unrecognizable, the probability that a building from half a century ago should still be standing was minimal, if not illusory. And nevertheless there it was, so little changed that Sara could recognize it even though there was no longer a boarding house there, but four floors of offices for failed or clandestine businessmen. On the white façade there were yellowing posters with red and blue lettering announcing bullfights, screenwriting workshops, meetings of Marxist cells, Dominican merengue festivals, poetry readings, Russian-for-beginners courses and football matches in the Olaya Herrera stadium. When we went up we found that Konrad and Josefina's room was now a calligraphy studio. A woman with her hair up and wearing bifocals received us, sitting in a swivel chair in front of an architect's table, under a halogen light that was the only luxury in the place. Her work was to write the names of graduates in Gothic letters for the four or five universities in central Bogotá. That's how she earned her living: putting strangers' names on sheets of translucent paper. She told us she worked freelance. No, she didn't know this building used to be a boarding house. No, as far as she knew the layout of the offices (which had once been rooms) had never been changed. Yes, she was happy in her work, she hadn't done any formal studies and had learned this craft by correspondence course. Every semester she wrote, or rather drew, a thousand or so names, and thus supported her two small children; she couldn't complain, she even earned more than her husband, who drove a taxi, a Chevette, what did we think, one of the new ones. She shook our hands to say goodbye. She had a thick callus on the middle finger of her right hand; the callus was covered with a stain of Indian ink, dark and symmetrical like a melanoma. As we walked towards the Parque de los Periodistas, Sara and I speculated about the room: where would Konrad and Josefina's bed have been, where would they have put the record player, if the bathroom door (this was unlikely) might be the same one. The absurd and self-indulgent idea that this could be of any importance distracted us for a while. When we left, after walking a couple of blocks in silence, Sara said, for no particular reason, 'During that time, we grew apart. I couldn't look him in the eye. I slighted him, I couldn't get it through my head that he could be capable of such a thing. And at the same time I understood very well, you know, the way everyone would understand. That mixture scared me, I don't know why. I can't explain what kind of fear it was. Fear of knowing I would have done the same. Or fear, precisely, of not having done it. There are many informers: you don't have to be at war to talk about someone else in certain circumstances. I grew distant from him, I pushed him aside, just like what's happening now, when this city is pushing him aside when he can't do anything about it. I started to see him as an undesirable. And suddenly I felt closer to him than to anyone else, it was that simple. I felt that from that moment on he would be able to understand me if I wanted to explain my life. That's the worst thing about being foreign.' And then she fell silent again.

I found out one day, without anyone taking the trouble to call and inform me, that Rosario University was going to remove my father's name from their list of illustrious alumni, that they were also going to withdraw his doctorate *honoris causa* – which my father had renounced at the end of the 1980s, when the university awarded the same distinction to Queen Sofia of Spain – and the granting of the Medal of Civic Merit would be cancelled, annulled, revoked (I don't know the applicable verb). That was how it was: the award had been decreed, as it was announced at the funeral, but the formal presentation hadn't yet been made, and the presenters, realizing or discovering that there was still time to retract, preferred not to present it. I didn't call the Court; I didn't find out to whom I could appeal, who to look for in the tangle of legislative or political bureaucracy, who to turn to if this were legally possible or what lawyer might be willing to take on such a case, who I could call, with more diplomatic intentions, to ask for explanations; I didn't demand official notification, nor a resolution, nor a copy of the decree annulling the previous decree: I preferred not to look for the document, whichever it was, that made my father the official pariah of the moment and guaranteed him what we'll all get sooner or later, his fifteen minutes as an untouchable. What I did keep is the newspaper clipping, because the incident, of course, was news: MEDAL OF CIVIC MERIT RETRACTED FOR UNBECOMING CONDUCT, ran the headline. 'There are internal pressures,' declared a source that preferred to remain anonymous. 'The reputation of the award would be called into question and granting it now would be a dishonour to those who have received it more deservingly.' I should say it didn't affect me too much, perhaps due to the anaesthetic effect of the letters that had arrived at the television station during the week following Angelina's interview, and that the station had very diligently forwarded to the apartment, without attaching too much importance to the fact that the addressee no longer existed (and in some cases without attaching importance to the fact that my father wasn't even the addressee, but merely the subject). There weren't many, but they were quite varied; in any case, there were enough to surprise me with the level of interest the public takes when it comes to insulting, its skill at assuming the position of victim and reacting as is expected in a respectable society. Decent Colombians, supportive Colombians, upright and indignant Colombians, Catholic Colombians for whom one betrayal is all betrayals: all condemned when there was condemning to be done, like good soldiers of collective morals. 'Dear sir, I would like to say I thought the interviewed young lady's bravery was *admirable* and thank you for speaking the truth. The world is definitely full of *villains* and they must be unmasked.' 'Doctor Santoro, I do not know you, but I know some like you. You are a hypocritical snitch, fucking backstabber, I hope you rot in hell, you son of a bitch.' There were some more objective letters, at once comforting and painfully disdainful. 'Let us not forget, gentlemen of the press, that this whole matter was but a tiny detail in wartime. Beside the six million, this was collateral damage.' There was even one addressed to me: 'Santoro, rest easy, keep writing and publishing your stuff, carry on acting the part of the great writer, we all know who you are now and the sort you come from. Your dad was nothing but a mediocrity and an impostor and you're the same, at the end of the day, a chip off the old block. When's your next book coming out? Signed: Your fan club.'

I didn't talk to Sara about this, as it would have annoyed her, and she, who had found out on her own about the matter of the medal, also decided not to mention it to me, in spite of our circuit through the streets of the centre – that retreat, somewhere between tourism and superstition, to the events of the 1940s – seeming to permit those subjects or even demand them. No, we didn't talk about that: not about the dishonour, or about the untouchable, or about the possible consequences the dishonour could have on the son of the untouchable. We didn't talk about the past my father had once tried to modify, in front of his rhetoric class, with the sole objective of defending himself against my book. We didn't talk about my father's death or about other dead people we would have liked to have with us then; we didn't talk any more about Enrique, the living person who wanted to be dead to Sara. When we returned to her apartment and she invited me to stay for lunch, and she went into the kitchen to fry some slices of plantain while she heated up a sort of goulash she'd made that morning, I thought, for no other reason than being back in her apartment, that Sara and I were alone, true, but we had each other, and what invaded me like a fever was a feeling of gratitude so strong I had to sit down on one of the sofas in the living room to wait for the heaviness, the dizziness to pass. And while we were having lunch, so late that Sara's head was starting to ache, this kind woman seemed to have noticed, because she looked at me with half a smile (the complicit glance of lovers who meet by chance at a dinner party). The complicity was a new feeling, at least for me; the sharing of interests and also of worries, having loved the same person so much had linked us in this way, had tied us, and ironically underlined the fact that Sara had been the one to prophesy the terrible deeds of the past, a sort of reverse Cassandra. I didn't know that could happen between two people, and the experience, that afternoon, was disconcerting, because it revealed the great lack I'd suffered growing up without a mother and how much I'd unknowingly missed. Sara was talking to me about the day I'd dropped off a copy of my book for my father. 'He called me immediately,' she told me. 'I had to go over to his house, I thought he was going to have some sort of attack or something, I hadn't seen him that bad since your mother's death.'

That's when I realized that my father had read the book as soon as he'd received it, and he'd done so with a fine-tooth comb and in record time, looking for declarations that could give him away and trying to read as fast as possible as if it wasn't already too late to remedy eventual damage, as if what he had in hand was not a published book but an uncorrected manuscript. 'He didn't find anything, but he found it all,' said Sara. 'The whole book seemed like a giant trail leading to him, pointing at him. Every time the Hotel Sabaneta is mentioned, he felt incriminated, discovered. Every time the blacklists are discussed in the book, lives damaged or simply affected by the lists, he felt the same. "I did something like that," he said. "They're going to find out. Thanks to this book of yours, they're going to find out. My life lasted this long, Sara, you two have just fucked up my life." I tried to put his mind at ease, but there was no way to get his fears out of his head. He said, "People who remember the Deressers are going to put two and two together. There are still people alive, people like us, who lived through all that. They're going to put two and two together. They're going to realize, Sara, they're going to know it was me, who did what I did. How could you betray me like this?" And then he insulted me, he who had always treated me like a protected little sister. "I should have expected it from you," he said. "You don't care what happens to me. You've always believed I deserve to be punished for what I did to old Konrad." And I told him it wasn't true, people make mistakes, were we never going to leave that behind? But he went on: "Yes, you've probably even prayed for me to get my just deserts, don't play innocent. But my own son? How could he do this to me?" He got so paranoid it was frightening. I tried to explain, and it didn't do the slightest bit of good. "He's not doing anything

247

to you, Gabriel, because he doesn't know anything. Your son doesn't know anything and nobody's going to tell him, least of all me. I'm not going to tell him, it's something from your past, not even mine, and your past doesn't belong to me. No, I'm not going to tell him, I haven't told him. And besides, it's not in the book. There is not a single sentence in the book that points to you." "The whole book points to me. It's a book about the lives of Germans and how Germans suffered during the war. I'm part of that. But this is not going to stop here, Sara. This book is an attack on me, no more, no less, an attempted homicide." "And what are you going to do?" I asked. It was a stupid question, because it could have only one answer. He was going to do what he'd always done: speak. But this time he spoke in writing. This time he conceded that his purposes required a more extended medium than words spoken in an auditorium. You know what he was like, Gabriel, you know your father's opinion of newspapers, of newscasts. The disdain he held them in, no? The poor man would have liked to live in a world where news passed by word of mouth, and one would walk down the street talking to people, saying things like, Did you know they killed Jaime Pardo? Did you hear that Gabriel Santoro gave a magnificent speech? And nevertheless he resorted to them, he resorted to one of his despised newspapers, he made use of them. Our book seemed like an attack to him, and he thought he could exercise the legitimate right of self-defence. The only way that occurred to him was to discredit you, ridicule you, and discredit and ridicule don't even count if they're not scattered all around as gossip. You know that. The funny thing about ridicule is that everyone talks, the victim feels like everyone's staring at him in the street even though it's not really like that. If he did such a thing, he wouldn't just sink the book, but he'd call attention to himself. But you can't talk reason to a psychotic. Gabriel the psychotic, Gabriel the mad genius. Did he tell you how he wrote the review?'

'No, we didn't talk about it. We were working on the reconciliation. The details didn't matter.'

'Well, I was with him. That was the day after his reading of your book and our chat. We went to the Supreme Court and he got one of the magistrates to lend him a secretary, and he took her to the hall where he gave his lectures. He asked her to sit up in the tiers, as if she were a student, and he dictated the review as if it were a class. It was fascinating to watch. Sorry for saying so, I know full well how much it hurt to see it published. But for me it was a spectacle, like seeing Baryshnikov dance. Your dad dictated it and didn't alter a single word. As if he had written a draft and was reading it out for a clean copy. With commas, full stops, dashes, parentheses, all dictated just the way it appeared in print, all in one go, without hesitating over a single word or changing an opinion or honing an idea. And the ideas in that review. The humour, the irony. The precision. The precision of the cruelty, sure, but cruelty also has its virtuosos. It was masterly.'

'I know,' I said. 'I saw him do that a couple of times. My dad had a computer in his head.'

'The worst thing is that nothing proved him wrong. Obviously, no one read between the lines, as he said, no one accused him of anything. People just noticed the book, commented on the father-and-son thing, and laughed a little . . . and then what was to come came to pass. But back then nothing happened. "You see?" he said to me later. "I was right about my strategy. It was terrible to have to do it, but I

249

was right. I escaped this time, Sara. I escaped by the skin of my teeth." Like madmen, like people who are ill. Like that German joke about a fellow who snaps his fingers all day long. His family takes him to see a psychiatrist and the psychiatrist asks him, Why do you snap your fingers all the time? And he says, To scare away the elephants. And the psychiatrist: But there are no elephants in Germany, my good sir. And the madman: You see, Doctor, see how well it works? Well, that's how your dad was. Your dad was the madman of the joke.'

While Sara was telling her German joke, I saw in her face the face of a little girl, the girl who had arrived in Colombia at the end of the 1930s. It was like a flash photo, a nanosecond of clarity when the wrinkles disappeared from around the smiling eyes. Yes, I had grown very fond of this woman, more than I'd ever suspected, and part of that fondness was a consequence of that which she had felt for the friend of her youth, her shadow brother, the fondness that years later had its refraction in me, preventing me, in some way, from the pathetic need to write letters to my father, turn into a beetle, ask permission to sleep in the castle. 'See, Doctor, see how well it works?' Sara repeated. 'I can imagine it perfectly. I think of your dad, I think of the madman of the joke, and they're the same person. The mad look on Gabriel's face sometimes.' In this memorial atmosphere of a private anniversary, the best thing I could think of to do was put on the record of German songs and ask my hostess to tell me about the one my father liked so much, to translate it for me and sum it up so I could understand it, and she told me about the spring that arrives, the girls who sing, the poet Otto Licht, whose name rhymes with the word 'poem'. '*Licht, Gedicht*,' said Sara, and laughed sadly. 'How could Gabriel not like that?' Later I asked her to write out the lyrics for me; although I can't now be sure, it's possible that I was already thinking of transcribing them into this book, as in fact I did.

Because it was after that day – after walking down Seventh Avenue and visiting what had been Konrad Deresser's boarding house, after passing in front of the pharmacy that no longer existed, which didn't make it invisible, where the old man had bought his pills, after sitting on the steps of the cathedral where they sang the *Te Deum* the day that, thousands of kilometres from the Plaza de Bolívar, the Second World War ended, after having been in the places I'd been in a thousand times and nevertheless didn't know, had never seen, which were as opaque and uncertain to me as the life of Gabriel Santoro – it was after all that, I say, that the idea of this report came into my head for the first time. That night I took a few notes, I sketched out a couple of lists of contents; I followed the few habits I've picked up, less as an aid than as an amulet, over the course of my journalistic career. And several months later, the notes had already filled a whole notebook and there were reams of documents piling up on my desk. One of those notes said: *Nothing would be as it is if they hadn't operated on him.* I read it two or three times, with the computer already turned on, and it seemed to me, looking back, that the phrase contained some truth, for perhaps my father would still be alive if he hadn't received the gift of the second life, accompanied, of course, by the obligation to make the most of it, by the need to redeem himself. It was that process I was interested in getting down in writing: the reasons a man who has been mistaken in his youth tries in old age to rectify his error, and the consequences that attempt can have on him and those around him:

especially, above all, the consequences it had for me, his son, the only person in the world liable to inherit his faults, but also his redemption. And in the process of doing so, I thought, in the process of writing about him, my father would stop being the false figure he himself had taken on, and would reclaim his position before me as our dead all do: leaving me as an inheritance the obligation to discover him, to interpret him, to find out who he had really been. And thinking about this, the rest came with the clarity of an explosion. I closed the notebook, as if I had this book memorized, and began to write about my father's sick heart.

Bogotá, February 1994

V

Postscript, 1995

A YEAR AFTER FINISHING IT, I published the book that you, reader, have just read. During that year several things happened; the most important, by a long way, was the death of Sara Guterman, who didn't live to see herself transformed for a second time into a character in a chronicle, and to whom I could not explain that the book's title, *The Informers*, referred to her as much as to my father, although the information each had supplied was of such a different nature. Her death occurred without pain or agony, just as predicted: the vein exploded, the blood inundated her brain, and in a matter of minutes Sara had died, lying in her bed and ready for a little siesta. It seems she had spent the morning rushing around from one side of Bogotá to the other, trying (without success) to mediate between the Goethe Institute and the cultural attaché of the German Embassy in organizing, with due anticipation, the commemorations of May 1995, the fiftieth anniversary of the end of the war. The German community of Bogotá was divided: some wanted the Embassy to take charge of the ceremonies, as an exorcism and also an atonement, or, at least, as a strategy to improve their image; for others, decisions over the quality and size of the anniversary should be left in the hands of the Colombian government, it was not a good idea to go around stepping on toes or reminding everyone, Germans and Colombians, of what everyone would have preferred (consciously, voluntarily) to forget with the passing years. In any case, the people who had lived through the war were fewer and fewer, and those still alive were the children and grandchildren of those Germans: people who, in spite of their surnames, had no affiliation whatsoever with the other country, had never visited it nor ever intended to do so, and in some cases hadn't even heard the language apart from the insults and interjections of an enraged grandfather. Among the things Sara had proposed and planned to carry out was an itinerant lecture – secondary schools, cultural associations, universities, German schools and Hebrew schools – that we would give together on the events related in *A Life in Exile* and, more importantly, on the events not related there, for at the time of writing Sara and I had decided by mutual consent to exclude a number of subjects, so as not to give her life story an inappropriate tone of grievance, but the discussion of which at a moment of anniversaries and commemorations seemed, more than permissible, pertinent and necessary. Since we thought we had time, since Sara's death occurred without any warning or decline, the only part of the lecture we'd managed to prepare was the selection of certain material. Sara looked through her Pandora's boxes and handed me a folder of well-chosen paragraphs, and well-chosen phrases under-lined within those paragraphs. She intended to comment publicly on many texts that she felt had been unjustly ignored until now, and among them whole sentences from the Minister of Foreign Affairs, López de Mesa (Jews had a 'parasitical orientation in life', and in Latin America there were 'many undesirable elements, most of them Jews'), but, thanks to the antagonistic aneurysm, none of that came to pass. Sara arrived home feeling tired one day, put a frozen chicken breast under a stream of running water and lay down to rest. She didn't wake up again. The downstairs neighbour thought it odd that twelve hours later the pipes were still making a noise; she went upstairs to see if Sara had a problem or if the apartment was flooded, and ended up calling her sons and asking them to come with a set of keys and open the door; and the next day, as soon as was possible, Sara was buried in the Jewish section of the Central Cemetery. After the Kaddish, someone, a bald man who spoke with a very pronounced accent – I'd become an expert on the subject, and knew what that implied: he was married to a German woman, not a Colombian, and he spoke to his children in German, not Spanish – said a few words that I liked: he compared Sara's life to a brick wall, and said that one could have placed a spirit level on top and the bubble would have stayed in the very centre, between the two lines, without ever moving from there. That was Sara: a solid and perfectly level wall. I felt that phrase did more justice to her memory than all the two hundred pages of my book, and I thought, for once, that it wouldn't be a bad thing to say so. But I didn't manage it, because as I tried to go over to the bald man, trying to think of how to explain who I was and why I'd liked his little elegy so much, I found myself face to face with Sara's eldest son, who turned the tables of the situation in an unpredictable way when he broke away from those attempting to give him their condolences to greet me, to hug me and say, 'I'm very sorry about your dad. My mum loved him very much, you know.' I thought he was giving me his condolences (although rather belatedly); I immediately realized that he wasn't referring to my father's death, but to his destroyed reputation.

Among the mourners were the owners of the Central Bookshop, Hans and Lilly Ungar. We said hello, I promised to go and see them one of these days, but, involved as I was in the writing of *The Informers*, never managed to do so. And, in

May, once the book was published, when I found a message on my answering machine in which Lilly invited me in a formal and rather peremptory tone to come to the bookshop, I thought the invitation was in some way related to Sara Guterman, or, at least, to that never-delivered lecture on the hidden anti-Semitism of Colombian politicians, for Hans Ungar (everyone knew this) was one of the most direct victims of the prohibitions López de Mesa used to minimize the number of Jews arriving in Colombia, and he often said in interviews, but also in casual conversations, that his parents had died in German concentration camps largely due to the impossibility of obtaining a Colombian visa for them such as the one he'd obtained and with which he'd entered the country, from his native Austria, in 1938. So anyway, when I arrived for the appointment I found them both, Hans and Lilly, sitting beside the solid grey table that functioned as the meeting place for the Germans of Bogotá and from which, with the help of a dial telephone and an old typewriter – a Remington Rand, tall and heavy like a scale model of a coliseum – they ran the bookshop. In the main display cabinet there were three copies of my book. Lilly was wearing a burgundy-coloured turtleneck sweater; Hans was wearing a tie and under his suit jacket he had put on an argyle sweater. On the table, beside a tall glass of water and a coffee cup stained with red lipstick, was the magazine *Semana*, which, exactly as Sara had suggested, had just published an article by way of commemoration, six pages (including an advertisement for South American Insurance) that there, lost among the rest of the news of a country not lacking in news, seemed liable to be overlooked.

The magazine was open to a page where there were two illustrations. On the left, a letter addressed to a certain Fritz

Moschell, and dated 16 July 1934, and underneath: *Document of the time: Everything to do with Germans was considered suspicious.* Almost the entire remaining space was taken up with a photograph of the Brandenburg Gate after the bombings. The caption, in this case, was: *Berlin destroyed: In Colombia the echoes of the conflict were barely felt.* It occurred to me then that this was the true reason for the meeting (for summoning me). Lilly offered me coffee; Hans, sitting beside us, seemed not to be listening to our conversation, and had his eyes fixed on the door to the bookshop and on the people who came in and out and asked for things and paid. After finishing her coffee, Lilly produced a piece of paper and I ended up helping her to correct a letter she intended to send to the magazine. 'In the article entitled "World War II a là Colombiana", published in your 9 May issue, I read that during the Second World War "López de Mesa's supposed anti-Semitism only complicated things". To anyone familiar with the circular that the Minister of Foreign Affairs sent to the Colombian consulates in 1939, who has read therein the order to raise "all objections humanly possible to granting visas to any more passports of Jewish elements", the Minister's anti-Semitism is much more than a supposition. I understand that the subject is a difficult one for Colombian citizens to discuss, but it should not be so in the media. For that reason I would like to make a small clarification . . .' This was just one of the interpolations I helped her to draft; when between the two of us we had finished writing the letter, and revised it to make sure there were no errors of any kind, Lilly folded the paper and put it in one of the drawers of her desk so carelessly, with such lack of interest, that I couldn't help but wonder whether the favour she'd asked of me was perhaps a pretext, and whether the idea of composing with my help a sort of tiny and already superfluous protest wasn't the way Lilly or Hans had invented to see me and to be closer to Sara Guterman, their recently deceased friend. After all, the Central Bookshop was the only bookshop that still had copies of *A Life in Exile*, in spite of the fact that seven years had passed since its publication. The Ungars had read the book; they'd thought it honest; Hans had even mentioned it on the radio, on an HJCK programme he contributed to every once in a while. But maybe I was mistaken; maybe my visit had nothing to do with Sara; maybe these suspicions were absurd, because, all things considered, the matter of the letter was perfectly plausible. There was the magazine, there were the Ungars, there was the draft of the letter; there was no reason to suspect they hadn't asked me there to correct it, just as I'd done.

It was only a few minutes before the bookshop closed for lunch, so I stood up and began to say goodbye. But then Estela, the serious-looking woman with a commanding voice who ran the till, came over and placed a pile of ten or twelve copies of *The Informers* on the table, and while Lilly asked me to sign them, and told me she hadn't read it yet but intended to as soon as she had a free weekend, Estela turned off half the lights, left and closed the door behind her. Without the street noise, the horns and motors, the bookshop fell so silent that I could have felt intimidated. Hans had stopped beside the table of German books, and through the green lenses of his glasses (the same ones he'd worn as long as I could remember) looked at them as any other customer might. 'He has read it,' Lilly told me quietly. 'He still doesn't know what to think. That's why he hasn't told you. A friend of his was on the list. It was at the end of the war and for something very silly, like requesting a book from the Cervantes Bookshop or something like that. How do you feel? What have people said to you?' I shrugged, as if to say I'd rather not embark on that conversation, and then she said, 'Hans knew them.'

'Who?'

'The Deressers.'

It wasn't so surprising, except that German and Austrian immigrants almost never formed part of the same circles: there were rivalries between them of the sort usual among the stateless when they notice (or believe they've noticed) that they have to dispute the right to the new territory. But it did indeed surprise me that Lilly or Hans might have known my father without me knowing. 'No, we never met him,' Lilly said when I asked her, looking at the keys of the Remington. 'Neither Hans nor I, I'm sure of that, he's told me several times.' For the second time I suffered an attack of paranoia. I thought Lilly was lying to me, that she had known my father and had also known his secret, the secret of his mistake, but over the years she'd managed to erase it from her life, to forget so completely that she could serve me as a customer in her bookshop without a single muscle in her face giving her away, she could talk to me about my first book without my noticing anything in her voice, and she could pretend, when she read my father's review of their friend Sara's life story, that she didn't know the subterranean motivations for his resentment. Was she lying? Was that possible? I wondered if I might have forever lost the capacity to trust people; whether finding out about my father's treachery and, to make it worse, having written and published the 250-page confession I'd just written and published had transformed me: made me paranoid, suspicious, wary, turned me into a pitiable, pathetic creature, able to see conspiracies in the affection of a woman as transparent as Lilly Ungar. Was I doomed? Had my father's double face contaminated me to the point of obliging me always to suspect deceit in the rest of humanity? Or had I been contaminated by the act of telling it in writing? Had writing *The Informers* been a mistake?

One of the first reviews of the book accused it, or accused me, of a deplorable mixture of narcissism and exhibitionism; and, in spite of the scant respect I had for the reviewer, in spite of his bull-necked prose, the obvious paucity of his reading and his crew-cut reasoning, in spite of the fact that each of his sentences revealed a lack of rhythm, grammar and syntax, in spite of the fact that he'd used his space for commentary to put his own inferiority complex (but calling it a complex would be flattery) and his literary failures (but calling them literary would be hyperbole) on display, in spite of his reproaches being little more than bar-room gossip and his praise being cocktail-party clichés, in the days that followed I couldn't get his accusations out of my head. Maybe transforming the private into the public was a perversion – accepted, it's true, in these days of voyeurs and busybodies, of gossips, of indiscretion – and publishing a confession of any sort was, deep down, a behaviour as sick as that of a man who exposes his thick cock to women in the street just for the pleasure of shocking them. After reading the book, and seeing himself included in it, my friend Jorge Mor had called me and said, 'You've got every right, Gabriel, you've got every right in the world to tell whatever you like. But I felt strange, as if I'd walked into your room and seen you fucking someone. By accident, without meaning to. Reading the book I felt embarrassed, and I hadn't done anything to be ashamed of. You oblige people to know what they might not want to know. Why?' I told him that no one was obliged to read the book; that writing a memoir or any sort of autobiography implied touching on private aspects of a life, and the reader knows that. 'Well, that's just it,' said Jorge. 'Why do you want to talk publicly about what's private? Hasn't it occurred to you that with this book you've done exactly what the girlfriend did to your dad, just more elegantly?' The attack took me by surprise, and I muttered a couple of rude replies and hung up, without trying to hide my fury. How dare he make such a comparison? In my book, I'd laid myself bare, I'd deliberately put myself in a position of vulnerability, I had refused to allow my father's errors to be forgotten: in many ways, I'd assumed responsibility for those errors. Because faults are inherited; guilt is inherited; one pays for what one's ancestors have done, everyone knows that. Was it not brave to confront this fact? Was it not, at least, commendable? And then my head filled with things my father had once said to me: he too had spoken to me about the private and the public, about the nobility of those who keep quiet and the parasitism of those who reveal. And he hadn't stopped there. *That's why you wrote it, so everyone would know how good you are.* My father returned from the dead to accuse me. *Look at me, admire me, I'm on the side of the good guys, I condemn, I denounce.* I'd used him: I'd taken advantage, for my own exhibitionist and egocentric objectives, of the most terrible thing that happened in his life. *Read me, love me, give me prizes for compassion, for goodness.* At that moment I was no more than a narcissist, sublimated by the false prestige of the printed word, it's true, but a narcissist when it came right down to it. Divulging my father's disgrace was no more than a subtle, renewed betrayal: Jorge was right. I asked myself: Would I have been capable of publishing this book if my father had survived the accident in Las Palmas? The answer was clear, and also humiliating.

I suddenly felt out of place, uncomfortable; talking to Lilly Ungar in the closed bookshop, I felt like an intruder. 'Maybe it was a bad thing to do,' I said, at the same time as I finished signing the last copy. 'Maybe I shouldn't have published this book.' And I told her about a strange thing that had happened to me that week: I was on the way out of one of the publicity events the book's publication compelled when a member of the audience, the only man in a bow tie in the whole auditorium, came over and asked me how Sara was, if I didn't think it necessary to force her to undergo the surgery, or at least convince her to move to a warmer climate, since her sons seemed completely uninterested in doing what they should to protect her life. I almost told him off, but then, in a matter of seconds, found myself telling him that Sara had died and about the funeral and how sad we'd been, because I thought the man was not just a reader, but that he knew her, that he was a relative or a friend of hers; and when I realized that wasn't the case it was too late to react, because my book was responsible for that intrusion and it was my fault that a stranger seemed to know or created the illusion of having known Sara. I was talking about that – of the invasions the book seemed to invite, of lost privacy, of narcissistic satisfaction, of the way the book had taken the place of my memories, of the probable embezzlement of other people's lives and among them my father's, of all those undesirable consequences of something as innocent as a confession, and of the absence, or the non-existence, of the desirable consequences that I had foreseen – when Lilly interrupted me. 'I didn't ask you here to write silly letters, dear, and much less to sign books,' she said, 'but I wanted to sound you out first, listen to you talk for a while. To see what state you were in, sweetie. To make sure I wasn't doing something stupid.' And she turned over an envelope that had been sitting on the desk the whole time, half hidden by the magazine *Semana* and the huge typewriter, and read out in her strong accent and guttural *r*s the words written on the front, under the stamp: *Señor Gabriel Santoro, care of Hans and Lilly Ungar*. It was a letter from Enrique Deresser. He'd read the book and asked me to go to see him.

The next day, at eight in the morning, I drove to Medellín, taking the highway from that inscrutably named place, Siberia. There was a four-hour journey between Bogotá and La Dorada, which marked the halfway point, and that was, at the time, one of the most inhospitable roads in the country, so I thought I'd do it without stopping, have lunch in La Dorada and then complete the second stage. I think I negotiated the route and its obstacles quite well. Leaving Bogotá means, among other feats, getting over a mountain range. 'Let's see if we can make the journey without anybody humming "Bolívar crosses the Andes",' my father used to say when he took my mother and me on a trip: that was one of the few verses of the Colombian national anthem he could listen to without getting indignant. (For me, too, leaving Bogotá has always been, more than tiresome, gruelling and torturous, but I've never been able satisfactorily to explain why I only feel comfortable in this fucking city, why I'm incapable of spending more than two weeks in any other city in the world. Everything I need is here; what isn't here strikes me as unnecessary. Perhaps this is another inheritance from my father: the will not to be expelled by this city so deft at expulsions.) I endured the stench of the cattle ranches, I endured the cold fog of the high plateaux and the violence of the following descent, the explosion in the nostrils of the aggressive smells and the silver onslaught of the *yarumo* trees and the uproar of the canaries and cardinals, I endured, as I crossed the Magdalena – that river with no fishermen or nets, because it no longer has any fish – the stupefying heat and the absence of wind. The second bridge was or is a sort of giant set of false teeth, metallic when the sun shone on the rails, fragile as old wood when crunching indecently under the weight of the cars. Before crossing the Magdalena, a soldier, probably stationed at the Air Force base – his helmet so loose that his voice echoed inside it – stopped me, asked for my papers, looked at them as if they were in another language and handed them back to me marked with the bellicose sweat of his hands, with a drop or two from his helmeted forehead. I didn't ask why he was stopping people so far from the base. He seemed young; he seemed to be afraid there, so near Honda and Cocorná and other unfortunate place names, so near the rumble, or the phantom rumble, of guerrilla attacks.

Anyone who has driven this route knows this is where you accelerate. Here, after crossing the river, cars go crazy. It's not known whether it's also fear (you have to avoid being stopped, being run off the road and forced out of your car), or if it's the twenty minutes of a straight strip of good road that, though not completely smooth, is decent and serviceable. In any case, needles scale speedometers hysterically; the strongest smell is not that of cow dung from the beasts sleeping beneath the trees, but that of burnt rubber: the rubber of tires ruined (tortured) by speed. I can say I did not snub tradition. It wasn't quite twelve when I parked in front of a restaurant, under a mango tree. Inside, two frenzied fans whipped the air, two white circles, almost translucent, flying a short distance from the low ceiling. The seats and tables were painted wooden boards nailed on top of four thin sticks: everything was designed to encourage the air to flow, everything willed the air to circulate because hot still air was the enemy. (The humidity condensed everywhere, and that seemed to obsess the owners of the place: that the water wouldn't evaporate.) In three-quarters of an hour I'd had lunch and started the engine again, as if I had a specific time to arrive, as if an interviewer was waiting to offer me a job. It was impossible not to think that my body, stuck in a car at eighty or a hundred kilometres per hour, was following the route that Angelina and my father had taken three years earlier, like the mime artists who follow unsuspecting people in Parque Santander. Time was a two-tiered bridge: they were on the bottom level, I was on the top. And at some point in this parallel journey, when the highway suddenly began to look familiar to me – there were landscapes I was sure I'd seen before in spite of this being the first time I'd made this journey – I thought that a fictitious memory had installed itself in my head from thinking and rethinking my father's journey while writing my book. I spent a good while trying to discover the cause of this trick of memory, until I finally figured it out: all this looked familiar to me because I'd seen it on television, a year ago. For an entire Sunday, Sara and I had been prisoners before every single news bulletin – at noon and at seven and at nine-thirty – hearing what was said without understanding, watching in silence and trembling, when a succession of figures, some with moustaches or beards, some with matt lipstick, with opinions and certainties, with rumours and eyewitness accounts, described or tried to explain how and why they'd killed him, if the own goal had been the cause or if it had been the argument in the car park, and how long it had taken, after six bullets from a 38-calibre pistol, for the football player, Andrés Escobar, to bleed to death.

Much later someone would ask me that question: Where were you when they killed Escobar? I'd been asked before: Where were you when they killed Galán, or Pizarro? I thought it was possible: a life ruled by the places a person is when someone else is murdered; yes, that life was mine, and that of many. I then remembered that date (4 July) when Sara and I devoted the day to following on television the convoy that the news programmes broadcast, fifteen or twenty windowless buses and canvas-roofed trucks going to the football player's funeral. On the broadcast was the thunder of the war planes that took off from the Palanquero base, the contrast of that noise with the silence of the people, and also, at least for an obsessive observer like me, the almost lyrical detail of the air that, displaced by propulsion of the engines, etched silver crests on the surface of the River Magdalena. Going to Escobar's funeral could be compassion or morbidity, pure rage or frivolous curiosity, but it had the value of the real, and I could understand it, and I'm sure that my father, more than understanding it, would have admired it, although he'd never been interested in football, at least not like me. (I have to say that my father was able to recite the names of the Santa Fe eleven of his day, because pronouncing 'Perazzo, Panzuto, Resnik and Campana' was pleasing to his ear, a sort of primitive verse like the melody of a drum.) And then, facing that televised route of that imitation of a funeral cortège, I felt the lack of a more solid reference to what I was observing. This often happens: when something interests me, I immediately feel the need to know physical facts to better appreciate it, and I lose interest if I don't manage to obtain them. If I'm interested in an author, I have to find out where he was born and when; if I go to bed with a new woman, I like to measure the diameter of her areolae, the distance between her belly button and the first hairs (and the women think it's a game, it seems romantic; they lend themselves to it without putting up any resistance). So at that very moment, from Sara's apartment, from Sara's telephone, I called Angelina Franco and asked her for the information I was lacking. She didn't understand at first, she reproached me for taking as a joke something as terrible as Escobar's murder, which for her – and she was right – marked a new *Now this country really is fucked* in the long history of fuck-ups, ever more serious, or lower, or more incomprehensible, or bleaker, that had filled the last several years in Colombia, the years of our adult life. But she must have noticed something in my tone of voice, or maybe I transmitted in some involuntary but nevertheless eloquent way that our incomprehension was not so different deep down, though it might seem so from outside; for in spite of not saying so right then, for me the Escobar thing was a memorandum (a yellow card, I thought later, more flippantly) that the country was sending me to emphasize, more than how impossible it was to understand Colombia, how illusory, how ingenuous was any intention of trying to do so by writing books that very few would read and did nothing but create problems for those who wrote them. In any case, Angelina gave way in the end, and assumed her role like a true cartographer. At that moment, she seemed to believe, the cortège's destination depended on the precision of her descriptions.

'Now they're at Puerto Triunfo,' she said. 'Now they're passing in front of the drug lord's zoo. Now they're at La Peñuela. That's where the air starts to smell like cement.' I remember at that moment Sara (who wasn't looking at me as if I were crazy: Sara had an extraordinary and sometimes worrying ability to accept the most arbitrary eccentricities) had brought me a glass of *lulo* juice, and I vaguely remember that I drank it with pleasure, and nevertheless the cement from the factories was the only valid reality for me: the juice, in my memory, didn't taste of *lulo*, but of cement. 'They're getting close to the Cave of the Condor,' Angelina was saying. 'There's frost on the stalagmites, Gabriel. There are ceiba trees and cedars that also have frost on them. You have to be careful up there and go slowly, because the road is slippery.' Yes, the road is slippery, and carries on being slippery for quite a way: Angelina, it seems, had offered this information as if it had nothing at all to do with my father's death. 'Now they're going down towards Las Palmas,' she went on. 'There's always a bit of mist there. On top of the walls are chamber pots and biscuit tins with geraniums. Whole lives spent planting geraniums in soda-biscuit tins, Gabriel. My parents did it, my grandparents did it, it's as if around there they hadn't yet discovered that flowerpots exist.' For an instant I stopped seeing the convoy on its way to the burial and began to see my father losing control of the car because of the fog, because of the slippery road or because of his defective hand, that hand unable to react adequately in an emergency (to control the steering wheel or put the car into second and get out of a perilous situation), and I think I actually shook my head, like in cartoons, to get rid of the images and concentrate, for once, on other people's pain. Later we saw on the news the images of people arriving at the Campos de Paz cemetery. We saw the flags – the tricoloured national ones and the green and white of the team – we saw the improvised banners made from sheets and spray paint, and we heard the nationalist slogans people chanted; and we began to foresee, in the tone of the broadcasters, in the looks on the faces of neighbours and the building's doorman, and even in the traffic on the streets, that particular atmosphere we get in Bogotá after a bomb or a notorious murder.

It was the last time I spoke to Angelina. At Christmas I received a horrendous card from her with a caption in English and a Santa Claus surrounded by glittery frost. Inside the card was a single phrase, 'With my best wishes for the festive season,' and her signature, halfway between infantile and baroque. There was also a piece of paper folded in half. It was a newspaper clipping cut out by a meticulous pair of scissors: a colour photograph of a flower-covered chair. On the back, carnations, daisies, geraniums and hibiscus formed a figure, vague at first, which after an instant became clearer. It was the dead footballer. Over his head, in three florid arches, was written: *HEAVEN IS FOR HUMBLE AND BRAVE LADS LIKE ANDRÉS ESCOBAR.* And in the blank space in the margin: 'A little memento of our last telephone encounter. 19.7.94. PS. Let's see if we can see each other live and in person one of these days.' I was moved that she'd thought of me when she saw the photo, and also that she'd gone to the trouble of getting a pair of scissors and cutting it out and buying a card and sticking the photo in it and putting it all in an envelope and putting it in the post, the kind of everyday conscientiousness that's always been beyond me. Yes, I was grateful for the gesture; however, I never called to tell her so, nor did I ever make any attempt to see her live and in person, and

Angelina disappeared from my life as so many others have: due to my inability to make contact, or to maintain it, due to my involuntary reluctance, due to that terrible ineptitude that prevents me from carrying on a sustained and constant interest – an interest that goes beyond the exchange of information, the questions I ask and the replies I expect and the articles I write with those replies – in people who appreciate me and whom I, in spite of myself, also appreciate. Only at a prudent distance can I maintain an interest in other people. If Sara hadn't died, I've thought on several occasions, we would have grown apart too, little by little, the way the waters subsided in the civil code. It was one of my father's favourite articles, which he'd memorized as a student and tended to repeat – no, recite – as if the pomposity of Doctor Andrés Bello, that nineteenth-century drafter of the code, was the best example of prose in the Spanish language; and now what is happening to me is that *the gradual and imperceptible subsidence of the waters* is so similar to the attachments in my life as to transform my life into the exposed land, which in the article is land gained by the proprietor, and in my life not so much. The gradual and imperceptible subsidence of the waters, that's the alluvium. Thus am I gradually left alone, thus have I been left alone.

Around four in the afternoon, after Puerto Triunfo and La Peñuela and the smell of cement and the Cave of the Condor, I arrived in Medellín. In spite of the precise directions in the letter (the description of an Ecopetrol station, of a fried-chicken restaurant, of the shop on the corner), I had to ask people in the street a couple of times to find the gated community where Enrique Deresser lived. There were three or four grey buildings lacking any decoration whatsoever, as

272

if the architects had decided that only ascetics would live there, or maybe people used to spending as little time at home as possible. In reality they looked like prefabricated constructions: there were too many windows and too few people looking out of them on to the patio, because that's what was between the buildings, a patio, a patch of cement where a couple of little girls were playing hopscotch (the lines drawn in pink chalk, the numbers in white). Trying to guess which building might be Deresser's, and whether I'd be able to keep an eye on my car from the window, I parked in the street and entered the estate through a little waist-high gate, without any security guard or doorman asking me where I was going, or requesting I leave a document, or phoning up to announce me. There was a little hut, but there was nobody in it. One of its windows was broken in the corner, and someone had tried to fix it with newspaper and insulating tape; the door had disappeared. The girls stopped hopping to look at me, not sidelong, not trying to hide the fact, but staring straight at me, scrutinizing me as if my evil intentions were obvious. I felt, although I didn't look up to confirm it, that all the women peering out of the windows were looking at me too. I found the building (or the *interior*, as it was described in the letter: interior B, apartment 501) and noticed that it had been a long time since I'd walked up so many flights of stairs when I had to stop on the fourth-floor landing to catch my breath, leaning against the wall, doubled over with my hands on my knees, so as not to arrive at Deresser's door panting, so as not to greet him with a sticky and sweaty handshake.

And then, I don't know why, I began to feel like I'd come to sit an exam and hadn't studied enough. Since anything at all might be waiting for me in Deresser's apartment, it was reasonable to assume that anything at all might be expected of me; I found myself wishing I had the folders of documents I'd relied on for the writing of *The Informers* in the back seat of my car. I felt vulnerable; if Deresser asked me a difficult question, Sara couldn't whisper the answer to me. Why did you write this, what's it based on, who are your witnesses, are you speculating? And I wouldn't be able to respond, because I had only written a report, while *he had lived it*: once again the superiority of living men over us, the simple talkers, the storytellers; we who, after all, devote ourselves to the cowardly and parasitic trade of telling other people's life stories, even if those other people are as close as a father or a good friend. When I was a child (I would have been about ten), I entered a story in a competition at school. I don't remember what it was about, but I do remember that we'd had to read *Leaf Storm* in Spanish class around then, and I thought it would be nice, or maybe just pretty, to put a dotted line under each paragraph like in my edition of that novel, and that was enough to make the teacher accuse me of cheating and dishonesty for having entered a story that an adult had written in the competition. It took me many years to understand that the dotted lines had given the story an inadvisably professional appearance; that imitating the outward signs of literary artifice had made it more persuasive, more sophisticated, and all that together had provoked the scepticism of an embittered woman. But that wasn't the important thing, but rather the impotence – that wasted word – that overcame me as I realized it was impossible to prove my authorship of the story, since *all the proofs were imaginary*. I feared the same thing would happen to me with Deresser. For an instant I lost all memory of my investigations, and no longer felt sure of what I'd written. I thought:

Did I make it all up? Did I exaggerate, manipulate, did I falsify reality and the lives of others? And if it was like that, why had I done it? Of course, not for my own benefit, since my father's disgrace, and that of my own name, had been confirmed in my book, although for me the confession had other and quite different effects. You're dishonest, Gabriel, a cheat. But what had been my crime? How would I be punished? Would the best strategy be to keep lying? What if Deresser read my mind? What if just by opening the door he became aware of the fraud?

But it wasn't Deresser who opened the door, but a young man, or in any case younger than me – at least, that was what his adolescent clothes suggested: he was wearing a T-shirt, tracksuit bottoms and running shoes, but it was obvious that he wasn't going jogging nor had he been – who shook my hand and made me follow him as if we already knew each other: he was one of those people able to skip over conventions and be at ease in a matter of seconds, without seeming deferential or cloying. More than that: this man was curt, too severe for his age, almost hostile. He told me, in this order, to follow him and to sit down, that they'd been waiting for me, that he'd bring me a Coke straight away, that they had no ice, he was very sorry, and that his name was Sergio, actually Sergio Andrés Felipe Lázaro, but everyone called him Sergio, not even Sergio Andrés, which would be normal in Medellín, where everyone used two names, so Sergio was his name and that's what I could call him too. And after all this he paused to explain what was missing in his speech: he was Enrique Deresser's son, a pleasure, delighted to meet me. He was, however, obviously not delighted with my visit, far from it; meeting me did not actually give him any pleasure whatsoever.

Enrique Deresser's son. Old man Konrad's grandson. Sergio went to the kitchen to get me a Coke while all the laws of genetics crowded into my head. He had black eyes, black hair, thick black eyebrows; but he also had the swimmer's shoulders and small, thin mouth and perfect nose I'd always assigned to my mental image of Enrique Deresser, the seducer of the Hotel Nueva Europa, the Don Juan of Duitama. What Sergio hadn't inherited, it would seem, was his father's and his grandfather's elegance: his diction and way of moving were those of a neighbourhood boxer, rough and somewhat coarse, as frank as they were crass. He was not unintelligent, that was more than apparent, but everything about him (it was obvious just watching him move, bring a glass, put it down on the table and sit down), down to the most banal gestures, seemed to say: I don't stop to think, I act. 'So, you're Santoro's son, the one who writes books,' he said to me. We were beside the window that overlooked the patio. The window was open, but covered by wisps of curtains that had been white in better days, so the light entered as if through translucent plastic, except when a breeze separated the curtains: then we could see the grey buildings across the way and a chunk of blue sky reflected in their windows. The armchair where Sergio had sat down was covered in a white sheet. The sofa where I was sitting didn't have a sheet, or it had been removed before my arrival.

'Yes, that's me,' I said. 'I'm really looking forward to meeting your dad.'

'Him too.'

'I was very pleased that he wrote to me.'

'Me, on the other hand, not so much,' he said. And since I couldn't think of a way to answer that immediately, he added, 'Shall I tell you the truth? If it were up to me, I would have torn that letter up. But he sent it on the sly.'

I wondered if it was hostility in his voice, or just discourtesy. His tracksuit bottoms had zips at the ankles; the zips were half open and revealed the thin grey socks of an office worker. 'Is Enrique here?' I asked. 'Is your dad home?'

His head answered no before his voice did.

'He went out early. He wasn't sure when you were going to come. Well, the truth is I told him you weren't going to come.'

'Why?'

'Because I thought you weren't going to come. Why else?'

His logic was impeccable. 'And is he coming back?' I said.

'No, sometimes he stays out to sleep under a bridge. Of course he's coming back.' Pause. 'You know what? I've read your books, both of them.'

'Oh good,' I said in my friendliest voice. 'And what did you think of them?'

'The first one I read for my dad. He gave it to me and said have a look at this to see what things were like back then. But he didn't tell me that lady had been a friend of his, or anything. The rest he told me after, so as not to influence me. At first it was as if it was nothing to do with him, you see what I mean?'

'No. Explain it to me.'

'My old man's a fair guy, he weighs everything up, you see? That's how he wanted me to read the book. And later he told me the rest.'

'About the lists . . .'

'Everything. All that shit, didn't spare me any of it. So, is that true what you put in this new book?'

'Which part?'

'That when you wrote the first one you didn't know anything. Is that true or pure shit?'

'It's true, Sergio,' I said. 'Everything is true. There's nothing that's not true in the book.'

'There is, don't exaggerate.'

'I'm not exaggerating. There's nothing.'

'Oh no? So what's all that shit about my dad living in Cuba or Panamá and I don't know where else? That's a total lie, yes or no? Or do you think we're in Panamá, sitting here?'

'That was speculation, not a lie. They're different things.'

'No, don't get clever with me, bro. All that stuff you wrote about my dad, all that about the wife and daughter, and how he fights with the daughter, all that's pure shit. Down to the last word, yes or no? I don't know why people do that kind of thing or what for. If you don't know something, go find out, don't make it up.' He stared at me with his mouth half open, as if weighing me up, the way boxers or gang members weigh each other up. 'You don't remember me, I can see that.'

'Have we met?'

'Weird, eh? Me, I remember you perfectly. I guess we're not the same.'

'That's for sure,' I said.

'I notice people more,' he said. 'You, on the other hand, do nothing but contemplate your own navel.'

It was him. It was Sergio Deresser, the son of Enrique and the grandson of Konrad (that genealogy was stuck to his voice and his image, his running shoes, his tracksuit bottoms). It was him. Seven years ago, after his father, unfortunately, had given him a book called *A Life in Exile* to read and had told him *this book's about me* though the book didn't mention him a single time; after he'd talked to him about a story of private cruelties – because such extreme cowardice is cruel, such drastic disloyalty as what Gabriel Santoro put into practice against his best friend and, to be exact, against a whole family who loved him, in whose house he'd spent more than one night, whose food he had eaten – after having got used to the transformation of his own surname and beginning to look at his father's life with fresh eyes, after all that, he ended up catching the early bus to Bogotá one day, and when he arrived he'd gone into the only phone booth there was in the station. After three calls he'd found out where the new Supreme Court was and the time of Doctor Santoro's seminar. And he went to hear him: he needed to know what the guy was like, if the treachery was visible on his face, if it was true, as his father said, that he was missing a hand; he needed to see whether his voice trembled when he spoke, if he seemed convinced, after the pathetic speech he'd spewed out in front of the most respectable people in the country, of being the great citizen everyone talked about. And when he got there, well, when he saw the washed-up, pitiful old man exercising an authority he no longer had, saying things too big for him, moving around with the self-confidence of a con man, as if he weren't the same person who'd pushed a whole family over the edge. And then the washed-up old man had begun to fabricate his own life, was there anything more ridiculous, was there any more complete or more convincing form of humiliation? 'You know the rest,' Sergio said to me. 'Or do you forget things too?' I hadn't forgotten: I'd spent nine days, or perhaps more, visiting my father's classroom, seeing him without being seen, and one of those days, that simple thing happened: Sergio arrived from Medellín and sat a few seats from where I was, maybe despising me in silence, praying he could one day let me know, notice and feel his disdain. No, Sergio Andrés Felipe Lázaro, I don't forget things, they simply

279

change over time; and we who remember, we who devote ourselves to remembering as a way of life, are obliged to keep pace with memory, which never stays still, just as happens when we walk beside someone taller.

'How did you recognize me?'

'I didn't recognize you, your book doesn't have a photo. I guessed, bro, I guessed. I didn't even imagine you'd be there. That occurred to me when your dad ran out, running as if he was shit-scared, as if he knew someone could stand up and say, All that's pure shit and you know it. I thought of doing that. I thought of standing up and shouting, You old bastard, old traitor. And it was like he'd read my mind. Did your dad know how to do those things?'

'What things?'

'Telepathy, things like that. He didn't, did he? No, he didn't, telepathy doesn't exist, and that's why you have to invent shit to write books instead of finding out the truth, and that's why your dad didn't know that I was getting the urge to shout, You old traitor, at him. A person can't read another person's mind, bro. If your dad could, he never would have gone to give that lecture. But there he was. And of course, he went running out as if he'd read my mind, and that was when someone said that's his son, what a shame, poor guy. I went out after you. I couldn't resist the urge to see your face.'

'And you saw it.'

'Of course I did. You were shit-scared too. Just like now, if you don't mind my saying so.'

'Did you tell Enrique?'

'No. What for? He wouldn't have liked that. He would have given me the same old sermon: there are things a real man never does,' said Sergio, but he didn't say what things he was referring to. 'We would have fought and that's not what I was after, right? I don't like fighting with my dad, I have respect for my old man, for your information. I can't say the same for you, brother.'

'Can you get me another Coke?'

'But of course, all you have to do is ask. That's what I'm here for, to wait on you.'

He went back into the kitchen. It had a swinging door, and through the little rectangular window I managed to see him setting the glass down on the Formica table and opening an old, orange-ish refrigerator and taking out of the white light (the image was almost magical, Sergio transformed for an instant into a sorcerer from a fairy tale) a plastic bottle. He did everything so lightly that I thought: He's enjoying himself. He's playing with me, and he's having fun, because he's been waiting for this moment for a long time. If I could get close to his face, I thought, I'd see him smiling; if I could hear his thoughts, this is what I'd hear: *A little while longer. Ten minutes, half an hour, a little while longer.* I was easy prey; I hadn't tried to defend myself; maybe I didn't know how, and, nothing could be worse in Sergio's hunting ground, that was obvious. I thought of telling him, I know what's going on here, you want to keep your rage intact, you don't want anyone to touch it, and if I talk to your dad maybe your rage won't be so justified. What if your dad and I end up as friends? What if he likes me? That'd be a problem for you, wouldn't it? These tantrums are important in your life. You're not going to let someone take them away, and that's why you're receiving me like this. You're a genetic case, recessive indignation. Then Sergio came back with my glass full to the brim (the surface of the liquid sparkled, bubbled, gurgled), sat down opposite me, invited me to drink. 'What's the matter, too much of a surprise? Well, at least you know who you're dealing with now. I'm no fucking coward, I meet you head on, I answer back. That's how it is, get it? This has to do with me, not just with my dad. He asked you to come, but not so you can start writing more lies. It's to clear up a couple of things. It's so you won't talk about what you don't know about.'

'I didn't write lies.'

'No, sorry,' he said. '*Speculations*. That's what they call them these days.'

'Why did it offend you so much, Sergio? I imagined that your dad might have gone to live in Cuba or Venezuela or one of five or six countries, doesn't matter which ones, because the idea wasn't to prove anything, just to suggest his situation. It was a way of showing interest in him, in how things had turned out in his life. What's so bad about that?'

'That it's not true, bro. Like it's not true that your dad's a victim. Or a hero either, and much less a martyr.'

'And he doesn't come over as one in the book.'

'In the book he's a victim.'

'Well, I don't agree,' I said. 'If you interpreted it like that, it's your problem. But I wrote something very different.'

'He was a bullshitter,' Sergio went on as if he hadn't heard me. 'When he was young and when he was old. A lifelong bullshitter.'

'You want a punch in the face?'

'Don't get pissed off, Santoro. Your dad was what he was. You're not going to change anything with your fists.'

Now he was getting into direct insults. For the first time I thought that this had all been a big mistake. What could I actually get out of this visit? The benefits seemed too intangible and in any case conjectural. Who was obliging me to stay? There outside was my car (it was visible from the window, I could find it just by stretching my neck). Why didn't I stand up and say goodbye, or leave without saying goodbye? Why didn't I force him to admit to Enrique Deresser that he'd thrown me out of the house with the violence of his comments, with personal attacks? Why didn't I put an end to the scene and later write an accusatory letter and let Sergio sort things out as best he could with his father? All this went through my head while I recognized how deceptive these ideas were: I would never do it, because years and years of working as a journalist had accustomed me to putting up with whatever I had to in order to get a fact, a reference, a confession, two words or a line that had some humanity or just a bit of colour, which could, finally, be written down and used in whatever article I happened to be working on. There was no article possible out of this encounter – this confrontation – with Enrique Deresser's son; nevertheless, there I stayed, putting up with his ex-aggerated disdain, his meticulous bravado, as if the betrayal had happened in the past week. (*Week*, I thought, *past*. But did these categories exist? Was it possible to say that time had moved in our case? What could it matter when the mistake, the denunciation and the amputation of a hand had already happened? The deeds were present; they were current, immediate, they lived among us; the deeds of our fathers accompanied us. Sergio, who talked and thought like the practical man he undoubtedly was, had realized this before I had; he had, at least, this advantage over me, and it was surely not the only one.) I thought: *It happened this past week. All through my father's life it had just happened.* I thought: *This is my inheritance. I've inherited it all.* Stupidly I looked at my right hand; I checked that it was where it always had been; I closed my fist, opened it, stretched my fingers, as if I were sitting in a donors' clinic and a nurse was taking blood; and in that instant I thought I was wasting my time and I should go, that nothing was worth this tension, hostility and invective.

Then, accompanied by his wife, in walked Enrique Deresser.

'I suppose that meeting her was my salvation. But that's how she is, Gabriel. She goes through life saving lives without even noticing. I've never known anyone like her: she doesn't have a single drop of wickedness in her head. If she wasn't as good in bed as she is in life, I probably would have got bored of her ages ago.'

We were outside, on the big patio inside the estate, very close to the chalk hopscotch the little girls had left; we'd sat down on a green bench – wrought-iron frame; wooden slats – that had its legs set into the pavement and its back to the window from which (I imagined) Sergio was spying on us with binoculars and a rum and Coke in his hand, trying to read our lips and make out our gestures. It wasn't completely dark yet; the street lights and the outdoor lights of the estate had come on, and the sky was no longer blue, but not black yet either, so you couldn't quite say that the lights were illuminating, but if they were turned off we would have been completely in the dark. The world, just then, was an indecisive thing; but Enrique Deresser had suggested we go downstairs, saying that talking about the past brings good luck if it's done in the open air, and making some falsely casual comment about the agreeable temperature, the sweet evening air, the calm of the patio now that the children had gone in and the adults hadn't yet come out to party. Rebeca, his wife, had greeted me with a kiss on the cheek when she introduced herself; unlike how I usually react, I'd liked the immediate intimacy at that moment, but I'd liked even more the carefree apology the woman offered in her Medellín accent: 'Forgive the familiarity, dear, but I've got my hands full.' She was carrying two plastic bags in her left hand and a string bag of oranges in her right; almost without stopping she went straight through to the kitchen. And before I knew it Enrique had taken me gently by the elbow and was leaning slightly on my arm to walk down the stairs, in spite of nothing in his body seeming to need it, while I did some quick sums in my head and came to the conclusion that this man was or was soon to be seventy-five years old. He hunched over a bit as he walked and seemed smaller than he was; he was wearing light cotton trousers and a short-sleeved shirt with two pockets (a cheap pen stuck out of the left pocket, and in the right was a shape I couldn't identify), and suede ankle boots with rubber soles (the ends of the laces were beginning to unravel). I didn't know if it was his shoes or his clothes, but Enrique gave off an animal smell that wasn't strong or unpleasant but was very noticeable. To play it safe, I didn't ask about it, and later learned that this smell was a mixture of horse sweat, stable sawdust and saddle leather. Since arriving in Medellín, Deresser had worked with *paso fino* horses, at first as a jack-of-all-trades (he wrote letters in German to breeders in the Black Forest, but he also brushed the horses' tails and manes and supported the penis for stallions servicing brood mares) and eventually, when he'd learned the trade, as a trainer. He didn't do it any more, he explained, because his back had aged badly, and after an afternoon's riding, or of standing in front of a young mare circling round a post, the muscles in his shoulders and waist protested for a whole week. But he still liked to spend time at the stables, talk to the new hands and give the animals sugar. It was sugar he had in his breast pocket: little packets that his rich friends stole from fine restaurants to give to him, and that he emptied into the palm of his hand so a horse's pink tongue would lick it off in one go as if the whole ritual were the best pastime in the world. 'Rebeca was the one who got me into horses,' said Enrique. 'Yes, it's no exaggeration to say that I owe everything to her. Her father was a great trainer. He worked for people with lots of money. In time it became drug money, of course. He died before he had to see that. Almost all horse people have touched drug money. But you look the other way, carry on doing your job, looking after your animals.'

So he never had left Colombia. 'My dad thought you had,' I told him.

'Maybe,' he replied, 'believing that was easier. Easier than looking for me, in any case. Easier than talking to me.' He paused and then said, 'But let's be fair: even if he had tried (and he didn't), he wouldn't have been able to find me. I left Bogotá at the end of '46. What was left for me in that city? The glass factory had closed down, or rather it had gone under. A whole lifetime's capital had turned into a pocketful of small change after the business had been blacklisted for three years, after the time Papa spent in the Sabaneta. For practical purposes, I was an orphan. My friends, well, you already know about my friends. But no, it wasn't really a matter of wondering why I should stay in Bogotá. It was a matter of wondering where to go. Because I didn't have a choice, you see. I hated Bogotá with a hatred I can't explain to you now. Bogotá was to blame for everything. Can I tell you something? I got hold of your dad's speech, in '88, the one at the Capitolio, you know? And I spent several days convinced he'd written it with me in mind, because it was everything I'd felt before, at least all the bad stuff.'

'And may I presume you gave it to Sergio?'

'Why are you speaking to me so formally?'

He was right. Who was I trying to fool with these linguistic diplomacies? We'd never set eyes on each other; we'd known each other all our lives. Enrique was relaxed with me and it wasn't a problem, but the idioms of his current life hadn't completely eradicated the diction of his birthplace, and he went back and forth between the straight-laced politeness of Bogotá and the offhand directness of his wife's city. 'Yes, I gave it to Sergio. That's been the most difficult thing about all this, showing my son how I felt. The lengths I've gone to in order to make him understand me, to get him to sense what it was like. Because it's not enough to explain this, you can imagine, you want others to experience what happened fifty years ago. How do you do that? It's impossible really. But you try, you invent strategies. I gave him your book. The speech. What comes to the son directly from his father isn't worth anything, because children don't believe their parents, not a word, and that's how it should be. So you have to turn everything around, no? Go through another door, take them by surprise. Raising a son is tough, but explaining to him who you are, what kind of life has made you who you are, is the toughest thing in the world. Besides, there are things, I don't know how to explain it to you, I've swallowed all this much better than he has. Obviously, because I've had half a century of it and he's just started. For him it's as if it happened yesterday. He treated you very badly, I'm sorry, you have to understand him.'

In October 1946, after trying to borrow money that he knew he'd never be able to pay back from the Society of Free

Germans, and receiving several negative responses, Enrique arranged to meet one of the members in the Café Windsor. Herr Ditterich hadn't wanted to talk about this in the presence of his colleagues, not wanting to appear sympathetic to the son of a man as suspicious as Konrad Deresser; but he knew his situation was difficult, and after all they were all emigrants, weren't they? Besides, young people had to help each other, Ditterich said to him, especially now that they were responsible for the reconstruction of the Fatherland. He gave him a letter of recommendation, told him who to ask for at the Cavalry School, and two weeks later Enrique left for Medellín. 'They wanted me to talk to a German, that was all, a business matter. That's where I met Rebeca.' Rebeca's father, wearing chaps, rode seven locally bred *paso fino* horses and a Lusitanian stallion, and a colonel from the School, in full uniform even though it was a Sunday, chose the stallion and five of the seven *paso finos*, and everyone went away happy. 'I exchanged three sentences with the owner of the horses. I didn't have to do anything. He was a young man, it was his first time in Latin America, and it wasn't that he was mistrustful, but he needed someone to speak to him in his language. The important thing was Rebeca, a girl of sixteen, flame-haired and so skinny she looked like a matchstick. For me, at that moment, she was like an angel, and a teasing, brazen angel, besides. She spent the whole lunch talking to me about her Viking ancestors like she was talking to a five-year-old, but touching my knee under the table. What am I saying touching me, rubbing up against me like a cat on heat.' Enrique – the Don Juan of Duitama – was talking as if now his former attractiveness surprised him, and I chose not to tell him what Sara Guterman had told me. 'I asked the angel if she could get me a job, and when I went back to Bogotá it was to pack up my things.' It wasn't a good idea to marry the boss's daughter, said Enrique, but that's what happened a year later. 'November, 1947. And here we are, as if we'd just been introduced. It's grotesque, really.'

'And in all those years you didn't have any more kids?'

'We didn't have any. Sergio is adopted.'

'Oh, I see.'

'The problem is mine. Don't ask me to explain it.'

The most conventional life possible: that was what his tone of voice and his still hands seemed to suggest, in spite of the fact that supporting the penis of an imported horse, or teaching it to trot to the rhythm of a Colombian folk dance weren't the most usual ways to earn a living. The conventional life had evolved with all its conventions for half a century; here, just eight hours by land from where my father had his own life, his own son and had endured the premature death of his wife, Enrique Deresser pretended (as my father pretended) that he'd forgotten certain wartime events or that those events had never happened. 'Of course I told Rebeca about my father,' he said. 'Everything was fresh in everyone's mind back then. In Medellín too there were Germans, Italians, even Japanese people who ended up more or less screwed, for more or less time, because of where they were from. There was a famous case, a certain Spadafora, an airline pilot who volunteered his services during the war against Peru. Every time he flew, the guy carried a little Indian box of saffron in his pocket. One of his aunts had bought it in a bazaar, the newspapers said, something like that. As an amulet, you know? Pilots are like that. So anyway, someone saw the little box and couldn't believe that wasn't the same swastika as Hitler's. And the information got to where it shouldn't have. Spadafora spent a fortune on lawyers, and yes, eventually he managed to get off the blacklist. But he'd fought against Peru, he'd fought on the side of Colombia, I don't know if you see my point.'

'Yeah, I do.'

'The thing is I told Rebeca the whole thing, and she wasn't at all surprised. Just the opposite, she spent half her life asking me to put right what could be put right. She wanted me to look for Mama, at least. Something I never did, of course, and if Rebeca didn't it was only out of respect. I closed the door and threw away the key, as they say. What am I going to do. I've never been one to impose on others. Maybe it's a flaw, I don't know.'

'But did you tell her about my dad?'

'I told her, yes. Sergio I told later, when your book about Sara came out. I don't know anything about books, but I liked the one you did about Sara. I was very sorry about her death. Although we'd never spoken again, it hit me hard. What was she like as an old lady? One time, at her family's hotel, we were arguing over something, something I said, and she made this face that I'd never seen. It was a blend of indignation and weariness, with a little bit of that personality that flees confrontations. It occurred to me that she'd look like that when she was old, and I told her. I've imagined her like that these last years, with that face. Indignant. Weary. But always agreeing with you. That's how Germans were back then. *Bloss nicht auffallen*, they said. Do you understand that?'

'I don't speak German.'

'Well, it's your loss. Don't stand out. Don't call attention to yourself. Go along with people. That's all contained in that phrase. It was a sort of command for them. Papa repeated it all the time. I came out different: I was mouthy and sometimes insolent, I liked conflict. It was much more than saying what I thought. I said it, but pounding the table or right in the face of my opponent, if necessary. Sara, in that, was a worthy representative of the immigrant community. And then later she was a worthy representative of Bogotá society. It could be a slogan for Bogotá, *Bloss nicht auffallen*, although only to your face. Behind your back people in Bogotá will tear you to shreds. Anyway, I'd like to see a photo of her, a recent one. Have you seen photos of her when she was young?'

'One or two.'

'And? Did she look like herself? Had she changed much?'

'The person in the photos was her. That's not always easy to see.'

'Exactly. Maybe I was right.'

'How did you hear she'd died?'

'The Ungars told me. Since they opened the Central I've ordered four or five books a year, books in German, always on horses, to keep in touch with the language. That's all I read. They told me. They called me as soon as they heard, that same night. I actually considered making the trip, going to the funeral, then I realized how absurd that would have been.'

'And my dad's funeral? Didn't you think of attending that one?'

'I found out too late. Just think, he was killed two or three hours after talking to me: it was the most absurd thing in the world. Even when I found out, two days after the funeral, not even then did I entirely believe it. It had to be someone else, someone with the same name. Because that Gabriel Santoro had been killed on the 23rd, the same day your dad and I had seen each other. No, it seemed impossible. First I thought it was you who'd died. What a terrible thing to say, I'm sorry, it's probably bad luck as well, but that's how it was. Then I thought there must be more than two people with that name in Colombia. A person invents things when they don't want to believe something, it's normal. I didn't want him to be dead, at least not after we talked, what we said, especially after what I said to him, or what I didn't say, yes, that more than anything, what I refused to say to him. And three hours later, he goes and gets himself killed. Sergio said, 'That's life, Dad. You just have to accept it.' I smacked him. I'd never hit him before in my life and I hit him when he said that to me.'

'I even thought maybe he'd never come here.'

'Of course he came,' said Enrique. 'And we were sitting right here. Here where you and I are. The only difference was that it was a Sunday and daytime. It was stifling. It had rained the night before, I remember that, and there were puddles here, we were surrounded by puddles, and even this bench was still a bit damp. But I didn't want to have him in my house, I can tell you now. I didn't want him stepping on my floor and sitting on my chairs, and much less eating my food. Quite primitive, no? An educated person like you must think that sounds pretty basic. Well, maybe it is. What I felt, in any case, was that letting him in, showing him the photos on the shelves, letting him pick up my books and leaf through them, showing him the rooms, the bed where I slept and made love to my wife . . . All that would contaminate me in some way, contaminate us. I had conserved the purity of my life, of my family for half a century, and I wasn't going to screw it all up now, as an old man, just because Gabriel Santoro decided to show up and sort out his conscience before he died. That's what I thought. Yes, the first thing that came into my head was: He's dying. He must have cancer, or even Aids; he's dying and he wants to leave everything all in order. I was disparaging towards him, Gabriel, and I regret that. I disparaged the effort he'd made. What he did, coming here to talk to me, not many people could do that. But our position at that moment was very different: he had thought a lot about me, or at least that's what he said. I, on the other hand, had erased him from my memory. I suppose that's how things go, don't you think? The one who causes the offence remembers more than the offended one. And that's why it was almost inevitable that I would be disparaging, and almost impossible for me to appreciate the enormity of what he was doing. Besides, it was enjoyable to be disparaging, why should I deny it? A person feels good, I felt good. It was a sudden satisfaction, a sort of surprise gift.

'As if that weren't enough, I didn't know about his operation. He didn't tell me, I don't know why, so I held on to the idea of him being ill. I spent our whole conversation looking at him, trying to find inflamed glands on his neck, or the shape of a colostomy bag under his shirt, those things you get used to seeing after a certain age, when every time you run into a friend it might be the last time you see him. I looked at his eyes to see if they were yellow. He thought I was giving him my whole attention. Because I looked at him, I looked at him closely, and what I looked at most, obviously, was his right hand. Gabriel had said hello when he arrived, but he hadn't offered me his hand. Of course, I knew very well why not, and at that moment I had enough tact not to look at it, but deep down, very deep down, I was shocked that he hadn't shaken my hand, I felt that he hadn't greeted me properly. If he'd offered me his left hand . . . or slapped me on the back (no, that's unthinkable). But none of that happened. There was no contact when we saw each other, and I felt it was missing. It was like the encounter started off on the wrong foot, you know? It's strange how shaking hands is so conciliatory, regardless of how we might actually feel. It's like defusing a bomb, I've always seen it like that: a handshake is a very strange ceremony, one of those things that should have died out by now, like bows and curtsies. But no: it hasn't gone out of style. We still go around all over the place squeezing other people's fingers, because it's like saying, I mean you no harm. You mean me no harm. Of course, then everyone harms everyone else, everyone betrays each other all the time, but that's beside the point. It helps. Anyway, it didn't happen like that with Gabriel. There was no conciliation to start with, the bomb remained active.

'And sitting here we began to tell each other about our lives. I told him what I've just told you. He told me about your mum, he chose to start there, I don't know why. "I confessed everything to her," he told me. "When I asked her to marry me, I also asked her to forgive me. It was a two-for-one offer, as they say." He never talked about me to anybody, he never wrote my name down anywhere, but he told her everything as soon as he could. "Confession is a great invention," your dad said. Half seriously, half in jest. "Priests are pretty cunning, Enrique. Those fellows know how things work." A person would think that the death of someone who knows an evil secret would be a liberation, just as the death of a witness frees the murderer. But your mother's death was just the opposite for Gabriel. "It was like my reprieve had been revoked." That's how he explained it to me. Gabriel hadn't changed at all in that respect: he said everything with a certain coolness, a certain cynicism, just like when we were young. As if it was nothing to do with him, as if he was talking about someone else. With him every word had its contents, but it was also a tool for looking down from on high, for keeping his distance. You'll know better than me what I'm talking about. When I told him I'd read your book about Sara he said, "Oh yes, very good, very original. But what's original isn't good, and vice versa." The same sentence you put in *The Informers*, isn't it? Well, with you one already knows: everything I say can be used against me. If I wasn't so old I'd think I had to be careful. But no. What do I need to be careful of now? What can I say at this age that could matter? What can they do to me if I tell? A person gets old and impunity lands on you, Gabriel, even if you don't want it. That was one of the things I said to your dad: "Why now? Who's going to benefit from your coming here on your knees at this stage of life?" And it was true. Was it going to do my father any good after forty years in the ground? Was it any use to my mama, who had to reinvent her life at forty-something, have children at an age when it can kill a woman? Reinventing yourself is painful, like surgery. After a certain point the challenge is overcome, the anaesthesia of the emotion, of the pride at overcoming it, wears off, and you start to feel the most savage pain, you realize you've lost a leg, or your appendix, or at least they'd opened up your skin and flesh, and that hurts even if they didn't find a tumour. I knew it because I'd been through that too. Through a reconstruction. Through the anguish of choices. It's a whole process: you can choose how you want to be, what you want to be, and even what you want to have been. That's the most tempting thing: to be another person. I had chosen to be the same but somewhere else. Change jobs but keep my name. "It's of use to you," Gabriel said to me. "It has to be of use to you to know that I've carried this all these years, that I could have forgotten and I haven't. I've remembered, Enrique, I've stayed in the hell of remembering." I told him not to be a martyr. A whole family had been ruined for one little word of his, so not to come here boasting of his memory. "There's something I'd like to know," he said then. "Was I lucky or unlucky? Did you pay them to kill me, or just to scare the shit out of me?"

'At that moment we were walking to the corner shop. Not that we needed anything, but there are conversations when you just stand up and start walking, because if you're walking you don't have to look each other in the eye all the time, and then it's just a matter of finding a destination for the stroll. Our destination was the corner shop. The closest place. Between here and there it's not very likely you'll get mugged, less so if you're not on your own, even less if it's Sunday and daytime. And the shop was neutral ground, one of those country places stuck in the middle of Medellín, with plastic tables out front, and those half-bottles of cheap liquor that drunks pile up in front of them as if they collected them. "I wanted you dead," I told Gabriel, "but I didn't pay them for that. I didn't even know there'd be machetes." I didn't say anything else and he didn't ask. Never in my life could I have imagined I'd say such a thing. Then I thought Gabriel had come to get me to say all those things that must have been a sin even just to say. He was there, sitting across from me with a beer. I didn't like it, I felt sort of threatened, understand? I'd begun that visit, or whatever you call an encounter like that, thinking: He's come looking for something. I just have to give it to him and he'll leave. Then, at some point in the conversation, I thought: We have a history in common. It's true that history isn't pure and isn't virginal; more than that, our history is very promiscuous. At the shop, on the other hand, surrounded by ten or fifteen identical drunks, all with their shirts open and moustaches, all armed though some didn't flaunt it, I began to think: We're wasting our time. What imbeciles. All this was just a farce. What is happening right here, today, this 23rd of December, the last Sunday before Christmas, is a big farce. The farce of someone who repents although they know it's of no use. The farce of making amends that do not exist, now do you understand? Like the morphine they give to a horse with a broken leg. Yes, a great farce, or not even that: a mediocre farce. I'd told Gabriel that I'd wanted him dead. I imagine one doesn't say these things just like that. And Gabriel knew it too, I suppose, he who had spoken so many strong words, words capable of destroying.

'I bought a packet of Pielrojas and a box of matches. I took out a cigarette and lit it before we left the shop. When we got back here, to the gate, I'd already finished it. Pielrojas don't last long. I offered Gabriel one and he told me in a reproachful tone that he'd quit and that I should quit too. That's when he told me about his heart and his bypass. "It's the best feeling in the world," he told me. "It's like being thirty again." We were standing there, you see the security hut? We were there, I'd taken out another cigarette and was in the process of lighting it, which isn't easy with the matches you get these days. They're not wood, they're not even cardboard, they're something like plastic. The heads fall off them, they bend in half. "But we're not thirty years old," I said. I kept trying to light my cigarette, although the wind blew out two matches and two more bent in half. "What a vice," said Gabriel. "As well as killing yourself smoking those things, you have to be a boy scout to get one lit. Let's go in, man, it won't be such an effort inside." And that was it: the idea of going into my house with Gabriel, Gabriel and I together, us and our promiscuous history, wouldn't fit in my head. I did what I did: what was necessary to protect me and protect my family. My reaction wasn't any more civilized than a cat marking its territory. I'm not making excuses, of course. Let's make that clear.

'I told him we should just say goodbye. That all this was futile, it had been futile from the start. Getting into his car in Bogotá had been, although it was painful to admit, a mistake. "None of this should have happened," I said. "It's a mistake that you're here. It's a mistake that we're talking the way we're talking. It would be a mistake, no, it would be a perversion for you to enter my house." His face changed. It hardened, crevices appeared around his eyes. He intimidated me and I pitied him. I can't really explain it. Gabriel had turned hostile and vulnerable at the same time. But I couldn't take it back. "It's in this life that all that happened, Gabriel, and you want to pretend it was in a different one. Well no, it's not possible. Look, I'm going to tell you the truth: I'd rather we just left it as it is." He asked me what I meant by that. I had gone through the gate and was standing on the other side of the rail, beside the hut but inside. I was on my premises, so to speak. From inside I closed the gate (I looked up at the window of my apartment, made sure no one was watching us) and explained it as best I could: "I'm saying don't come back and don't call me, don't try to put the world to rights, because in the world are people who aren't interested. I'm saying the world doesn't revolve around your guilt. What's the matter, don't you sleep well? Buy some pills. Ghosts wake you up? Say a prayer. No, Gabriel, it's not that easy, you're not going to buy your peace of mind so cheaply, I'm not a discount store. Like I said: don't come back, don't call me, and please, please, please, let's pretend you never came. It's too late for these rectifications. If you want to make amends, you're going to have to do it on your own." I thought: Now he's going to speak, and I was scared. I knew all too well what he was capable of when he spoke. But he didn't, as incredible as it may seem. He didn't speak, didn't defend himself, didn't try to convince me of anything. For once in his life, he kept quiet. He accepted his failure. It was like a failed law. A law of forgive and forget, the amnesty decreed by a retreating dictator. It all collapsed on him in a matter of seconds. I won't deny he accepted it gracefully. I understood a lot of things when I read your book, Gabriel, but there was one thing in particular that shocked me at first and has carried on troubling me. I'm going to tell you what I understood: I understood that looking for me, coming to Medellín, coming to see me, trying to talk to me, all that for your dad was part of his great plan for personal reconstruction, I don't know how else to say it. And I destroyed it. If I'd read your book before, if I'd known what was behind his visit, maybe I wouldn't have said what I said. But of course, that's impossible, isn't it? It's an absurd hypothesis. That's a book and the other was life. The life went first and then came the book. Does this seem stupid what I'm saying? That's how it always is. That doesn't change. Later in books we see the important things. But by the time we see them it's already too late. That's the trouble, Gabriel, forgive my frankness, but that's the fucking trouble with books.'

Staying for dinner was the most natural thing in the world; also, at that hour of the night, the least reasonable. Rebeca had leaned out of the living-room window (calling Enrique, with a mixture of authority and tenderness, she'd included me without mentioning me); and soon, as the old man took my arm to climb the stairs, and a whiff of sawdust and animal sweat reached my face, I thought that accepting the invitation would be reckless, because after dinner it would be too late to return to Bogotá – that was obvious – but perhaps I could find a hotel. And then my head decided to do what it so often does: pretend it hadn't heard these last ideas. Curiosity, and the satisfaction of my curiosity, weren't taking orders from any kind of cheap good sense (the danger of the road at night, the risk of not finding a room). I wanted to keep seeing, keep hearing, even when what I saw and heard during the meal was the elaborate accumulation of normality I'd expected. But nothing was normal in this man, I thought, and one would have to be especially dim not to notice that: this normal life, the prudent and bland happiness of his old age, was marred from within – I won't say *poisoned*, although that was the first word that occurred to me – and under the table with its lace tablecloth, and above the unbreakable plates on which the food looked like another decoration moved the facts, the nasty facts, the facts that don't change even if everything else changes. Enrique wasn't from here; he'd fled here; by surname and by nature, though not by soil, Enrique was a foreigner. None of which prevented him from requesting with each of his gestures: be nice to them, forgive the triviality of their lives, their insignificance. And that's why watching him lift his fork to his mouth was fascinating: Enrique lifted a mound of ground beef, chewed a piece of onion, washed it down with a sip of *lulo* juice, smiled at Rebeca and took her hand, made banal remarks and she replied with equally banal ones, and for me it was as if they were reciting the Book of Revelation. If I blink, I'll miss a verse; if I go to the bathroom, I'll miss a whole chapter.

Sergio hadn't stayed for dinner. The disdain he felt for me (for my father, whose name I shared, for my dishonest book) had been so obvious that his parents didn't even insist when he began to say goodbye, without giving himself time to make up an excuse, and in two shakes he'd grabbed the jacket of his tracksuit and was gone. 'His girlfriend's an artist, like you,' said Rebeca. 'She paints. She paints fruit, land-scapes, you know better than I do what they call those pictures. They sell them on Sundays at Unicentro. Sergio's as proud as a peacock.' While Rebeca prepared a herbal tea for after the meal, Enrique went downstairs by himself to smoke a cigarette, just as he'd done, as I learned, every night for the last thirty years. 'Habit's stronger than he is. If he doesn't do the same thing at the same time, his day's ruined. Like your dad.' She looked at me as she said this; she didn't wink at me, but she might just as well have done. 'You can't imagine what it was like watching him read your book, Gabriel. He'd suddenly close it and say, He's like me, Rebeca, Gabriel's like me. How funny. Or sometimes he'd say just the opposite: Just look at him, he's still such a bastard, look how he behaves.'

'You never met him, did you?'

I already knew the answer, but I wanted her to confirm it.

'No, that one didn't want me to meet him,' she said, pursing her lips, kissing the air in the direction of her husband. 'He hid me away as if I had chicken pox, you know? The feeble one of the house. Look,' she went on after a pause, 'don't you take the blame for things he did, it's not fair. You forget that, you live your life.' She wiped her hands on her apron and gave me an affectionate pat. It was the first time she'd touched me with her hand (that moment is always memorable). 'You don't mind my meddling?'

'Of course not.'

'Good, because that's how I am. Nothing I can do about it.'

When Enrique came back up, I'd finished my tea and Rebeca had put the Yellow Pages (a brick of newsprint with card covers, the spine scratched, the corners bent with use) on my lap. 'What's going on?' asked Enrique when he came in. 'He wants to look for a hotel,' said Rebeca. 'Oh,' he said, as if the idea of my leaving had never crossed his mind. 'A hotel, right.' I called the Intercontinental, although it was a bit expensive, because it was more likely I'd find a room available at this hour. I made the reservation, gave my credit-card number, and when I hung up asked my hosts how to get there from where we were. 'I'm going to draw you a little map,' said Rebeca. 'You have to cross the city,' and she got down to work, biting her tongue while she drew streets and numbers and arrows on a piece of squared paper, putting all her weight on to the felt-tip pen. Enrique said to me, 'Come here, I want to show you something while she finishes that. The poor dear takes her time over these things.'

He took me to their room. It was a narrow space, so much so that there was only one bedside table; on the other side of the bed, the matching table wouldn't have fitted (or it would have blocked the closet door, an unpainted Triplex board, so flat and plain that it made me think of cartoon shipwrecks). In one corner, on a sort of drinks trolley that could be moved away from or near the bed, adjusted to the whims or myopia of old age, was a television, an old set with imitation wood grain, and on top of the television was a desk calendar with pictures of *paso fino* horses. I saw that the bedside table was

Rebeca's dominion, even though the photo beneath the lamp was not of her husband as matrimonial bedsides theoretically required, but of herself, somewhat younger but already without a trace of red left in her hair: the photo would be ten or fifteen years old, and had been taken beside a small swimming pool that didn't look too clean. 'That's in Santa Fe de Antioquia,' Enrique told me, as he took out of the drawer what at first appeared to be a photo album and turned out to be a ring binder. 'We go every December. Some friends rent us their house.' He opened the rings of the binder and took out a few pages, which weren't pages but plastic sleeves that contained the pages (or photographs, or cuttings) protected from sweaty fingers and the humidity of the atmosphere. 'You already know this, although you don't know you know it,' Enrique said to me. What was inside the sleeve was a typewritten, formal letter, without a single correction; to make out the letters I had to press the tip of my index finger against the plastic, and I felt like a child learning the difficult habit of following a line, interpreting it, connecting it to the next one.

Bogotá, 6 January 1944

Honourable Senators Pedro J. Navarro, Leonardo Lozano Pardo and José de la Vega:

My name is Margarita Lloreda de Deresser. I was born in Cali to a traditionally Liberal family. My father was the late Julio Alberto Lloreda Duque, engineer by profession and consultant on public works for the government of the late Doctor Olaya Herrera.

The reason for this letter is none other than to request your intercession on my behalf and that of my family in the light of the situation which I here relate:

In 1919 I married Konrad Deresser, a German citizen. The marriage has remained solid under the eyes of God since then and we have one son, Enrique, a young man of exemplary conduct who is now twenty-three years of age.

Due to his nationality my husband has seen his name included in the 'blacklist' of the government of the United States of America, which as your honours undoubtedly are aware brings terrible consequences for any individual or business, and our case has not been different. In the space of the few weeks since the unjust inclusion on the 'list' we have been brought to a state of crisis which appears to have no escape and will without a doubt soon bankrupt us.

However, my husband has never had, does not have, nor will he ever have any sympathy for the government currently in power in Germany, for which reason his inclusion on the list is unfair and unjustified and due to nothing but rumours without any basis in fact.

My husband is the proprietor of a small family business, Cristales Deresser, dedicated to the

'Does it end here?' I said. 'Don't you have the rest?'

Enrique took out another of the plastic-sleeved pages. 'Don't get in a state,' he said sarcastically. 'The world's not going to end just yet.'

manufacture and commercial sale of window panes and all kinds of glass. The total capital does not exceed 8,000 pesos and we have no more than three full-time employees, all of whom are Colombian.

My husband, furthermore, is part of the broad German community that arrived in Colombia at the beginning of the century and since then has loyally abided by all the laws of our country. He has distinguished himself among the people of Bogotá by the strictness and honesty of his morals and habits, as so often occurs with members of this race of elevated qualities. And in spite of having always felt proud of his origins my husband has never prevented me from raising my son in the religious and civic values of our Colombia, in the Catholic church and our valued democracy, which today we see under threat. Which my husband regrets as much as all Colombian citizenry of which he considers himself a part.

With all due respect I ask your honours, not only in my name but in the name of the rest of the German families who find themselves in analogous situations, that you intercede before the Government so that our names may be removed from the aforementioned list and our civil and economic rights may be restored. My husband and many other German citizens are suffering the consequences of the place where they were born by virtue of Providence but not of their actions or deeds. Deeds and actions that have always been in accordance with the laws and customs of this nation which has taken them in so generously.

I thank you in advance for the attention you can give this matter. And awaiting demonstrations of your goodwill, I remain,

Yours faithfully,
Margarita Lloreda de Deresser

'How did you get it?'

'By asking,' said Enrique. 'As simple as that. Yes, I thought it was strange too. But then I thought: What's so strange? Those papers are of no interest to anybody. There are hundreds of letters like this, thousands, it's not like they're irreplaceable. There was a fire a few years ago. Many of them went up in smoke. Do you think anyone cared? Waste paper, that's what those archives were. The civil servant who gave it to me confessed the truth. They cut those papers into strips and put them on the desk so people who get fingerprinted have something to wipe off the ink with.'

'And you went to Bogotá, you requested it, and they gave it to you?'

'You're surprised, aren't you? What did you think, that Sara Guterman was the only obsessive? No, Sara is an amateur next to me. I've taken this matter very seriously indeed. I'm no dilettante. If there were a guild of document collectors, I'd be the president, don't doubt it for a second.'

'Oh, you're into that,' said Rebeca as she came in. In her hand were the directions, streets and avenues that would take me to the hotel, which, of course, I now had no desire to get to. 'Poor thing, he has no one to show his toys to.'

'I do have,' said Enrique, 'but I don't want to. This isn't for any old nobody.'

'I don't suppose I can take them with me,' I said. 'Even if I brought them back first thing tomorrow morning.'

'You suppose right. These papers don't leave this house while I'm alive.'

I said I understood (and I wasn't lying). But that was the letter Sara Guterman had told me about. And Enrique had it. He'd shown it to me. *I had seen it.* In the middle of that family archaeology, I thought the tacit agreement that Enrique and his wife had arrived at was tremendous: they both spoke of that letter lightly, as if that way they could neutralize the gravity of its contents. I, for one, didn't want to enter into the game. What was radiating from the paper, from Margarita Deresser's signature, even from the date, prevented me.

'If you lost one of these papers, if you damaged it, I'd have no choice but to kill you,' said Enrique. 'Like spies in movies. I like you, man, I don't want to kill you.'

'Me neither,' I said, handing back the second page of the letter. I stood up and went over to Rebeca to kiss her goodbye. 'Well, thank you for everything,' I was saying.

'But if you want,' Enrique interrupted me, 'you could sleep here.'

'No, no. I've already made a reservation.'

'So cancel it.'

'I don't want to inconvenience you.'

'The inconvenience will be all yours,' said Rebeca. 'The sofa's hard as a rock.'

'There's something else,' said Enrique. 'There's something else I'd like to do with you. I haven't been able to do it on my own, and who better than you to go with me?'

And he told me about how often he'd driven on the road up to Las Palmas, thinking all the time he'd go and look at the site of the accident, thinking of parking the car by the side of the road and walking down like a tourist on the mountainside, if that was possible. No, he'd never been able to: each time he'd kept on going, and a couple of times he'd reached the extreme – ridiculous, yes, he knew it – of turning up the volume on the car radio so as not to hear the urgency of his own meddling thoughts.

'What I propose is that we go there tomorrow,' he said. 'It's on your way to Bogotá, you're going to have to pass by there in any case.'

'I don't know if I want to.'

'We'll leave early and we won't stay long, I promise, or we'll stay as long as you want.'

'I don't know if I want to go through that, Enrique.'

'And then you go home. Go and look, nothing more. To see if I can clear it up once and for all.'

'Clear what up?' I asked.

'What do you think, Gabriel? The doubt, man, this damned doubt.'

From the moment Enrique and Rebeca said goodnight, from the moment they went to their room, less than four metres from the sofa where I was spending the night, and closed the door, I knew I wouldn't be able to sleep that night. With time I've trained myself to recognize nights of insomnia long before trying to force myself to get to sleep, and so I've stopped wasting the time that gets wasted like that. I turned off the living-room light but not the floor lamp, and in the half-darkness, sitting on the cushion that Rebeca had put in a pillowcase for me, spent a long while thinking of my father, of the forgiveness he'd been denied, of the journey he'd begun after that refusal and never finished, and I couldn't help but think that my presence that night in Enrique Deresser's house was one of the ways that life has of mocking people: the same life that had denied my father the only redemption possible, and along the way denied me the right to inherit that redemption, had now arranged that I, the disinherited, should be a guest for a night of the one who had refused to absolve us. The light poured straight down from the lampshade, illuminating only the circular space below it, the rest of the room remained in darkness (its objects vaguely distinguishable: the dining table and its chairs in disorder, the chest of drawers at the entrance, the frames of the photos, the paintings – or rather, posters – on the walls, which in the darkness weren't white, but grey); and nevertheless I had to stand up and walk around in the tiny space, because the same electricity in my eyes and limbs, the same static that kept me awake, wouldn't let me keep still.

The window exhausted its possibilities almost immediately: outside, nothing was happening, not in the windows of the other buildings, all black and blind, not in the street, where my car still survived, not on the patio, where the chalk squares of the hopscotch reflected the dusty light of the street lamps. In the photos on top of the chest of drawers, Sergio appeared touching a pony's nose and making a disgusted face, Rebeca and Enrique posed on a bridge – I knew there was a famous bridge near Santa Fe de Antioquia, and assumed that bridge and the one in the photo were the same one – and a woman, younger than them but too old to be, for example, Sergio's girlfriend, hugged Rebeca at a party holding a little glass of anisette in her free hand. All this was difficult to see in the darkness, just as the German titles of the ten or twelve paperbacks I found in the first drawer were difficult to see (and to understand), abandoned along with sets of screwdrivers, pots of glue, packets of sugar, two or three syringes with their caps, two or three rusty buckles. In the kitchen I opened and closed cupboard doors trying not to make noise; I found a glass jar of biscuits and ate one, and I took out a bottle of cold water from the fridge, and poured myself a glass (I had to go through jams and boxes of tea before I found one). On the door was a magnet in the shape of a horseshoe and another with the crest of Atlético Nacional. There wasn't anything else: no names, no lists, no messages. With my glass of cold water in my hand I went back to the illuminated corner of the sofa. It must have been almost midnight. I put

Enrique's binder on the cushion, so the light would hit it at an angle and the reflection on the plastic wouldn't block out the letters, and found myself once again, like so many times in my life, involved in the examination of other people's documents, but not with the impartiality of other times, instead overexcited and nervous and at the same time tired like on the day after an intense drinking session. 'Tomorrow you'll give them back to me,' Enrique had said, 'but tonight you can take your time over them.'

'But can't I photocopy them?' I'd said, because Margarita's letter alone had stimulated me as if I'd come across an auction of Demosthenes' toga. 'Can't I get up early, find a shop and photocopy them?'

'These letters are mine and my family's,' Enrique said. For the first time, his tone of voice had a tinge of reproach. 'No one else has any reason to be interested.'

'They interest me. I want to have them –'

He cut me off. 'You haven't understood. They're not for you to have.' And after an uncomfortable silence he went on, as if apologizing for protecting his territory: 'It's that I don't want them to end up in a book,' he said. 'Out of reserve, or privacy, call it what you will. I'm very fond of these letters, and part of my affection comes from knowing that no one else has them, that they're mine, that no one else knows them. If they were published, something would be lost, Gabriel, something very big would be lost for me. I'm not sure if I've made myself clear.'

I said he had. He'd made himself clear, yes, sir, clear as day. And as soon as I opened the album and turned three or four pages I understood his anxiety, the fear of the damage this collection could suffer in careless hands. In plastic sleeves, after the one in which Margarita had asked the senators for help, were several of the letters, eight or ten, that old Konrad had sent to his family – first to his wife, and then to his son – from the Hotel Sabaneta concentration camp. There wasn't more, but that was everything. 'They're not for you to have,' Enrique had told me: that had been his subtle way of saying, *You are forbidden from appropriating them; you, who steal everything, aren't going to rob me of this.* He was my host; I was his guest. By giving them to me, allowing me access to them even if only for one night, he had trusted me. But things didn't turn out the way we both would have preferred: as soon as I read the first letter I knew I'd end up betraying that trust, and when I got halfway through the second I set about the task of betraying it.

Sergio could arrive at any moment. I put my shoes back on, looked for my jacket on the chair by the entrance, and with jacket and shoes I went to the door where the Deressers were sleeping. I held my breath, to hear better, and after ten or twenty seconds I discerned the rhythmic breathing of two sleeping people; I thought it might just be one, it was possible that, like me, one of them might be having a bad night; but there was no way to confirm it, and what is not possible to confirm should never be considered. I tried to fix the door so it would look closed from the outside. When I seemed to have managed it, I went down the stairs in darkness, and on my way from the door of the building to that of my car, I walked across the chalk hopscotch by accident. I didn't know if I'd ruined it, but I didn't stop to find out. I got into my car, not through the driver's door, but on the passenger side, I got my notebook out of the glove compartment, a pen out of my jacket, turned on the little roof light and got down to work. I found that the letters were arranged backwards: the most recent ones first, the oldest ones later. Only when I got to the last ones in the archive did I understand the particular effect this reading caused, this reversed chronology.

The following are the letters I transcribed:

Fusa, 6 August 1944

Son,

Today the ones who are being deported have left the hotel. Heinrich Stock, Heider and Max Focke. Stock was a propagandist, one of the hard-liners, that is what everyone said.

Last Sunday their families came as usual and everything was just like always and on Tuesday the order arrived and today they took them. They are going to travel to Buenaventura and from there board a ship to the USA. They say that from the USA some are going to Germany and some will stay in other camps.

The only thing I do not want is to return to Germany. The war is already lost.

Señores censors, this is not a code.

It seems they are going to bring skittles. But every day we hear something different.

They said they were going to give us more than four beers a day.

Here the people have a reason to get out. What am I going to get out for?

Papa

Fusagasugá, 25 June 1944

My dear son,

Now it is five o'clock and we're all in the dining room writing our letters. Sundays are the most terrible days for me. The mass does not help me at all, just the opposite,

312

making me think how far away God is from me. I feel confused. Which is my religion and which is my country? These are the two things a person can ask for and I do not know who I can ask for anything.

This is what is called total ABANDONMENT.

All day I speak in my language with people from my land but we are in another land. Forgive me if this seems silly to you. On Sundays I generally write silliness. On weekdays we are in the coffee plantations and we tend the gardens but on Sundays we do not. The agricultural work distracts us but on Sundays there is too much free time. Today I sat out on the terrace and watched the cars arriving from Bogotá with families. Everyone sat by the pool with their families. Has ours failed for ever? I don't even want to think that. Who am I without you two? Nobody. To keep myself entertained, I started thinking about how many of those people I had sold windows to. Twenty-three. Kraus still owes me, incredible. I have lost the ability to sleep. I don't want to complain too much but that's how it is. Tomorrow the bell will ring at six and I know now that I will have been awake for two hours by then. I sleep for four hours at best. From nine-thirty we cannot make noise and those hours of silence and darkness are the worst. Tell me how things are at home. Tell me if you have had news of your mother and do not lie to me about this. Please, do not abandon me as well.

Your papa,
Konrad

Fusagasugá, 26 May 1944
Dear son,

Your mama will come back sooner or later. I have taken a little while to write to you because I did not want to tell

313

you lies. One is too optimistic in moments of emotion and your letter left me floored, I will not deny it. I could be destroyed but I am not. Do you know why? Because later when I calmed down I was thinking what was in truth most probable and I arrived at this conclusion. Your mama is going to come back because we are a family. I do not have the slightest doubt and I do not make mistakes when it comes to judging someone. Have patience that everything will come in due time with God's help.

You tell me that she went through terrible days. I have also had some terrible days because it is not easy to be separated. Of course what she did is an act of egotism and that is rare in her, always such a generous person. That is why I am sure that she will reconsider. There is nothing that time cannot fix and one day we will be together again all three of us. I give you my word.

Your papa who loves you,
Konrad

Hotel Sabaneta, 21 April 1944
My dear and adored Marguerite,

I would like you to come and live in Fusa. Here in the hotel there are people who have their families in Fusa and they can go and see them every day and even stay and sleep with them. When they go they are escorted by a policeman and when they come back too. But they sleep with their wives and can see their children. The houses in Fusa are very expensive because now everyone wants a house in Fusa and there are people here with lots of money. But if we make an effort we can find a cheap little place for you to live. Enrique can stay in Bogotá. How good it would be to sleep next to you again. I know we do not have money but something could be done, as they say hope is the last thing to die.

Here one lives without serious problems so do not worry about me. There is not much to do because it is forbidden to have a radio. They do not even let us listen to music and for me listening to music would help a little because I could be distracted. One of the employees in the hotel likes me and he is the one who helps me to write my letters. Let us see if I can ask him for a radio or if he will let me go in his room to listen to music for a while.

I love you always.

Yours,

Konrad

Hotel Sabaneta, Fusagasugá, 9 April 1944

My adored Marguerite,

You never like me to write to you in German and now you are in luck because in this place German is forbidden for correspondence. All letters must be in Spanish and have to pass through a horrible censorship. We submit them open and a person in charge reads them and asks for explanations. They will be looking for spies. But of course here we are all spies, simply for having surnames that they cannot pronounce. They gave us medical examinations as if we had contagious diseases. Being German is a contagious disease. We can still speak it. At least that is not forbidden.

There was a Catholic mass last week but I only found out today. It was Father Baumann. If they say masses here maybe it will not all be so bad and anyway there is only one God. Father Baumann reminded me very much of Gabriel. I told Gabriel that if he wanted he could come

and practise here instead of going always to the Gutermans. It would break the tedium for me. And he could
hear Father Baumann because Gabriel is Catholic. Remind him, please. But do not insist if he does not want to.

Well, I hope you have not stopped looking for help.
Someone has to understand that all this is a mistake and that I
have done nothing wrong. This is how this country pays me
back for loving it as I have loved it. Colombia is the most
ungrateful country that God has placed on the face of the
earth. And I am not the only one to say so. At meals this is the
topic of conversation. What happens is that here there are
wolves in sheep's clothing and that is the problem for those
of us who have ended up here. That the others know I am
not like them. My love, the important thing is that you
believe me. The rest does not matter. What Enrique thinks
matters very little if you believe me.

I will write to you as much as they allow here and hope
I do not bore you.

Yours,

Konrad

When the last letter in the archive, the first that Konrad
Deresser wrote from the Hotel Sabaneta, was transcribed
into my notebook, I took a couple of minutes to recover
from the blow of everydayness: the letters had been the
best testimony of those ordinary days, unbearably ordinary,
that in an ordinary city had been spent in an extraordinary
time and place; the letters had been, for that very reason,
the best testimony of the error committed by my father.
This alone had forced me to steal them; as if that weren't
enough, there was also this paragraph in the middle,
dropped in there, between two pathetic appeals destined

for a Margarita who perhaps already, at that moment, had ceased to be with her husband: that neutral paragraph like the net on a tennis court, that mentioned my father's name (which was enough to make it unique and valuable) and to me seemed to contain impossible images. *Practise* in that paragraph was a long and malleable verb, and a word made of burnt rubber. I spent a while thinking about *The Mastersingers of Nuremberg*, and I put the anecdote of the radio station together with the lost cover I'd found at my father's apartment. Suddenly my father had a violin pressed against his neck, and he was practising; or rather he received singing lessons from old Konrad or learned vocal tricks to control his diaphragm better, because old Konrad knew about things like that. I imagined my father getting on buses or into other people's cars with his violin case hanging from his shoulder, and I tried to speculate about the moment he decided to give the instrument up. I managed to think all those things before I sensed that the paragraph did not refer to the learning of instruments or breath control, but of the German language.

Was that possible? My father learning German from such a young age? My head began to look for signs in the life of the Gabriel Santoro I had known, but it was late, and investigative work in the mental archives is exhausting and not always reliable. It would be better to turn to my current informer, Enrique Deresser, although that would have to wait till the next day.

I put my notebook back in the glove compartment. Before getting out of the car, I looked at all the corners of the street, making sure Sergio was nowhere to be seen. I walked back to the building as if someone were following me, and towards five, still dressed, I managed to get to sleep for a couple of hours without remembering what I'd dreamt. But maybe I dreamt of my father speaking German.

I woke up to the gurgling of a coffee maker. I mustn't have opened my eyes straight away, because later, when I finally managed it, Enrique Deresser was standing in front of me, asking to be taken out for a walk like a dog with a leash in its mouth; he didn't have a leash in his mouth, but a cup of coffee in his hand, and he didn't want to go for a walk, but to the place where, according to the Highways Authority reports, a friend from his youth had died in an accident. His collection of letters was no longer beside the sofa, where I had left it the night before. It was already put away, it was in a safe place now, it had been put out of reach of thieves. Enrique handed me the hot cup.

'OK, I'll wait for you downstairs,' he said. 'I'm going to get some *buñuelos*. If you want I'll get you some too.'

'*Buñuelos*?'

'To eat on the way. So we don't waste time having breakfast.'

And that's how it went, of course: Enrique wasn't prepared to put the business off a second longer than necessary. With the steering wheel in my left hand and holding a ball of hot dough between the fingers of my right, I followed his directions and found myself, after going up some steep, urban, unevenly paved streets (concrete squares bordered with lines of tar), leaving the city and going up into the mountains. My passenger's knees banged against the glove compartment: I hadn't realized Enrique was so tall, or his legs so long, until that moment, but didn't say anything for fear of provoking a conversation that might somehow lead him to open the glove compartment and find my notebook and leaf through it out of curiosity and come across the words I'd stolen from him and his family. But that didn't seem probable: Enrique was concentrating on other things, his gaze fixed on the trucks we passed and on the curves of the road, that ribbon of dark, sinuous cement that became unpredictable a few metres in front of the car and disappeared from sight in the rear-view mirror. At one point, Enrique raised his index finger and tapped the windshield.

'Geraniums in biscuit tins,' he said.

'What about them?'

'You mention them in your book.'

And then he was silent again, as if he didn't understand something that for me was obvious: he'd begun to interpret a good part of his world through something he'd read. He yawned, once or twice, to relieve the pressure on his ears. I did the same and discovered that the altitude had blocked them a little. That can happen before you notice, because the ascent is not so drastic, and the process is quite similar, one thinks, to how an old man gradually goes deaf. Going up into Bogotá causes a sudden deafness, like the result of a childhood illness; that ascent, up to Las Palmas, was like the progressive and natural deafness of old age. I was thinking about that when Enrique tapped the windshield again and told me to pull over, that we'd arrived. The car slowed down and the tires skidded on the loose gravel of the verge, and the unpleasant parking-lights signal started beeping. On my left was the highway, which always seems more dangerous when you're still, and on my right floated the green stain of some bushes, so sparse that among their leaves you could make out the air of the valley and the violent drop of the mountainside. And that's when, maybe because of the sensation of farewell provoked by being with someone in an unmoving car, maybe because of the

319

slightly eccentric way the surrounding landscape united us – turned us into confidants or accomplices – I asked Enrique what I'd been wanting to ask him since the night before. 'Of course he spoke German,' he said. 'Spoke it like a native. He learned it at the Nueva Europa. That was his school. Peter, Sara, they were his teachers. The accent he picked up from them; people with a good ear have no problems, and Gabriel had a better ear than Mozart. In your book there are important things and unimportant things. Among the unimportant things, what surprised me most was that Gabriel had forgotten his German. He must have wanted to forget it. Until that day when he started singing '*Veronika*', no? Sara loved that song, I remember perfectly. And Gabriel pretending he'd started studying it in old age, that he'd only been studying the language for a few months. All that you put in the book. I read it but I couldn't believe it. The man who used to recite speeches from the Reichstag pretending he didn't know German. Don't tell me it's not ironic.'

'Tell me about it. Sara didn't say much about that.'

'That would be because there's not much to tell,' said Enrique. 'I remember very well a conversation, one of the last I witnessed between them . . . Gabriel asked my father to explain a couple of references that came up in the speeches. My father did it gladly, like a teacher. That was the closest they ever were. It wasn't a friendship, no. Gabriel didn't betray a friendship with Papa, but he did betray something. I don't know what to call it; there has to be a name to apply to the spot where he stuck the knife in. Those speeches, I don't know if you know them. No, I wouldn't dare say that Gabriel learned German to understand them, but it would be very naive to think it wasn't one of the benefits. In any case, it's normal that Sara wouldn't have mentioned it, I think.

Gabriel never committed the error of taking those guilty enthusiasms to the Nueva Europa. He was a sensible fellow, after all, and he had his head screwed on straight. He could study them, but he did it in secret and with shame. Maybe he would have liked my father to be a little more ashamed. Me too, of course. How I despised him. Oh, yes, I came to despise my father. What cowards. We were both very cowardly.' It wasn't difficult to imagine that he'd been re-reading old Konrad's letters the morning my father had come to visit him; I imagined how fresh the resentment would have felt, the daily updating of the disdain; I imagined Enrique going over in his head the text he knew by heart while my father performed his little speech of contrition. But most of all I imagined the course of a life encumbered with the documentary reconstruction of scenes from the other life. That's what Enrique had devoted himself to: the documents he had collected were his place in the world. I thought that was why he had thrown them at me almost en masse, because he thought I would receive the same peace, and with that Enrique turned into a sort of small messiah, an ad hoc saviour, and the documents were his gospel. 'Yes, Gabriel used to go to the Nueva Europa to practise his German,' said Enrique, and narrowed his eyes. 'Sometimes I think it might have been there. Isn't that horrible? Not just contemplating that possibility, I don't mean only that: isn't it horrible that we'll never know where it happened? That moment weighs on us, Gabriel, and we're never going to know how it went. No matter how many of my father's letters I've saved. No matter how much information Sara Guterman might have given you, we're missing that information. Tell me something, have you imagined the scene?'

'I've tried,' I told him. 'But the places from those years

hardly exist any more. I never saw the Nueva Europa, for example.'

'I've reconstructed it as if I'd been there. I'm walking along the upper corridor and I see him downstairs, sitting with the fellow from the Embassy or the police, but I keep going to my room. How could I imagine it? I don't even stop to try to see who Gabriel's talking to. I don't even think about it. I see him without thinking. I don't wonder: Who could that be? Is he practising his German? Gabriel would sit down to talk to the Germans, he liked to swap languages. The Germans would come away with three or four new phrases in Spanish, quite happy. So in that image I could have wondered if he was swapping languages. But I don't wonder anything. My eyes pass over Gabriel. Between those two and me there is a glass door, a whole patio and a fountain making fountain noises. So I could say I try to hear what they're saying and I can't. But it's not like that. In the scene that I imagine, I don't try to hear anything. Normal, don't you think? You go somewhere you go every day, see your friend sitting and doing what he's been doing as long as you've known him: talking. How are you going to imagine?'

'You can't,' I said.

'I know you've always wanted more details,' he said. 'But closer than this we can't get, I'm telling you. The details change, that's true. Sometimes there's rain splashing into the fountain's pool, other times there isn't. There are the little fishes, there are the coins people throw in. Sometimes I see Sara busy with customers at the reception desk, and I curse her for not suspecting anything either. I've been carrying this around for a long time, son. And I think you're strong. I don't think it'll hurt you to help me a little. After all, you're the one who's written about this, you're the one who's dealt with it, and the land belongs to he who works it. No one has as much information as you. Sara was the last, but she can't help me now. Use the information, Gabriel, do me that favour. In ten years, if I'm still alive, come back here, and we'll discuss our points of view, you can tell me about your scene. Tell me if your father chose the place or if he adapted to what they asked. If he informed with pleasure or if he had conflicting emotions. If in the interview he denies that he speaks German, or if it's precisely because of that, because he speaks German, that they credit what he says. Does he think of Sara? Does he feel that by accusing my father he's defending her from something? The questions are endless. I have my own hypothesis. I'm not going to tell you, so as not to influence you.' There again was the impulse to make light of things that I'd witnessed the night before, the strategy that transformed everything into a game to defend himself against the pain of the facts. He had spent fifty years living with the betrayal. In those terms – I thought – I was a recent arrival. Deresser would have been planning this ambush in advance, a long while in advance – since the publication of my book, for example. And everything, the invitation to go to see him, the description of my father's visit, the access he'd allowed me to all his documents, everything was paving the way to this instant: the instant when he got rid of half the weight of his life and transferred it to another person; the instant of a tiny liberty, obtained in old age and almost by chance. 'This is what I wanted to request of you,' he said. '*That you think.* I've spent too many years; this is as far as I've got. Now it's your turn. But I will warn you, no matter how early you get up you won't see what isn't there. No matter how much you think about that scene the sun won't come up any earlier. Anyway, you understand me now. It's impossible to complete the scene.' After a while, he added, 'Is there anything else you wanted to know?'

I wanted to say to him, Is there something you know for certain, by any chance? Is there anything in my father's life that has just a single aspect?

But instead I said, 'For now no. If there is anything else, I'll let you know.'

'OK. So, time for what we came for, don't you think?'

'I think so.'

'Let's not use up the whole morning talking about the past,' he said. 'Let's be realistic. You and I are alone. These stories don't matter to anyone any more.'

We got out of the car and found ourselves in the noisy and too bright world of outside, and we began to walk forward, along the verge, skirting around the line where the mountain dropped off into the abyss and where there are no containment rails or artificial protection of any kind: men depend on the will of the stones and the tree trunks and the breeze-block or adobe houses to keep from going over the precipice. The air was dense and humid and the deciduous smell of the vegetation filled it the way a basin gets filled. I began to sweat: my palms and the back of my neck were damp, my watchstrap stuck to my wrist.

We had walked thirty or forty metres when Enrique stopped me. With his hands on his hips and panting (eyebrows raised, the corners of his mouth open like the gills of a dying trout), he took a deep breath and said, 'Here it is.'

Here it was. Here was the place where my father's car had gone over the edge. This landscape was the last thing he'd seen in his life, with the probable exception of some lights bearing down on him or the bodywork of a bus that pushed him off the road. While I approached the edge of the slope and focused on some bushes torn out by their roots, broken branches and disturbed soil, on the nature that had preferred not to regenerate in all those years, Enrique was looking at the road, which at that spot twisted less (or its bends were not so sharp), and was perhaps thinking, as I was thinking as I looked at it, that this was another of the illusions generated by stillness: from the side, everything seems straighter and, especially, seems *straighter for longer*, and you'd never think that something might be unpredictable for the cars passing, a barefoot pedestrian, a frightened dog. If a bus appeared round this bend, I thought Enrique was thinking, the driver of a car would see it; if he didn't see it, because of the dense darkness that must cover this road at night, or because of some distraction (the distraction that comes from a recent sadness, the disappointment of bad news), the most likely thing was that a person with normal reflexes would manage to steer out of its way. Because the width of the road, at that point, seemed to allow it; because the speed a car could have reached on its way up was not great. At that point, thought Enrique, an accident was rather improbable.

Yes, that was what Enrique was thinking. No doubt about it. Who says it's not possible to read other people's minds?

The previous afternoon, his son had practically assaulted me for speculating about his life (and doing so, on top of everything, in the midst of that apology for treachery that was my book); but this time, at least, it wasn't speculation. I could read Enrique's thoughts, one by one, as if he had spat them out onto the asphalt after thinking them. Enrique was standing facing the fatal curve, and I was watching him and I could have even closed my eyes and listened to the progress of his thoughts . . . but the bus, Enrique was thinking, could have appeared around the bend at the moment Gabriel was trying to find a radio station, but the bus might have had its lights turned off, to conserve energy from the battery as they often do, but Gabriel's bad hand might have been the reason his reaction hadn't been effective, but his heart might have failed from the sudden jolt of the fright, and in that case Gabriel would have been dead when his car went over the edge . . . but what about the driver's intentions, what about the possibility of suicide, was it not possible that the bus driver was desperate, disappointed, a man at the end of his tether? Had the bus driver never committed any errors in his life, and was it not possible that he'd tried to mend them and someone had denied him the redress? These possibilities exist, Enrique Deresser was thinking, no one can take them away from me. By now Gabriel's son has figured it out, now he knows why I brought him here, why we've come to see the place where Gabriel swerved into the abyss, where he preferred to bring it all to a close because it was all a farce, because his life had been a farce, that's what he felt. Nothing would have been easier for me than misleading him, telling him no, none of that, stop feeling you're so important, stop believing your guilt makes you unique, that you invented the desire to make amends, that really is arrogance, Gabriel Santoro, that really is a cheap farce, not the other thing, the other is a life with enough time, and everyone, given enough time, is going to fuck up over and over again; he'll make a mistake and put it right and make another mistake, you give anyone time and that's what you'll see, one fuck-up after another, amends and more amends, fuck-up and amends, fuck-up and amends, until time runs out . . . because we don't learn, Enrique Deresser was thinking, nobody ever learns, that's the biggest fallacy of all, that we learn; we really would be hoodwinked if we believed that one, Gabriel Santoro, and you more than anybody. You thought you'd learned, that you'd made one mistake and it was as if you'd been immunized, isn't that so? Well no, the evidence indicates the opposite, Mr big-shot lawyer. Everything indicates that there is no possible vaccine: you stay sick and you'll be sick for your whole fucking life and your whole fucking death. Not even in death will you be freed from the fuck-ups you've committed. That's why you don't need to run yourself off the road and take a whole busload of people with you along with I don't know how many passengers. You won't fix anything by doing that and you'll have to bear as many crosses as there were deaths in the accident. To the dead man from the beginning you'll add the dead at the end. Is that what you want? Is fucking up the lives of a few people travelling in a bus your idea of retribution? Because if that's how it is I can't help you, Gabriel Santoro. Nothing I say will be sufficient if your idea is so strong, if you're so set on closure to bring it to a close like this. If you're ready to screw the rest of us just make sure you're good and screwed. That's what Enrique Deresser was thinking as he looked at the bend that wasn't so sharp in the road that wasn't so dangerous, while he was imagining the quantity of things that would have to happen at the same time so the accident would have been an accident instead of the voluntary closure, without pomp or circumstance, of a farcical life, of that giant blind knot that had been the undeserved life of Gabriel Santoro. That, finally, was what he was thinking, while Gabriel Santoro's son, behind him, seemed to be waiting for some sort of verdict, because he was aware that this was a trial: he was the definitive audience for the last trial of his dead father, held on the soft shoulder of a mountain road, between the smell of rotting tropical fruit and the tubercular rattles of exhausts and the abrupt gusts of passing cars that descended into Medellín at frightening speeds and those that came up towards unpredictable destinations, because after this road a thousand routes were possible and Bogotá was just one of them. But it was the one that Gabriel Santoro would have taken if his car had not gone over the edge, and it would also be the one that Gabriel Santoro's son would take as soon as he confirmed that Enrique Deresser wasn't to blame: because in this trial Enrique Deresser also stood accused, and his summing-up should prove that the road was dangerous, that the night had been dark, that the bend was sharp and the visibility bad, that a mutilated hand doesn't react well in emergencies, that a recently repaired heart is fragile and cannot bear violent emotions, that a tired old man has bad reflexes, and more so when he'd lost in a single day a lover and a friend from his youth who perhaps, between the two of them, might have been able to bring him back to life.

Historical Afterword

COLOMBIA'S RELATIONS with the countries involved in the Second World War are quite complex. The following lines are an attempt to explain some of the historical context for the non-Colombian reader.

The 1938 presidential elections in Colombia were won by the Liberal candidate Eduardo Santos. At that time the government of the United States was striving to increase its diplomatic and military presence in Latin America, convinced that the ideology of National Socialism had started to gain supporters in those countries. When the war broke out, in September 1939, concern centred on the most important strategic zones, one of which was the Panamá Canal and neighbouring countries, particularly Colombia. In 1940 the US government began to request Colombia's collaboration, and in 1941 President Santos agreed a series of secret accords with the US that included the construction of military bases on the Caribbean coast and the American right to intervene militarily in case of emergency. It was as part of this collaboration with the US in its fight against the Axis that the Colombian government accepted the implementation of 'blacklists'.

The official name of the document was the 'Proclaimed List of Certain Blocked Nationals', and its objective, in all of Latin America, was to prevent the economic and commercial activity of persons and companies opposed to US defence policies. It should be noted that the government's fears were well founded, as sympathy for European Fascism had gained support in those years: several Germans and Colombians were arrested for distributing Nazi propaganda; Laureano Gómez, one of the most influential Conservative politicians, was a known admirer of Franco and self-confessed enemy of the United States; and in 1942 the authorities became aware of the existence of an organized Nazi Party in Colombia, with headquarters in the Caribbean city of Barranquilla and pivotal support in several Colombian cities.

The blacklist, drawn up by the American State Department, was created in July 1941. On 8 December, as a consequence of the Japanese bombing of Pearl Harbor, Colombia broke off diplomatic relations with the Axis nations. By May 1942, the section of the blacklist destined for Colombia named six hundred and thirty people. Inclusion meant a sort of civil death: the impossibility of carrying out any economic activity whatsoever and sanctions on those who maintained economic relations with any blacklisted person. Updating the lists was the responsibility of the US Embassy, which initially relied on its own personnel, but soon found itself overwhelmed by the work and eventually set up a network of informers to report on any suspicious activity. Those reports were not always well founded: the use of rumour or simple prejudice resulted in excesses of all kinds.

Meanwhile, the US government continued to press for the confinement of the citizens they considered dangerous or suspected of subversive activities. In 1942 another Liberal, Alfonso López Pumarejo, was elected President. López tried to resist these measures, but in 1943 something happened that changed the rules of the game: the attack by a German submarine on the Colombian schooner *Resolute*, sinking it and killing half its crew. The government's reaction was to declare a 'state of belligerence', a concept halfway between breaking off diplomatic relations and a declaration of war. As a secondary effect of this new situation, in March 1944, López's government opened the detention centres. The principal one was the Hotel Sabaneta, a luxury hotel located in the small city of Fusagasugá, a two-hour journey from the capital, Bogotá. Criteria for confinement to these centres were as confused as in the case of the blacklists, as the authorities fell back on citizens' reputations. The Hotel Sabaneta functioned as a detention centre until 1946, months after the war had ended.

Notes

4 *Gaitán, Jorge Eliécer* (1898–1948): Leader of the Liberal Party and presidential candidate, famous for his talents as an orator. His assassination on 9 April 1948 split Colombian history in two, and for many is the distant origin of the violence the country would experience during the rest of the twentieth century.

11 *Bolívar, Simón* (1783–1830): Known in Latin America as The Liberator, Bolívar is the most notable of the leaders who led the Latin American colonies to independence from Spain during the first decades of the nineteenth century. He died in Santa Marta, Colombia, and his final journey from Bogotá is recounted in *The General in his Labyrinth*, by Gabriel García Márquez.

12 *Rojas Pinilla, Gustavo* (1900–75): General of the Colombian army who, after taking power by means of a *coup d'état*, installed a dictatorship that lasted from 1953 to 1957.

12 *Lleras Restrepo, Carlos* (1908–94): Liberal politician. Minister of the Treasury between 1942 and 1944 and President of Colombia from 1966 to 1970.

20 *SCADTA (Sociedad Colombo-Alemana de Transportes Aéreos)*: Colombian–German Air Transport Society. One of the first aviation companies in Latin America, founded in 1919 by Colombian and German partners. During World War II, the fact that there were German citizens among the shareholders was a source of concern to the Colombian and US governments.

21 *Olaya Herrera, Enrique* (1880–1937): Liberal politician. President of Colombia from 1930 to 1934.

29 *Caballero, Lucas* (1914–81): Colombian writer, journalist and caricaturist whose opinion columns, published under the pseudonym Klim, were among the most read of the time.

39 *Los Tres Elefantes*: Department store with branches in several Colombian cities. In 1990 the branch in the Niza shopping centre in Bogotá was the target of one of the bloodiest terrorist attacks committed by the Medellín Cartel, leaving twenty people dead.

39 *Centro 93*: Bogotá shopping centre. It was the target of a terrorist attack in 1993, attributed to the Medellín Cartel, which killed eleven people.

56 *Troco* (Tropical Oil Company): US-owned petroleum company that operated in Colombia from 1921 to 1951, when its concession reverted to the Colombian state.

136 *Buss und Bettag*: Wednesday, eleven days before Advent, observed in Germany as a day of penance.

142 *La vorágine (The Vortex)*: Atmospheric protest novel concerning the Amazon rubber industry by José Eustasio Rivera (1888–1928), published in 1924. It is probably the most important Colombian novel prior to Gabriel García Márquez's *One Hundred Years of Solitude*.

142 *Emil Pruefert*: Head of the Nazi Party of Colombia from 1936.

143 *Arciniegas, Germán* (1900–99): Renowned Colombian historian and essayist. He was Minister of Education in Eduardo Santos's government, from 1941 to 1942, and during Alfonso López's second government, from 1945 to 1946.

165 *Villarreal, José María* (1910–99): Conservative politician. Governor of Boyacá during the final years of the Second World War and later Minister of Commerce under Laureano Gómez. He was also Colombia's Ambassador in London and Tokyo.

166 *godo*: Formerly derogatory slang term for Conservative.

170 *Pantano de Vargas*: Battle on 25 July 1819 in which Simón Bolívar, in command of the Colombian army, defeated the Spanish general José María Barreiro and achieved independence from Spain.

204 *Gómez, Laureano* (1889–1965): Principal Conservative politician of the war years, famous for his ferocious opposition to US policies and for his sympathy for the regime of Francisco Franco. He was President of Colombia from 1950 to 1953 and was deposed by the *coup d'état* that brought General Gustavo Rojas Pinilla to power.

215 *NI (No Information), KN (Known Nazi)*: Secret codes used in the intelligence reports on possible subversive activities, according to FBI director J. Edgar Hoover's instructions. Other codes were: BN (Believed Nazi); BF (Believed Fascist); KF (Known Fascist); BSL (British Statutory List).

268 *Escobar, Andrés* (1967–94): Colombian football player murdered in confusing circumstances. During the 1994 FIFA World Cup, Escobar scored an own goal that resulted in Colombia's elimination from the tournament. Back in Medellín he was murdered after a fight in a bar apparently occasioned by an argument about the goal.

268 *Galán, Luis Carlos* (1943–89): Liberal politician and presidential candidate on two occasions. He was assassinated on 18 August 1989.

268 *Pizarro Leongómez, Carlos* (1951–90): Commander in chief of M-19, Colombian guerrilla group that was active from late 1973 or early 1974 to 1990. He led M-19 to demobilization and disarmament, and was to stand as presidential candidate. He was assassinated on 26 April 1990.

274 *Leaf Storm*: Gabriel García Márquez's first novel (*La hojarasca*, 1954).

A NOTE ON THE AUTHOR

Juan Gabriel Vásquez was born in Bogotá in 1973. He studied Latin American literature at the Sorbonne between 1996 and 1998, and now lives in Barcelona. His stories have appeared in anthologies in Germany, France, Spain and Colombia, and he has translated works by E. M. Forster and Victor Hugo, among others, into Spanish. His essays, reviews and reportage have appeared in various magazines and literary supplements. He was recently nominated as one of the Bogotá 39, South America's most promising writers of the new generation. The Informers is his first novel to be translated into English.

A NOTE ON THE TRANSLATOR

Anne McLean has translated Latin American and Spanish novels, short stories, memoirs and other writings by authors including Julio Cortázar, Ignacio Martínez de Pisón, Carmen Martín Gaite and Tomás Eloy Martínez. Her translation of *Soldiers of Salamis* by Javier Cercas was awarded the Premio Valle Inclán and the *Independent* Foreign Fiction Prize in 2004.

A NOTE ON THE TYPE

The text of this book is set in Bembo. This type was first used in 1495 by the Venetian printer Aldus Manutius for Cardinal Bembo's *De Aetna*, and was cut for Manutius by Francesco Griffo. It was one of the types used by Claude Garamond (1480–1561) as a model for his Romain de l'Université, and so it was the forerunner of what became standard European type for the following two centuries. Its modern form follows the original types and was designed for Monotype in 1929.